HUNTER'S PURSUIT

Author's Edition

by

KIM BALDWIN

2005

HUNTER'S PURSUIT

ISBN 1-933110-09-0

This Trade Paperback Original Is Published By
Bold Strokes Books, Inc.,
Philadelphia, Pa, USA

First Edition: March 2005

Credits
Executive Editor: Stacia Seaman
Production Design: Stacia Seaman
Cover Design By Sheri (GRAPHICARTIST2020@HOTMAIL.COM)

What Reviewers Say About BOLD STROKES' Authors

❧

KIM BALDWIN

"Her…crisply written action scenes, juxtaposition of plotlines, and smart dialogue make this a story the reader will absolutely enjoy and long remember." – **Arlene Germain**, book reviewer for the *Lambda Book Report* and the *Midwest Book Review*

❧

ROSE BEECHAM

"…a mystery writer with a delightful sense of humor, as well as an eye for an interesting array of characters…" – *MegaScene*

"…her characters seem fully capable of walking away from the particulars of whodunit and engaging the reader in other aspects of their lives." – *Lambda Book Report*

"…creates believable characters in compelling situations, with enough humor to provide effective counterpoint to the work of detecting." – *Bay Area Reporter*

❧

JANE FLETCHER

"…a natural gift for rich storytelling and world-building…one of the best fantasy writers at work today." – **Jean Stewart**, author of the *Isis* series

❧

RADCLY*f*FE

"Powerful characters, engrossing plot, and intelligent writing…" – **Cameron Abbott,** author of *To the Edge* and *An Inexpressible State of Grace*

"…well-honed storytelling skills…solid prose and sure-handedness of the narrative…" – **Elizabeth Flynn**, *Lambda Book Report*

"…well-plotted…lovely romance...I couldn't turn the pages fast enough!" – **Ann Bannon**, author of *The Beebo Brinker Chronicles.*

"…a consummate artist in crafting classic romance fiction…her numerous best selling works exemplify the splendor and power of Sapphic passion…" – **Yvette Murray, PhD**, *Reader's Raves*

Acknowledgments

I'd like to express my appreciation to several dear friends who read along as I wrote this manuscript and offered their ideas, encouragement, and tactful feedback: Linda Harding, K.L., and Kat Yancey Gilmore and Marsha Walton, who contributed their copy-editor skills early on and deserve special thanks.

I must also acknowledge Margaret A. Helms, whose insights and suggestions made Hunter's Pursuit a much better book; she taught me lessons about writing fiction that will last a lifetime. I'm deeply grateful.

Most of all, my heartfelt appreciation goes out to Radclyffe and Lee, the forces behind Bold Strokes Books, who made my first novel the book I always wanted it to be and opened the doors to an exciting future and long association. I hope I do you proud! And also many thanks to my wonderful copy editor, Stacia Seaman, whose attention to detail is absolutely unparalleled. And last but not least, to Sheri for a killer cover. I'm extremely fortunate to have been invited to be among such a talented bunch of women.

Finally, to my soul mate and partner, M. This book would not have been possible without you, and is dedicated to you with all my love.

Kim Baldwin 2005

Dedication

For M.,
My Kindred Spirit

CHAPTER ONE

Hunter hated the smell of blood, the pungent, metallic scent that seemed to creep into her skin and linger there for days. But experience had taught her how to deal with it. She took shallow breaths as she stood over the chrome kitchen sink, searching the bloody clothes she'd cut off the young woman now lying unconscious in her bedroom. She was looking for a wallet, some ID, some hint to her patient's identity, but there was nothing to indicate who the woman was or what she was doing way the hell out in the middle of nowhere. In the pockets of the woman's jeans, shirt, and coat, Hunter found a few bills, some coins, and a small plain key ring containing three keys. Nothing else. She checked the labels on the clothes. No help there. The first person Hunter had ever brought to her underground bunker was a mystery. The only clue was a license plate number.

She wanted to berate herself for rescuing the woman, an action contrary to her better judgment. A lot of people wanted Hunter dead. Bringing an outsider to her hideaway was an unnecessary risk.

But she found it hard to feel threatened by the stranger who lay unmoving in the next room. She wasn't sure why. It wasn't just because the woman seemed harmless and was currently incapacitated. Hunter had exceptional instincts for danger, honed by years of training in the martial arts. And she knew better than anyone that appearances could be deceiving. But despite all the unanswered questions surrounding the woman, Hunter wasn't unduly alarmed by tonight's turn of events. She couldn't explain it. It was just a feeling.

In her line of work, gut feelings could save your life—or get you killed.

Hunter was not her real name, but it was an apt pseudonym. A freelance bounty hunter and assassin for hire, she was a gifted chameleon, fluent in several languages and renowned for her resourcefulness.

She had an exotic but indistinguishable look about her. Her even features and lightly bronzed complexion could suggest a Mediterranean heritage, or Latin, or maybe even Native American, and she used the ambiguity to her advantage. Last month, her hair was black and she spoke Spanish. This week it was medium brown. Very close to her natural color for the first time in a long time. She used to like the challenge of becoming someone new, but she found she missed recognizing the face that looked back at her in the mirror.

Hunter discarded the bloody clothes, washed up, and went to her desk to fire up her computer.

The bunker had a simple floor plan. The main living area was a 30 by 30 foot concrete room, with a kitchen in the northwest corner and a desk in the southwest corner. The living room took up most of the eastern half of the room. The eastern wall consisted of built-in bookshelves, all jammed with books, beyond which lay a hidden room where Hunter stored her weapons and surveillance equipment. Two doors in the southeast corner led to a bedroom and bath.

Her desk faced the room. Behind it, set into the wall, was a trio of security monitors. All were dark at the moment. Hunter hacked into the state police database and typed in **Michigan License MAK 214**. While she waited for the registration information, she rubbed her eyes and went over again the bizarre turn of events that had touched off her current situation.

The safe house was well hidden, cut into a hillside in an unpopulated region of northern Michigan just a few miles south of the Lake Superior shoreline. The densely wooded area was hilly and pocketed with small bogs, which made overland travel difficult even under the best circumstances. And fierce nor'easters sweeping down from Canada the last two weeks had created whiteout lake-effect blizzards that made negotiating even short distances impossible.

Tonight had been Hunter's first opportunity to go outside in many days, and she had relished the chance to venture out into the clear, cloudless night despite temperatures near zero. She'd decided to cure her cabin fever with a hunting expedition and had been successful—the body of a small deer rested on the sled she pulled behind her.

On her journey home, Hunter paused on a high ridge. As she rested, she spotted lights in the valley below on the only road in the area, a two-lane going north/south. North, it led to a small village—Wolf Point. But the village's antique stores and restaurants, motels, and boat rentals were shuttered up from Labor Day to Memorial Day, so the road was unused this time of year except by the occasional snowmobile venturing out of Tawa, a city thirty miles to the south.

Hunter raised her rifle to one shoulder and peered through its high-powered scope. These weren't snowmobile headlights. It was a car—traveling impossibly fast in the deep snow of the unplowed road. In another minute it would pass just below her. *He'll never make the curve at that speed,* Hunter thought as she watched the sedan's progress.

The car careened past, fishtailed, and clipped a tree before flipping twice and coming to rest at the bottom of a small ravine. One headlight canted crazily upward. The other was dark.

Almost before it stopped, Hunter tossed down the rifle and pulled the deer's body from the toboggan. She jumped aboard the sled and sent it hurtling down toward the wreckage. Flames erupted from the vehicle's engine just as she dug in her heels to brake.

It took a couple of minutes to douse the fire with snow. One or two more to get the door open. A woman, unconscious, was pinned in the driver's seat. *You can't afford to get involved,* Hunter's instincts screamed, but the woman's face was bleeding and one arm was turned at an unnatural angle. She would probably freeze to death unless Hunter intervened.

Hunter leaned into the car with her small pocket flashlight, looking for a way to extricate the driver. She could smell a musky perfume mixed with the acrid scent of blood. The woman stirred and cried out in pain, and the sound pierced Hunter's armor. She had to help.

She bent back the mangled steering wheel and managed to

get the driver out, cradling the woman in her arms to move her the short distance to the sled.

As soon as Hunter lifted her, the woman sighed and buried her face in Hunter's neck. She reached up with her uninjured arm and touched her rescuer's cheek. It was like a lover's caress—so sweet and gentle and so unexpected that Hunter froze for a moment.

No one ever touched her like that. Or at least, no one had for a very long time.

She was surprised to discover what a lasting impression that brief caress had made. *You liked it, didn't you? You liked it very much.*

Hunter glanced at the photograph on her desk, studying the faces of the happy family pictured there. *You used to pet my cheek like that, didn't you?* She felt a twinge of regret for the choices she'd made. It was an emotion she rarely allowed herself to feel but was growing increasingly familiar with. She'd been thinking a lot lately about the past, and about retirement.

There was really no reason for her to work anymore. She had plenty of money and nothing to prove to anyone. And her conscience was beginning to nag at her after remaining mostly dormant much of her adult life. Even the righteous kills no longer held any satisfaction. And the worst parts of her past—the jobs she'd hated but had been forced to take—those kills had begun to give her nightmares.

A soft chime from her computer drew her back to the present.

In her haste to get the stranger back to the bunker, Hunter had given the wrecked sedan only a cursory inspection, but she'd seen no purse and the glove compartment was empty. The license plate was all she had to go on in trying to establish her patient's identity.

It told her the car was stolen.

According to the Michigan State Police database, the car had been reported stolen in Detroit on 2/24/05. The blue Sebring sedan was registered to a sixty-nine-year-old Ann Arbor man named Douglas Dunn. It had been taken from a gas station while its owner was inside paying for his tank of gas.

The car had been stolen a week ago, hundreds of miles away.

Curiouser and curiouser, Hunter thought, frowning. She rose from her chair to check on her mysterious patient.

The injured woman stirred, caught halfway between sleep and wakefulness. Something seemed to be holding her down, pressing against her chest. It cut into her side with every breath. She felt too warm and her body ached. But the worst was the shooting pain in her head. She tried to force her mind to a place without pain. An impossible task. But after a time, she fell back into the black void of sleep.

Hunter touched her hand to the woman's forehead. Feverish. She backed away and settled into an overstuffed chair she'd pulled beside the bed and studied the woman who lay unmoving under a heavy fleece blanket tucked around her like a cocoon.

Her patient was 5 foot 4 or so, with a firm, well-toned body. She looked to be about twenty-five, ten years younger than Hunter, and she was probably quite attractive, but it was hard to tell for sure at the moment. Bandages hid much of her face and the areas that were exposed were puffy and bruised. Her nose had been broken, blackening both eyes, and there was a small lump behind one ear. Her shoulder-length blond hair was matted with dried blood, and a three-inch gash on her forehead had been closed with several neat stitches of dental floss. Her left arm was set with a makeshift splint, her left knee was wrapped in an Ace bandage, and her rib cage had been tightly taped when Hunter felt at least two, and probably three, cracked ribs.

Hunter had taken several classes for paramedics. She'd received a multitude of injuries over the years in her job, sometimes in countries where doctors were scarce, other times in places where stabbings and gunshot wounds required physicians to contact law enforcement. So she treated her own injuries when she could.

But it had been quite another experience altogether to treat this stranger. She'd tried to be clinical about it. Detached. Detached was something she was normally very good at.

But she couldn't help but notice when she stripped off the woman's clothes what soft skin lay beneath. Pale and fair, where Hunter was dark. The silky flesh unmarked, except for two scars. One an inch long, above her right eye, and a raised, jagged one on her abdomen that Hunter found herself lightly tracing with a fingertip, as if by doing so she could discern the injury that had caused it.

As she gently probed the stranger's ribs for injuries, Hunter's eyes strayed to the woman's full, round breasts, nipples pink and hard in the cool bunker.

She took her time examining and treating the woman.

She couldn't remember the last time she'd been quite this turned on.

Something brought the injured woman back to the edge of consciousness, a murky place where the relentless drumming in her head overshadowed the pain elsewhere in her body. She struggled to open her eyes, fighting hazily to learn the circumstances of her pain, but she could see nothing.

All was black. And still. There was only the pain. Horrible, horrible pain. *Dear God, make it stop!* She couldn't move. *Where am I?* Her mind was unable to tell her where she was or how she got there. A rush of panic washed over her. *Am I dead? Can you be in pain when you're dead? Am I in hell?*

She had to move her body. To connect again with the real world. She tried to raise her arms to throw off the confining covers, but the effort brought a sharp new pain to her left forearm, momentarily eclipsing the throbbing in her head. She gasped aloud, a raspy sound that seemed to come from very far away.

"Can you hear me?"

A voice! A human voice! A woman, very near. I'm not dead. And someone is with me. Knowing she was not alone, wherever she was, pushed back the panic a little.

"Can you hear me?" the voice asked again. It was low and melodious. Soothing.

She wanted to answer. The voice was a lifeline. A beacon in her black world. But it was an effort. "What?" The word came out as a croak. "Where...?"

"You're safe," said the voice. "Everything is all right."

The words had a calming effect. The panic receded somewhat. *Hospital. Must be in the hospital. What happened?* She wanted to talk, but her throat was swollen and dry. Her tongue was made of sandpaper. "Can't..." she tried again. Her head pounded away, relentless.

"Try to drink a little. I'll help you."

Gentle arms lifted the woman's head and shoulders—a movement that amplified her pain.

"Stop!" she screamed.

Her upward progress was halted, and the low voice spoke again, a whisper close to her ear. "Try to relax and focus on your breathing. It will help against the pain. In...and out. In...and out. That's good. Now I'm going to give you some water. You must try and drink some."

Slender fingertips gently parted her swollen lips and guided a plastic straw between them. She sucked on it and felt cool water flood her mouth and throat, relieving a bit of her discomfort. After a few sips, she released the straw and was laid gently back against the mattress.

"What happened?" Speaking took tremendous effort. The sound seemed to reverberate in her head.

"I know you must feel like hell," said the voice, suspended in the darkness to her right. "You got banged up pretty good. A broken wrist, some cracked ribs, maybe a concussion."

"Where am I?" Another wave of pain assaulted the woman's already throbbing head.

"You're in my home...a long way from the nearest doctor, and it's impossible to move you. There's no phone here, but I really think you'll be fine. You need to rest now."

"Can't...see," the woman rasped. She tried to swallow. Coughed.

The gentle hands cupped the back of her head, bringing it up very slowly, and reinserted the straw between her lips. She sucked eagerly on it. The cool water seemed to dull the throbbing in her head.

"Your eyes are swollen shut, and the room is dark to help you sleep. Don't worry about all that now. Give the swelling time to go down. Get some rest," the voice urged before moving away.

Wait! Don't go! Don't leave me alone! What's happened to me? Who are you? But she was alone again, she could feel it. Silence. Darkness. The fear began to creep back in, just a little.

Focus on your breathing, the voice had said. And so she did. In...and out. In...and out.

A nice voice, she thought hazily. A caring, kind voice. Her mind conjured it up again. There was a hint of an accent, wasn't there? Sexy. It was a distraction from the pain. From her disorientation. In...and out. In...and out. She surrendered to the voice and drifted back into an emptiness devoid of dreams.

She'll have more questions when she wakes up, Hunter thought as she returned to her living room. *I better start thinking about what I'm going to tell her, who I'm going to be. Nothing too elaborate. Keep it simple. Of course, the bunker does make things a little more complicated.*

She had adopted a number of personalities over the years. Heiress, Pilot, Chef. The heiress identity had gotten her close to a rich Italian shipping magnate whose secret business involved the transporting of illicit human flesh to high-paying clients who used them for sex and servitude. Girls and boys, most not yet sixteen. She felt no remorse when she put a gun to the man's head.

Not the heiress, she decided. *Maybe the chef?* She went to her refrigerator and pulled the door open. There were a few apples, two eggs, and a half brick of cheese—the only remnants of the perishables she'd brought in by snowmobile three weeks earlier. She usually stayed in the bunker between jobs. *Nah. Can't be the chef. Even one eccentric enough to have a bunker home would still have more in her icebox.*

The food situation wasn't as dire as it appeared. A door off the kitchen led to a large pantry, twelve feet long by eight feet wide. Deep shelves held a large variety of dried and canned goods and staples like flour and sugar, powdered milk and eggs.

I should go back to pick up the deer, especially since I have another mouth to feed. Hope nothing's gotten to it. She was glad she had field dressed the animal and that the temperature outside was well below freezing. She also needed to retrieve her rifle. *Wouldn't hurt to have another look at that car, either.*

She headed back to her desk and picked up the remote control as she dropped into the chair and turned to face the monitors. She clicked on the first one and studied the security camera's image of the forested area just outside the well-hidden entrance. The tracks from the sled were still visible. *That's pretty easy to follow, if someone has an inclination to.*

She wasn't expecting company. But this was apparently a night for the unexpected, so she didn't like having a clear trail from the wreck right to her front door. *What the hell was she doing out on that road?*

Hunter flipped off the monitor and wheeled around to face the desk. She reached for her computer keyboard and opened her instant message program, selecting "Kenny" from her list of contacts.

Kenny Foster was the closest thing she had to family. They'd met seven years ago at the Academy. She was a veteran by then, but still living on the grounds.

He was ten years younger, and still a new recruit. At first, Hunter regarded Kenny as nothing more than another link in the chain of computer whiz kids who were common at the Academy. They came and went with startling frequency—most of them geeky, adolescent boys who leered at her and hit on her mercilessly until they learned who she was.

Kenny was different. He had a genius level IQ and a maturity that belied his age. Though he too had a hideous crush on her, he hid it well most of the time and never approached her about it or spoke to her at all. But she caught him watching her surreptitiously when they crossed paths at the cafeteria or elsewhere on the grounds.

He began to get a reputation at the school—a difficult task in an environment of overachievers. He had a special gift with computers, and it was rumored he could crack into any database or computer in the world. Despite his tender age, he began to be assigned some top-level jobs. His first assignment in the field was under Hunter's supervision, and it was fortunate it was or he'd not have made it back.

When she learned they would be working together, Hunter sought him out. She found him alone on a bench on the grounds and joined him. She was a little intrigued by the baby-faced, slightly built teenager. She'd heard about his technical skills but knew very little else about him.

"You don't look old enough to drink," she said by way of greeting.

"Good disguise, huh? I'm really forty-two and balding."

She laughed.

"We're going to be working together, I hear," he said. "I don't want you to think I can't take care of myself because I can."

"Glad to hear it."

"I scored a 92 on my marksmanship test yesterday."

"Impressive," she said.

"Getting there. But I don't think I'll ever have your consistency. Did you ever get less than a perfect score when you were in training?"

She smiled at him. So he'd hacked into her file. "What else do you know about me?"

"You're twenty-eight and single," he offered. "You speak six languages fluently: English, Greek, French, Spanish, German, and Arabic. And you know a smattering of Italian, Portuguese, Russian, Chinese, and Japanese. You have black belts in several martial arts disciplines, and you're an expert fencer. And you weren't born in this country, but I couldn't track down where you were born, or what your real name is."

"Pretty good," she said. "Now what about you?"

"I'm eighteen," he said. "Good at computers and math, but not much else, I'm sorry to say."

"Parents? Family?"

"Dead," he said, without elaborating.

She looked into his eyes and saw herself—a solitary orphan

with pathetic social skills and no direction. He was a kindred spirit.

"Mine too," she revealed. But the memories were still too painful.

There was another long silence.

"You'll do fine," Hunter said, getting to her feet. "I'll keep an eye out for you."

She had done just that, and brought him home alive.

Afterward, at her urging, he decided to remain in the relative safety of the computer room and kept his ear to the ground. That suited Hunter fine. She didn't have to worry about his well-being, and she had a faithful ally in the inner sanctum. Two years later, when she escaped the Academy, she took Kenny with her.

There was nothing he wouldn't do for her.

She typed: **Hey buddy, checking in. Anything interesting on the pipeline these days?**

She glanced again at the photo on the desk while she waited. Her guest wouldn't be up and around for a while, but she thought it best to put it away. Avoid questions. She opened the bottom drawer and put the photo face down atop a pile of file folders. Then she locked the desk and pocketed the key.

A chime from her computer drew her attention back to the monitor. The reply from Kenny read: **Shit yes, Hunter. You're in danger! I've been trying to reach you for two days—someone's put a million dollar contract out on you. Don't know who yet, or whether anyone's gonna try to collect. Working on it. Be careful.**

Hunter took a deep breath and let it out slowly, forcing herself to relax against the tension building between her shoulder blades. She typed: **Keep me posted, but quit worrying. I'm safe.**

Yeah, right. Where have I heard that before?

Hunter stared at her computer screen. *Someone puts a million-dollar price tag on your head one day, and the next—a woman shows up on your lonely road. With no ID. Driving a stolen car like the devil himself was after her.* The hair stood up on the back of her neck.

You should rest, she told herself. *She'll be out for a while, and you should be sharp for question-and-answer time.*

Hunter lay down on the leather couch in the living room. *Let's just say for a moment she isn't after me. This is just some weird coincidence. Whoever this woman is, what the hell am I going to tell her?*

She closed her eyes and began to take deep, even breaths. As she drifted off, her mind considered and rejected several more identities. *Law enforcement. Personal trainer. Musician. Possible. But the security monitors would be kind of hard to explain. Gardener. Architect. Paramedic. That one's not bad. But a paramedic would have a phone and a pager. And better medical supplies. No, it should be a job where I could be working from home. Maybe something connected to the Internet...*

The dream began as it always did. She was opening the door to his bedroom. Everything was going smoothly. The layout of the house had been exactly as described. She had only to dispatch her target and get the hell out of there. No muss, no fuss.

His outline under the covers was clearly visible in the moonlight streaming in through the window beside the bed. The blankets were in disarray. Like Hunter, he was a restless sleeper. But he didn't stir as she approached the bed, and his soft snoring satisfied her that he was well and truly asleep.

She didn't know his name. She knew nothing of him at all, except that he was alone in the house, and he had to die. Garner thought it best, in the beginning, to give her as little information as possible.

So she put the gun to his head. But before she could pull the trigger, there was a noise behind her. She whirled around. A figure stood silhouetted in the doorway.

It was only her third assignment, and it was the first time things didn't go exactly as expected. She did as she'd been taught. It had been drilled into her, over and over again. Leave no witnesses.

She raised the gun and fired at the silhouette, then spun back to the bed and fired again as the sleeping figure came awake. The man in the bed made no further movement or noise. But the other did not die immediately. There was a sound from the doorway, a soft moan of pain.

Hunter had to be sure. She pulled out her flashlight and approached the dark figure on the floor. The flashlight's bright narrow beam found a teenaged boy. Tall. Blond. Young. Fifteen or sixteen, probably. He had pajamas on, and there were braces on his teeth. Blood was pumping out of him at a furious pace from the hole in his chest, and Hunter knew he would die soon.

"Dad!" the boy moaned. He reached out with a bloody hand and grasped the cuff of Hunter's pants. "Dad!"

Hunter woke from the dream as she always did, thrashing about in a cold sweat, trying to shake the boy off, heart pounding.

She never knew the boy's name. But he haunted her still.

Hunter lay on the couch, feeling not at all rested from her nap. Her eyes scanned the wall of bookshelves facing her, and she considered what lay behind them. The secret chamber that housed her arsenal. Her mind returned to her search for the right identity. *And just how would you ever begin to explain the tools of your trade?*

It was that thought that gave her the answer she was looking for. The persona that was perhaps closest to her heart was perfect for her current situation. It would explain the bunker, the isolated location, even the security monitors. The tools that were behind the wall—some of them anyway—would be the perfect window dressing to the story. So would the bunker's décor.

She went to the bookshelves and removed a first edition of *The Secret Garden* from a high shelf. She stood on her tiptoes and pressed the button that was hidden behind it. A loud click confirmed the unlocking of the center panel, which she swung open to reveal her armory. She ignored the safes that contained her weapons and moved to the one that housed her surveillance equipment.

Hunter opened the safe and pulled out a high-powered spotting scope, her night-vision goggles, and her 35mm and digital cameras. She placed them on the coffee table in front of the couch. Her large-format field camera and tripod were set up in a corner of the living room before she closed the bookshelf panel and locked it again.

She was pleased with her solution, and not just because her photographer identity would explain the bunker and its contents. *I don't want to lie to her if I don't have to,* she realized, *and this is close to the truth.* The admission startled her. She was a practiced liar, and did it well. *Why don't I want to lie to her?*

She had no answer for that. There was just something about the woman that she found intriguing. The stranger brought out a gentle, nurturing side of Hunter that she wasn't aware she was even capable of. And she had certainly stimulated Hunter's libido.

Resigning herself to the unfamiliar feelings, Hunter began thinking about how she would introduce herself to her guest. She swore long ago she would never tell anyone her real name again, yet she didn't want to use Hunter, either. She didn't know what the woman was doing there, or who she was. It wouldn't be prudent to admit her real identity.

And there was another reason.

You just don't want to be Hunter anymore, do you? Hunter is ruthless. Unfeeling. And that's not what you want to be with her.

No immediate solution came to mind.

She returned to her computer to check in with Kenny. **Anything new?** she typed.

His response came at once. **Yes. At least two takers on your contract. Our old friend Otter, and a woman—no ID on her yet. Still don't know who is behind it. More soon, I hope.**

A woman? Oh, Lord. This just gets better, Hunter thought. Her head began to throb.

Her gut feeling still refused to acknowledge that the woman in the next room might be dangerous. But she had to admit that she wasn't altogether certain her hormones weren't clouding her judgment. She vowed not to let her guard down.

She returned to the bedroom. The only light spilled in through the half-open door. She checked the woman's forehead again. The fever seemed to be gone, but the woman moaned softly in her sleep, apparently in pain.

Hunter untucked the blanket on the left side of the bed and pulled it back to check the makeshift splint she'd wrapped around her patient's left wrist. *Not a bad job, if I do say so myself. That'll heal just fine.*

She started to cover the woman again, but froze when she caught sight of something she had missed earlier while treating the woman's injuries. *Damn. How could I not have noticed that? Probably because you were staring at her breasts.* Hunter frowned. She felt a sharp pang of disappointment. *I bet someone is looking for her.*

CHAPTER TWO

Six days earlier

S cout had been tracking her quarry for four days. The trail had led her to St. Ignace, just north of the Mackinac Bridge, the five-mile span that joins the two peninsulas of Michigan. Here the trail had turned cold, so she was checking places she knew that Hunter was known to frequent before hiding out—groceries, car rentals, and post offices.

Scout had done her research. She was certain she was well ahead of anyone else trying to collect on the million-dollar contract. Not that many would even try. Although Hunter's reputation had been exaggerated over the years, it was not entirely false. But Scout was confident she would prevail. *I know how you think, Hunter— because I'm just like you. That gives me an advantage. That's how I'll catch you. And no one is more motivated than I am.*

She parked the stolen Sebring sedan behind a small post office, next to a battered red pickup that probably belonged to the clerk. There was only one other car, parked directly in front of the main entrance. She waited until it pulled away.

Stepping into the small alcove, she paused to study the clerk behind the glass door ahead of her. Perfect. Piece of cake. Scout unzipped her coat and opened the top three buttons of her blouse.

The clerk was middle-aged and balding, with a bit of a paunch. Part of a tattoo peeked out from his rolled-up cuff. He looked up when the door opening triggered a little bell.

Scout put on a smile sure to melt any man and sashayed toward him. "Hi there," she said, leaning forward across the narrow counter. "Can I steal a few minutes of your time? I'm new around here and I bet you are just the guy I need to talk to." She reached out and touched his arm. "Whatcha say, sugar? Help a girl out?"

The clerk almost managed to hide his surprise. "I'm all yours, beautiful." He grinned.

"I'm looking for a girlfriend of mine," Scout purred. "She's the memorable type. Tall. Pretty." She reached into a pocket and withdrew a small photograph. It looked like a driver's license or mug shot photo. Face front, plain background. Hunter wasn't smiling.

Scout handed it to the clerk. "I haven't seen her in a while. Her hair might be different," she said, studying his face.

One of Scout's best talents was reading people. She noticed the tiny changes in body language that signaled when someone was hiding something or lying. She'd seen the man's eyes widen just slightly in recognition when he looked at the photo. Yet he did not readily admit he'd seen Hunter.

"She was in here waiting for a package?" she encouraged, giving his arm a little caress.

"Well, honey..." he finally said, a leer spreading across his face, "I may need to think about that a while. I get off in an hour, how about we go get a drink and talk about it?"

"Look...I'm in a hurry now to find her, but I'll take you up on that when I'm done with my little errand."

The clerk scarcely heard her. He was too distracted by her cleavage—her breasts barely contained within a lacy red bra that peeked out of her tailored silk blouse. He licked his lips as his eyes traveled upward, taking in her fair skin and tousled blond hair. Meeting her eyes again, he gave her a wink. "Now, I'm sure whatever it is can wait until my memory comes back. Maybe I need a little incentive."

Scout's flirtatious façade evaporated. The pouty smile disappeared. Her eyes narrowed to slits. "How's this?" she snapped, moving before he could react. She pinned down his arm with the hand she had casually caressed him with, cutting into his wrist with sharp fingernails. Her other hand brought a small but razor-sharp knife to his throat.

Oh, Jesus. He felt it nick his skin, drawing blood. He froze. She was at least a head shorter than he was, but he knew immediately not to resist. "Hey, now, no need to get upset, lady," he stuttered. "I was just trying to be friendly. I didn't—"

"Shut up. Just tell me what you know." Scout pressed the knife against his throat again, this cut a little longer and deeper. A small stream of blood trickled down his neck, mixing with his sweat. Her face moved to within inches of his, and he could see a savage determination in her eyes.

"She came in here a couple of weeks ago. Three weeks, maybe. She was around a couple of days, waiting for a general delivery package." He paused and felt another jab from the knife. "The name was Mary Green, I think. She got tired of waiting, told me to forward it on when it arrived. I did, couple of days later. Some place farther north of here." The words rushed out. He was sweating profusely.

"Where exactly?" she urged, still only inches from his face. She pressed the knifepoint against his jugular.

"I really don't remember," the man shrieked.

Scout could taste his panic. "You will."

Two hours later, in a small run-down motel called the Vagabond, Scout relaxed on room seven's queen-sized bed. Her back, cushioned by worn pillows, rested against the headboard, and her legs were stretched out in front of her, crossed at the ankles. She was eating takeout Chinese food with chopsticks. Beside her, a laptop computer displayed pictures of quaint log cabins for rent, each equipped with a fireplace, kitchen, and hot tub.

It took her about an hour of searching the Internet to find what she was looking for, and her final choice had nothing to do with amenities. She unplugged the phone line from her laptop and replaced it in the phone, then picked up the receiver and dialed.

"Star View Cabins," a female voice on the other end answered.

"Hey there," Scout responded with a convincing Southern drawl. "I'd like to reserve a cabin for my husband Boots and I for a second honeymoon. I'm fixin' to surprise him. Y'all got somethin' available right away?" As she spoke, Scout cracked open her fortune cookie. *People find it difficult to resist your persuasive manner.* A grin spread across her face.

"As a matter of fact, we do. We had a snowmobile group just cancel."

Scout glanced at the laptop. "I read on your Web site that your cabins are really secluded, is that right?"

"Yes, indeed. All the cabins are well away from each other, and the resort is accessible only by snowmobile this time of year. Will you be bringing your own or would you like me to arrange transportation out of Tawa for you?"

"We'll have our own, thanks. I'd like to reserve your most remote cabin for two weeks, starting tomorrow night. And can you lay in a supply of groceries and put a note on my booking that we don't want to be disturbed? Just charge everything to my credit card." Scout's voice dropped to a conspiratorial whisper. "I'm gonna make Boots unplug his pager and I'm leaving the cell phone at home."

"That's no problem at all. May I have the number on your credit card?"

"You bet. The name is Douglas Dunn." She read off the number. *Serves him right,* Scout thought. *What idiot leaves credit card receipts in his glove compartment?*

She hung up the phone, humming happily to herself. *You're mine, Hunter. All mine. Wherever you're hiding, I'll find you.*

CHAPTER THREE

A chorus of tympanis pounded away in her head as she came awake. *Stop that infernal drumming. I can't think.* She tried to remember where she was and what had happened to her. *Feels like I've been dropped off a cliff and then run over.*

Bits and pieces came to her. She'd been hurt. The voice. *I remember the voice.* A warm, reassuring voice had taken care of her. Made her feel safe. She longed to hear it again.

She fought to open her eyes. One swollen lid obeyed and cracked open enough for her to see she was in a darkened room. A bedroom, unfamiliar. Light spilled in through a half-open door opposite the bed. *Where am I? What is this place?* She tried to turn her head to look around, but the effort amplified the insistent throbbing behind her eyes. She took a deep breath and a stabbing pain cut into her side.

"Ow! Damn!"

The woman heard a yawn from somewhere off to her right, close by, and then came the rich, low voice she remembered. "Are you all right? Where does it hurt?"

The voice was a tonic. She had to see the face behind it. She tried again to turn her head. But the pain was unbearable, and she slumped back against the pillow. "My head is killing me," she rasped out, wincing in pain. She heard a drawer open and the sound of water being poured. "Who are you?"

"I'm going to help you take some ibuprofen," the voice said, ignoring her question. "Try to drink as much of the water as you can."

A hand slipped beneath her neck, then moved to support the back of her head. It was a large hand, strong, but it cradled her

KIM BALDWIN

with caring gentleness. Another hand came into her narrow field of vision. Two long fingers and a thumb held small brown tablets to her lips.

She opened her mouth, extending the tip of her tongue, and felt the tablets placed there. She saw the hand withdraw briefly, and then it was back with a glass of water, the fingers guiding the straw into her mouth. She downed most of the contents of the glass. Her mind urged the voice to speak again. As she relaxed and released the straw, it did.

"Well done. Think you can manage some soup? You need to get your strength back."

"Yes. Hungry," she answered. She was shrugging off the haze. Her mind was becoming clearer, and the water hitting her stomach seemed to bring it back to life.

"That's a good sign. Rest for a bit. I'll be back and wake you when it's ready. Chicken noodle okay?"

"Yes, thanks," she managed, absently adding, "My favorite."

She heard the squeak of a chair cushion beside her, and then she saw the retreating back of the woman behind the soothing voice. Her caretaker reached the door and pulled it open, pausing to turn back for another look. For an instant she was silhouetted in the doorway.

She had long legs, a lean, athletic build, and she was tall. Broad shoulders tapered to a thin waist and trim but shapely hips. She was somehow bigger than life. A presence. The woman in the bed involuntarily sucked in a deep breath at the sight. She ignored the pain the movement caused in her side. The door closed, plunging the room into darkness again.

Nice. Very nice, she thought. *Great voice and incredible body.*

She dozed.

The next thing she knew she felt that hand under her head again. A strong enfolding arm followed the hand; this time she was brought slowly up to a half-seated position. Pillows were jammed behind her back, but the arm remained around her shoulders, supporting her weight. She could feel the presence of her rescuer beside and slightly behind her, but she was unable to turn to look her in the face. She wanted to, very much.

The room was still darkened, but enough light came in through the open doorway to allow her to see that a small rectangular tray had been placed over her lap. It held a bowl of soup, spoon, and napkin, and a mug of weak tea. As she sat up, the blanket slipped down a bit, exposing her upper chest to cool air. She shivered. She realized for the first time she was naked, and the knowledge sent a faint flush to her cheeks. *How long have I been out?* she wondered. *And how long has she been taking care of me?*

She went to cover herself and only then realized that her left arm was in a splint. It screamed in protest when she tried to move it. She gasped.

Her caretaker reached around her and pulled the blanket back up, tucking it around her chin. "I'll feed you," the voice said softly, so close to her ear that she could feel the warm breath of the words move her hair.

"Who are you?" the woman asked again, as the napkin was tucked beneath her chin.

"Eat first, then we'll talk."

Neither spoke for several minutes while the injured woman sipped the soup. She could see just a bit out of her other eye now, and was glad for the return of her depth perception.

She studied the hand as it fed her. Long fingers, tanned skin. Short fingernails. No polish, no jewelry. *A handsome hand*, she thought.

After the tea was gone, and near the end of the bowl of soup, she broke the silence, asking between spoonfuls, "Will you tell me again what happened? I can't seem to remember." She felt much more lucid now, despite the persistent pain in her head. It was easier to talk, and she could feel her strength returning.

The body she was leaning against stiffened, and there was a pause before the low voice spoke again.

"You were in a car accident. I saw it happen, got you out, and brought you to my home. We're a long way from a town or doctor."

"A car accident? Did I hit something?"

"No, your car went off the road and flipped over. You were going pretty fast, and the road wasn't plowed. What's the last thing you recall?"

She closed her eyes. She'd been trying to remember. Her brow creased in concentration. "Where am I?" she asked. "I mean, what state is this?" She was still having a hard time conjuring up anything about the accident.

"You're in Michigan. The Upper Peninsula, near Lake Superior. You don't remember that?"

She tried to focus. Everything she remembered seemed inconsequential. She liked chicken noodle soup, for one thing. *It's my favorite. I know that.* The thought consoled her a little.

I've been to Paris. She could see sidewalk cafes, and patisseries with glass display cases filled with delicate desserts. *I had a puppy when I was small.* But she couldn't recall the dog's name. *I make a mean Bundt cake, and I drink way too much coffee. Someone is always kidding me about that, but who? Who?* It hit her. Her name.

She felt her stomach drop suddenly as the realization struck home. *Who am I?* A sudden panic washed over her. *Oh, my God, I can't remember my name.* Her breathing accelerated. *Or where I live.* She searched her mind for some solid bit of information. Her home, her family. Nothing.

"What is it?" the voice said. The arm that supported her tightened its hold. "You're hyperventilating. Try to slow your breathing."

She wanted to comply, but it was several moments before she calmed enough to speak. "I don't remember...anything. Nothing important, anyway. Why can't I remember my name?" Saying the words, admitting it aloud, increased the sense of panic. Her eyes welled with tears. She tried to turn her body, forgetting for a moment about her injuries. The shooting pain in her head stopped her cold. "Who am I? Do you know who I am?"

The woman supporting her shifted position, and she was soon enfolded in strong arms.

"No, I'm sorry," the voice whispered beside her ear, as a hand gently petted her back. "But don't worry. You'll remember, or we'll find out somehow."

She began to cry, burying her face into her rescuer's soft cotton pullover. It was too much to absorb at once. Too overwhelming to think that the memories of her life had been wiped out. The only thing that was keeping absolute terror at bay was this kind Samaritan who had taken her in.

"Everything will be all right, you'll see."

She had no reason to believe the words, but she wanted to, desperately. She clung to the voice and the arms that embraced her, weeping softly until a more urgent need asserted itself.

"I have to...use the bathroom," she whispered. She felt the embrace loosen, and then she was lowered back to the bed.

"I'll help you," the voice said, out of her range of view. "I have a pan for you to use. You'll need to help me get it under you... but try not to put weight on your left leg. Your knee got banged up in the accident."

Cool air hit her body as the blanket was peeled back, and she put her weight mostly on her right leg, lifting her hips so the shallow plastic pan could be placed beneath her. Mortified by her vulnerable position, she took a moment to empty her bladder. Soon it was over, the pan was removed, and the blanket tucked again around her. She had kept her eyes closed throughout most of the process in her embarrassment.

Her exertions and full stomach made her suddenly very tired. She yawned.

"Sleep now, I'll be back to check on you in a while."

She was nearly there when a last conscious thought occurred to her. *Wait, what's your name?* she wanted to ask, but she was already asleep.

Hunter returned to her computer to see if there was anything more from Kenny, particularly about the people who were after her. Intuitively, she believed that her patient's apparent amnesia was no act.

Kenny's reply was immediate. **Otter is in Michigan, don't know where. Got a little on the woman. She's short, blond, pretty. Did a recent hit in the Mideast. Has a thing for knives, uses lots of identities. No one knows her real name.**

Hunter bristled. Nah, it couldn't be. She could spot an

assassin at a hundred yards. She'd know if one were lying in her bed. Wouldn't she?

What's happening to me?

Hunter had very large "personal space" requirements and was far from the nurturing sort. She rarely allowed anyone within her reach, unless she was initiating the contact. And that contact was usually either violent or for the rare purpose of quick, anonymous sexual gratification. She had always been a solitary individual and had resigned herself to the fact she would always stand apart from the rest of the world.

But something was different now. She had thought herself incapable of the sorts of things she was now doing and feeling. But she'd not only readily embraced the woman—she'd enjoyed it. Very much. Enjoyed the physical closeness. The act of comforting another human being.

And something else. Her libido had made itself known again, stirring up the mental image of the naked body beneath the sheets.

Hunter wasn't yet ready to try to articulate what it all meant. She felt a little out of control. But it wasn't an altogether unpleasant experience.

She admitted to herself that no matter how much she was drawn to the stranger, nothing would likely happen between them. She was what she was, after all. *Who could care about me, with the life I've led and the things I've done?* And there were far too many unknowns about her guest. She knew there was no future in it. Still, she found an unusual peace with her unexpected company. She'd enjoy what she had, as long as she could.

She thought some more about the questions that were sure to come up the next time the woman woke up, and the answers she would give.

With that thought, she heard the woman's voice call out tentatively from the other room.

"Hello?"

Chapter Four

Two days earlier

Tawa was a small tourist town, catering to a year-round stream of outdoor types. Springtime brought bird-watchers, and summer invited campers, hikers, and boaters. Fall drew deer hunters, and winter heralded the arrival of snowmobile and cross-country ski crowds.

As a result, Tawa was well equipped with a number of small motels and cabins, some well away from the town itself. It was toward one group of such cabins that a brand new Ski-doo snowmobile now raced.

Scout tried to dissipate her growing frustration. She'd spent the last three days trying to pick up some trace of Hunter. There were a lot of places to check, and so far she'd found no one who remembered seeing her quarry. She'd questioned all the clerks at the local post office, and none recalled seeing the woman in the photograph or a package addressed to Mary Green.

She was certain that Hunter would isolate herself. So she concentrated her search on the more remote inns and cabins around Tawa. She'd put a lot of miles on the snowmobile she bought at a small dealership in town, once again charging it to the sedan owner's credit card. But her stakeouts had turned up no sign of Hunter, and she began to wonder if her target had moved on. She didn't think so—Hunter had this destination in mind, she was sure. For the first time, it occurred to Scout that maybe Hunter had a permanent place in the area.

She eased back on the snowmobile's throttle as she approached the isolated cabin she'd been staying in, then braked in front of the door and shut off the engine. When she did, she could hear the faraway sound of a helicopter. Her eyes scanned the sky. The sound was coming nearer, but the trees around the cabin prevented her from seeing it. The sound changed, becoming constant, then abruptly stopped. *It's at the lodge.* She started up the snowmobile again and headed off in that direction.

When her snowmobile emerged from the woods about a half mile away, she spotted the helicopter. It was parked in a small clearing just outside the log-and-stone lodge that served as the central office for the Star View resort.

Her suspicions were confirmed when she saw three men carrying supplies from the helicopter to the lodge. *That's how they supply these remote places—with helicopters. There can't be more than a couple of them at most out here in this godforsaken place.* She watched from some distance away, the snowmobile engine idling. The men finished with their task and went into the lodge. Not a good time to talk to the pilot. But soon, very soon.

Scout headed back to her cabin to plot her next move. She was closing in on Hunter. She could feel it.

Chapter Five

When Hunter's patient awoke again, she tried to stretch and winced at a dull pain in her knee. The throbbing behind her ear was tolerable, and she could move her head without the shooting pain she had experienced earlier. Her eyes felt crusty and swollen, but she could see well enough to take in her surroundings. The room was still dim, illuminated only by a shaft of light coming in through the open door.

She looked toward the dark leather easy chair where her benefactor had been seated. A small sigh of disappointment escaped her lips as she realized she was alone.

Her eyes began to take in the rest of the room. There were no windows. She was in a comfortable antique bed that sat quite high off the floor. Oak, in a simple Shaker style she found very pleasing. There was a matching table next to the bed. It had two drawers and a shelf full of books. She couldn't read the titles in the dim light. On the table were a lamp, a pitcher and glass, and assorted first aid supplies, neatly arranged: ointments and gauze, tape and scissors, a bottle of ibuprofen.

A large dresser that also matched the bed completed the furniture in the room. There was nothing on the dresser—no photographs or knickknacks. The walls held a few large framed pictures. Photographs, she thought, but she couldn't see any of them clearly. Except for the pictures, the room had a Spartan, impersonal feel to it. Like a hotel room.

The silence was deafening. No T.V. noise from the other room. No sounds at all. *Did she leave?*

She didn't want to be alone. She felt claustrophobic. She

ached to hear the voice again and see the woman who belonged to it. Clearing her throat, she called out, "Hello?"

Hunter hesitated briefly with her hand on the doorknob, composing herself, before stepping into the room and walking to the bedside table.

The stranger's eyes followed her. She had propped herself up on her good arm to get a better look at the woman who had saved her, but Hunter was backlit again as she crossed the room and she doubted that the woman could make out her features.

Hunter kept her eyes averted as she crossed the room with a quiet ease—seemingly relaxed, but her heart rate had accelerated. She was on guard again, and trying to subdue the nervous excitement she felt at her first real face-to-face meeting with her guest. She turned on the lamp, which brightened the room considerably. Then she dropped into the chair beside the bed and brought her eyes up to meet the woman's.

They stared openly at each other, certainly longer than was typical or polite, neither speaking. Hunter held her breath. So did the stranger. A shy grin spread across the woman's face.

Even with the bruises and bandages, the stranger was beautiful when she smiled. It was an easy, friendly smile that lit up the woman's face, and Hunter was instantly captivated by it. But what she was feeling was so alien to her she didn't quite know what to do. Her eyes were drawn to the woman's lips. She couldn't stop herself from imagining what it would be like to kiss those full, smiling lips. She felt a skittering of excitement run up her spine. She smiled back at the stranger.

"I know you, don't I?" the woman said. She cocked her head, her smile widening. "I'm sure I know you."

Hunter was stunned. Momentarily speechless. *She knows you because she came here to kill you!* her instincts screamed.

But even if it was true, the woman obviously didn't remember. Hunter could tell. The stranger was smiling at her with such a hopeful expression on her face, so certain she would agree, that

Hunter almost regretted having to tell her she was wrong. "I'm sorry. I'm pretty certain we've never met." *I'd remember you.*

The woman's smile faded. "Are you sure? You seem so... familiar."

Hunter nodded. "I'm sorry."

She stared off into space as she considered what Hunter had said. "Maybe it's just wishful thinking, then," she said finally. She fought back tears. "I wish I did know you. It feels as though I do."

"Perhaps I just remind you of someone." *Or you've seen my picture.*

"Maybe so," the woman sighed. Her shoulders slumped forward, her disappointment evident. "I'm not sure of anything at the moment."

"Well, you're going to be my guest for a while," Hunter said, leaning forward to encourage the woman to look at her. "I can't move you right now anyway, and that will give us time to try to find out who you are and where you belong." She smiled reassuringly at the stranger. Her face did not betray her doubts.

The woman met her eyes and seemed to relax. "Thank you," she said. "For saving me, for taking care of me. For..." *making me feel at home,* she wanted to say, but chose "...for everything."

"My pleasure," Hunter replied. *That's certainly an understatement.* An image of the woman's naked body flashed into her mind. She suddenly felt much too warm. She cleared her throat and looked away. "I mean—I'm happy to help. Just let me know what you need," she stammered, trying to regain her composure.

The woman noticed the faint reddening of Hunter's bronzed skin. Taking advantage of the opportunity to study her rescuer unobserved, she took in the finely sculpted features, high cheekbones, and the sensual curve of Hunter's lips. Thick, shiny brown hair cut in a layered shag fell just below her collar. *You're just...breathtaking...that's the word. I sure wish I did know you.* "What's your name?"

"Call me Kat," Hunter said. "It's a nickname I haven't used in a long while," she explained vaguely. "But I kind of miss it." There was a sadness in her voice that told the stranger there was more to the story, but Hunter didn't elaborate.

Hunter had never thought she'd want to hear that nickname

again. She had buried it in shame many years ago. But something had whispered the name in her ear, and for the first time in a long time, it felt right.

"I'm very pleased to meet you, Kat." The woman's voice was soft, almost reverent, the name spoken with such a tenderness that it reminded Hunter of a time long ago.

For a moment, Hunter imagined she was Kat the innocent again, and not an assassin. They were just two strangers meeting for the first time, and anything was possible. But a nagging inner voice snapped her back to reality. *You don't know who she is. Remember that. And you are what you are. You can't erase your past.*

"What about you?" Kat asked. "I know you don't remember your name, but we need to start somewhere. What would you like me to call you? Any names spring to mind?"

The woman pursed her lips and closed her eyes in concentration. After a moment, she opened them again and shook her head. "Nothing. Wait! I had to have a driver's license with me, didn't I? Didn't you find a wallet or anything?"

Kat rose from the chair and put one hand into a pocket of her jeans. She placed its contents on the bed and sat back down. "This was all you had on you."

The woman glanced at the bills—a ten, two fives, and three ones—and scattered coins before reaching for the small key ring that lay piled with them. The plain ring contained three keys. There was a small one, unmarked, that looked like it might open a padlock and a car key with a logo etched on it she couldn't identify. The third looked like it might be a house key.

Before she could ask, Kat volunteered, "The big key is to a Mazda vehicle of some kind, which is not what you were driving when you crashed. You were in a dark blue Sebring sedan."

The woman gripped the keys lightly in the palm of her hand. "None of this is ringing a bell. What about my clothes?"

"No help there either," Kat answered. "I'm afraid I had to cut them off you."

The woman stared off into space and said nothing for a long while. Finally, almost to herself, she whispered, "Well, that's just jake."

"Jake?"

The faraway look didn't change. The woman took in a deep breath and exhaled it slowly. "Just an expression," she sighed.

"What's it mean?" asked Kat.

The woman in the bed looked at her again and forced a half smile before answering. "It means everything's all right...just dandy."

"Ah," Kat said, "I see. You were being facetious. Sometimes slang escapes me, I'm afraid."

"You know, that's not too bad, actually," the woman said. "Jake, I mean—as a name, until we can think of a better one."

"Or until you remember," Kat added, rising and moving around the bed. "Jake it is." *I need to go back out to the crash site and really give the car a going-over,* she thought to herself. *There's got to be something there to tell me whether you're a bounty hunter or not.* She came up on Jake's left side and motioned for her to relax and lie flat again. "We do have one clue," she said, hesitating only a moment before reaching down to roll the blanket back from that side of the bed.

She kept Jake's torso covered but exposed the splinted left arm. Supporting the arm as she did so, Kat put her fingers under the woman's left hand and raised it up off the bed. She watched with feigned detachment as Jake stared at the plain gold wedding ring on her finger.

CHAPTER SIX

Evan Garner tapped well-manicured fingernails on his mahogany desk, an expansive monstrosity that had been polished to a high gloss. He stared at his computer screen, which displayed the first page of a top-secret dossier on the bounty hunter known only as Hunter.

Garner's large office was richly appointed. The wall behind him contained a bank of TV monitors—all muted at the moment, but tuned to the major broadcast networks and CNN. Another wall was a thick glass window to the outside world; the view was of a busy but unremarkable suburb of Washington, D.C. Across the room from the desk sat a matching mahogany conference table that could seat a dozen people comfortably, and there was also a sitting area with a burgundy leather couch and two matching easy chairs.

There were two sharp raps on Garner's door and a brawny man of about forty stepped into the room. He was clean-cut, clean-shaven, and impeccably dressed in a dark blue suit and conservative gray tie, just like his boss. The suit had been tailored to minimize the well-developed muscles of his arms, shoulders, and chest. Garner demanded that his employees have as few distinguishing features as possible so they could blend into the background in any situation.

"You're late, Thomas," Garner barked. "Better make it worth my wait. What's the latest?" Most men would be afraid to use that tone with Thomas Maynard, but Garner's burly bodyguard was loyal and respectful beyond reason.

"Sorry, Mr. Garner," Thomas said. "Well, sir, we think Hunter's in Michigan. Otter tracked her as far as Detroit and then lost her." Beads of sweat appeared on Thomas's forehead. "The chick—Scout—she went to Detroit too, and from there to a little town in the Upper Peninsula called Tawa. It's out in the middle of nowhere."

He had his boss's full attention. "Well? Has Scout found Hunter?" Garner demanded.

Thomas flinched. "We don't know, sir. Scout hasn't checked in like she's supposed to. We're getting her location from the tracking device. It hasn't moved from Tawa in three days, so we think she may be on to something. We tried calling her cell phone, but no one answers."

Garner glared at him. "Three days? And no one has followed up to see if she just dumped the damn cell phone?" He got a little louder with each word, finally shouting the last two.

"Sir, she wouldn't do that, would she? You made it clear she couldn't collect on the million unless—"

"She doesn't care about the money, Thomas, or she would be calling in like she was told." Garner enjoyed talking down to his underlings. "Take care of it now. Get somebody there as soon as you can."

The bodyguard stepped to a phone on the conference table and dialed, then spoke softly into the receiver. They had a man already in Detroit on other business. Frank would be dispatched to Tawa as soon as he could rent a private plane. Thomas thought his boss was a genius for putting tracking devices into the cell phones they issued the bounty hunters.

She was one creepy bitch, Garner thought, as he recalled the day Scout had showed up at his door. That she had made it to his office was a testament to her tracking skills. The million-dollar contract she'd come to inquire about had been very discreetly issued, sorted through layers of filters to hide the identity of the person behind it. Interested parties were to send an e-mail; they would be contacted with further details.

Garner had never heard of her, and that was saying a lot, for he knew most of the players in her business. But her tactic had impressed him even as it unsettled him. And he was so anxious to neutralize Hunter he would not turn anyone away from trying to collect on the contract.

But he knew there was a lot the woman wasn't saying. She

didn't ask questions about the money. She just wanted a good photo of Hunter and whatever details she could get about Hunter's likely whereabouts and known habits.

He recalled now that she had never agreed to the stipulation that she check in every twenty-four hours on the cell. She'd just smiled at him as she pocketed the phone. It was a disturbing smile. Almost feral. The thing that had bothered him most, however, was how anxious—almost gleeful—she seemed to be to go after Hunter, even after he had warned her about her target's considerable skills.

Otter, the other bounty hunter who was going to try to collect on the contract, was also anxious to begin the chase, even though he knew firsthand of Hunter's abilities. But Garner was not surprised to see Otter turn up. He knew the man needed money, and he also knew that Otter had personal reasons for going after Hunter, whatever the risk.

Thomas hung up the phone. He walked the few steps from the conference table to stand again before his boss's desk, awaiting further instructions.

"Contact Otter and tell him to head to Tawa. Fill him in on Scout. Has anyone else expressed interest in the contract?" Garner asked.

"No, sir. Six others answered the ad, but when they found out who the target was, they declined."

Garner nodded. "That's all."

As Thomas departed, Garner rose from his chair and walked to the windows. He looked outside, but his gaze was unfocused. A part of him regretted having to eliminate Hunter. They'd been close once. But it needed to be done. There was no alternative.

Chapter Seven

I'm...married?" Jake asked, staring at the ring. "How can I be married and not remember that?" The gold band should have given her comfort. It was a tangible sign that she belonged somewhere, was tied to someone...someone who probably was looking for her, worried about her, missing her. But the ring only amplified her confusion and frustration. "How could I forget a husband?" *Or is it a husband at all? I'm obviously attracted to Kat. Could I have a...a wife somewhere?*

"Someone must be looking for you," Kat said.

Their eyes met. The revelation stood like a wall between them. *How can I feel so drawn to you,* Jake wondered, *if I'm committed to someone else?*

Kat returned to her chair, all the while studying Jake's face. She was convinced the amnesia was real.

"I don't remember a...a spouse," Jake said. "How can I not?"

"I wouldn't worry about it. You hit your head pretty hard when you crashed. Give it time, you'll remember," Kat said. She tried to sound encouraging, but the effort fell flat.

Jake looked at Kat. At that moment, anyway, she didn't want to remember any more than Kat wanted her to. In the emptiness of her amnesia, she wanted to latch on to the only thing that made her feel safe—this enigmatic woman who had rescued her. But the ring could not be ignored. She propped herself up again.

"How can I have a whole life I don't remember? How is that possible? I must have a home somewhere. A family. A job." A tremor laced the edge of Jake's voice. She looked to Kat, her eyes beseeching Kat for answers.

KIM BALDWIN

"Let's try something. Lie down and close your eyes. Try to relax," Kat urged.

Jake nodded and settled back into the pillows.

"Take a deep breath. Try to clear your mind," Kat said. "See if any images at all come to you. A face, perhaps—mother, father. Your boss. Maybe a school chum?"

Jake tried. She set her mind adrift. But she could see no parents. No spouse. No best friend. The only image was that puppy she'd had. A mutt, part German shepherd. But she still couldn't recall his name. "Nothing, really. I had a dog once, long ago, but that's all." She opened her eyes.

"Well, it's something," Kat said. "Don't be discouraged. Try again. See if you can imagine an event. Maybe that will trigger something. Thanksgiving dinner when you were growing up. Opening Christmas presents. Blowing out candles on a birthday cake."

Jake closed her eyes again and tried to do as Kat instructed, but any image she conjured up seemed forced and unreal. More like images from a movie she'd seen, perhaps. Not her own memories. "Nope," she said, after several moments of trying.

"Okay, how about a place? Your living room, maybe, or kitchen. The place where you work. Maybe you can get a glimpse of what you did for a living." Kat tried to keep her expression and voice neutral.

Jake once again closed her eyes. After a few seconds, the image of the Parisian patisserie came again to mind. It was like a picture postcard—a snapshot with no context—but it seemed real, as though she'd experienced it firsthand. She could see the rows of pastries and tortes and vaguely remembered finding it difficult to make a selection. That picture was followed by another. People on a subway train. She had studied their faces and could see them again now. An older man with a mustache, reading a London newspaper. Then a series of images flashed by. The crowded, noisy street bazaar in Cairo. A craftsman hammering a copper plate. A rug vendor. A filthy stall where a toothless merchant smoking a hookah sold grilled pigeons on bamboo skewers. She could smell the smoke mixed with the prevailing odor of unwashed bodies. That was all. There was nothing more. She opened her eyes and the images disappeared. "I think I've traveled a lot," she said, with a hopeful tone in her voice that hadn't been there before.

Kat leaned toward Jake. "What did you see?"

"Well, I think I've been to Paris," Jake said. "I can remember shopping in a pastry shop. And I've been on the London underground. And at a street market—in Cairo, I'm pretty sure."

Cairo? Kat's instincts warned her not to react to the news, but Kenny's e-mail rang in her mind. The woman who was after her had done a job in the Middle East.

"Well, you should be encouraged," Kat said. "But perhaps that's enough for now, you shouldn't push yourself." *And I need some distance.* "Why don't you try to think about something else for a while, or rest a bit, while I make us something to eat. Are you hungry?"

"Yes, I am. That would be great."

"I'll see what I can scrounge up. Are you allergic to anything, any foods I should avoid?" Kat asked without thinking.

Blond eyebrows furrowed. Jake didn't answer immediately. "I don't think so," she said, drawing the word out. "Sure hope not, anyway." She looked back up at Kat with a forced smile.

Kat nodded and left.

Jake decided to take Kat's advice and put aside her past for a while. She took another look at the room, its furnishings now illuminated.

She could see that the framed pictures she'd noticed earlier were indeed photographs—nature photographs, and good ones. The wall to her left held three; the first was a vivid sunset over a lake, the vibrant streaks of pinks and purples mirrored in the water below. The next was an equally colorful shot of the aurora borealis, or northern lights—curtains of blue and green and a hint of yellow spread across a night sky. And beside that, a brilliant display of autumnal color. Sugar maples adorned with fiery reds, oranges, and yellows lined a forest trail partially obscured by a thin layer of equally colorful leaves.

On the wall to Jake's right was a grouping of animal photographs: a black bear and cub, a coyote, a fox with a litter of kits, and an animal she couldn't identify—a mink or a weasel, maybe. And hanging above the dresser across from her was a majestic photo of a bald eagle in flight.

The pictures provided bursts of color on an otherwise muted palette. The whole room was gray: the walls, the floor, even the ceiling. *It's a concrete room,* she realized. *That's odd. Like a basement or something.* And there was no clock in the room. No TV. No stereo. No phone. Weird.

The room made Jake feel even more disoriented and confused. The whole situation conjured up question after question with no answers in sight.

The woman who had saved her had been nothing but kind and considerate. But there was a lot she wasn't saying. *And who's to say that what she's told you is the truth?* Jake wondered for the first time. The thought was terrifying. *She could tell you anything and you wouldn't know any better, would you? You don't know her real name, or where you are, or how you got here. Or even when and how you got hurt.*

A part of Jake wanted to march into the other room and demand to know exactly where the hell she was and what had happened to her. But she was in no physical shape to be making demands.

And despite all the unanswered questions, there was something about Kat that made Jake want to trust her. *She saved your life and took you in. Nursed you back to health. What would she have to gain by lying?* she asked herself. *Maybe she's just a little eccentric. Not everyone has a television and a phone. And she did say we're a long way from the nearest town.*

She wanted so much to believe Kat. She had little else to believe in at the moment. And she couldn't deny she was powerfully attracted to the woman who had rescued her. She was anxious to get to know her better.

She pictured Kat bringing her here and stripping off her clothes to treat her. The idea of this stranger's hands on her naked body, especially while she was out cold, should have made her feel a bit uncomfortable. But she found the opposite to be true. The image was exciting. Provocative. Still, she was feeling a little too exposed and vulnerable in her current state.

"Kat?" she called out. Almost before the word left her mouth, her benefactor appeared in the doorway—so fast that Jake jumped and the blanket slipped, nearly exposing her breasts. She grappled for the covers.

Kat looked chagrined and a flush colored her cheeks. "Sorry, I, uh...I didn't mean to startle you," she stammered. "Whatcha need?"

"Do you have something I might put on?" Jake asked. "I'm feeling a little, uh..."

"Of course." Kat came into the room and moved toward the dresser before Jake could finish. She removed a large T-shirt from a drawer and held it up for inspection. It was dark blue and plain, displaying no hot vacation destination, no alma mater insignia, no clues at all about its owner. Probably comfortably loose on Kat, it would make a short dress for her guest. "This okay?"

Jake nodded, and Kat took the shirt over to the bed.

"Let me help you put it on," Kat said. She tried to appear nonchalant, but her hands were shaking, just a little, as she stood over Jake, staring at her bare shoulders and the hint of cleavage she could see. *Those breasts are dangerous weapons.*

"I can probably manage myself," Jake stuttered. She could feel herself blushing. "But thank you."

Kat gave her a half smile and a tiny nod and handed her the shirt. "Let me know if you need anything else. Dinner will be in an hour or so." She turned on her heels and left, closing the door behind her.

As soon as she was alone, Jake pushed back the blanket, exposing her nakedness. She shivered as she stretched stiff arms and shoulders, careful with her splinted arm. She felt weak and shaky.

Her eyes fell again to the plain gold band she wore. She pulled it off with difficulty, noting the deep impression it had made on her finger.

She looked inside for an inscription.

Kat returned to the kitchen and put her mind to work on what she could conjure up for dinner with her limited ingredients. She was a creative chef, having learned a variety of techniques in a crash course at Le Cordon Bleu cooking academy in Paris two years earlier. The class was originally a means of getting close to a target, a paranoid drug dealer with a taste for fine food, but Kat had inadvertently discovered her fondness for cooking.

Tonight she found herself wanting to come up with something special for her guest. It was a challenge given her resources. She stepped into the pantry and scanned the shelves, selecting and then rejecting first one recipe idea, then another, stymied always by a missing key ingredient.

Finally she found a few combinations she thought would work and carried an armful of supplies back into the kitchen. First she made a simple dough and set it aside to rise. Then she chopped and grated several ingredients and dumped them into a cooking pot and set it on the stove.

As she worked, Jake dominated her thoughts. The smart move would be to keep her distance from the mysterious woman, but even as Kat devised a plan to return Jake to civilization, she found herself enveloped in a whimsical daydream about the two of them riding out the winter alone in the bunker.

Kat shook off the fantasy and checked on dinner. She gave the pot a stir before retiring to the living room.

She needed her music.

Jake read the words engraved on the inside of the wedding band for a third time. "Always and forever – S." *Who are you, my forgotten mate?* she wondered. *Steve? Stan? Sue?* The inscription made her feel guilty about her fascination with the woman in the next room and her own inability to recall anything about this S.

Jake's capricious memory loss left her feeling confused and afraid. She could not remember faces or names from her past. But she felt she hadn't lost the essence of herself—her beliefs, her sense of right and wrong, the core of her character. She believed that she held fidelity and the vows of marriage to be sacred, even if she could not recall making the commitment. She was torn between a conscience that urged fidelity to a spouse she couldn't remember and the undeniable attraction she felt toward the woman who had saved her.

Jake relaxed against the pillow, closing her eyes and trying to think of all the names she could—male and female—that started with S, hoping one would knock something loose in the logjam of her memory. Sid, Sean, Sylvia, Sandy, Serena, Stuart, Sally, Stacia...

Music. Sweet, haunting music. First it accompanied Jake's dream, whatever the dream was, for it was immediately forgotten as soon as reality took over. Then she realized she wasn't imagining the sad, soulful voice of a cello. The rich, fluid sound, played without accompaniment, rang with emotion, telling a story without words.

Jake listened with her eyes closed, letting the music embrace her. It struck a chord deep within her. She understood it perfectly. It was the story of love and loss, regret and longing. She'd surely never heard anything so beautiful.

Soon it was over, and there was silence. After a minute or two, the cello played again, and it wasn't long before Jake realized she recognized this piece. It was a suite by Bach. She smiled. She somehow knew that music was an important part of her life, and the certainty of that pleased her.

There was silence again. Jake waited, hoping it would resume.

❖

She hadn't remembered dozing off. It seemed that she slept too much, though she couldn't be sure how much time had elapsed since she'd been brought here. She had no watch. But the sleep had done her good, because she felt markedly better after each nap. She stretched and brought her hand to her face, fingering the bandages on her nose and cheek, feeling the stitches in her forehead. *Glad I wasn't awake for that. What can't this woman do?*

She called out, "Kat?"

KIM BALDWIN

The door opened after only a moment and her host stood framed in the doorway. "Something you need?"

"I've never heard anything more beautiful," Jake said. "It was you playing, wasn't it? Not a recording?"

Kat reddened slightly. She looked at the floor and nodded.

"I know the last piece," Jake said. "Bach—the first of his six suites for cello, right?"

Kat looked at Jake and her eyebrows rose. "You know music. That's not something a lot of people would probably recognize."

Jake nodded. "I think it's important to me." Her eyes held Kat's. "Your playing...it really touched me. Especially the piece just before the Bach." She closed her eyes, remembering. "Such emotion. Grief...love...longing. It was wonderful. It really touched me."

Kat said nothing, staring at the other woman, her look of surprise quickly masked when Jake opened her eyes again.

"I've never heard it before. I'm sure I would remember," Jake said. "Well, I think I would, amnesia or not. Who is the composer?"

She understood. Kat didn't speak for a long time. She wrote music because it was the only way she knew to express her feelings. The only way she knew to deal with emotions she fought, but that sometimes welled up in her unexpectedly. She had never shared her music with anyone because it was just too...intimate. Personal.

But although Kat hadn't intended Jake to hear her play, she found it didn't bother her that she had. She wanted to get to know this woman, as much as that was possible. She sensed that Jake wanted that too. Kat would not speak of her growing feelings, and there was much she could not reveal of her life, her past. But perhaps her music had shared things about herself she could never verbalize. It seemed so. Jake certainly seemed to understand the music.

Finally Kat spoke. "I wrote it." It was a big admission for her. It was the first time she'd given someone a glimpse at her innermost feelings in many years.

Jake's jaw dropped. "You? You wrote that? That's amazing. What a gift you have. Does it have a name?"

Kat shook her head. "No," she said. "It's only for me." She

looked at Jake with a masked expression, but her voice was gentle when she continued. "I mean...I've never played for anyone before. I thought you were asleep."

"You've never played for anyone? Ever?"

Kat shook her head.

"Then I feel very honored. You're good enough to be with any symphony," Jake replied. "And that piece was just extraordinary. Have you written anything else?"

Kat shrugged. "A few things."

"I hope you'll let me hear them one day." Jake looked directly at Kat in a way that left Kat feeling uncomfortably exposed.

Kat looked away. "Perhaps," she said. "Right now I need to finish dinner. It won't be much longer." She turned and left without meeting Jake's eyes again.

It was only after she had gone that Jake remembered the other reason she'd summoned Kat.

She really wanted to see herself in a mirror.

❖

Kat reappeared in the doorway carrying the lap tray she'd used earlier. A spicy-sweet aroma filled the room. Jake's stomach growled. Until then, she hadn't realized how hungry she was.

Kat helped Jake sit up and positioned the tray across her lap. "I've got lots of food, but kind of a limited supply of ingredients," she said, nodding toward the food to encourage Jake to dig in. "I hope it's all right."

Jake surveyed the contents of the tray. A large basket of pita bread was nestled beside a shallow dish of hummus, its creamy surface garnished with a splash of olive oil and a dusting of paprika. Two bowls held an aromatic stew she didn't recognize.

Jake attacked the food with gusto. "It's wonderful," she said. "Hummus I've had, but not as good as this. And the bread is still warm. You made it from scratch?" she managed between mouthfuls.

"Yes," Kat replied, reaching down to pull the easy chair close to the bed. She dropped into it and reached for a piece of pita. "I had to improvise a little, but I think everything turned out okay."

She was going to ask Jake if she needed help eating, but it was apparent the woman was managing just fine.

"What is this?" Jake asked, sampling from one of the bowls.

"Fakorizo," Kat answered automatically, reaching for the other bowl. Her authentic pronunciation of the dish, with a slight rolling of the *r*, drew Jake's attention.

"Greek?"

"Yes, Greek," Kat replied, her mood suddenly serious, her appetite gone. She put the bowl back on the tray.

Jake instantly regretted that her simple question had seemed to trigger something painful to Kat. Pretending to ignore the sudden change in her host, Jake dug into her bowl. The fakorizo was delicious. A medley of orzo, tomatoes, onions, and lentils, it had an unusual spicy sweetness. Glancing surreptitiously at Kat, Jake let several purrs of delight escape her lips as she chewed slowly, savoring the taste.

But Kat's mind was obviously elsewhere. She stared off into space, saying nothing.

Finally stuffed, Jake leaned back against the pillows and took a deep breath. "That was just fabulous. Thank you for going to so much trouble."

That brought Kat back from her musings. "No trouble. Glad you enjoyed it."

They looked at each other in companionable silence for a long moment before Jake grinned and asked, "So, you're a paramedic chef who plays a mean cello when she's not saving damsels in distress?"

Kat laughed out loud.

It was an unexpected treat for Jake—she loved the warm, low chuckle and accompanying full smile, though she wished it had lasted longer.

Too soon, Kat's smile faded, and her eyes grew a little sad. "It's kind of hard to describe what I am," she said, suddenly serious again. "A lot of things, to be sure."

Jake nodded, hoping she would elaborate.

"One of the things I like most to do," Kat said, gesturing with one hand toward the photos hanging on the wall, "is take pictures. These were all taken within a fairly short distance of here."

"You really are a woman of many talents," Jake replied, studying the photos again in light of this revelation. She wanted to hear Kat laugh again. "Do you do everything perfectly?" she teased.

Kat tried to smile, but her eyes were sad. She didn't reply.

"These are all—well, just...splendid, that's what they are," Jake proclaimed after a moment. "So you're a photographer, then? For a magazine?"

"Sometimes for magazines, yes. I do mostly freelance work."

"Well, you certainly have a good eye," Jake said. *But why are you so evasive with every answer?* When it was apparent Kat would volunteer no more, Jake prodded, "I'd love to see more of your work."

"That can be arranged. There's more in the other room, when you're able to get up and around a bit."

Mention of the other room piqued Jake's curiosity. Maybe there was more she could learn about Kat out there. It also drew Jake's attention back to the odd feature of the room she was in. "Is your whole house made of concrete? Or are we in a basement or something?"

"Well, it is a little unusual," Kat replied. "We're underground. This is a bunker, built into the side of a hill."

Jake cocked her head. "A bunker?"

"It's a retreat of mine. And a particularly good base for a nature photographer, as you can see. Lots of wildlife right outside. The house is built into the hill mostly to hide it." All true. "It's kind of like a big hunter's blind, only I mostly hunt with a camera instead of a gun." Kat still didn't understand why she wanted to avoid lying to Jake. She just did. "And it's very energy efficient because it's underground," she explained vaguely. *You're giving away too much.*

"Well, it is certainly very...different," Jake said, inviting further comment, but none was forthcoming. After a long silence, she tried again. "You said we're a long way away from a town. Don't you get lonely here by yourself?"

Kat shrugged. She couldn't bring herself to answer truthfully. *I didn't know how lonely I was until you showed up.* "I travel a lot. And I have a couple of other places. I split my time between them."

Kat didn't elaborate, and Jake sensed this was a topic she probably shouldn't pursue—at the moment, anyway. *Do you have someone else waiting for you in those other places?* she wondered. The thought was unsettling.

But though she was terribly curious about Kat's life, there was something else on her mind.

"Do you have a mirror?" she asked, bringing her hand up to touch the stitches on her forehead again. "I'd like to get a look at myself." She remembered vaguely what she looked like, but she really needed an up-close reminder. She was torn about whether she wanted the experience to jar her memory or not.

"Yes, of course," Kat answered. "But I'm afraid the only one I have is bolted to the bathroom wall."

"Well, I could use a trip there," Jake said. "I mean, I think I can make it, if you'll help me. I really hate bedpans."

"Sure," Kat answered. "I can do that. Give me just a minute." She rose from the chair, took the tray from the bed, and left the room. In a moment, she was back, hesitating at the side of the bed only briefly before she reached down to peel back the blankets.

Before Jake realized what was happening, Kat leaned down, put one arm under her legs and the other behind her back, and lifted her with apparent effortlessness. Jake was cradled securely, her head against Kat's chest. She inhaled deeply, relishing for a moment the unexpected sense of safety and security she felt enfolded in the other woman's arms. Then she exhaled, a long, slow breath that sounded like a sigh. For a moment, neither woman spoke, and Kat didn't move.

Jake tilted her head up and met Kat's eyes. Their faces were only a few inches apart. "I could probably walk, with help," she stammered. Her heart was racing. *But this is much nicer.*

"No need," Kat answered, breaking eye contact and stepping toward the doorway. *I can't be this close to her,* she thought, willing herself to take steady, even breaths.

"You're very strong," Jake said playfully.

"Mmm-hmm," came Kat's reply, accompanied by a bit of a smirk. "I'm a big girl."

"I noticed," Jake replied before she could stop herself.

Kat laughed and carried Jake into the bathroom. En route, Jake had a quick glimpse of the outer room. Her eyes took in the living room, the wall filled with books, the cello. A large camera on a tripod in the corner.

The bathroom had a shower, a sink with oak cabinets beneath, and a toilet. Kat set Jake gently on the commode and retreated to the doorway. "Call me when you're ready," she said, and closed the door.

Jake glanced around the room. There was a large mirror over the sink on the wall to her right, and to her left was another grouping of animal photographs. She smiled, realizing they were all critters associated with water—a beaver, an otter, and a muskrat. It made her think back to the groupings in the bedroom, and she wondered whether there was a commonality there that she'd missed. Then it hit her. They were all meat eaters. Predators.

When she called out that she was finished, Kat came in and leaned down to pick her up as before. But this time Jake anticipated the action. She raised her good arm as she was lifted and draped it behind Kat's back. Her hand came up to rest on Kat's shoulder, just where it met the base of her neck. As she was hoisted into the air, Jake's hand gently squeezed into the softly muscled shoulder.

The action caused Kat to tighten her grip on Jake ever so slightly. It seemed a more intimate position even than the one they had been in earlier, and it was beginning to make Kat a bit uncomfortable. She felt a little light-headed as her pulse went into overdrive. She was certain that Jake could feel her heart pounding through the blood vessels in her neck.

She needed a distraction. She walked to the mirror and turned sideways so the woman in her arms could see herself. Kat turned her head toward the mirror too, wanting to witness Jake's reaction. It was a mistake, and Kat knew it immediately.

CHAPTER EIGHT

The visual tableau of them reflected in the mirror—their faces close together, arms enfolding each other, seen only from above waist level—made it appear they were entwined in a lovers' embrace.

The image made Kat acutely aware of Jake's soft skin under her hands. And she was fixated on the small hand pressing gently into the base of her neck. Kat closed her eyes. A tremor raced through her body. She was certain Jake noticed.

Jake glanced at herself only long enough to think, *Yes, I know you.* She was mesmerized by the image of them together. The vision sent a scorching rush of heat through her body. She looked at the woman who held her just in time to see Kat's eyes close tight, an unreadable expression on her face.

Jake gently squeezed Kat's shoulder, a gesture that was almost a caress.

Kat's eyes shot open.

Their eyes met. Neither woman spoke for several heartbeats.

Finally, Kat looked away. She cleared her throat, not thoroughly trusting her voice at the moment, and managed only two words. "So...familiar?"

"Yes," Jake answered. She looked at their reflection again. Kat would not meet her eyes. After a moment, Jake said, "I kind of had an idea what I looked like. It's reassuring, despite the fact I look like a raccoon."

A trace of a smile appeared on Kat's face at that, and her eyes met Jake's again.

"But seeing myself didn't stir up any memories of my past," Jake said.

Both women relaxed a bit at that, relief reflected on their faces. Kat just nodded and carried Jake back to the bedroom. Once again Jake glimpsed the living room, kitchen, and office. She wanted to get a better look at the rest of the place, but she didn't want to impose further on Kat. Not at the moment, anyway. *She must be getting tired of lugging me around. Though she really looks like it's no effort at all. She's not even breathing hard.* Jake could feel Kat's taut muscles beneath her hand.

Kat focused on taking even, steady breaths. She was anxious to distance herself from the raw sexuality of Jake's body. Her nerves simply couldn't take it.

As they neared the bed, Jake suddenly gripped Kat's shoulder again and said, "Wait."

Kat froze and looked reluctantly toward the blonde, her face only inches away.

But Jake wasn't looking at her. She was looking at the two large photographs hanging above the bed.

One was a close-up of a lynx, eyes half closed, lazing in the sun in a meadow dotted with purple wildflowers. The other was an equally impressive shot of a bobcat, his brown, spotted coat vividly outlined against a snowy backdrop. "They're wonderful. I hadn't seen them before," Jake said. "I notice you have a kind of theme going in the different rooms. Water beasts in the bathroom. And predators in here, right?"

Kat nodded. "You're very observant, aren't you?"

"What's in the other room?" Jake asked.

"You'll see soon enough," Kat said, setting Jake back on the tan flannel sheets. She pulled the fleece blanket up again to cover her. "Right now, you need to rest. And I'm going to go out for a bit. I won't be long." She gave Jake a little smile as she reached over to shut off the lamp.

She was halfway to the door when Jake's voice stopped her. "Kat?"

She paused and turned back toward the bed.

"Thanks again. Sorry I'm so much trouble," Jake said.

"You're no trouble," Kat lied as she left. Jake could turn out to be nothing but trouble. Kat felt it.

❖

Jake closed her eyes and settled back into the pillow, but she knew she wouldn't sleep immediately. Her heart still hammered in her chest. It had started pounding during the seconds? minutes? while they were standing in front of the mirror. *Sure seemed like a long time, but I bet it wasn't. I guess that's what you call chemistry.*

Her mind jumped to a place she didn't want it to. *Did I—could I—have felt this with the person I married?* She didn't want to think about being married. But something kept reminding her of it. *And what about children?* That thought hadn't occurred to her until now. *Surely you can't forget your own children.*

Though Jake sensed her attraction to Kat was mutual, she would not act on it. Not while there were so many variables outstanding, so many questions unanswered. *Who knows how much the situation and my amnesia might be screwing with my emotions. Besides, if I have a spouse, surely my feelings for Kat will disappear when my memory returns. Won't they?*

CHAPTER NINE

In his younger days, he was called Otter because of his appearance. He had a lean and lanky frame then, and a habit of wearing his dark hair slicked back with copious amounts of hair grease. He had the same dark eyes as his namesake; lifeless eyes, the eyes of a predator. And he had an otter's temperament. Playful one minute, jovial, but capable of sudden, unspeakable viciousness.

His hairstyle hadn't changed much, but he combed it more to one side now in an unsuccessful effort to cover a bald spot. The lean physique was gone too, replaced by the softened flesh and paunch of middle age. But he still had a clever mind and infinite patience—tools essential to his chosen profession.

He'd been out of prison for six months, living in fleabag hotels and picking up whatever odd jobs he could. It was hard to get back into his old line of work. He had been out of touch for seven years, and too many others were now competing for the same contracts. He also lacked the money to invest in the kind of surveillance equipment and other toys that were needed on the bigger jobs.

So he answered the ad for this contract not expecting to collect on it. It was one of the biggest he'd ever heard of, for one thing, so he was certain it would attract a lot of takers better equipped than he was. But he'd lucked out, perhaps because of his past association with Garner. He'd not only been given the opportunity, he'd been provided with enough cash up front to take care of his immediate needs, including the rental of the dark green Ford Explorer he was driving.

He wanted the million, of course. It would set him up for life. But he'd almost have taken the contract for nothing when he found out who the target was. The icy bitch he held responsible for his incarceration.

Otter hadn't liked Hunter from their first meeting, and that dislike had turned to loathing when she had left him stranded during the job they did together, taking away his only means of escape.

He spent his time in prison dreaming of revenge. He hadn't tried to find her since his release only because he had no idea where she might be and he lacked the resources to look. Otter knew how dangerous Hunter was and would proceed cautiously, but his overpowering need for vengeance and the million-dollar reward overrode any misgivings he might have had about going up against her.

He could see a green mileage sign that indicated Tawa was just another twenty miles down the road.

I'm coming, bitch. He licked his lips in nervous anticipation. *It's payback time.*

CHAPTER TEN

K at suited up in her parka and arctic boots. She was standing in a concrete-lined tunnel some twenty feet long that connected the living area of her bunker to an underground garage. From this connecting chamber there was also a small offshoot tunnel that went straight up. Ladder rungs led up through the smaller passageway, which was just large enough for a person to pass through. It was her emergency exit and had never been used.

She used the tunnel as a giant storage closet. Pegs in the walls held a variety of coats, and along the floor were snowshoes, snow boots, and hiking boots. A couple of large military-surplus metal drums contained gloves, hats, scarves, and other odds and ends.

Once she was appropriately garbed for the bitter cold outside, she walked down the tunnel to the two-inch-thick steel door that led to the concrete garage that housed her generator, water pumping system, and snowmobile. She unlocked the door by punching a series of numbers into a security keypad in the wall. The steel door and long tunnel effectively insulated the living room from the constant, droning noise of the generator. The machine was hydroelectric, powered by a small stream that ran through the hill. Next to the generator was a large, well-equipped toolbox. Kat opened it and withdrew a small metal pry bar and jammed it into one of her pockets.

Kat glanced at the snowmobile. It would cut her time to and from the crash site by at least an hour, but it would also create a much more visible trail. She'd checked the monitors before suiting up and knew that a thin layer of new snow had partially covered the track her sled had made when she'd brought Jake back to the bunker.

But it was still visible. And it wasn't snowing at the moment. Kat glanced at her watch. Three a.m. She was surprised to discover it had been just over forty-eight hours since she'd rescued Jake. She'd lost all track of time. *No wonder I'm so tired.* She decided to walk. She was still a bit unnerved by the way she was responding to Jake, and she wanted some time alone to ponder what was happening. She punched more numbers into another keypad—this one on the wall leading to the outside—and a large panel slid open, revealing the dark night beyond.

Kat retrieved the toboggan and stepped outside with it, breathing deeply of the fresh air. She opened a small hidden keypad on the outside of the panel and punched in the code to close the doorway behind her.

From the outside, the entrance was well camouflaged. An intruder would have to be within ten feet to tell it wasn't the natural slab of rock and moss that it appeared to be from a distance.

She'd brought a flashlight, but the bright moon lit her surroundings well enough for her to avoid obstacles on her way to the wreck. She set off toward the road at a fast clip, torn about whether she hoped to find clues in the wreck that would jar Jake's memory.

Jake wasn't sure how long she had slept, but her bladder was full again and in urgent need of relief. She called out Kat's name and waited expectantly, trying a second time, a little louder, when some time had passed with no response.

Pretty soon she could ignore it no longer. She leaned over and turned on the light, then peeled back the covers and slid her legs over the side of the bed. She dropped the short distance to the floor, trying to keep her weight off her left knee.

The concrete floor was cold against her bare feet. She shivered under the thin T-shirt. She hopped over to the dresser, debating with herself only a moment before opening one of the drawers. It seemed like an invasion of her host's privacy, but Jake was freezing, and her discomfort outweighed the nigglings of her conscience.

The drawer she opened contained socks and underwear. The

socks, all black or navy, were neatly paired and arranged in a tidy row. Underwear and bras—also dark colored and most of them silk—were folded in tidy piles. *Kind of a neat freak, aren't you?* Jake resisted the urge to touch the smooth fabrics, but she couldn't stop herself from briefly imagining Kat wearing them.

She picked out a thick pair of soft cotton socks, closed the drawer, and leaned against the dresser to put them on. Doing so meant flexing her injured knee and putting weight on it, a task that sent a sharp pain to the joint. She waited for it to subside, then opened the next drawer down.

This one contained T-shirts, also meticulously folded and stacked. Jake gave in to her curiosity and glanced through them, but all were as nondescript as the one she wore. The next drawer contained sweatshirts and heavy pullovers. Like the T-shirts, they were plain and dark colored: black, brown, burgundy, navy, charcoal, and dark green. *So you're not a pastel kind of gal,* Jake thought.

She reached for a sweatshirt. She was glad it was much too large for her, for it easily slipped over her splint and extended well below her waist. Warmer now, she shut the drawer and moved toward the doorway, the pain in her knee intensifying with every tentative, limping step.

She negotiated the few steps into the bathroom and relieved herself, then made her way to the sink, glancing at herself in the mirror again as she washed her hands. Without Kat's distracting presence this time, Jake took a few minutes to examine her injuries. The bruising around her eyes was a dark bluish purple, with streaks of mottled yellow. *Not a particularly attractive shade on me.*

She also noticed for the first time the clotted blood in her hair. She ran some water and tried to wash out as much as she could one-handed, careful not to wet the bandages on her face. She was happy with the result, but the prolonged time on her feet was taking its toll. Her knee had begun to throb, and she felt a little light-headed. *Better get back to bed.*

Jake wanted to explore a bit more, but it would have to wait until she was stronger. She hobbled back to bed, finding it momentarily difficult to maneuver herself back onto the high surface with her bad knee and splinted arm. Finally she lay back, exhausted from her efforts, and relaxed into the pillow. Despite the ache in her knee, she was soon fast asleep.

Kat began her inspection of the crash site by raking the high-powered halogen flashlight beam over a wide area around the wrecked car. An inch or two of new snow had fallen, obscuring anything small that might have been thrown from the vehicle when it flipped over, so she knew any search of the ground could only be perfunctory at best.

She moved to the driver's door, still ajar from the rescue two nights previous. A light dusting of snow had blown into the car through the door and rear windshield, which had shattered when the vehicle flipped over. Kat crawled into the sedan and began a meticulous examination, checking the glove compartment again, and under the seats, the floor mats, over the visor. She found a few odds and ends. Some fast-food wrappers. Kleenex. A map of Michigan. A tube of Chapstick. A pair of gloves—women's size small. The gloves were thin leather and form fitting. Not very appropriate for winter, Kat noted. *But very much like the ones I wear when I'm on a job and don't want to leave fingerprints.*

She could find no car registration, title, or insurance information. The car key, still in the ignition, was on a small ring with several others. Kat pulled it out to examine it more closely. There were six keys in all, in a variety of shapes and sizes but with no markings to tell what they opened or operated. There was nothing in the interior of the car to help conclusively establish Jake's identity.

She carried the keys to the back of the car and ran her flashlight over the trunk, which had been partially caved in. The ignition key fit in the lock and turned, but the compartment remained stubbornly closed. Kat took the metal pry bar out of her pocket and popped the trunk.

Shining her flashlight inside, she quickly dismissed the spare tire, jack, and toolbox that dominated the space. Her eyes were drawn to a silver case. One she was well familiar with. It was an expensive Pelican case—indestructible, waterproof, and essentially jimmy-proof. She owned several herself and used them for transporting weapons and delicate camera equipment. This one was a little more than two feet long, less than half that in width.

The case was locked. She tried the keys on the key ring she'd taken from the car. The third one fit neatly into the lock and turned. She took a deep breath before she opened it, suspecting what she would find inside. She wasn't disappointed. The contents confirmed her worst fears.

She stood for several long moments staring down at a photo of herself. It lay atop a high-powered sniper rifle, neatly disassembled and packaged in a custom-cut foam interior. It was an AWC M91 BDR. A premier takedown rifle. She had one almost exactly like it back in her weapons room, but hers was tactical black and this one was NATO green. The case had cutouts to fit the stock, sling, barrel, scope, torque wrench, and cleaning kit.

Kat felt as though she'd been punched in the stomach. Her mind accepted what she'd tried so hard to resist. Jake was the bounty hunter who was after her. But the rest of her still refused to believe it. She couldn't understand how the seemingly gentle woman she'd been tending to, had felt such an attraction to, was a paid killer, just like she was. She'd known a lot of them in her time, and she just couldn't wrap her mind around Jake being a member of that cold and ruthless fraternity.

Kat knew almost immediately that what she should do and what she would do about this revelation were two entirely different things. She would not ordinarily hesitate to kill another bounty hunter foolish enough to come after her. But that was impossible with Jake.

Another option would be to transport Jake by sled to Tawa and leave her at the small clinic there. But without sedatives, it would be a painful, arduous trip for the injured woman. And she'd also then know the route to the bunker, meaning Kat would have to abandon it and move to another safe house.

Kat didn't care for that choice either, and not because she bemoaned the loss of her favorite hideaway. *Unbelievable,* she thought, shaking her head. *Jake was on her way to kill me and I still want to protect her and get to know her. What the hell is happening to me?*

Suddenly a new thought occurred to her. *What if Jake never regains her memory?* Kat considered the possibilities. If she didn't tell Jake what she knew, and if Jake never remembered, what then?

And maybe she isn't married after all, she considered. Few in her line of work were, for a number of obvious reasons. And Kat herself had been known to wear a wedding ring as part of a disguise for a job.

Could this new knowledge change everything? Despite their evidently mutual attraction, Kat had refused to allow herself to really consider any possible relationship with Jake. *But she's just like me. Maybe she'll understand me and accept what I do.* A tiny flicker of something ignited in her. It was hope, an emotion she was unable to recognize. *If she doesn't regain her memory, is there a chance for us?*

Her decision made, she closed the Pelican case and loaded it on the sled, then headed toward the hill where she'd left her own rifle and the deer carcass. That logical inner voice that usually guided her actions tried to warn her against what she was about to do. *What if she does remember? What if she wakes up one day and wants to kill you?* Kat was surprised at how much she wanted to ignore the voice.

The first hint of dawn was breaking as Kat returned to the bunker and checked in on Jake. Her patient was sound asleep, her face relaxed and serene, but her hair was wildly mussed, the blunt-cut strands sticking up in all directions. *She just looks so damn cute. How the hell can she be an assassin?*

She didn't dwell on the fact that it appeared as though Jake was out to kill her; she just couldn't believe her instincts about this woman were so far off base. There were still some things that didn't fit, true. Like where the hell had Jake been going and why was she driving so fast? The lack of ID now made more sense, and so did the stolen car. *But there was no way she could have known I was out on that hillside that night.*

She left Jake to sleep and retrieved the two rifles from where she'd left them in the tunnel. She put them both in her weapons room after spending a considerable amount of time drying and cleaning the rifle she'd left in the snow. Then she spent an hour or so cutting up the deer. Something had gotten to the carcass, probably a coyote or fox, but a large portion was still untouched. There was enough for several meals. Most went into the freezer, but two tenderloins were set in the fridge to thaw for tomorrow's dinner.

Kat went into the bathroom to wash up and glanced into the mirror. There were dark circles under her eyes. She needed sleep. And soon. But she had to smile faintly at herself despite the uncertainty ahead. *Maybe everything will be just fine,* she lied to herself. *If only Jake just never gets her memory back.*

Kat had taken three steps toward the bedroom when she froze, ears cocked. Had she heard something? A moment later she heard it again. A cry of pain from behind the closed bedroom door.

CHAPTER ELEVEN

Otter had only been in Tawa twenty-four hours and he was already sick of the place. He hated small towns. There was never any action. Otter liked to gamble, and he had some cash left from the advance he'd been given for expenses. He'd been able to find out absolutely nothing about Hunter's whereabouts. But he had learned that Michigan was crawling with casinos. There seemed to be one on each of the numerous Indian reservations in the state, and the nearest one was only an hour and a half away. He was getting really tempted to take a detour from the job and see what his luck was like.

As much as Otter wanted to collect on the million and his long-dreamed-of revenge against Hunter, the closer he got to her the more he unconsciously sought to put off the deadly confrontation. He'd kill her, all right, and be happy doing it. But that didn't stop him from having a bad case of nerves when he thought of meeting her face-to-face.

Otter decided to hang out at a tavern he'd spotted near his hotel. He'd maybe shoot some pool and get a few beers while he thought about the casinos some more. He'd been so broke since he'd gotten out of prison he was going to enjoy having a few dollars in his pocket. He slipped his .38 revolver into its shoulder holster and grabbed the hotel key off the table beside the bed.

He was really hoping he'd get another lead on Hunter from Garner, but maybe if he chatted up some of the local boys, they'd remember seeing the bitch.

❖

Thomas knocked twice on Evan Garner's door before entering. He closed the door behind him and waited for his boss to acknowledge him.

"Well?" Garner asked, not looking up from the papers he was reading.

"Frank's in Tawa, sir. He followed the homing device in Scout's phone as far as he could. He just called in on his cell."

"And?" Garner glared at him.

"Well, sir, he's stuck waiting for a tow truck. He was following the signal on some two-lane out of town and got stuck in deep snow. He'll have to go back to town to get a snowmobile to get any farther. It may be a little while before we know more."

"Come back when you've something to tell me," Garner instructed. "And Thomas, keep the word out about the contract. See if we can't generate some more interest." The more the merrier. Garner dismissed his aide with a wave of his hand.

Thomas felt a little sorry for Hunter. He liked her and thought her a hell of a good-looking dame. But Garner sure was determined to see her dead. The brawny bodyguard wondered what Hunter might have done to prompt the boss to want to eliminate his former number-one protégé.

CHAPTER TWELVE

Kat dashed through the bedroom door when she heard the cry.

Jake moaned in her sleep, thrashing about, heedless of her injuries. She cried, "No! Stop!" then let out an agonized wail of pain.

Kat gently held Jake's shoulders to the bed, trying to calm her and keep her from injuring herself further, all the while calling to her in a soft, soothing voice. "It's all right. Everything's fine. You're safe. It's just a nightmare." *What are you dreaming about, Jake? Whose face haunts you?*

She stroked Jake's upper arms, trying to gently wake her. She noted Jake was now wearing a sweatshirt and wondered how she'd gotten out of bed to get it.

Jake's eyes shot open. She looked terrified. She was sweating, breathing heavily, and still caught in the grip of her nightmare.

Kat continued to absently caress her arms, looking down at her with concerned eyes. "You're all right. It was just a bad dream. I have them, too." *Why did you just volunteer that?* "Want to talk about it?"

Jake's eyes focused on Kat, and relief replaced the fear coursing through her. She tried to recall what the dream was about, but it was already hazy. The rush of adrenaline it had triggered was waning, and it left her feeling groggy, almost hungover. "I...I can't remember."

Kat felt a rush of relief. "Well, you're fine now," she said. She pulled her hands away from Jake and nodded toward the sweatshirt. "So someone got out of bed?" she said with a smirk.

Kat's expression chased away the remnants of Jake's anxiety.

"Yes," she admitted. She blushed at the recollection of discovering Kat's silk bras and panties. "Nature called, and I had to answer," she said. "And I was kind of chilly. Hope you don't mind."

"I don't. I just can't believe you made it there and back yourself." Kat pushed aside the alarm bells going off in her head at the realization that Jake had been going through her things. She wasn't snooping. She was just cold.

"That may not have been real smart, in retrospect," Jake said. "Think it aggravated my knee some."

"Let's have a look." Kat moved to the left side of the bed. "It's time for me to check your bandages anyway, though I must say you're looking better otherwise. The swelling on your face has gone down." She peeled back the blanket and examined Jake's knee, which had swollen again. "Doesn't look too bad, but it needs some ice. And you shouldn't try that again," she scolded gently. "Sorry I wasn't here to help you."

Kat loosened the bandage and left the room to make up an ice bag. After that was done, she checked Jake's splint.

"I'd like to examine your ribs now. Can I help you sit up?"

Jake nodded, and Kat slid her arm beneath Jake's shoulders, supporting her and helping her to lean back on some pillows placed against the headboard. Once she was settled, Kat moved in front of her so they were facing each other. Jake shifted her weight and lifted the T-shirt and sweatshirt with her good hand, exposing her bandaged abdomen. She held the material so that it would cover her breasts. The blanket covered her from the waist down.

Without a word, Kat reached out to remove the long strips of material wrapped around Jake's midsection as Jake leaned slightly forward. In order to unwrap the bandage, Kat leaned toward Jake as well, her arms around and behind her. Their faces were only inches apart. Neither looked at the other, their nervousness palpable.

Kat tried to keep her hands from shaking. Her palms were sweating. The proximity to Jake was exquisitely excruciating.

Each experience that brought them close together was more difficult than the last.

Finally Kat got to bare flesh. As Kat's nimble fingers gently probed Jake's rib cage, her hand brushed up against the bottom swell of Jake's breast.

Both women froze.

Kat looked into Jake's eyes, just inches from hers. Then her gaze dropped a few inches to Jake's lips. She longed to close the distance and claim those lips. She hungered for it. She couldn't stop herself. She didn't want to.

Jake held her breath. The touch against her breast had electrified her, and she saw something different in Kat's eyes. A yearning that matched her own. The pupils were enlarged, the lids hooded with desire. Kat's eyes were fixed on her lips, and the smoldering eroticism of her gaze shot through Jake and pinned her in place.

Kat moistened her lips.

CHAPTER THIRTEEN

Otter was perched on a high bar stool in an establishment that most just called Dugan's. The neon sign outside said Dugan's Authentic Irish Pub and Grub. The proprietor, a plump Norwegian with a droopy mustache, polished glasses behind the bar. He'd bought the place a couple of years earlier and kept the name, even though the former owner took many of the authentic Irish decorations with him when he left. It would have cost too much to replace the sign. Now all that was left was the Bass Ale on tap, the Wednesday lunch special—corned beef and cabbage—and a lot of cheap green paper shamrocks tacked to the walls.

There were about twenty other people in Dugan's at the moment. A few were shooting pool at the two tables in the back, and three couples sat at tables eating sandwiches or the special of the day. The rest were on bar stools watching the latest sports scores on ESPN. The place did draw in the occasional curious or thirsty tourist, but it was a neighborhood bar and everyone in it at the moment was a regular, except for Otter.

He was on his third beer and had had no luck pumping the locals. No one had seen Hunter. He was patient. He decided to stop trying for the moment. He was content to get a pleasant buzz from the beer and maybe put a few dollars on a game of pool later.

A small bell tinkled—the door opening to admit another thirsty patron. Otter, bored, turned at the sound and glanced around. The newcomer was a tall, thin man dressed in the tan insulated Carhartt overalls that pegged him as a farmer or at least someone who worked outside a lot. He had a weather-beaten face that was deeply lined though he was probably only in his forties. He walked to the bar and stood two bar stools down from Otter as he waved at the bartender.

"Hey, Karl, gimme a draft, wouldja?" the man said, unzipping the top of his coveralls. He set his hat and gloves on the bar.

"How's it going, Marty?" the bartender replied, drawing the beer and setting it in front of the man.

"Same old, same old," Marty said. "Been up on the roof shoveling snow. Got an ice dam up there again this year, and it's been leaking into my den. Would've gotten my TV if I hadn't caught it when I did." He sipped his beer and glanced up at the latest hockey scores. "Heard anything more about what happened to Sam?"

"Not really," Karl replied. "Mike was in yesterday. Said they still don't have much. Sam told him just before he died that he was meeting with a woman client. You know Sam—said she sounded sexy on the phone and wanted to take a sightseeing tour, just her alone, so he was looking forward to it. That's about all they have to go on."

Otter, who'd been only half listening, tuned in to the conversation beside him while appearing outwardly to take no notice of the two men. He stared at the TV but didn't see it, waiting for the bartender to continue.

"The sheriff called in the state police to fingerprint Sam's office," Karl said. "But they said it was useless. Too many customers been in and out of there, and you know that place never got cleaned."

"What about Riley?" Marty asked.

"Up in Canada on some job the last week or so, they think. Probably doesn't know yet."

"They ever find the knife?"

"Nope," said the bartender. "And there was nothing in Sam's stuff about the client. The last page of his appointment book had been ripped out."

Marty shook his head. "Hard to believe a woman could do that."

"Yeah," Karl replied, moving away to the end of the bar to fill a waitress's drink order.

Otter turned to Marty. "Get a little excitement here?" he asked.

Marty turned to look at Otter and nodded. "Yeah, friend of ours was killed a few days ago. Got his throat cut. Hell of a way to go." He wore a mournful expression and shook his head again as if he still had trouble comprehending the news. "Couldn't have had much in the cash register. Summer and fall were really his busy seasons. He had a helicopter and did mostly tourist flights up over Lake Superior and back."

Otter's expression remained impassive, but his heartbeat had doubled with the latest bit of news. "And they think a woman did it?" he asked.

"Yeah," Marty said. "Sam didn't do much this time of year except make occasional deliveries to places out in the sticks. He had a route of regular stops. But he didn't have any the day he died. Only some woman tourist he was supposed to take up to the lake. He was good with the women, y'know. Got a lot of pretty clients to go out with him."

"Well, I'm sorry about your friend," Otter said. "Where'd all this happen?"

Marty nodded at the condolences. "A little airstrip north of town," he said. "Nothing much else around. That's why they don't have much to go on. Nobody saw anything."

Otter got up from his bar stool and placed a few bills on the counter, then turned to leave. He paused beside Marty and said, "Don't worry. What comes around, goes around—someone will find her." *And that someone will be me.*

CHAPTER FOURTEEN

Desire coursed through Jake. She could still feel the brief touch of Kat's hand on her breast. She closed her eyes and leaned slightly forward, encouraging Kat to close the distance between them. She trembled in anticipation.

A shrill alarm broke the silence.

Kat snapped to attention and bolted from the room.

Drat, Jake thought. Her heart racing, she waited expectantly for Kat's return. Her mind teetered between wondering what the alarm meant and wondering whether the two of them would acknowledge and pursue what had obviously been about to happen.

Her mind unwillingly went back to the ring on her finger. It seemed alien to her. An unwelcome obstacle to her growing feelings for Kat. She wanted to take it off and forget about it, but her conscience stopped her. *It signifies a promise made. And you keep your promises,* it nagged at her. She ran her hand through her hair in frustration and felt where odd sections had dried, sticking hurly-burly in every direction. She closed her eyes, chagrined at what she must look like and embarrassed that Kat was seeing her at her worst.

When she looked up again, she spotted Kat standing in the doorway, an apologetic half smile on her face.

"Sorry about that," Kat said. "I have an alarm system to alert me when something really big gets within a certain distance of the bunker. You know, might be something unusual...something worth shooting," she added. "Just a deer this time."

Jake nodded but said nothing, hoping Kat would pick up where they were before the interruption.

But Kat wouldn't look at her. She took up her place beside

the bed and resumed her rebandaging of Jake's ribs. Once that was done, she examined Jake's face, removing the bandages except for the one across her broken nose. She applied an antibiotic ointment to a couple of areas and left them open to the air to heal. When she was finished, she backed off a couple of feet, putting distance between them and finally meeting Jake's eyes. "You should rest," she said. "It's the best thing for you right now, and I could do with a nap myself."

Jake started to protest. Her body still burned with desire, every nerve ending raw and exposed. She would not sleep any time soon.

But Kat was behaving so differently now, so detached and inscrutable, that Jake knew the moment was gone. She sighed. "All right," she said. "Wait a minute—I'm taking your bed, aren't I?"

"Not a problem," Kat replied. "I've a couch in the other room." She turned off the lamp. "Sweet dreams."

When Kat shut the door behind her, the room went absolutely black.

Jake could not relax. She was wide awake, and as the minutes passed, the darkness seemed to close in on her. It was too quiet. She felt incredibly small and vulnerable. The room was her amnesia, swallowing her whole. She yearned for Kat's return.

Kat slept fitfully. Her mind was preoccupied with analyzing the unfamiliar emotions she had felt before the alarm went off. She had lived her entire adult life somewhat estranged from the world, shutting down emotionally after her family was taken from her. She'd never allowed herself to experience true intimacy with anyone. Certainly she was no virgin, but her sexual rendezvous were all about release and gratification, never affection. They were quick and anonymous, and often a little rough. She seduced strangers, or allowed herself to be seduced, when her pent-up energy demanded an outlet or in the infrequent times when she could not ignore the loneliness that had become an integral part of her.

But what she felt for Jake was more than simple lust. Her mysterious guest totally captivated her and evoked feelings of tenderness, protectiveness, of...belonging. She'd never experienced such things with anyone, and it terrified her even as it excited her.

Kat tossed and turned until midafternoon and then gave up trying to sleep. She got up and headed to the bedroom, leaving the door slightly ajar to provide enough light for her to see. She crossed to the dresser and removed clean underwear, socks, a navy pullover, and a pair of jeans. She noted with some satisfaction that only a pair of socks and sweatshirt were missing from her things, just as Jake had said. The rest appeared not to have been disturbed. Kat could not resist moving to the bed to check on her patient, who was sleeping soundly, snoring softly because of her broken nose. Kat reached out and lightly brushed hair from Jake's forehead, marveling not for the first time at how soft her skin was. It begged to be touched. *This is not good. Not good at all. You're just getting in deeper and deeper. Look at yourself, all touchy-feely all of a sudden!*

As she went about her routine of showering and getting dressed, Kat found herself preoccupied with planning what she would cook for Jake. What power did Kat's guest have over her to make a simple thing like cooking so complicated?

Jake awakened to one of her favorite smells. Freshly brewed coffee. An enticing, earthy fragrance that beckoned her with an elusive familiarity. A necessary part of her daily routine, she was certain, but it triggered no specific memory. She opened her eyes just as Kat set a tray on the end of the bed. The coffee competed with another delicious aroma and set Jake's mouth watering.

When Kat turned on the lamp, she could see that Jake was already awake and watching her. "It's afternoon, but I was kind of in the mood for breakfast, so I made coffee and blueberry pancakes. I hope that's all right."

"It smells wonderful," Jake said, sitting up.

After positioning the tray across Jake's lap, Kat took her seat in the easy chair beside the bed.

"Where's yours?" Jake asked as she took a sip of coffee. She recognized it as a Kona blend, rich and dark and full bodied. "This is so good. I'm a bit of a coffee addict, I think."

"I've already eaten," Kat replied, taking a second cup from the tray. "Just coffee for me. Do you take cream and sugar? I'm afraid I only have powdered milk."

Jake poured warm maple syrup from a small glass pitcher over the stack of flapjacks. "No thanks, black is fine." As Jake devoured her flapjacks, she stole sidelong glances at Kat. From the furrow on Kat's brow, Jake guessed that something was on her host's mind. She put her fork aside and faced Kat. "Want to talk about it?" she asked.

Kat said nothing immediately. She shifted position in the chair, looking down at the floor. She avoided Jake's knowing gaze. "I went back to your car last night and searched it. I'm afraid there was nothing there to help identify you. I'm sorry."

Jake was surprised that Kat had revisited the crash site without telling her about it first. *And at night? That's weird. We really must be out in the country if the car is still there. Why the hell would I have been on such an isolated road?* But despite her questions, Jake felt oddly relieved at the news, as if her subconscious really did not want her to remember who she was.

What if she never remembered? What if there was no way to verify her identity? Part of Jake wanted it that way so she could toss the wedding ring out into the snow and explore her feelings for Kat. But it was a silly fantasy. Anyone could be found.

Jake met Kat's eyes. "Can't the police trace the license plate and tell me who I am? Or at least who owns the car. I have to know them."

"That's a possibility, but we'll have to wait until the weather is better and you're healed some more before we try to get you into town."

Jake nodded. There had to be an answer out there to the mystery of the wedding ring. But what if she met her husband and still couldn't remember him? Despite her respect for the sanctity of marriage, how could she be expected to be faithful to vows she never remembered taking—to be wife to someone she didn't even know?

Jake realized that despite her overpowering attraction to

Kat—or perhaps because of it—she now believed her spouse was a husband, not a wife. When she'd thought Kat was going to kiss her, she knew that what she was feeling was somehow different than what she was used to. The thought of lying with Kat and touching her soft skin...exploring the curves of her body...her breasts...aroused Jake in a way she knew was unprecedented. She felt a flutter in her chest as she imagined it, like she was a teenager discovering sex for the first time.

Her images of her sexual history were indistinct, but she sensed she'd been with men, not women. The thought of sex with men felt...vivid. Real. But although Kat seemed somehow familiar to her, the idea that she'd been intimate with a woman before seemed...kind of unreal. She felt naïve when she tried to imagine it. And she was a little afraid that if she was right about the desire she'd seen in Kat's eyes—and if they gave in to this powerful attraction that seemed to be pulling them together—would she know what to do?

Jake was relieved there could be no immediate answers. She wanted to put off searching for someone she didn't remember to give her time to get to know this woman she was so drawn to; to explore whatever was happening between them. She realized she hadn't spoken in several minutes, and Kat hadn't broken the quiet. She glanced up to see Kat watching her, an expression of gentle concern on her face.

Jake tried to smile. "I'm okay." She shrugged. "I mean, I've been wondering what I'll do if we find out who I am, and I still don't remember. Can't imagine picking up right where I left off if my spouse is a stranger to me." She sighed, looking away, and ran her fingers through her hair again. "So in a way, I'm not in a real hurry to find out who I am from the police. I'd rather remember on my own. But I know any family I have must be worried about me." She sighed. "Nothing we can do about it at the moment. Got any more of that delicious Kona?"

"Yes. Plenty. I'll bring back the carafe." Kat set their mugs down on the bedside table and took the tray from Jake's lap. "You know, you should think about a real name for yourself...just in case you don't get your memory back. And I have some ideas about that. Be right back." She headed for the door.

"I'm not going anywhere," Jake answered. She wouldn't have if she could.

Kat returned with the coffee and a small pile of books. She tossed the books on the bed next to Jake and refilled both of their cups.

Jake scanned the covers. There was a dictionary, the Audubon Society Field Guide to North American birds, a guide to wildflower identification, and one entitled *Michigan Trees*.

"Thought we might get some ideas leafing through these," Kat explained, reaching for the bird book and settling back into the chair. "Lots of names come from nature: Robin, Phoebe, Iris, Violet. We can toss out a few and see if anything hits you."

Jake thought it an inspired plan. "What a scathingly brilliant idea!" she proclaimed with a grin, reaching for the dictionary.

Kat chuckled, recognizing the reference. "Thanks, Hayley," she commented dryly. She'd seen *The Trouble with Angels* too.

Jake looked through the dictionary, flipping randomly among the pages. She recognized immediately what a whimsical task this could be. Her eyes seemed to fall on words that, when considered as names, seemed absurdly humorous. Furl. Fume. Funk. Heave. She glanced over at Kat.

Her host seemed to be taking the task a bit more seriously. Kat's face was furrowed in concentration as she flipped through pages, shaking her head.

Maybe this isn't such a good idea, Kat thought as she scanned the bird book. Nearly every species that jumped out at her was absolutely ludicrous as a person's name. Butterball. Bufflehead. Booby. Canvasback. Cuckoo. Godwit. Grosbeak. She considered Wren and Widgeon; she kind of liked how they sounded, but neither seemed right for the woman in question. She tossed the bird book back on the bed and reached for the one on wildflowers instead, glancing up to find Jake watching her. "Nothing really grabbed me," she explained a bit sheepishly.

"Me neither," Jake agreed. "Well, why don't I just toss out some words at random and see how they sound? Leave it to fate?"

She quirked an eyebrow as a mischievous grin spread across her face.

What's she up to? "All right," Kat said.

Jake made a ceremonious show of flipping the dictionary open on her lap. She closed her eyes and dramatically flexed her index finger before jabbing it on a random entry. She bent over the book to see what she'd landed on and announced, "Gimlet!"

Kat grinned. Why was this silly game becoming so much fun?

Jake repeated the selection process. This time her finger landed on..."Fococcia!"

Kat chuckled. "Could make for some interesting nicknames."

Jake looked momentarily confused, but as she mentally sounded out the options, her cheeks flushed.

Kat's smile broadened. She snatched the dictionary from Jake's lap. "Let me have a go," she said, then went through the same dramatic selection process, finger poised over a random entry. She jabbed blindly at the page, then peered at her choice. "Opaline?"

Jake giggled. "Fine if I was ninety and living in a nice little rest home in Opa Lacka." She held out her hand for the dictionary. "My turn."

Kat grinned and relinquished the book. As their fingers touched briefly in the exchange, a spark flashed between them.

Jake swallowed hard and tried to refocus on the book in her hand. "Uh," she stammered. "Okay, let's try that again." She opened the book and blindly selected "Auger?"

Kat cocked her head. "Actually, I don't think that's too bad. Kind of catchy. But not you. Doesn't suit you," she declared.

"All right, I'll take your word for that," Jake replied. Kat's response had made Jake realize just how much Kat's opinion in this really mattered to her. She would immediately reject any name if Kat didn't like it.

It didn't make sense. Jake had imagined herself as too independent to be concerned with a total stranger's opinions of such things. It seemed the more time she spent with Kat, the more confused she was about her identity. She made no move immediately to return the book to Kat, lost for a moment in a concentrated effort to remember her past.

Kat noticed the change. "Jake? You okay?"

Jake didn't answer right away. She stared off into space, squinting her eyes as if that would help her clear the block in her memory and see beyond it. Finally she looked at Kat and shrugged. "Sorry. Trying to remember. But it's so damn frustrating. I sort of sense things about my life. They feel like long-ago memories, where you can recall vague generalities but have forgotten the details. I've been to a prom, but I can't tell you where I went to school. I love macaroni and cheese, but I can't see my mother's face and tell you if she ever made it for me." She sighed. "Better than remembering nothing at all, I guess. But it's maddening." She handed the book back to Kat and forced a smile. "C'mon, your turn. Pick a good one."

Kat nodded, wishing Jake would laugh again. She loved that laugh—it was lilting, and light, and very infectious. She hadn't laughed very much in her life and it felt really, really good. She poised her fingertip over the dictionary, squinting her eyes for effect, and landed on, "Mucosa!"

Simultaneously, they both said, "Eew," then erupted into laughter. Jake roared until tears streamed down her face.

Kat struggled to contain herself, but every time she looked at Jake, they burst into giggles again.

Finally, after several minutes, Jake leaned forward and took the book. "I have *got* to do better," she said, selecting blindly from the big tome. "Scrumptious?" she read aloud, then blushed. She couldn't look at Kat.

But that was all right because Kat couldn't look at her either. She stared at the wall, a light flush warming her cheeks. Determined to regain control, she blindly reached for the book and cleared her throat, not commenting at all on Jake's selection. She poised her own finger over a page. She chose. She looked down. Her light flush went full dark scarlet in an instant, just as Jake glanced back up at her.

"Well?" Jake urged. "Don't keep me in suspense. What's my new name?"

CHAPTER FIFTEEN

Thomas was relieved to have some good news for his boss for a change. Evan Garner had been growing increasingly sarcastic and terse with each hour that had passed since they'd last heard from Frank, the man they'd sent to Tawa. Thomas had seen it before. It was how Garner manifested his impatience, and it wasn't good. It usually meant his boss was about to erupt, and he would pick the nearest scapegoat if the real target of his frustration—in this case Hunter—wasn't available.

Since it was intended to be a reconnaissance mission only, they had not dispatched their best man to Michigan. They expected only to find out what had happened to Scout—but Garner knew the man might also stumble on Hunter in the process. So the operative had to be expendable.

So they had sent Frank, a large man who followed orders well if they were spelled out in detail. He was quick for his size and skilled at several methods of killing. He was not nearly smart enough to go up against Hunter, but few were, and he wasn't really expected to see her face-to-face.

Thomas rapped twice on Garner's office door and pushed it open.

His boss stared at him as he entered the room. "Frank found the car Scout was driving, boss. It was wrecked off a little road, miles away from anything. Flipped over into a ditch."

"Wrecked?" Garner asked, his curiosity overcoming his bad mood.

"Yeah, door was open, and the trunk. No sign of the broad, but there is some kind of track leading off into the woods, probably from a sled. Frank followed it for a ways, but he said it was slow going on the snowmobile, so he turned back. Needed better lights and warmer clothes. The homing signal ended at the car. Frank thinks Scout's phone must be under the wreck somewhere in the snow. He can't find it." Thomas paused. "He tried to call from the crash site, but his cell phone was out of range so he had to go back to town. He wanted to know do you want him to follow the track. I told him stay put while I check with you."

Garner considered that a moment. "Have him relay to you precisely where the car is, so we can find it again if anything... unfortunate happens to Frank. Then tell him to follow the track and report back as soon as he can."

"Right, boss."

"And Thomas," Garner said, catching him at the door. "Remind Frank that if he does meet up with Hunter, the million is his if he kills her."

Thomas nodded and shut the door behind him.

A smug grin spread across Garner's lips. He was already thinking about how he would celebrate when he could go back outside, unafraid of an ambush from Hunter. He knew better than anyone not to underestimate his former protégé. He'd been living in this secure building and sleeping in his office since he'd issued the contract on her life, and he'd continue to do so until she was eliminated. Even now he didn't feel completely safe. His inner sanctum was familiar territory to Hunter, and she might be bold enough to meet Garner on his own turf.

He hated to give up the million dollars cash, half of it out of his own hefty bank account and half skimmed from accounts he controlled as administrator of the Academy. But business had been very good the last few years. They had had no shortage of assignments, almost all of them bringing in six figures. He knew he'd get no real peace of mind until she was dead. *We're closing in, Hunter. Can your damned intuition feel it?*

CHAPTER SIXTEEN

Jake leaned toward Kat. She tried to see what entry Kat had selected, but the dictionary was too far away. "Kat?"

Kat's blush deepened. She briefly considered substituting any other word on the page in front of her. But she knew Jake would see through the ruse. She sighed, submitting. Her voice was unexpectedly husky when she answered. "Smooch."

"Ah," Jake replied, as a flash of heat suffused her body. "Do you think that suits me?" she wondered. She wasn't aware she'd said it aloud.

Kat didn't answer. She couldn't speak. Her mouth was suddenly parchment dry. Her rapid heartbeat drummed in her ears.

The heat and energy that surrounded them drew their eyes to each other. Kat felt exposed. Every nerve ending was raw. She knew Jake could see how much she ached to kiss her, caress her. She wanted to give in to this voracious and unrelenting craving that was pulling them together.

Jake sucked in a breath when she gazed into Kat's eyes and saw the same unmasked yearning she had seen there earlier. Pupils dilated with arousal were boring into her. The heat running through her body became a fireball.

The anticipation was almost painful.

Kat licked her lips. She struggled to regain some sense of control. But it was impossible when she saw her own ardor reflected in Jake's eyes, eyes that shimmered with wet desire.

It was Jake who broke the silence, although the word that escaped her lips did so without her knowledge or consent. Her body and her soul conspired to remove whatever restraint was holding Kat in her chair. "Please," Jake whispered.

An involuntary moan escaped Kat's lips at the confirmation of their mutual need. She had to shut her eyes momentarily against the hammering of her heart in her chest. When she opened them again, she saw Jake's hand extended to her, her eyes beseeching Kat to close the distance between them. She was powerless against those eyes.

Kat rose from the chair. She moved to the bed, drawn toward Jake like a moth to a bonfire. Jake's outstretched hand found her waist. Delicate fingers closed on a belt loop and tugged her closer.

Kat sat on the edge of the bed, facing Jake. Her hand came up to stroke Jake's face—a soft caress along the line of her jaw—before it cupped the back of her neck, long fingers wrapped in soft blond locks. She pulled Jake's face to hers gently as she leaned forward to close the final inches between them.

The kiss began so gently, so tentatively, that it belied the raging inferno that enveloped them both. *So soft,* Kat's mind crooned. *So wonderfully, exquisitely soft.* Her body hummed with the adrenaline pouring through her, demanding more, seeking deeper contact. She had never felt so alive. She had no further conscious thought, so intent was she on the sensations coursing through her. Her blood was on fire.

Jake's aching need blossomed under the kiss, scorching her, sending her internal temperature soaring. *More,* her body begged. Her tongue answered, the tip reaching past her own parted lips to taste the edge of Kat's mouth, seeking entry, teasing but insistent.

Kat could not contain the breathy groan that answered Jake's oral seduction. She melted into the kiss, parting her lips to allow Jake entry, tongues meeting in sweet caresses—tasting, exploring. The kiss deepened, and Jake tugged Kat's body closer. Her arm encircled Kat's waist.

Finally they had to break apart to breathe.

Kat pulled Jake's head against her chest in a close embrace. One arm gently encircled her. The other absently stroked her hair. Kat breathed erratically. Rational thought had vanished at Jake's whispered plea, and she had surrendered fully to her emotions. It was something she ordinarily would never have allowed herself.

But she had always relied heavily on her extraordinary sense of intuition. It set her apart. She could see things, feel things, know things that others could not. Sometimes even she didn't fully understand how she knew. But her intuition had never yet been wrong. And it fairly shouted at her now that despite all evidence to the contrary, this was meant to be.

Jake trembled. Her cheek against Kat's chest, she could hear the rapid, pounding pulse of Kat's heartbeat. It mirrored her own and was a deeply comforting sound. Jake felt profoundly grateful that Kat was apparently experiencing the same unbelievably intense reaction to their kiss that she was. Memory loss notwithstanding, she knew she was treading on unfamiliar ground. She couldn't believe she'd ever before felt such a powerful connection to another human being.

Neither spoke, both so overwhelmed by the physical and emotional sensations that poured over them, enveloped them, swallowed them whole. This was ecstasy. But would it last?

CHAPTER SEVENTEEN

Frank kept his mind focused on the million-dollar payoff that awaited the person who got Hunter. It was the only thing that kept him pushing on, cursing, following a godforsaken path in the snow that he had long ago decided had to have been made by a masochist.

Frank was a city boy, born and bred. He grew up in Las Vegas, a place he still retreated to whenever he had some free time. He had never been camping, fishing, or hunting in his life. His passions were poker, craps, and nights in the company of a certain redheaded showgirl at the MGM Grand. This outdoorsy crap didn't suit him at all.

His assignment had been one nightmare after another. First he'd gotten stuck in the snow in the rental car and had to wait two hours for a tow truck. At least he'd had plenty of gas and had been able to run the heater while he waited. He'd have been in a lot of trouble otherwise, dressed in his customary suit and tie and only moderately heavy overcoat, shiny dress oxfords, and leather driving gloves.

He'd picked up a heavy sweater, insulated gloves, and a pair of cheap pull-on boots at a Wal-Mart near the snowmobile rental place. Driving the snowmobile to the crash site had actually been kind of fun, at least for the first several minutes. It was a bit like operating a motorcycle, which Frank had tried on a few occasions. The road was mostly straight and even, and he'd covered the thirty miles from Tawa in less than two hours, stopping only occasionally to verify with a handheld monitor that he was still heading toward the homing signal emanating from Scout's cell phone.

He'd spent a long time at the crash site, trying in vain to

locate the phone and then following one of the two sled trails that led from the wreck. The track had gone up a hill, then down the other side, where it converged with the other trail that led from the smashed car.

He followed the track for several minutes, cursing the cold. It had long ago seeped through his thin pants and even into his new gloves and boots. He began to lose feeling in his fingertips, and that really worried him. The track led into a vast wooded area devoid of any sign of civilization whatsoever. He began to regret not asking the snowmobile shop how far the machine could travel on a single tank of gas. When the sled trail went into a thicket of trees too dense for the snowmobile to follow, he gave up and headed back the way he came.

Back in Tawa, after he'd called in his report and fortified himself with a couple of roast beef sandwiches, he'd gone shopping at an outdoor supply store. This time he outfitted himself in a thick insulated snowmobile suit, a fleece-lined Gore-Tex cap, Sorel boots, and oversized mittens that reminded Frank of boxing gloves.

All the items were purchased on the advice of an obliging clerk, a teenaged kid with acne who obviously considered his customer one of the oddest tourists he'd ever seen. Frank had also picked up a powerful flashlight and extra batteries, a water bottle, several candy bars, and a red five-gallon gasoline container, which he filled and strapped to the back of the snowmobile.

He was warm again and more anxious to resume the search now that he had the money as an added incentive. When he'd been sent on this errand, he'd only been told to locate the homing device and the woman it had been given to. But Thomas had just informed him that Hunter might be in the vicinity and that she was worth a million dollars dead. It was the first he'd heard of the contract on her life—Frank had been working on a small matter in Detroit when he'd gotten the call to divert to Tawa.

He had heard of Hunter's exploits, of course, but he was sure a lot of it was just exaggeration. No woman could be that good. So he had no qualms about going after her, although he'd wished it had happened in a warm city and not the damned arctic wilderness.

It took him several hours to follow the track to its end. Several times, the sled trail went where the snowmobile could not, so he had to seek out alternate routes on foot for the heavy machine. It got even harder to follow once it began to get dark. Finally the trail ended abruptly, outside the sheer rock face of a hill. It was obviously a secret entrance of some sort. He began searching for a way in.

❖

Jake relaxed into Kat's embrace. Her heartbeat began to return to normal. She wanted to ask Kat what would happen now, but she was a bit afraid to speak and spoil the moment. Her head was cradled against Kat's breast; she felt immensely safe in the haven of the other woman's arms. Kat continued to gently stroke her hair, while Jake's hand caressed the small of Kat's back.

Both women froze when the shrill alarm again pierced the silence. Kat regained her equilibrium first and reluctantly loosened their embrace. She looked at Jake and shrugged. "Sorry, I'll turn that off. Be right back."

Jake nodded, releasing Kat and following her every move with a small, shy smile on her face. "Don't be long," she whispered, but Kat was already through the doorway.

Annoyed at the interruption, Kat strode to the desk and snatched up the remote control, turning off the alarm and turning on the bank of monitors. Although she'd placed her motion sensor five feet off the ground and close to the wall, far from any game trail, a deer did on rare occasion set off the alarm. But she couldn't understand how it could happen twice in such close succession unless the sensors needed adjustment.

Her answer came as monitor number three flickered to life. Darkness had fallen, but the camera outside the main entrance, equipped with night-vision capability, presented a clear image of a figure examining the camouflaged door panel with a high-beam flashlight. Years of training and experience kicked in at the sight. Kat retreated back into the shadows and Hunter took over.

❖

Jake knew something was horribly wrong the instant Kat

reappeared in the bedroom doorway. The relaxed, gentle demeanor she had exhibited just moments ago was gone. Her face wore a serious, resolute expression now, and energy fairly crackled around her as she strode purposefully to the bed. She was commanding. Intimidating. Powerful. The muscle along the sculpted line of her jaw twitched as she gritted her teeth in determination. Her eyes were cold and distant.

"I can't explain right now, but I need you to stay right here. Don't try to get out of bed." Kat's voice was businesslike. Firm. But she leaned over the bed as she spoke and put her hand on Jake's uninjured arm. She gave it a gentle squeeze. "Trust me. Okay?"

Jake didn't hesitate. "Whatever you say."

Kat went to the dresser and pulled out some clothes.

"What is it, Kat? Is everything all right?"

Kat paused and turned to look at her. Her face softened. "Nothing for you to worry about." Without further elaboration, she turned and left, closing the door behind her.

Kat briefly considered giving Jake a gun to use in the unlikely event that the intruder got past her. But Kat was unsure how she would react to the offer. *It might distress Jake more than necessary— she may not even remember how to use one. Or maybe she will. Do you really want to arm her and then have her memory come back?* Kat decided against it, and that made her even more determined to stop the intruder quickly and quietly outside the bunker. She'd think about what to tell Jake later.

She opened the hidden room and stepped inside. She stripped off the clothes she was wearing and put on the heavy insulated underwear and insulated white coveralls she'd taken from the dresser.

She opened the largest gun safe, lips pursed in concentration as she considered what weapons to take with her. She pulled out her 9mm Glock automatic and extra clips and stuffed them into the pocket of her coveralls. A .38 revolver came next, housed in a holster she strapped to her right ankle. And finally, a Spyderco knife, tucked into another pocket. She left the room and closed it up again.

Grabbing her night-vision goggles from the coffee table, she jogged to the tunnel. She pulled a white balaclava from a peg on the wall and put it on. It covered her face and neck, leaving only her eyes exposed. The goggles came next. She parked them on her forehead, then pulled on her white Mickey Mouse boots and laced them up. Finally, she fished in one of the army barrels for a thick pair of white gloves and put them on.

She moved to the rungs on the wall and began to climb. Forty feet up, the rungs ended at a circular steel hatch that looked like those found on submarines. It had a metal handle that Kat pushed to unlock the hatch and a large ring that she grabbed on to and turned counterclockwise to open the round door. She had to use every bit of her considerable muscle to get it to move. It made more noise than she would have liked, but that couldn't be helped.

She decided to wait a few minutes where she was in case the intruder heard the noise and decided to investigate. The emergency exit would remain well concealed as long as she didn't open the hatch. Once she did, the movement of the snow above it would mark the spot and make it much too visible.

She was confident the intruder could not get in the main entrance. She would wait until he had enough time to get up the hill, satisfy his curiosity, and return down the hill. She wanted to meet him away from this opening, as there was no way to lock it from the outside. She just hoped there wasn't more than one intruder.

As she waited, her mind drifted back to Jake. Her icy demeanor thawed just a little as she remembered the incredible sensations of the kiss. *Don't think about that now. It's a distraction you don't need.*

❖

Frank had found the security panel that would open the main door to the bunker. He stared at it, wondering if touching it would set off some kind of alarm or something to alert whoever was on the other side of the wall. He didn't like to have to make decisions like this, especially if Hunter might be in there. Exaggerated reputation or not, he still didn't want her to take him by surprise.

He chewed his lip, staring at the panel. He heard a soft, metallic grinding sound from somewhere up above him and to the right. He glanced around, suddenly feeling too exposed where he was. He stayed close to the wall, hoping whoever was above him couldn't see that far over the edge. Hugging the surface of the wall, he began moving away from the sound, hoping to circle around the hill a ways before he came up the other side. Maybe he'd get the chance to come up behind whoever was up there and get the drop on them.

Jake wished to God the room had a clock. Time seemed to drag on and on, but she had no idea how much of it had really elapsed. It seemed as though Kat had been gone an awfully long while. Twenty minutes? Thirty? But Jake knew her growing anxiety was probably skewing her ability to tell time, and it might have been only half that. She had taken Kat at her word that there was no time to explain, but now she wished she had tried at least to ask how long Kat might be gone. The wait was excruciating.

Jake considered how little she really knew about the woman who had so totally captivated her. The transformation in Kat after the second alarm was startling and a bit unsettling. Steely self-assurance radiated off her, and she appeared to be almost a different person entirely. The change had been so profound and unexpected Jake could not help wondering what could possibly have triggered it. Certainly more than another wayward deer.

She started to count, marking off the wait in minutes, because it was something for her mind to do other than worry about Kat and think about how much she needed to visit the bathroom. Kat had asked her not to get out of bed, and she was trying very hard to comply. But she knew her resolve was crumbling. Her bladder was screaming for relief. Could there really be any harm in just walking a few feet to the room next door?

CHAPTER EIGHTEEN

It was to Frank both a blessing and a curse that the hill he was climbing was heavily wooded. He could sneak up on whatever had made the noise by moving from tree to tree. That made him feel much less vulnerable. On the other hand, it made it hell to try to see anything or anyone. A thick cloud layer obscured whatever moonlight might have penetrated to the forest floor. There could be someone hidden behind any of the trees around him.

He tried to move as quietly as possible while spending as little time as he could in the open areas between trees. He paused behind every other tree, listening, as he neared the top of the rise. He heard no further sounds at all, except a very faint, far-off cry—a lone coyote. The plaintive sound went on sporadically for a couple of minutes, and then all was silent again. Frank wrongly thought wolf when he heard it, and he immediately wondered if a wolf would go after a man. He was really beginning to hate this assignment, million dollars or no million dollars.

His face and ears were freezing, and that was distracting him a bit. He'd never been so cold. He'd exposed his ears to the frigid air so he could hear better. He figured he must be close to the place he'd heard the noise coming from, but he was really only guessing. Frank stood as still and quiet as he could for a long while, listening, peering into the darkness. He started to wonder if he'd really heard something. The noise had sounded metallic, and he could see there was nothing around him except woods and snow.

He fished a candy bar out of his pocket. As he ate, he became more convinced that he must have just imagined he heard something. *Who knows what kind of things are out here with me and what noises they make?* he thought uneasily. He was no coward. He had confronted lots of dangerous situations in his line of work. Still, he liked knowing what he was up against.

He stayed there a long time despite his growing anxiety, because the alternative would be for him to return to the more exposed area of the rock wall and deal with the security panel again. He wasn't quite ready for that yet.

Kat thought that enough time had probably elapsed for the intruder to have investigated the area and left, but still she waited beneath the closed hatch. That sixth sense of hers urged caution and she obeyed, even though various parts of her body complained about the long time she remained suspended on the ladder rungs. She tried to stretch out her muscles, stimulating the blood flow so she would be ready to face whoever was outside.

Too warm now, she unzipped the coveralls to let in the cool air and pulled up the balaclava so it no longer covered her face. She would wait a while longer, although her muscles twitched in anticipation of the confrontation ahead.

Jake couldn't stand it any longer. If she didn't move now, right now, she wasn't sure she could prevent an accident. Certainly Kat would understand—she had been in such a hurry to respond to the alarm she hadn't stopped to consider Jake might need to use the bathroom.

Jake moved her legs over one side of the bed. Trying very hard not to put any weight at all on her bad knee, she slid down to the floor. She hopped to the doorway, opened the door, and continued through the bathroom door to the commode, balancing better on one foot than she expected and getting to her destination just in time.

The relief was enormous. She washed her hands and headed to the bathroom door. Peering out, she glanced around the outer room and got her first real long look at the rest of Kat's retreat. To her right were large built–in bookcases filled with books. She took in the leather couch and easy chair and the small kitchen opposite the bookshelves. It was a lovely room, but few knickknacks were apparent. The only real decorations were the pictures on the walls—more animal and bird photographs. Kat's cello case sat against the wall to Jake's left. Beyond that, and in front of her, was a large desk.

Jake's eyes were drawn to the only movement in the room—a slight flicker that came from one of the monitors set into the wall behind the desk. Intrigued, Jake moved toward them, momentarily forgetting her promise to Kat. The monitors had an odd green tint to them; they weren't televisions. Each held a static picture, and Jake realized they must be images from security cameras.

Standing in front of them, she could see that the first one showed a large rock wall and a bit of forest around it. The second camera was focused on a long, narrow corridor of some kind—she could see hats and coats hanging on pegs. The third monitor displayed a small clearing in the woods surrounded by a thick growth of trees. Jake's eyes were drawn to movement in the last monitor.

One of the dark shadows in the monitor separated itself from the longer shadow that had concealed it. Jake stared, fascinated, as the shadow came into slightly better view of the camera. She could see now it was a person, though it was hard to be sure if it was male or female because the figure was clad in a one-piece suit. A snowmobile suit, she realized. She suspected it was a man because of the disproportionately large upper body.

The man appeared to be eating something. One hand kept going to his mouth. It looked like the he was waiting, hiding, pressed up against the tree like that. *Where is Kat?* Jake worried.

A flicker to her left brought her attention to the second monitor. *There she is,* Jake thought with relief. Kat was climbing down rungs at the edge of the screen and skipped the last couple to land gracefully on her feet in the corridor. Then she bounced up and down with nervous energy, stretching her arms and arching her back. Jake tried to look closer at Kat's surroundings in the monitor. *Where are you?*

Jake pried her eyes away from the screen long enough to glance around the room she was in. There were two doors besides the ones to the bedroom and bathroom. One was on the other side of the room, next to the refrigerator. The other, probably the exit door because of the locks on it, was set into the wall between the desk and the kitchen. *Are you on the other side of that door?*

Jake suddenly remembered her promise, and she was a bit concerned that Kat would come through the door and find she had left the bedroom. But she was even more worried about Kat's safety, given the figure that was evidently waiting outside in the woods. *He set off the alarm,* Jake realized. That certainly explained Kat's sudden change in demeanor. *She knows he's out there.*

She turned back to the monitors, waiting for something to happen, her sense of anxiety growing. *Kat said we were a long way from civilization. Who is he and what does he want?*

She watched, transfixed, as Kat calmly pulled a large handgun from the pocket of her white overalls and with practiced efficiency checked the clip. "Who are you really?" Jake whispered, wide-eyed.

CHAPTER NINETEEN

Evan Garner hated being trapped in his office. It was making him claustrophobic. He paced back and forth in front of the large wall of windows.

They had heard nothing from Frank for several hours. Garner was now admitting to himself it might have been a mistake to have sent the man to Tawa. He'd thought of Frank as just another willing gun to throw at Hunter—an expendable one, if things went badly.

But now he worried that if Frank did find Hunter, she would kill him and then run, and that could make everything much more difficult. She knew how to disappear. Worse yet, it might send her straight to his office.

He pressed a button on the intercom on his desk.

Thomas responded at once. "Yes, sir?"

"Call Otter," Garner instructed. "Fill him in about Frank and the location of the wrecked car. Tell him to get a snowmobile and try to follow the track and see what the hell has happened."

"Right away, sir," Thomas responded.

Damn your eyes, Hunter, Garner thought. *I wish I didn't have to kill you. But you leave me no other choice.*

It had taken Otter several minutes to break into the helicopter office. He was a bit out of practice at picking locks. He'd had to break the yellow police tape on the door, but he wasn't worried he'd be caught. The place was out in the middle of nowhere, just as the guy at the bar had described, and he was pretty sure a small town like Tawa wouldn't have the manpower to keep it under surveillance.

Otter stepped across the doorway and into the small customer waiting area. It had a half dozen cheap plastic chairs that reminded him of the ones in prison. On a narrow coffee table was an assortment of old magazines, mostly *Sports Illustrated* but a few hunting and fishing titles as well. He went behind the long counter that ran parallel to the back wall. Atop it was a cash register, which had been emptied, and small stands displaying the owner's business cards and brochures outlining services and rates.

Shelves beneath the counter held an untidy assortment of magazines, manuals, invoices, and what looked like a lost-and-found depository—a cardboard box containing sunglasses and gloves, hats and pens, an umbrella, children's toys, a small notebook, and a key ring with keys.

Otter moved behind the counter to a door that led into a small office. He shined the beam of his flashlight around before he stepped into the room. He spotted a desk and chair, filing cabinet, and a small TV on a stand in one corner. The owner was evidently not fussy about neatness. There was a thick coating of dust on the TV and piles of papers on the desk, and the wastebasket beside it was nearly overflowing with fast-food wrappers. Personal items were scattered here and there. On the filing cabinet were several trophies and framed pictures. Along one wall were piles of cardboard boxes, their tops open and contents spilling out like the police had gone haphazardly through them. Hanging on the wall were several framed photographs, most aerial shots evidently taken from the helicopter.

In the middle of the room, on the concrete floor, was the white chalk outline of a body, and what appeared to be a very large dried bloodstain around where the head and neck of the victim had lain.

Otter stepped around the outline and went to the desk. He opened the drawers and poked through their contents. Letters and invoices, old bills, and check stubs. A pint bottle of Jack Daniel's, nearly empty. A half-eaten bag of potato chips.

Next he tackled the filing cabinet. It contained several folders, organized by date. He frowned. All the files were more than six months old. There was a large blank space in the drawer that logically should have contained the more recent ones, so he suspected the police had taken them.

At first glance, there seemed to be nothing here that could lead him to Hunter. But he was certain she had to have been responsible for this. The only thing he couldn't figure was why, especially since the helicopter still stood parked outside.

Otter nearly jumped through his skin when his cell phone rang in his pocket. His nerves were on edge. It rang again. "Yeah?" he answered in a clipped voice. He listened for several minutes. A smile spread across his face. "Right on it," he answered, shutting off the phone and making his way out of the office.

Not a bad way to travel, he remembered, glancing at the helicopter as he returned to his car. But the big machines would always remind him of Hunter's betrayal. He relished the opportunity to finally settle the score.

CHAPTER TWENTY

Jake watched as Kat's image on the screen cocked her head as if she was listening for something. Jake's eyes darted to the third monitor. While she'd been watching Kat, the man behind the tree had disappeared. Jake narrowed her eyes, staring hard at the monitor, praying to see some movement that would tell her what had happened to him. Had he just darted behind the tree he was standing next to? Or had he gone?

She looked back to the middle screen.

Kat was moving now too—she pulled a white ski mask over her face and neck, then slid an odd-looking pair of goggles over her eyes. She moved to the right of the screen and then up out of view, like she was climbing a ladder.

Now Jake could see neither person, and her anxiety doubled. She was tempted to go through the exit door, see if Kat was there and warn her about what she'd seen on the monitor. But she was held in place, both by her promise and by her uncertainty over what she was witnessing.

Kat had looked so comfortable—casual, almost—handling the gun. It was very disconcerting to Jake and didn't fit at all with the image she held of the woman. Nature photographer, cello player, cook, rescuer. Maybe she was in the military or law enforcement somewhere, she surmised. Or maybe something not quite so innocuous.

There was movement now on the third screen. In the clearing in the forest, the snow moved. *No, that's not it,* she realized. Something was under the snow. A large circular object rose perpendicular to the ground, and the snow that had been around it fell away. Kat emerged from the ground. *It's the exit,* Jake realized, amazed at how well concealed it had been. *Watch out, Kat. He's out there somewhere,* her mind screamed in warning. *Jesus, what the hell is going on here?*

Frank had convinced himself that whatever he thought he'd heard must have been some weird bird or animal. He'd pulled down his cap to cover his ears again. They'd gotten so cold they positively ached. He'd read stories about how people had lost toes and fingers to frostbite, and he worried about his face—particularly his ears and his nose, which ran profusely in the chill air.

He was glad at least it wasn't snowing. He could follow his own tracks back to the rock wall. He knew he could get lost out here way too easily.

He was less cautious going down the hill than he had been coming up, no longer concerned that someone might be watching him. *No one else is stupid enough to be out here,* he told himself. He headed back toward the rock wall, not at all looking forward to trying to crack the security panel. He was pretty good at picking most locks, but any kind of electronic device was beyond him. He just had to hope he'd get lucky.

Kat sensed, finally, that it was safe to emerge from the emergency exit. She cracked the hatch and snow cascaded into the tunnel around her. She climbed up and out, adjusted her goggles, and quickly scanned the area for the intruder. Satisfied, she closed the hatch and quickly kicked snow over it, trying to obscure the entrance as best as she could. Staying low and moving quickly, she headed to the nearest big tree and concealed herself behind it, listening. She heard soft sounds, not far down the hill. The crunching of boots and the rustling sound of nylon against nylon. She hurried noiselessly toward it.

There was a chance, she knew, that the intruder could be a snowmobiler or hunter who found her sled tracks leading from the crash site and got nosy.

Or maybe someone had discovered the wreck and called the police. The man could be a deputy investigating the stolen car. Either option would be real trouble for her. She didn't want to kill an innocent man or policeman, yet she had to protect the bunker as long as Jake could not be moved. Kat had to find out who the intruder was and whether he had revealed the location of the bunker to anyone else.

She followed the sounds, finally glimpsing the man through the trees. He was making his way back to the main entrance. She closed in on him, studying him. He was large and muscular, but she could not see his face to tell whether she recognized him. He plodded noisily along, his nylon snowmobile suit making the rustling sounds she'd heard, and he was sniffling loudly.

Suddenly the big man tripped and fell headlong into the deep snow, flailing his arms. He rose to his feet, cursing loudly, and Kat resisted the urge to laugh. A few minutes later, he was back standing before the security panel at the rock wall. He turned on a flashlight and scanned the area with it, then removed his right mitten and began punching numbers into the panel.

Kat crept up behind him, every muscle in her body taut in anticipation. She reached for her Glock as she approached her target.

Frank was randomly hitting numbers on the keypad, hoping he wasn't triggering an alarm, when two things happened simultaneously.

He heard a low female voice directly behind him say "Freeze," and cold metal was pressed firmly against the back of his neck. It was wedged into the narrow space between his cap and the collar of his snowsuit.

He did as he was told. The fingers on his exposed hand were beginning to freeze, but he took no notice. He kept the flashlight trained on the panel. *Hunter,* he thought nervously, and despite the cold, he began to sweat a little inside the insulated suit.

Her voice came again, beside his ear, as the cold metal nudged his neck for emphasis. "Who are you?"

"Uh...uh," Frank stammered, stalling for time. Why the hell hadn't he anticipated this? He couldn't admit who he was and what he was doing here. His delay in answering prompted another firm prod from the gun. "My name is John. I...I'm lost," he said.

"Try again," the voice said.

She cocked the gun, the sound echoing loudly in his ears despite the cap he wore. He began to sweat in earnest now.

Frank found his voice and tried to keep it steady. "I was following some tracks, just out snowmobiling," he lied.

"Don't believe you. Who are you working for?"

"No one," Frank said, too quickly.

A long sigh from behind him. "You don't lie very well." A hand reached around him and took the flashlight from his left hand. "Raise your hands above your head," the voice instructed.

Frank obeyed. When he did, the mitten he'd been holding under his left arm fell to the ground. His right hand was nearly numb now from the cold, but he resisted the urge to flex his fingers to restore the blood flow.

The cold metal was removed from Frank's neck. "Turn around, very slowly."

He did as he was told. As soon as he turned, the bright beam of the flashlight blinded him, shining directly into his eyes. He squinted against the glare.

"Take your hat off. Move slowly," the voice said from in front of him.

Frank removed his cap and dropped it in the snow. His mind worked furiously trying to come up with an explanation for his presence, but he could think of nothing convincing. It was Hunter, he knew it was, and he suddenly found himself trying to recall details of the stories he'd heard about her. Everyone talked about her reflexes, he remembered. Said she could move faster than you could see. His mouth was dry.

"Let's try this once more," the voice said, drawing closer. "What's your name?"

He took a deep breath to calm his nerves before he answered. "Frank," he said. Still squinting, he lowered his eyes. He could barely make out the silhouette of her lower body. She was four or five feet away, out of his reach.

"Very good. Now back up, Frank," the voice commanded. "Up against the wall."

He obeyed, retreating by small, slow steps until his back was against the hard surface. He waited for her to say something. A minute passed in uncomfortable silence. Trying to feign a nonchalance he didn't feel, Frank shrugged and opened his mouth. "Look, lady, you got me all wrong—" he began, but his next words were cut off in his throat.

Before he knew what had happened, she was upon him. One large, strong hand tightened around his larynx, cutting off his air. Her thumb dug hard into the pulse point at the base of his jaw, effectively pinning him against the wall. In a reflex action, he struggled against the iron grip and started to bring his hands down, but the second he did that, she tightened her hold until he began to see stars. *Damn, she's strong,* he thought fuzzily. His lungs screamed for air. He was going to black out.

He stopped fighting her and put his hands back up. When he did, she loosened her grip enough for him to suck in some sweet air. Then she tightened her hold again slightly, pushing upward against his windpipe until he couldn't breathe at all unless he was on his tiptoes. The back of his head pressed painfully against the wall. The sharp edge of the security panel cut into his lower back.

"No more lies now, Frank."

"Okay, Okay," he wheezed. He was having a hard time talking through the excruciating pressure on his windpipe, and he had lost all feeling in his right hand. He was in real trouble here, he realized. And she was getting impatient. "Look, I'm just out here to find someone." He gasped for air. "Sorry to have bothered you. Obviously she's not here." He was past thinking about the money now. He just wanted the hell out of here.

Kat felt fairly relaxed, considering the current circumstances. She knew now that this man was probably no real immediate threat to her or to Jake. He didn't seem to have either the brains or the imagination to get himself out of his current predicament, and he seemed to be alone.

But she still had to find out who he was and what he knew, and more importantly, she then had to decide what to do with him. Part of the latter decision would depend on whether he had told anyone the location of the bunker.

She hoped he'd give up the information willingly. Sometimes big brutes like this had a high tolerance for pain, like she did. She didn't think he was operating on his own. He was the type who took orders. And if she was right about who sent him, she knew Frank would try at least for a while to resist giving up the full story. Evan Garner could be ruthless with underlings who betrayed him. The contract on her life was proof of that, wasn't it?

Kat let several seconds elapse in silence. She smiled a little when she could feel the desired response. Frank's pulse rate beneath her thumb increased. She squeezed his larynx until he coughed in pain. "Who are you looking for, Frank?"

He blinked against the aching pressure on his throat and the blinding light held directly in front of his eyes. "A woman. Blond. Had a car wreck," he rasped out.

"I'm listening," Kat urged.

"Tracks from the wreck led here," he said. He paused, considering how much to tell her.

Kat squeezed his throat again and pressed the flashlight forcefully against the bridge of his nose. A sharp outcropping of rock on the wall behind him cut into his scalp. "Don't make me beg for every tidbit, Frank," she warned.

"I'm a private investigator," he said hoarsely, "working for the woman's husband." Frank didn't think the story would pass. He knew he lied poorly. But he feared what Hunter would do if she learned the truth. He was rather surprised when she didn't immediately call him on it.

Kat's muscled forearm began to tire from the pressure she was putting on Frank's larynx. She thought the man was lying, but what if he wasn't? Had Jake's husband somehow tracked them down through the car? She had nearly convinced herself that the wedding ring was merely a prop Jake used as a bounty hunter. Was that only wishful thinking?

"Okay, Mr. Private Eye," she said playfully, never altering the steely grip around Frank's throat. "Time for show-and-tell. First

I want the names of the client and the wife. Then I'll want to see your P.I. license, because I'm just sure you're the law-abiding type and carry it with you like you should."

Frank tried to swallow. An impossible task at the moment, even if his mouth wasn't sandpaper. "Uh," he stammered, "Uh, I don't have my license. It's back in my car."

"Of course it is," she said agreeably. She kneed him in the groin.

He groaned loudly and slumped forward against the excruciating, blinding pain. Her hand remained locked against his throat, increasing his agony. He fought to remain conscious.

After a couple of minutes, the pain had subsided enough for him to focus. He wished he could feel his right hand enough to risk some move against her. His left was a problem now as well; it was going numb from being held so long in the air. That blow had angered Frank and dampened his fear. He wanted so badly to hurt this bitch now. Screw the money—that would just be a bonus. Rage poured through his body.

Just as he had about mustered his courage to try something, she kneed him again.

"Calm down, Frank," Kat said, nearly supporting his full weight against her hand as he slumped forward in response to the second jarring blow. She had felt his pulse increase beneath her thumb after she'd kicked him the first time, and she'd correctly identified the strong, rapid pounding as an adrenaline rush. She knew he'd been about to lash out at her. It was why she favored the neck grip she was using on him, in fact. It was a debilitating hold that enabled her to get a good idea of what her victim's heart rate was doing. And that helped her predict their behavior.

But her forearm had begun to ache from the strain of holding him. She knew now he was lying about being a P.I., and she wanted to get this over with.

"You need to resist the urge to fight me, Frank. I won't hurt you any more if you just start cooperating and tell me the truth." She eased up just slightly against his throat so that he could take deeper breaths.

He stood on rubbery legs. Holding his hands even slightly

aloft now took tremendous effort. At least for the moment, the fight was gone from him.

"You trying to earn a million dollars tonight, Frank?"

He jumped a little, startled at the question, but didn't ask her to explain it. Instead, he closed his eyes and took a deep breath. "I came here because I was ordered to follow the trail from the car," he volunteered. "To find a missing blonde," he reiterated through clenched teeth. "That's the truth." There was a long pause before he continued. "I know who you are, Hunter, but I came here to find Scout. She was the one out to collect on the money."

Kat nodded to herself. This finally was the truth. There were two more things she wanted to know. "What can you tell me about this Scout?"

He was surprised at the question. "Isn't she here?"

She tightened her grip on his neck. "I get to ask the questions, Frank," she scolded. "Tell me about Scout."

"Okay, enough," he choked. "Sorry."

She loosened her grip again just enough so he could breathe.

"She's a bounty hunter, like you. Didn't check in for several days so the boss sent me looking for her. He put a tracking device in her phone, and I followed it to the crash site. That's honest to God all I know."

"You know nothing else about her? Her real name, where she's from?" Kat prodded.

"No. Only what I told you," he insisted.

"When was the last time you checked in with Garner?"

So she knows about him, too, Frank thought with deep disappointment. *Figures.* She knew about the money. He didn't want to answer, because he knew when he did, Hunter would have no further use for him. She'd have to kill him because he knew where the bunker was. So he had nothing left to lose. He'd have to take any chance he got to get out of this. If only she'd relax her grip just a bit more. The pain between his legs had dulled to a low throbbing. He tried to wiggle his fingers, hoping she wouldn't notice. He could not feel his right hand at all. It seemed detached from his body.

"When, Frank?" Kat repeated.

"Several hours ago," Frank wheezed, exaggerating his

discomfort in the hope it would get her to loosen her grip. "Not sure, exactly."

Kat knew she couldn't hold him much longer. She was afraid her forearm would soon tremble against the strain. "Do they know where you are?"

"They kn-know where the car is," he admitted, stuttering slightly. It was a speech impediment he'd overcome as a child that only resurfaced now because of his extreme stress. "They don't know about this place. M-m-my cell wouldn't reach," he finished.

That's that, Frank thought absently. *Now or never.* With a quickness born of desperation, he brought both hands together, then down hard, aiming blindly for where he imagined Hunter's head was. He tried to ignore the choking agony in his windpipe.

Pain flashed up his arms as he contacted with something solid. Suddenly the bright light was no longer in his eyes, and her grip was gone. Still blinded from the flashlight, he blinked furiously, reaching out for her. He gripped coarse material and tried to pull her toward him in a bear hug.

Kat fought back with an elbow to his face that broke his nose.

Blood poured from both of his nostrils, and his rage flared anew. He fought for his life. Frank threw wild punches with both hands, making contact only rarely, thankful that the more frequent hits to his own body were being cushioned somewhat by the thick padding of the snowmobile suit. His eyesight was coming back. He grabbed for her, and they struggled against each other, locked in a violent embrace until they toppled over into the deep snow.

Frank was momentarily distracted by the shock of his exposed face and neck being enveloped in the knee-deep powder. He relaxed his grip on Hunter's right arm.

Kat yanked her revolver from its holster and brought it down hard against the side of Frank's head.

He stopped moving.

CHAPTER TWENTY-ONE

Jake was frantic with worry. She had witnessed most of Kat's interrogation of the intruder outside the bunker, staring stunned at the monitor as her enigmatic friend subdued the man against the rock wall. Kat looked to have the situation under control, but Jake sorely wished she could hear the conversation between the two.

Suddenly, the man fought back. Jake saw him hit Kat hard against the side of her head. The flashlight went flying and the two were flailing away at each other, locked in a desperate struggle that propelled both their bodies outside camera range.

Jake waited, her heart pounding in her ears, her anxiety an enormous weight in her chest, but neither Kat nor the intruder immediately reappeared in the monitor.

Jake didn't think at all about what she did next. She hobbled to the exit door of the living room, her promise to Kat forgotten, overtaken by her concern for her rescuer's safety. Once through the door, she glanced around the tunnel, taking in the big steel door at the other end, the clothes and boots along the wall, and, immediately to her right, the ladder rungs that led up to the exit she'd seen Kat emerge from.

Jake yanked a pair of black insulated coveralls from a peg on the wall. They were much too large for her, so she rolled cuffs at her ankles and wrists. All the footwear was several sizes too big as well. She pulled on a pair of boots, then fished around in one of the army barrels and pulled out gloves and scarves, stuffing the material into the boots to make them fit more snugly. She donned a pair of heavy woolen gloves and a hat and, trying to ignore the pain in her knee and wrist, struggled to scale the ladder rungs. She was out of the emergency exit a couple of minutes later. *I'm coming, Kat. Hang on.*

Kat stayed where she had fallen for several moments to catch her breath. Then she got to her knees and unzipped her coveralls enough to jam her right hand beneath her left armpit to warm it up. It was nearly blue from its long exposure to the frigid temperatures.

She leaned over Frank's supine body. He was out cold. *Dumb shit*, she thought, aiming the crude sentiment at the man before her, but also acknowledging that she had left herself open for his attack. She hadn't wanted to hurt him—he was just a hired gun—but he'd left her no choice.

She had a lot to do now. She looked up at the sky. A thick layer of clouds obscured the moon and stars. If it snowed soon, the bunker might be safe for at least a while longer. She wanted to check the forecast, but first she had to get rid of all evidence of Frank's being at the bunker.

She got slowly to her feet. The big man had clocked her a good one to the side of her face when he'd hit her. A small cut beneath her eye was bleeding profusely, and there would be a large, ugly bruise across her cheek and jaw. She felt the blood running down her face but ignored it.

Her hand had warmed sufficiently for her to regain the use of her fingers. She flexed the sore muscles of her forearm. Standing at Frank's shoulders, she leaned down to take one of his wrists in each of her hands. Grunting slightly from the effort, she pulled him toward the rock wall entrance several feet away. Heavy though he was, the task was not as difficult as it might have been because his nylon suit slid over the snow with little resistance.

Once at the panel, she keyed in the access code and hauled Frank into the generator room. She removed a roll of duct tape from her toolbox and trussed him up, securing his feet and his hands behind him. Then she searched the pockets of his snowsuit.

She found a cell phone, which she immediately took apart to render useless and check for a homing device. To her relief, there was none. She also found a gun—a .44 magnum—extra ammunition, a jackknife, a candy bar, and a map of Michigan. She stuffed the weapons into the pockets of her coveralls.

She unzipped his snowsuit and thoroughly searched the clothes he wore underneath. She leafed through his wallet before she stuffed it into her pocket. When that was done, she went back outside the bunker and retrieved Frank's flashlight, still lit under several inches of snow.

She used it to find her night-vision goggles, which she'd removed just before she snuck up on him. She followed the tracks he'd made until she came to his rental snowmobile a short distance away. The key was in the ignition. She drove it through the rock wall entrance and parked it beside her own machine. She closed the hidden door again.

Frank would be coming around any minute.

Jake pushed herself up through the emergency exit and shut the hatch behind her, cutting off the small amount of light from the tunnel and plunging her into darkness. She waited a minute for her eyes to adjust, then began searching for the tracks Kat had made.

She remembered the way Kat had gone after leaving the exit, so she headed in the same direction. It was very difficult to see, especially once she entered the edge of the forest. Finally, she stumbled across a trail in the snow she could barely make out. She moved with agonizing slowness because of her knee, but the adrenaline pouring through her body propelled her on.

She had gone only thirty feet or so into the woods when the silence was broken by the high-pitched whine of a snowmobile. She froze at the sound, which seemed to be coming from some distance away, farther down the hill she was descending and off to her left. What did it mean? Was the intruder leaving, and if so, what had become of Kat? Her heart sped up. She headed directly toward the sound, leaving the tracks she had been following.

Jake had hobbled quite some distance when the roar of the snowmobile ended as abruptly as it had begun. She stood still, listening, and heard another faint sound from the same general direction. Then all was silent again.

Jake was momentarily torn about whether to continue forward or backtrack to regain the foot trail she'd been following. She was in the deepest, blackest part of the forest, and it was nearly impossible to make out her own tracks. She decided the safest route would be to return the way she'd come and try to pick up Kat's trail again.

She saw a faint path veering off to the right. She followed it, confident she would soon catch up to her friend. She knew from watching the monitors that it had taken Kat only six or eight minutes to travel from the exit to the wall where she had confronted the intruder. But Jake knew it would take her much longer. Pain shot through her knee. She limped forward at an ever-slower pace.

The snow was deep enough, and it was dark enough, that Jake couldn't see individual prints in the snow, just a line cut through the soft powder. But she just had to be on Kat's trail. Didn't she?

CHAPTER TWENTY-TWO

Frank groaned. What the hell? His head ached something fierce. He wanted to touch the spot that hurt worst, but he couldn't move his hands. Or his feet.

Then he remembered, and came fully awake. Hunter. He forced his eyes open, thin slits against the throbbing pain. He was lying on his side on a concrete floor. A pair of boots walked away from him.

Frank tilted his head to see the rest of her. Tall. Dark hair. She had her back to him and was searching the pack that had been strapped to his snowmobile.

He glanced around. A small electric heater, placed out of his reach, blew warm air in his direction but with little effect. A water bottle lay nearby. Beyond that a generator and two snowmobiles—one of them his rental.

His eyes drifted back to Hunter.

She was watching him. Her face was stone. Expressionless. Blood dripped from a gash on her cheek. The front of her white snowsuit was spattered with it. She studied him in silence, her eyes boring into his, until Frank withered under her unrelenting glare and looked away.

"That was really dumb, Frank. You said you know who I am," Kat chided in an almost friendly voice.

"Aw, Hunter, I had to try." Frank tested the bindings at his hands and feet. Shit.

"What am I going to do with you, Frank?" She stepped closer, looming over him, until he had to strain his neck painfully to see her face.

"Probably nothing I'm going to like," he managed.

"You may be surprised."

The chitchatty tone she was using was beginning to rattle Frank. His breathing picked up, and he started chewing on the inside of his cheek.

She leaned down until her face was only a foot from his. "Still think you can collect on the million, Frank?" she hissed. Her eyes were predatory. She bared her teeth in a savage smile.

He didn't like that look at all.

Frank turned his head away from her. "Told you, I was just looking for the woman. She was the one who was after you. Not me. I don't want to get in your business." He didn't care about the money anymore, so he hoped it sounded like the truth.

She seemed to consider his answer. She paced around him for a long moment before speaking again.

"Frank, what do you think of Garner? Do you like working for him?" Her voice was gentle now, soothing.

Frank's bushy eyebrows knitted together, and it took a moment for the question to register. *Where is this going?* "Well, he's not a bad boss," he volunteered.

"What does he pay you? Enough for you to do what you want to do?"

Frank looked up at her. The wild expression was gone. She was calmly awaiting his answer. "The pay is okay. A grand a week, bonuses sometimes."

"Frank, this is your lucky day. I'm going to offer you a one-time-only incredible deal." She said it like she was offering him some grand prize on a game show.

The statement made him less afraid, and Frank was intrigued despite himself. *Is she serious?* He struggled to sit up but couldn't manage with his hands and feet tied.

She came up behind him, took hold under his armpits, and pulled him up to a seated position. She did it like it was no strain at all. Frank was impressed.

"You're going to be my patient and cooperative guest for a little while," Kat said, looking down at him. "And in return for your best behavior, I'm going to give you enough cash to take a nice, long vacation someplace warm when you leave here. How does that sound?" She cocked her head. The predatory smile was back, warning him to accept.

He began to see why she had the reputation she did. "Whatever you say, Hunter."

She nodded. "Good boy. Think you can forget where you are and how you got here?"

Maybe she really is serious. Might she actually let me go? He looked her right in the eyes. "That's honestly no problem. The woods aren't my thing, Hunter. I seriously doubt I could find this again even if I wanted to." He paused a beat. "And I really don't want to find it again."

"That's the right answer, Frank. Don't make me regret my generous impulse."

Frank hoped she was being square with him and not keeping him alive for some purpose down the road. He didn't have much choice in the matter, really, unless some opportunity presented itself. "Good as gold, don't worry. And if you keep up your end, once I leave, I was never here." Screw Garner.

"I knew you were smart." Kat looked away from him for the first time to glance around the room. She believed Frank, but not enough to let her guard down. She went to the steel door that separated the garage from the connecting tunnel and keyed a set of numbers into the security panel beside it. She opened the door and looked back at Frank. "Don't move a muscle, now. I'll be back before you know it." Then she was gone.

He took her at her word and stayed where he was.

Kat grabbed a stuff sack from the bottom of one of the army barrels in the tunnel. It contained a down sleeping bag and pillow. In her haste, she didn't notice that a pair of boots and a set of coveralls were missing from among the stores of gear in the hall.

She returned to the generator room and spread the sleeping bag in an empty corner, Frank's water bottle beside it. She pointed her portable heater in that direction, but kept it well out of reach. It wasn't doing much to heat the large room, but it would take the edge off and Frank would be comfortable in his snowsuit.

Kat took a long length of chain from her snowmobile—the solid, heavy one she used to pull the sled—and took it to the corner. She threaded it through a metal ring embedded in the concrete wall.

Then she found a shorter, lighter chain in her toolbox, along with two sturdy padlocks, and laid them out next to the bag.

Frank watched her every move.

Now she was ready for him. She took two firm handholds at the back of the collar of his nylon snowsuit and pulled him a few feet along the concrete floor until he was next to the sleeping bag. She put the small chain around his hands and feet over the duct tape and secured it to the larger chain with both padlocks. He could move around only a few feet.

"I know that's not very comfortable, Frank. But it'll have to do for right now," she said.

Kat took her toolbox and the tool kits from both snowmobiles into the tunnel. After a final glance around for anything else he might be able to use, she nodded once to Frank. "Be good now, I'll see you in a little while." She left through the steel door, closing it behind her.

Kat stood for a few moments in the tunnel with her back pressed up against the door. She wanted to check the weather forecast; she should do that next. Then fix herself up a little bit before she went to talk to Jake. *That'll give me a little time to decide what I'm going to tell her.*

Despite his inexperience on snowmobiles, Otter had made good time getting to the crash site on the snowmobile he'd rented. He followed the trail out of Tawa that Frank had made.

He sat on the parked Polaris and swept his flashlight across the landscape. Two snowmobile tracks led away from the wrecked sedan. They came together not far away and led off into the woods. Frank had followed Hunter and gotten caught. That's why he hadn't come back. Otter was sure of it. He just had to follow Frank's trail.

Satisfied with his assessment, Otter pulled a raspberry turnover and thermos of coffee from the storage compartment of his snowmobile. He had already wasted a lot of time renting the machine and finding warm enough clothing. But Otter was rusty and Hunter would be expecting trouble. Exhaustion could get him killed.

After a short break, he put away the thermos and started up the snowmobile. *These damn things make too much noise. Probably how Frank got caught.* But if he was to go any distance at all, Otter didn't want to be doing it on foot.

As he set off on the machine, his mind drifted back to the last time he'd seen Hunter.

He ran toward the helicopter. It was more than a hundred feet away and already twenty feet in the air. Hunter was at the controls. He waved his arms for her to pick him up. He couldn't make out her features, but he was sure she had seen him just before she turned the chopper and sped away.

Otter had always preferred to hit his targets from a distance. He was an expert marksman, at least in his heyday. But this one he wanted to do up close. He wanted to make absolutely certain Hunter knew just who it was who killed her.

Fifteen minutes after leaving the exit hatch, Jake found her forward progress slowed to a near crawl. Her knee was killing her. The adrenaline surge had worn off, and walking in the heavy, oversized boots was torturous.

She paused on the trail to listen, but the night was absolutely quiet. Surely, she thought, she must be getting very near to the rock wall she'd seen on the monitor, so the fact that she still couldn't hear any trace of Kat was very disconcerting. She thought about calling out Kat's name but was afraid the intruder might still be nearby.

Jake didn't know she was lost yet. She worried only that Kat had been knocked unconscious in the snow—or worse. She took a deep breath and pushed ahead, wincing with every agonizing step. She had started to sweat under her coveralls.

There in the dark night, in the depth of the forest, she didn't immediately notice it had begun to snow.

CHAPTER TWENTY-THREE

K at came back into the living room and was about to sit down at her desk to check the weather forecast when she noticed the bedroom door was open. She had very deliberately closed it, she was certain. The bathroom door was open as well. The only sound she could hear was the very faint hum of the refrigerator across the room. A tingle of apprehension crept up her spine as she moved toward the bedroom.

She saw that Jake was not in bed, but nothing appeared to have been disturbed. She darted to the bathroom door and looked inside. Where the hell was Jake? She checked the pantry. She even opened the weapons room to eliminate that possibility. There was nowhere else. Jake was gone.

She looked over at the three monitors. Her heart sank.

She saw me. She saw everything. Did I scare her? Did she run?

Kat thought it unlikely that Jake had slipped out of the main entrance during the only time the door had been open and unattended—the couple of minutes that she'd been away retrieving Frank's snowmobile. Jake had to have gone through the emergency entrance.

She can't have gotten far with that knee. She wondered what Jake had been wearing when she left. Temperatures outside were in the teens. She went into the bedroom and opened the dresser drawers. Nothing missing that she could tell. She went into the tunnel and studied the hanging gear and footwear. She realized that her black winter coveralls were gone, and an old but fairly well-insulated pair of boots. That eased her mind only slightly.

Kat detoured to the weapons room to retrieve a small handheld

GPS—global positioning system device—which she often used to find her way back to the bunker when she was out hunting or photographing wildlife.

She returned to the tunnel and fished through one of the barrels for a wool cap. And she picked up her night-vision goggles and Frank's flashlight. She wondered what Jake was thinking, out there in the cold, alone. *She must have been very afraid to have gone out like that, in the shape she's in.*

Kat's heart clenched at the knowledge. She'd been thinking only of protecting Jake. *When I find her, can I make her understand?*

Suddenly another possibility occurred to her. *Did Jake regain her memory? Is that why she left?* She rejected the idea. It was doubtful Jake had suddenly remembered who she was and then bolted, all in the space of a few minutes, after what had occurred between them. No. Jake had to have seen everything on the monitors and been upset by it, she decided.

Kat climbed the rungs of the emergency exit. She had no idea what she would tell Jake to explain what had happened and why. She knew she'd better start figuring that out. Kat had no doubt she would find her, but it might take a while—she didn't know how fast Jake might be able to move, and how far. And she didn't know how much of a lead Jake had, but it was possibly a half hour or more.

Would Jake answer if Kat called out her name, or would she run and hide?

As she popped the hatch, Kat considered whether she should leave it open or closed. If Jake changed her mind and came back to the bunker, she'd only know how to find that entrance—and she wouldn't see it unless the hatch was open. But unlocked and ajar, it left the bunker vulnerable to anyone who might be following Frank.

She emerged into the cold night. She was startled to find it was snowing lightly. *Be careful what you wish for.*

The snow made the decision for her. She decided to take the risk and leave the hatch open. She couldn't leave Jake with no way to get back in.

❖

Jake had stopped again. She was now sweating heavily beneath the insulated coveralls. Her exertions had left her panting and tired to the bone. The pain in her knee was unbearable.

She was worried. She had at first tried to ignore the anxious inner voice that told her she had gone too far, it couldn't be this way. But she finally had to admit it must be true. She was lost.

Going after Kat had been an impetuous, foolish act, she admitted in retrospect. She had no idea where to go and was in no shape to be tramping around in the wilderness in subfreezing temperatures. But given the circumstances, she knew she'd probably do the same again. She knew that despite the many unknowns about her mysterious friend, if Kat was in trouble, that's where she should be. It was as simple as that, or felt like it was.

But that impulse had put her square in the center of trouble. She knew she had to try to return the way she'd come, but the prospect of reversing and traveling the same long course again was daunting in her current state.

She needed to rest a minute first. Get the weight off her knee. A few steps off the path, she spotted a large fallen tree that would serve as an adequate bench. She brushed the snow from it and sat down, glad for the momentary relief for her knee. She wondered if she should put snow on it to help with the swelling. *Probably not in this cold,* she decided.

She would wait here for only a few minutes to get her strength back. She was so tired she found it hard to focus.

Kat was grateful it hadn't been snowing long; she could still make out Jake's trail in the snow. She scanned the area thoroughly with her night-vision goggles. Nothing. She parked them on her forehead.

She took out the flashlight and shone the bright light along the trench in the snow and followed it. She came to the jag Jake had made when she'd heard the snowmobile. Kat knew the detour had gone directly toward the main entrance of the bunker. It couldn't be far, and she wondered about that. Had Jake left the bunker early enough to have heard some of her interrogation of Frank at the wall below?

The trail ended abruptly, and Kat realized Jake had backtracked, so she did as well. She nearly missed where Jake had turned off onto the game trail, but at each intersection she came to, she gently blew away the upper powder on the trail to see the shape of the prints in the more solid snow beneath. She saw the boot imprint and recognized the tread. She hurried where she could. She was afraid the falling snow would make her task much more difficult. Soon she was far from the bunker.

Kat paused to catch her breath. It was tough going through the knee-deep snow. She heard the faint drone of an engine. Her senses went on high alert, trying to pinpoint the source of the noise, but it was difficult. She thought it came from the same general direction as the bunker.

Kat wondered whether Frank had gotten free and was fleeing on one of the snowmobiles. If he was, she thought, he was a hell of a lot smarter than she'd given him credit for.

Probably not, she decided. It could be another of Garner's men coming to collect on the contract. She hoped that wasn't the case, but she had no intention of turning from her search for Jake. She just had to hurry. She really hoped now that Jake wouldn't try to evade her and would come back to the bunker willingly. There wasn't a moment to lose.

Otter cut the engine on the snowmobile. Though it was only snowing lightly, the accumulation was making it more and more difficult to follow Frank's trail. He realized with a sense of alarm that his route back would also soon be impossible to follow if the snow kept up.

He hadn't seen any lights since he'd left the main road. No sign of civilization at all, for that matter. He'd just been on a slow, difficult trail through the woods, a path that seemed to lead nowhere. He'd brought extra gasoline, but not enough for running around lost if the route became obscured in front and behind. He had to make a decision soon. Continue on or return the way he came. Even if he found Hunter and killed her, it wouldn't do him much good to die in the process.

On the other hand, a million is worth a hefty risk, he figured. Hunter had to be somewhere, probably somewhere nice and warm where he could rest up and figure out how to get back to town. He'd make her give him directions—just before he killed her. *There may never be another opportunity like this. This trail is your big payoff. You have to go forward.* He started the engine, committed to finding her at any cost.

❖

Jake was so fatigued from her trek through the snow that she dozed off momentarily and nearly toppled off the fallen tree. She jolted awake, berating herself for her carelessness. *That can get you killed.* She wondered what had happened to Kat and said a prayer that her new friend was safe and unhurt.

She knew she should start heading back. She tried flexing her knee, but it felt as though the short period of inactivity had done it more harm than good. It had stiffened up, and any movement in the joint at all sent wrenching pain up and down her leg. She couldn't imagine how she could stand on it. But she had to try.

Jake slid carefully off the log, putting her weight on her good leg. She tried to hobble the few steps back to the trail she'd made but paid dearly for every bit of forward movement. The pain in her knee was so bad now she could not stop from crying, and Jake began to doubt she could make it all the way back to the bunker.

She threw herself forward in clumsy, lurching movements, trying to keep as much weight off the knee as possible. She looked around for a stick she might use as a crutch or cane, but any that might have been on the ground were hidden completely by snow, and there were no low-hanging branches that might suffice. She fought on until a misstep caused her to careen forward, off balance.

She tried to stop her fall by throwing out her hands. When her splinted left arm hit the ground, the pain was so intense she nearly blacked out. She lay where she had fallen, rolling over to face upward toward the sky, sucking in deep breaths against the pain.

She began sobbing. Great heaving sobs. They were cries of pain, of frustration over her memory loss, of anxiety over what might have happened to Kat, over the foolishness that had put her in this situation. But mostly they were the result of sheer exhaustion. She didn't think she could go on.

She closed her eyes. It was comfortable lying there in the snow. Peaceful.

CHAPTER TWENTY-FOUR

Jake felt hazy, foggy. Like when she woke up at Kat's after the crash. What she wanted more than anything was to hear that soothing, low voice again. It had made her feel safe and protected from the first moment she'd heard it. *I hope you're all right, Kat.*

She remembered the intensity of their last moments together. Before the alarm changed everything. Her body felt heated from the memory of their kiss. She relived it, took comfort in it, relaxed into it. She was just drifting off when she felt herself being lifted into the air. *Nice dream.* Then she was truly asleep.

Kat was grateful for Jake's pain. It helped her locate the woman. It was getting very hard to see Jake's trail even with the flashlight because of the accumulation of new-fallen snow. Kat had turned off the light a short while ago and was using her night-vision goggles because she was afraid Jake would hide if she saw someone pursuing her.

Kat paused in her tracks when she heard something break the silence of the night. It was Jake, sobbing, and the sound sent a deep ache of regret to her very core. She felt responsible for causing it. She felt guilty, too, for any momentary doubts about Jake's intentions. She'd obviously not run because she'd gotten her memory back. She must have been upset by what she'd seen.

Kat continued forward toward the sounds, approaching as quietly as she could. When she got within fifteen feet or so, Jake went quiet. Kat froze. She listened. She crept closer. She leaned over Jake's prone body. With her goggles on, Kat could see Jake's eyes were closed. She heard her deep, even breathing and realized she was asleep. Perfect. She'd much rather deal with all of this later at the bunker. She lifted Jake gently but firmly in her arms. *Meanwhile, I can think some more about what I'm going to tell you.*

She started back, moving as quickly as she could. *Stay asleep, Jake. Just stay asleep.*

Otter followed the snowmobile tracks with growing anxiety. He could barely make out the slight depression in the snow. He was peering so intently at the track just in front of the sled that he was almost upon the rock wall before he knew it. It stood some twenty to twenty-five feet in front of him. His initial confusion at the sight of the trail dead-ending was quickly replaced by a shrewd appreciation for Hunter's camouflaged entrance.

He cut the engine and turned off the headlight, plunging him into darkness. He cursed himself for not keeping an eye further forward. Hunter had probably discovered Frank just this way— he'd driven right up on her hideout.

Otter looked around. He could see no cameras. Not that he probably would. It was too dark and there were too many trees around to hide them in. He shrank back against an enormous oak, hiding in its shadow, and waited for a few minutes, his eyes scanning the surrounding area. When nothing happened, he took out a small flashlight with a bright, narrow beam and approached the rock wall.

He flashed the light back and forth along the ground in front of him. The snow in the whole area was flattened by tracks. There had been a lot going on at this spot, but a thin layer of new snow told him no one had been here in the last several minutes. He searched the rock wall for a way in, concentrating on the area that had the largest concentration of tracks.

He was rewarded with the quick discovery of the security panel.

Just a few feet from where Otter stood, Frank lay on the other side of the wall on the sleeping bag, studying the room he was in. There wasn't much to see. The snowmobiles and generator were lined up along the opposite wall, some ten feet out of his reach. Two small bulbs attached to the generator provided enough light for him to see the rest of the room was nothing but solid concrete, except for the two doors: the panel they'd come through from outside and the steel door Hunter had gone through. Both needed security codes to access.

Frank believed that Hunter meant it when she said she'd reward him for being patient and cooperative. But still he worked at his bindings as surreptitiously as possible, afraid she might be watching him with hidden cameras. His eyes were alert as he strained against the chains and duct tape.

Kat paused on the trek back to the bunker in an open space where the trail seemed to disappear. She made wide sweeps in the snow with her feet, clearing a small area before she gently set Jake down. She kept her left arm behind Jake's shoulders and sat down beside her, resting Jake's head against her chest. Jake stirred but didn't awaken.

Kat flexed her sore arm a few times before retrieving her GPS device from her coveralls. She sighted in their current position and checked the direction and distance to the bunker, whose coordinates were preprogrammed into the instrument.

As she put the GPS away, she studied Jake's face, composed and serene in sleep. The woman's earlier sobs of pain rang in Kat's ears. It was wrenching, the ache she felt at having frightened Jake into running from her. She could think of no convincing explanation she could offer to Jake for what had happened, except some version of the truth. She didn't know precisely what Jake had seen and what she'd heard. *But how much of the truth do I te'l her?* That would depend a lot, Kat guessed, on what Jake's reaction was when she woke up.

Kat's mind went back to the engine sounds she'd heard earlier. She had to get moving. The long night wasn't over yet. Kat scooped Jake up and started off in the direction of the bunker.

Otter stared at the security panel. He studied its housing and how it was affixed to the wall. But he didn't dare touch it, afraid it would alert Hunter of his presence. He wished now he'd spent more of his prison sentence reading up on electronic gadgetry. He'd never been good at it, and there had been too many advances while he'd been serving his time.

He stepped away from the wall and shined his flashlight beam around the area, searching in an ever-expanding circle. He could barely make out a single foot trail that led away from the wall, around the hill. He didn't really want to wander far from the snowmobile. It was still snowing and he knew he could easily lose his way. But he had committed himself to this. The way back to the crash site was surely covered up by now, so he had to find a way into Hunter's hideout.

He began following the foot trail. It was very hard to see near the exposed rock wall but a bit easier once it led into the woods, where the new snow hadn't accumulated quite as much. Otter followed it for several minutes, up the hill and through the dense woods. He was startled to see a light through the trees in front of him.

When he crested the hill, he found the source. In the clearing just ahead, a large round metal hatch stood wide open, light pouring from within. He approached with caution. *This is just too easy. A trap?*

Chapter Twenty-Five

Otter crept up to the hatch. He unzipped his insulated coat and drew his .38 revolver from its shoulder holster. It had been a long time since he had carried a gun, but it still felt familiar in his hand. He peeked down the hatch and listened for any sound from below. Nothing. He put his flashlight away. It was going to be difficult to descend the ladder with the gun. He'd just have to proceed slowly, alert for any sound or movement beneath him.

He started down, pausing every couple of rungs to listen. He was soon in the tunnel. He noted the doors at each end—the big steel one with another security panel next to it and the other, with no locks that he could see. He spotted a security camera mounted on the wall, high above the door with no locks. He hustled to get beneath it, out of its range of sight. He stood in front of the door. Gun at the ready, he very slowly tried the knob.

It surprised him when it turned. He heard the click of the mechanism and eased the door open. He glanced inside. He stepped into the doorway, using the door as a partial shield, expecting to see Hunter leap out at him at any moment. *She's too damn good at that,* he remembered with a shudder. His eyes took in the large living room, the bookcases and couch, the desk and monitors, the kitchen, and the three doors in the room, all of which were open.

When another minute had passed with no sound or movement from inside, he slipped over the threshold and crept toward the corner where the two doors stood open. Every muscle was alert. His heart was racing. His eyes were everywhere. When he got to the bedroom door, he glanced inside. Nothing. He repeated the careful inspection at the bathroom door. He checked the shower.

He crossed the living room to the pantry and checked that

room as well. He relaxed slightly. The place appeared to be empty. Was Hunter out pursing Frank? Or disposing of his body? Otter wondered. It certainly seemed careless of Hunter to leave an entrance standing open. But what other explanation could there be?

He would wait for her. Surprise her. Finally get revenge for all those years in prison. He glanced around. Where to hide? His eyes fell on the monitors. He recognized all three views: the tunnel, the clearing where he'd found the open hatch, and the rock wall. *Damn good thing she wasn't here when I drove up. She'd have ambushed me before I ever found the hatch.*

Just as he was finishing that thought, Otter saw movement in the first monitor. It was...a person. Someone tall. Hunter. He smiled. *My timing is better than the last time I saw you.* He took a couple of steps closer to the screen. He saw Hunter go to the security panel, but she had her back turned away from the camera. The wall slid open. She stepped inside where he couldn't see her but was gone only a minute or two. She went back outside but was soon out of camera range again.

Otter worried briefly that she might find his snowmobile. But Hunter returned almost at once, and this time she carried a body. She went by so quickly it was hard to tell much about the burden she was toting. But he knew it could not have been Frank, who'd been described to him as a big guy. The body Hunter carried was smaller. He realized it probably was a woman. *She killed that Scout chick Thomas told me about. When did she get here?*

Once Hunter was inside again, the wall slid back into place.

You're coming, Otter breathed, assessing his potential hiding spots. He decided to wait in the pantry, with the door left slightly open as it was when he arrived. He thought it was the least likely place she'd go immediately. That would give him time to observe her and plan his moment of attack. Perhaps he wouldn't want to spring on her the moment she arrived. She would probably be on high alert after confronting Frank and Scout.

He hurried through the pantry door and positioned himself behind the wall, comforted by the gun in his hand. He peered through the narrow opening between the door and the frame and tried to remain calm. The anticipation was both dreadful and delicious.

❖

Kat was physically spent by the time she arrived back at the bunker with Jake. She'd immediately dismissed the thought of getting back in through the open emergency hatch. It would be impossible to carry Jake through the narrow opening. That meant she would have to go in through the generator room. She didn't like that option because it meant she'd have to go by Frank. She didn't want him to know about Jake's presence, and there was always the chance he might have gotten free from his confinement and be waiting for her return.

But she had little choice. She needed to get inside immediately. She'd just have to hope that she could get by Frank quickly with a still-sleeping Jake.

As she emerged from the woods near the rock wall, she glanced down. She saw tracks from a boot tread she didn't recognize. They were very fresh and easy to see, and they led off toward the emergency exit. *You had to leave the damn hatch open. That explains the engine I heard.*

She realized she'd have to put herself in view of the security camera if she was to get inside the main entrance with Jake. She wanted to disable it, but it was in a tree and virtually inaccessible. The branches were slick with snow and ice.

Kat laid Jake down next to a large tree after clearing away as much snow as she could. A quick surveillance of the area turned up Otter's snowmobile, which had nothing on it to identify the owner. The keys were still in the ignition. She pocketed them.

She moved toward the rock wall, punching the numbers in while she turned her back to the camera and withdrew her Glock from the pocket of her coveralls. She slipped inside and glanced toward the corner, reassured that a startled Frank was still securely trussed up.

She took in the rest of the small chamber. Nothing was disturbed. There was nowhere for someone to hide, and she could see from the green light on the panel next to the steel door that no one had come through it while she was gone.

She turned to her prisoner and glared at him. "Face the corner, Frank, and close your eyes. I don't want to hear a peep out of you for the next few minutes."

He rolled over awkwardly, curious about the change in her demeanor, but said nothing.

Kat pocketed her Glock and went back outside. She scooped Jake up in her arms and returned to the generator room. She glanced toward the corner. Frank lay perfectly still, eyes averted.

Kat shifted Jake's weight in her arms so she could extend her right hand to punch in the security code first at the exterior door, to close it, then at the steel door, to gain access to the tunnel. She glanced frequently at Frank as she completed these tasks to make sure he wasn't moving. Her arms were more tired than she'd ever remembered. But the adrenaline pouring through her gave her renewed energy.

Once the steel door was unlocked, she shifted Jake's weight again, hefting the woman over her left shoulder. It freed up Kat's right hand and arm. She glanced again at Frank as she withdrew her gun from her coveralls. He hadn't moved.

She opened the door a few inches and peered in. There was no one in the tunnel. As she pushed the door open, Kat could feel Jake stir.

The blonde mumbled something and started thrashing about. She was waking up. At the worst possible moment.

"Shh," Kat said softly over her shoulder, but it was no use.

Jake tried to raise her head up to see where she was and what was happening.

Kat stepped over the threshold into the tunnel and shut the door behind her. She shoved the Glock back into her pocket and lowered Jake to the floor with her back propped up in the corner near the steel door. She knelt in front of Jake so that they were face-to-face.

Kat stiffened even as her eyes sought Jake's. She expected Jake to become frightened—panicky even, perhaps—at finding herself back at the bunker.

But Jake's expression went from one of hazy confusion to

happy recognition when their eyes met and she registered where she was and who she was with.

Before Kat could speak or react, Jake reached out with her good arm and pulled Kat into an awkward embrace. "You're all right! Thank God. Thank God." Jake pulled her to arm's length and studied her face. "But you're hurt," she cried, seeing the cut on Kat's face and the blood on her face and clothes.

Kat was dumbfounded. This was not at all the reaction she'd expected. "It's nothing," she said, smiling a little. She fought to subdue the joy she felt at the embrace and tender words. While the obvious caring and concern in Jake's voice reassured her, now was not the time for explanations.

"We have a lot to talk about," Kat began, her eyes not leaving Jake's. "But we can't right now. Someone may be in the bunker. It's a very dangerous situation. Jake, I have to ask you...again," she emphasized, with mild rebuke in her voice, "to trust me. You must stay here and not make a sound until I come back." She didn't wait for a reply. There was no time. She grabbed a couple of coats from the wall and laid them behind and over Jake. They would keep her warm and help conceal her.

As she leaned over Jake to tuck the heavy coats around her, Jake reached up and put her hand around the back of Kat's neck.

Jake pulled their heads close together until her mouth was only a couple of inches from Kat's ear. "I promise to do exactly as you say this time. I do trust you. Please be careful." She held Kat there, their cheeks touching, for just a moment.

"I will," Kat whispered back. She pulled away reluctantly as Jake released her grasp on the back of her neck. They looked at each other a moment, then a small smile crept first over Kat's face, then Jake's.

Despite their perilous situation, both had had their greatest fears alleviated, so they could not help but smile a little in sheer relief.

Kat turned without further word and approached the door to the living room. She stopped outside and removed her boots. She grasped the doorknob with her left hand as she pulled out her Glock with the other. She didn't look at Jake.

Hunter couldn't have distractions.

She turned the knob, unlatching the door. She stepped to the side, her back against the wall for protection, and inched the door inward. She craned her head around the door frame to see inside the living room. All was quiet. After a few moments, she ducked down and slipped inside, crouching behind the waist-high kitchen counter that protruded several feet into the room.

Her sixth sense of alarm was ringing loudly in her ears. *Someone's here.* She knew it. She could feel it. She was in an exposed position if they were in either the bedroom or bathroom to her right. She doubted that the intruder had found the weapons room, so that left the pantry as the only other place to hide. Three choices. She poked her head up in a quick motion to take in the pantry door on the other side of the counter, some fifteen feet away. It was open a few inches, but she knew she'd gone in there herself when she was looking for Jake. *Did I close it?* She couldn't remember. She'd been in too much of a hurry.

She stared at the two open doorways to her right, with her gun aimed in that direction. She listened. She waited. She tried not to think of Jake. She risked a glance toward the monitors. She could barely make Jake out in the picture on the first screen. Covered by coats, lying in the corner farthest from the camera, she looked like a pile of discarded clothes.

Kat returned her focus to the situation at hand. She waited some more, but could detect no sound from any of the rooms the intruder might be in.

❖

Otter had learned some measure of patience in prison. At the moment, however, he could barely contain his fevered energy. The object of his long obsession was within striking distance.

He saw the door open and Hunter's quick glance over the counter in his direction. Seeing her close up, even for that brief instant, sent his heart racing. He took long, deep breaths to calm himself but remained frozen in place, afraid the slightest movement would alert her to his presence.

He aimed his gun at the place he'd seen her raise her head, waiting for it to reappear like a pop-up target in a carnival shooting gallery.

He was disappointed but not surprised that she appeared to know someone had broken in and was waiting for her. She'd taken care of two other assassins tonight, after all. But Otter knew her better than the others did. And that, he told himself, gave him an advantage. He knew how extraordinarily patient she was. She would wait as long as she needed to, to gain an advantage in a difficult situation.

Well, he could be patient too. She had to come out in the open eventually to search for him. When she did, he'd be ready.

Kat crouched uncomfortably behind the counter for several long minutes, senses on high alert. Every now and then she would venture another glance away from the bedroom and bathroom doors to the monitors to make sure Jake hadn't moved.

Ordinarily, in a situation such as this, she would simply wait out her adversary. She'd find a way to use their often rash offensive attack against them somehow. But she had to think of Jake. She hadn't had time to really assess her injuries, but she knew Jake had to be in pretty bad shape to have collapsed in the snow. And who knew what Frank might be up to.

She needed to push this to a confrontation, but she had to do it in a way that would put her in a more advantageous position than she was in now. After a moment, the solution came to her. She crept backward toward the open door to the tunnel, her eyes pinned to the bedroom and bathroom doors, expecting the intruder to show himself if she made any noise whatsoever. *You're a smart one, aren't you?*

She made it through the door and pulled it closed again. Pocketing the gun, she grabbed a light jacket off the wall and threw it over the security camera to put it out of commission. Then she hurried to Jake.

"You okay?"

"Don't worry about me," Jake said.

"Can't help it," Kat responded. "Hang in there. I think I know a way to take care of this."

She retrieved her flashlight. "It's going to get very dark in here. Don't be afraid."

Jake nodded.

Kat punched in the security code and went through the steel door, not bothering to shut it behind her. She glanced at Frank as she entered the generator room. He was still facing the wall. She said nothing but went directly to the generator and shut it down, plunging the bunker into absolute darkness. She switched on the flashlight and returned to the tunnel, shutting the heavy door behind her and venturing a quick last look at Jake.

Kat went to the door to the living room, turned off the flashlight, and began to strip. She peeled off the white coveralls and the thermal underwear that covered her legs. When her naked flesh was exposed, she finally noticed how cold it had gotten in the tunnel. She turned on the flashlight and flashed it upward to see the hatch still standing open. She scaled the ladder rungs to pull it closed and lock it. Descending back into the tunnel, she set the flashlight on the ground at her feet. She peeled off her thermal top, then her socks.

❖

Jake hurt everywhere. The fall had done further damage to her broken arm, and her knee was so swollen and painful she tried very hard not to move at all. That part wasn't too·difficult at the moment. She was frozen in place, watching Kat.

After a few moments in darkness, the only sounds the rustling of clothes, the flashlight had come back on and Jake had seen Kat climb the exit tunnel, clad only in black silk panties and a top that looked like the long underwear her brother wore.

My brother? Jake gasped. A sudden image of a fair-haired young man flashed into her mind, along with a scattering of information. It was sort of like channel surfing and landing on a

TV movie in progress, staying tuned only long enough to get a little of the story.

I have a brother. Harding. Everyone calls him Hardy but me. I call him Hardy-har-har sometimes because he makes me laugh. He wears flannel shirts and ratty long underwear when he goes fishing. That was about all she could remember at the moment. But a lot more seemed right at the edge of her consciousness.

Her surprise and relief at the recollection was interrupted when her attention was drawn by a sound. Kat, setting down the flashlight. Jake watched with fascination as Kat removed her top and peeled off her socks. She was left standing in the chill air dressed only in black silk briefs and a matching bra. Jake was mesmerized. The woman was magnificent. The light from below illuminated Kat in a way that definitely seemed erotic to Jake, despite the absurdity of that at the moment. But she had no time to really appreciate the sight.

She watched as Kat leaned down to retrieve a gun from her coveralls and stepped to the door to the living room. The flashlight clicked off. The tunnel was pitch-black again.

❖

Kat paused at the door, her eyes closed. There was no ambient light whatsoever in the bunker, so her night-vision goggles were useless. She was fully reliant now on her other keen senses and home turf advantage.

Ready or not, here I come, Kat's inner voice chanted. As much as she had grown weary of a life of violent confrontations, she was exhilarated over the battle that lay beyond the door. She would protect Jake at all cost. Every nerve ending sang in anticipation, her remaining senses hypersensitive to every stimulus. No one had ever violated the sanctity of her safe house. She'd make them very sorry they did.

CHAPTER TWENTY-SIX

Otter chewed his fingernails when he was nervous. He had gnawed his left thumb nearly raw waiting for Hunter, wondering where she had gone. *What's she up to?*

The bunker went dark.

Shit. He waited for his eyes to adjust. They didn't. He couldn't see his hand in front of his face. *Shit, shit, SHIT.* He had his flashlight in his hand before he realized he couldn't use it. It would make him an instant target.

But he didn't put it away. The feel of it comforted him. As he listened for any sound from outside the pantry door, he tried to imagine Hunter's next move. He knew she had extraordinary eyesight, but he didn't believe anyone could see in this darkness. That meant she was either operating completely blind or, more likely, she had some sort of newfangled equipment to help her see in the pitch-black. She'd always been big on the latest high-tech gizmos and gadgets.

He cursed her under his breath as he considered his options. The pantry now felt more like a snare than a sanctuary. *Although on second thought, maybe there's something in here I can use.* He fumbled for the doorknob and pulled the door shut as quietly as he could. He turned on the flashlight and scanned the shelves along the walls. Using the flashlight was an enormous risk. But he couldn't just wait for Hunter to find him.

His thin lips curled into a wry grin. He snatched a few items from the shelves and cut the light. After laying his trap, he opened the door a few inches to where it had been previously. Otter held his breath and waited, listening at the crack. *It won't be long now.*

❖

Kat snuck back into the living room, pausing to ease the door closed behind her. She breathed deeply, sniffing the air. Listening. She crept noiselessly to the wall to her immediate right and then slowly forward to the corner with the desk. She traced the wall with her left hand and held the gun in her right. Her fingers skimmed across the security monitors as she came upon them and turned the corner. She paused and listened again for another minute. Though she sensed no one within several feet of her, Kat's instinct told her to proceed slowly.

She continued her silent trek along the wall toward the bedroom door. She slowed when she approached the space where she knew her cello case would be and stepped around it. She paused and listened at the threshold of the bedroom, then stepped inside and navigated the perimeter of that room, stopping periodically to focus her senses on her immediate surroundings. She moved around the bed, finding the chair and table with remembered ease. She'd blindly traveled the route from bed to bathroom often in the middle of the night, so that leg of her journey was familiar.

She examined the bathroom in the same methodical way, following the wall, making periodic stops with her senses scanning for the intruder. Then she was out in the living room again, moving along the wall with the bookcases. She paused to listen outside the weapons room. There still had been no sound in the bunker. If the intruder hadn't changed locations when the lights went out, then he had to be in the pantry.

Kat left the wall and crossed the center of the living room, giving the pantry door a wide berth. She found the kitchen counter with her outstretched left hand and used it as her tactile guidepost, drawing her along past the sink and the stove to the refrigerator, which stood just outside the pantry door.

She and Otter were now just a few feet apart. Kat stood with her back pressed against the fridge, her senses expanding into the space around her, probing silently. She held her gun at the ready, fingertip caressing the trigger.

Kat's sixth sense had already told her the intruder was very near, but it was her keen sense of smell that gave her the first solid evidence of the man who had invaded her sanctuary. When she detected a slightly sour aroma only inches away, she knew she had him. Even the pros perspired.

She knew he was waiting on the other side of the door.

She crept three feet to her right and threw herself forward, hitting the door with her right shoulder with unbelievable force. She felt the impact of the door slamming against the intruder's body just before she lost her footing and went down hard. Her Glock flew from her hand.

When the door slammed into him, Otter was propelled backward—hard, into the wall of shelves behind him. He got the wind knocked out of him but good, and he lost his gun and flashlight. The shelves collapsed, spilling their contents on and around him. The commotion was deafening. A heavy jar glanced off his head.

He lay on the cement floor where he landed, struggling to breathe. His need for air overtook everything else.

His hand went to his forehead where the jar had impacted. The skin was unbroken, but a lump had already started to form. His movement shifted the shelving piled on top of him. The noise was loud in his ears, and he suddenly felt extremely vulnerable. He froze and listened intently. He could hear Hunter's labored breathing several feet away.

Otter took a second to regroup. He seemed to be in one piece, but Hunter sounded injured. This could be his only chance to overpower her.

Otter threw off the boards and cans and groped around on the floor, searching for his gun and his flashlight. He found nothing but packets of grains, cans of vegetables, boxes of pasta. He paused after several seconds of searching to listen. He could no longer hear her heavy gasps for breath or anything else. He didn't know where she was.

Silence.

Shit.

❖

Kat was already trying to analyze what it was the intruder had put on the floor even as her legs went out from under her. Some sort of dried beans or peas, maybe, she thought, her arms pinwheeling as she careened sideways. Her rib cage slammed into the sharp corner of a shelf. She landed on her back and doubled up against the sharp pain in her side. It was hard to breathe. Each expansion of her lungs brought new pain.

She knew that the intruder had obviously gone down as well, but the resulting cacophony had died. All was quiet now except for Kat's raspy gulps for air.

Another flurry of sounds erupted from the corner where the man had fallen. Cans clattered against each other. One rolled across the floor in her direction. He was searching for something, probably a gun. *Protect Jake,* her instincts whispered. Kat would deal with the pain later. Now she had to survive.

She rose to a crouch. She reached around her with both hands, feeling for a weapon, as she fought to quiet her breathing.

She scuttled crablike several feet to the left without making a sound, picking up several cans along the way. She cradled them in her left arm while her right swept outward in search of her gun. The intruder had gone quiet.

Kat hefted a can in her right hand and waited, holding her breath, extending her hearing until she heard a faint sound. A whisper—maybe the intruder's clothes or his breathing. It didn't really matter. She lobbed the can as hard as she could directly at the noise.

She was rewarded by a satisfying thunk that was immediately followed by a muttered curse. Then all was silent again. She lobbed a second can at the same spot. Another thunk. Then shuffling noises as her target attempted to evade further attack. Kat smiled. She fired another can at the retreating sounds, eliciting another thwack of impact and another curse, this one louder than the first.

She heard him grappling around for something to throw back at her, so she was flat on the floor at least a second or two before the first can came her way. It sailed far above her and three feet to her right. More followed, thrown in a random pattern of rage. Kat was glad for the clatter. It masked her own search for her Glock. She crawled a couple of feet more to her left until she was against a wall. She ransacked the lower shelves for more ammunition.

Her hands found more cans and jars. She focused on her adversary's noisy effort to return fire. She rocketed a steady stream of cans and bottles at the spot. Most hit their target.

The man tried hard to be quiet under her assault, but he apparently couldn't help the occasional grunt of pain when something hit a particularly vulnerable spot.

Kat adjusted her aim accordingly.

She began creeping closer to his position. She inched her way along the wall, grabbing items off the shelves, keeping up her incessant barrage. Once in a while she would hear something sail by her ear and crash against the wall behind her, but the intruder was now spending more time protecting himself than trying to retaliate.

Otter was in trouble, and he knew it. Several of the damn cans had hit him pretty squarely in the head. One opened up a gash above his eye. And the last one had hit him hard in his lower abdomen as he'd been trying to retreat, shuffling backward on his rear end. *Just a few inches lower,* he gulped as he crouched in the corner, trying to shield both his face and groin from further assault. He knew she was closing in. But she wasn't hitting him with every single throw, so he knew Hunter was operating blind too. There might still be a chance he'd come out of this.

He knew he had to make a move. In desperation, Otter fell to his hands and knees, searching wildly around him, heedless of the noise. The floor here was sticky. He smelled maple syrup and the stench of dead fish. He felt something cold and metallic in the pool of syrupy goo. His hand closed around his .38.

Even as another can hit him in the shoulder, Otter smiled. He pointed the gun in Hunter's direction. He cocked it and pulled the trigger.

CHAPTER TWENTY-SEVEN

Kat was in her windup to pitch another can at him when she heard the gun cock. She dove forward. The bullet whizzed by just above her. Right where her left eye had been a second earlier.

Before Otter could pull the trigger a second time, she was upon him. She threw herself at him headfirst and sent him sailing into the corner. His head cracked against something, and he saw stars for a moment. Kat recovered more quickly. Her left hand found the gun in his right hand and she wrenched it from him. Her right hand found his neck and tightened around it, pinning him against the wall.

"Who are you?" Kat demanded. She pressed her thumb hard into the pulse point at the top of Otter's jaw, below her ear. Her other hand rammed the gun convincingly into his rib cage. He winced.

"Just an old friend, Hunter. Came by to look you up," Otter choked.

"Big mistake, little man," Kat said. She tightened her hold on his neck until he could no longer breathe at all. He struggled, wrapping his arms around her, flailing against her despite the gun. But she held him fast and took his blows until his efforts stopped and he grew still.

She released her grip and Otter slumped to the floor. She shifted the gun to her right hand and reached out with her left, finding his head and skimming over it until she found just the spot she wanted. She marked the spot with her left hand while she brought the gun down with her right. He'd be out for a long while now. And have one hell of a headache when he did come to.

Kat got up and felt her way to the door. Her body was still

energized with adrenaline, but the fatigue she'd been fighting for hours was reasserting itself. She still had much to do before she could relax.

She returned to the tunnel and felt around for her clothes. She wiped her sticky hands on the garments, found her flashlight, and flicked it on. She found Jake and crouched down beside her. "Everything is okay now," Kat said. "I'm going to turn the lights back on, I'll be right back." She touched Jake's cheek before she found her way to the steel door.

Once through it, she shone the light toward Frank. She caught him scrambling to return to his corner. While she was gone, he had moved to the end of the chain, a few feet farther into the room. And he had managed to unravel a little of the duct tape around his hands, but the chains still had him securely bound. He froze when the light hit him.

Kat said nothing as she proceeded to the generator. As soon as the flashlight was off him, Frank continued his mad scramble back to the corner. He was there by the time she flipped the switch, illuminating the room again.

He ventured a look at her, afraid of her reaction to his efforts to break free. His eyes went wide as he took in the sight of her, but he dared not open his mouth.

She glared at him with a fierce, feral energy that made him wish he'd never heard of Garner.

Whatever had just happened—and from the sight of her it had been something he'd like to have witnessed—it certainly hadn't helped her mood that she'd caught him trying to get away. He shrank into the corner and dropped his eyes. He heard her leave, slamming the steel door behind her. Frank inhaled greedily. He hadn't been aware he'd been holding his breath.

Kat returned to the tunnel, consciously trying to calm herself and dissipate some of the savage energy that gripped her. She didn't want to be Hunter when she dealt with Jake. She wanted to be Kat again. Once through the door, she tried to smile reassuringly as she looked down at her friend. She was surprised to find Jake staring up at her with wide eyes. *Oh my God, does she remember?*

❖

Jake stared at Kat, eyeing her up and down, her look of bewilderment turning into one of amusement. Then her face grew serious as she focused on Kat's shoulder. "You're bleeding."

Kat followed Jake's eyes, for the first time looking down at herself. Nearly every inch of her naked flesh was covered with food. Her left side was slathered with maple syrup. Her right leg had smears of mustard. Spots of flour and cornmeal dotted her lightly bronzed face and arms. Her silk briefs were soaked on one side and clung to her like a second skin. Her shoulder, the object of Jake's concerned gaze, had a large red smear that looked like blood.

Kat casually reached up with one hand to scoop up a bit of the substance with one fingertip. Then, her eyes on Jake, she put the finger in her mouth and sucked on it in what was, in Jake's mind, a most seductive manner. After a moment, Kat winked at Jake and withdrew the finger. "Hot sauce," she announced. "You missed one heck of a food fight."

She seemed so nonchalant about the whole affair that Jake relaxed a little. "Do I get details?"

"Later," Kat promised. "Right now we need to get you back in bed. Then I have a few loose ends to tie up." She crouched down and lifted Jake.

Jake shrieked in pain.

The sound shot through Kat and she froze. "I'm sorry," she whispered.

Jake took deep breaths to fight the throbbing in her knee and the shooting pain in her arm. "Not your fault," she managed. "My own stupidity. I was in no shape to try to go after you."

"Go after me?" Kat asked as she carried Jake toward the living room.

"Thought you were in trouble." Jake closed her eyes against the pain. When she opened them again, they were in the bedroom and she was being lowered onto the bed. "I seem to have a knack for getting myself into bad situations that you have to come get me out of."

A half smile formed on Kat's lips. "I wouldn't mind a nap and a hot meal before the next crisis," she said as she examined Jake's wrist. She glanced at Jake. "But this is not your fault. It's mine."

Kat continued her evaluation of Jake's injuries without further elaboration. She gently probed Jake's knee, which had swollen badly on one side.

Jake put her hand on Kat's arm, forcing the other woman's full attention. She held it there until Kat looked directly at her. "It's time for some answers," she said, in a voice that brooked no argument. "What aren't you telling me?"

"I've got a couple of things to attend to first that can't wait," Kat answered, looking away. "It won't take long. I'll bring back some ice for that knee and reset your wrist. We'll talk then."

She turned to leave, but the sound of Jake's voice caught her at the doorway.

"Kat?"

Kat turned to face her.

"I remembered something."

Kat's sharp intake of breath was the only outward sign of her shock at Jake's revelation. She felt as though she'd been kicked in the gut, but her face betrayed none of her inner turmoil.

"I have a brother," Jake said. "His name is Hardy. Not much else yet. But maybe my memory is coming back." She had a hopeful expression on her face.

Kat nodded and forced a smile. "That's good news."

Jake saw that Kat's heart wasn't in the sentiment and wondered why she didn't seem pleased at the news. But before she could ask, Kat was gone.

Kat's heart sank as she leaned against the bedroom door, absorbing Jake's news. *Will you still want to kill me when you remember who you are?* Kat refused to believe that was possible and felt guilty for doubting Jake. Jake had apparently risked her own life going out into the snow, all because she thought Kat was in trouble.

She couldn't think about all that right now. She forced Jake's news out of her mind. She had work to do. She went to the pantry and surveyed the chaos.

Otter was sprawled on the floor, still out cold. He was bleeding from a cut above his eye. There was another above his ear, but neither looked too bad. His face was already swollen from the blows he'd taken. She'd been spot-on with several of her throws.

Otter looked a lot older than Kat remembered. Heavier too. Still the greasy hair, but a lot less of it. Although Kenny had warned her about Otter, she was still a little surprised to see him. She didn't think he had the brains or the nerve to get this far.

Her mind flashed back to the last time she'd seen him.

She was still working for Garner then. He had put her in charge of a three-man team whose mission was to rescue a kidnap victim—a six-year-old girl—and execute her kidnappers.

Hunter flew into Albany, New York, a day ahead of the rest of the team to get a preview of the walled private estate where the girl was being held. The mansion and its sprawling grounds were nestled in a river valley an hour away in the Catskills.

Hunter studied the place for three hours through night-vision binoculars from a hillside on the adjacent property. There were lights on in several second-story rooms, though it was after midnight. Figures passed by the windows. All men, never the girl. Sentries patrolled at irregular intervals. They'd meet up and have a smoke, chat a while.

Hunter took it all in and added it to the information Garner had given her about their mission. She had blueprints of the interior and a picture of the little girl. And she had several photos of the two men she was to assassinate. They were behind the kidnapping. She didn't know what their motivation was. It didn't matter. Her two targets had at least a dozen friends with them, and many of them were armed.

Kenny's plane touched down an hour before Otter's, so Hunter got a chance to brief the teenager over a sandwich at the airport bar. He asked all the right questions and regarded their mission with the same seriousness that she did. By the time Otter joined them,

Hunter had developed a healthy respect for Kenny's intelligence and maturity.

Otter was another matter. Hunter and Kenny found him in baggage claim just as he was retrieving his bag.

"Well, well, well. Nice to meet you." Otter licked his lips as his eyes traveled the length of Hunter, settling on her breasts. "I got to thank the boss. He's never hooked me up with a hottie like you before, sweetheart."

"Stick to business, Otter," Hunter said. She turned and headed toward the exit.

"Aw, c'mon, dollface. We got lots of time to get acquainted," Otter persisted. He leered at Hunter as the trio emerged outside. "Hey, kid, take a hike, huh? Meet us at the hotel."

Kenny slowed his steps, uncertain what to do.

Hunter turned and glared at Otter. "Look, little man," she snarled. "Put your eyes back in your head and shut your mouth or I'll shut it for you. We've got a job to do."

His good humor disappeared. He stepped a foot closer, invading her personal space. "I ain't taking orders from no broad," he spat.

They stood there a moment, glowering at each other. Kenny remained off to one side, watching.

Hunter pulled out her cell phone and started to dial.

"Hey, wait a minute," Otter said, backing away when he realized who she was calling. "I didn't mean nothing by it, no harm done."

She closed the phone and put it in her pocket. "Let's go."

They spent the next couple of hours discussing the operation over dinner in Hunter's hotel room, the blueprints spread out in front of them.

At 1:00 a.m., Hunter flew them by helicopter to a clearing not far from the hill where she'd studied the estate.

Kenny got them past the computerized security system and inside a rear entrance while Hunter and Otter took out three guards.

They crept up a back stairway in the darkness, toward the second-floor rooms where Hunter had seen the lights. They paused at the top of the stairwell. Two guards were in the hall, playing cards at a small table.

Hunter and Otter knocked them out before they could raise an alarm.

Hunter listened at the door of the first room they came to. Silence. She twisted the knob and eased the door open. A library or study. No one inside.

She started to close the door, but Otter's hand on her arm stopped her. He waved his gun toward the desk in the room. Behind it, on the wall, a cabinet door stood open. Within was a safe.

Hunter had already seen it. She glared at Otter and shook her head as she closed the door to the room.

He gripped her arm harder. "Five minutes," he whispered.

She shook him off and clamped her hand over his mouth.

He pushed her away, but did not speak again.

She continued toward the next room, looking back over her shoulder to make sure Otter was behind her. Kenny hung back.

Hunter entered this room as she had the other. The door open a crack, she could see a guard in profile, looking out the window. Propped against the sill was a semiautomatic rifle.

She nudged the door open another inch. She could see the end of a bed. Another inch. There was the girl, asleep.

Hunter turned. Otter was directly behind her. She motioned toward the girl, then looked at Otter to make sure he understood.

He nodded.

She eased the door open and took in the rest of the room at a glance to ensure there were no other guards. The man at the window hadn't heard them.

Hunter overpowered him before he could react. She joined Otter as he was gathering the girl in his arms and gently shook the girl awake.

"Hi, Sally," Hunter whispered. "I'm a friend of your daddy, and I've come to take you home to him. You have to be real quiet, though, all right? Don't make a sound, now." She smiled and put her finger to her lips.

The girl nodded solemnly.

"Wait at the stairwell," Hunter whispered in Otter's ear. He nodded and left with the girl, her arms wrapped around his neck. Hunter motioned for Kenny to follow him.

Everything was going as planned. Hunter headed toward the master bedrooms.

She had to hit four bedrooms before she found both of the men whose faces she had memorized. Neither woke. They never would again.

It had taken five minutes.

When she returned to the stairwell, she was not entirely surprised to find the girl now in Kenny's arms, Otter nowhere to be seen.

"Library," Kenny whispered.

She nodded.

Otter was at the safe, his attention on the dial between his fingertips. He never heard Hunter slip back into the room.

"Come on, you little shit, or I'm leaving your ass," she hissed.

He was startled but not deterred. "Almost got it," he said in a low voice, not turning around, but Hunter was already out the door.

She took the girl from Kenny, and they headed back down the stairwell.

They were crossing over the threshold when alarms rang out. They broke into a run.

The safe was wired, Hunter realized as she sprinted across the lawn, Kenny close behind. She could hear him panting for air.

Lights went on everywhere all at once, illuminating the house and grounds.

They were sitting ducks.

Shots rang out. A bullet hit the sod just ahead of her, blasting bits of earth and turf into the air.

They reached the wall and scaled it, passing the girl between them. A bullet slammed into the stonework a foot to the left of Kenny's head.

Gasping for air, they scrambled up the hill. Halfway to the top, Hunter took a look back.

Otter was far behind, still inside the wall. He was being

pursued by three men on foot. Two other men were shooting at them with rifles from the second floor.

They were almost over the rise when Kenny fell.

The little girl screamed.

"Let's ride piggyback. Hold on tight, now," Hunter told Sally as she pulled her onto her back.

She reached down and pulled Kenny to his feet. He'd been shot in the side but was still conscious, and stumbled forward with her support.

Hunter got the girl and Kenny belted into the helicopter just as Otter came over the hill. She scrambled into the pilot's seat and pulled on her night-vision goggles. Otter was laboring under the weight of a bulky sack. The men behind him were closing in and had their guns out.

Hunter started up the chopper.

Otter was too far away. There was nothing she could do. The girl was their priority, and he had sealed his own fate.

She lifted off.

Ping! A bullet ricocheted off the bottom of the copter.

She hit the throttle.

Hunter saw Otter drop his bag and wave his arms at her just before he fell. She couldn't tell whether he'd stumbled or been shot.

She'd later learned from Garner that Otter was sent to prison for his part in the raid. But she had no regrets about leaving him behind. The greedy bastard had nearly gotten them all killed.

Bet you have a bone or two to pick with me over that, she mused, looking down at Otter's supine form. He was as covered with syrup and flour and other unrecognizable foodstuffs as she was. And he stank.

She searched him and found a box of ammo for his .38. Her own gun was on a shelf next to a jar of peanut butter. She went to the weapons room and got two sets of handcuffs and a ring of keys, which she temporarily stuck into one of Otter's pockets since she didn't have any of her own.

She grabbed hold of him and dragged him through the living room and tunnel and into the generator room.

"Got some company for you, Frank," Kat said cheerily as she

took out one set of handcuffs and secured Otter's hands behind his back. "Although I don't expect him to be quite as cooperative as you have been." She looked up from her task to glare at him. Her voice turned menacing. "Most of the time, that is."

Frank averted his eyes and kept quiet.

"You can get back in my good graces, though," Kat continued. "Just keep an eye on Otter here, and start hollering real loud if he manages to get farther than you did in trying to escape."

She pulled Otter over to the corner next to Frank and laid him out on his side. The two men made an odd pair. Frank had to be almost a foot taller than Otter and outweighed him by more than a hundred pounds.

She used the second pair of cuffs on Frank, replacing the chain and duct tape. He could move his hands more freely now. He flexed his fingers, restoring some of the circulation he'd lost, and nodded to her in appreciation for the small reprieve.

Kat threaded the chain that had been on Frank's wrists through his handcuffs and then through Otter's, binding them together back to back. There was less than four feet of slack between them. With the padlock, she secured that chain to the heavy one attached to the wall.

She didn't speak again until she finished and headed toward the door. "I'll be back in a while to feed you and let you move around a bit, Frank." She paused at the doorway and turned to look at him. Her eyes were cold, her voice threatening. "Don't disappoint me again."

Frank looked down at the unconscious man beside him. Otter's face was swollen and bruised, and he was covered with smears of food. At least he'd find out what the hell had happened. In different circumstances, Hunter in her underwear covered with food might make for an interesting story, but Frank knew he'd never have the guts to tell this one. At least not as it really happened.

A fetid aroma assaulted his nostrils. Frank leaned into Otter, sniffing. Maple syrup, and...fish. Dead fish. He eyed the short length of chain between them and groaned.

Chapter Twenty-Eight

Kat headed to the kitchen for ice for Jake's knee. A chill ran through her, and she glanced down again at her near-naked body. She really wanted to shower and put on some warm clothes, but Jake came first.

As she entered the bedroom with the bag of ice, she was not surprised to find Jake sprawled on her back in the middle of the bed, sound asleep. She was still clad in the coveralls, boots on her feet. Kat removed the boots, smiling a little at the myriad of things that had been jammed into them to make them fit better.

She unzipped the coveralls and helped Jake out of them as gently as she could, but Jake stirred and groaned.

"Shh. Go back to sleep," Kat whispered. She reached down to smooth a strand of errant blond hair on the sleeping woman's forehead, her fingertips lingering to caress Jake's cheek.

Jake sighed, a contented mewling sound, and drifted back off without ever opening her eyes.

Kat put the ice bag on Jake's knee and covered her with the fleece blanket, tucking her in like a pampered child.

Kat got a lot accomplished in the hour Jake napped. She took a long, hot shower and put on clean jeans and a sweatshirt. It helped to refresh her and reduce some of the fatigue she was fighting.

Then she tended to Frank, heating up a bowl of soup for him and letting him eat, stretch, and relieve himself outside the main entrance. All of it was done under her careful scrutiny, her Glock held casually in one hand as though it were a natural extension of her arm. Although his bladder had been full an hour earlier, it took Frank a moment to get going under Hunter's unwavering stare.

Otter stirred only once during the proceedings. He groaned but didn't awaken.

Once that chore was finished, Kat spent a few minutes on her computer looking at radar and satellite pictures of the weather front that was dumping snow on the Upper Peninsula. The area was expected to get another eight inches or more over the next thirty-six hours, and the winds were expected to increase. It would create whiteout conditions and significant drifting. *That should make it impossible for anyone else to follow Frank and Otter's snowmobile tracks to the bunker.*

Kat realized she was absolutely starving. She had burned up a lot of energy during the last several hours, and her body was craving compensation. She headed for the kitchen. From what she'd seen of Jake's appetite so far, she knew she should probably make enough for an army.

Kat took out the venison tenderloins she'd set in the fridge and seared them in a cast-iron skillet before setting them in the oven to finish cooking. She surveyed the mess in the pantry to see what had survived the battle with Otter.

She had lost a good bit of her stores, she realized, taking a more complete mental inventory than she'd allowed herself earlier. Several of the cans were dented but salvageable. But the rack that held her bins of flour, cornmeal, rice, and dried potatoes had been overturned, and Otter had scattered nearly all her stock of dried peas and beans on the floor in his successful effort to trip her up. About half of her bottled stores—mustard, ketchup, dressings, salsas, and syrups—had been used as ammo. She regretted most the loss of the two bottles of Blue Front Barbecue Sauce she'd brought all the way from Florida.

It would be hard to feed four people for very long on what remained.

Kat's stomach rumbled as she reached for a box of macaroni and cheese, so she took two boxes off the shelf. Then she rummaged around the mess on the floor until she found a couple of cans of fruit.

This will be fun to clean up, she thought, sniffing the air with a grimace. The room smelled...fishy. She spotted the broken remains of an economy-sized bottle of Thai fish sauce on the floor, right where Otter had been lying.

She grinned. Otter hated fish.

❖

Kat wolfed down a healthy portion of the makeshift meal she'd thrown together. The rest she put on a tray and carried to the bedroom. She set it down on the bedside table and gently shook Jake awake.

Jake grumbled at the touch, protesting the interruption of a rather erotic dream she was having, until she opened her eyes and saw the object of her fantasies in the flesh. Then she came quickly awake, her nose immediately trying to identify the source of a tantalizing aroma. She turned her head, saw the tray, and her smile widened. Forgetting her injuries for a moment, she tried to prop herself up to eat.

The pain in her knee and wrist was unbearable. "Ow! OwOwOwOwOwOwOw!" Finally the worst of it abated. She felt a hand on her shoulder and looked up to see Kat leaning over her.

"Sorry, I should have warned you not to try to move," Kat said. "Your knee is full of fluid, and I think you've broken your wrist in a new place."

"Oh, that's just great." Jake shook her head and blew out a long breath of exasperation.

"Don't worry, we'll get you fixed up and feeling better," Kat said. "Let me help you sit up to eat. You need to get your strength back. We'll deal with your injuries after you do." She got Jake into a more comfortable position, her back against the headboard of the bed, and set the tray in front of her.

The venison, already cut into bite-sized portions, shared a plate with a generous pile of macaroni and cheese. The tenderloin had been finished in a sauce made of red wine and dried cherries. There was also a small plate of canned pear and peach segments, and a glass of merlot.

"This really looks and smells wonderful," Jake said, reaching for her fork. "I can't believe how hungry I am."

"I'm not surprised," Kat answered. "You covered a few miles out there. It must have been incredibly difficult with your knee."

Jake stopped chewing for a moment to look at Kat, who had dropped into the chair beside the bed. Dark circles rimmed Kat's eyes. She looked absolutely exhausted. Jake pictured Kat walking those same long miles in the dark, in the snow, to find her...then walking them yet again while carrying her.

"I'm sorry, Kat," Jake said. "I know I should have stayed put, like you asked me to." She put the fork down, her appetite momentarily forgotten. "I tried to, but I finally just had to get up to pee. And when I was coming back, I saw the TVs. I saw you fighting that man, and I thought you were in trouble and needed help." After a long pause, she added, "But apparently you didn't." Jake was obviously curious about what had happened, but she wanted Kat to volunteer the information.

Kat nodded toward the food. "Eat that before it gets cold."

Jake reached for the fork and resumed eating, slower this time. She watched Kat, hoping for an explanation.

Kat fidgeted under Jake's unwavering stare. She closed her eyes, gathering her thoughts. She knew she could delay no longer. She was about to make a leap of faith—an action virtually unknown to her.

"Jake," she began, her voice unexpectedly husky. She sat forward in the chair and looked at Jake. Her throat went dry. She swallowed hard. "There are a lot of things about myself I haven't told you." She paused. "That I haven't told anyone." Another pause. She bit her lip. "A lot of unpleasant things, things that most people wouldn't understand." She looked away again and stared at the floor. She held her hands tightly together on her lap.

"The work that I do, the real work, I mean—nature photography is more my avocation..." She took her time, careful to choose the right words. "The real work I do is very dangerous and very secretive. I guess you could say I hunt down people who are big problems. Problems that individuals can't deal with alone or that governments turn a blind eye to. Some that law enforcement can't do anything about...who have to be dealt with...outside the law."

Kat's throat constricted. She forced herself to look at Jake.

She had to see what Jake's reaction would be. "Sometimes," she continued, her expression a mask, "I have to kill people."

Jake's eyebrows furrowed as the news registered. But she did not shy away from Kat. And when she spoke, her voice was calm, her tone more curious than alarmed. "Did you have to kill the man I saw you fighting with?"

"No," Kat responded, avoiding Jake's eyes again. She took a deep breath. Opening up to Jake made her feel exposed. Vulnerable. But a measure of relief washed over her at Jake's mild reaction to her news. "I didn't kill him. Or the other one," she added as an afterthought. "They're both fine."

"The other one?" Jake's eyebrows shot up and her eyes got wide.

"Uh, yeah," Kat admitted. She'd forgotten Jake had never seen Otter—she must have assumed the food fight in the dark had been with the same intruder Kat had fought with on the monitor.

"Yeah, there were two," Kat said. "They're both okay, just trussed up for the moment in the other room." She nodded in the direction of the door. "The generator room, on the other side of the tunnel." She paused, clearly disarmed by the change in subject at such a critical point in her confession. "I'll get back to them in a minute."

Jake nodded, her attention fully on Kat. Her look was expectant. Her food was cold. She didn't notice.

Kat cleared her throat. She looked at the floor. She wiped sweaty palms against her jeans, stalling while she considered what she would say next. Jake didn't seem horrified by her profession. Kat wondered whether it was because some part of Jake still inherently recognized the job, even with her amnesia.

Kat hadn't planned on ever telling her new friend about what she had learned about Jake's real identity. But she was reconsidering that now. *I still don't want to lie to you, do I?*

"Jake," she said, leaning back in the chair. "You said you remembered your brother. Have you remembered anything else?"

It took Jake a moment to register what she thought was an abrupt change in subject. "No. I just had a picture of him. A name, an impression that we're pretty close. Why? What does that have to do with what's going on? Who are those men?" She wished Kat would get back to what she'd been talking about.

But Kat wouldn't look at her. And she acted as though she hadn't heard Jake's question. "Have you recalled anything at all about what you might have done—what job you might have had or skills you used in your past?"

Jake took a deep breath to calm her irritation with the continued questioning. Not that she didn't care about her past. Certainly she did. But she really couldn't remember anything else, and Kat seemed to be deliberately avoiding further talk about her own life and these "unpleasant things" that she said she had done.

"I really don't remember anything about that," Jake said. "Just what I've told you before. I think I've traveled a lot. Why? Why all these questions?"

Kat bit her lip, nodding slightly. She stared at the door opposite her chair, as if to bolt to it at any moment. Her next question really seemed to come out of left field. "Do you remember if you've ever held a gun? Or fired one?"

Jake frowned. *Do you know something about who I am that you're not telling me?* She tried to visualize herself with a gun. A pistol. Then a rifle. At a shooting range, or hunting animals. She shrugged. "Doesn't seem familiar. I don't think so. But I just don't know."

"Okay," Kat said, nodding as if in agreement. As though Jake's answer settled more questions in her mind than just the one she'd asked.

Jake's curiosity could be contained no longer. She leaned toward Kat, reaching out her hand to touch the other woman's arm. Kat had to look at her. "What aren't you telling me, Kat?" "Am I a policewoman or something? Are you?"

Kat's face clearly showed how unexpected that question was. She flinched and blushed deep red, as though she were a child caught in a lie. She looked away.

"No, Jake, we're not law enforcement." Her low voice sounded apologetic, and a little sad. "We're bounty hunters. Mercenaries. We're in the business of hunting people down for money. So are the two men tied up in the other room. They're here hunting for me. To kill me."

Jake gaped at Kat, her eyes wide in shock, her mind unable to immediately grasp all that she had heard. "We?" she finally asked. "I'm a...a bounty hunter, too?"

Kat still couldn't meet her eyes. "I think so, yes." A long moment passed before she added, "I think you came out here to kill me too."

CHAPTER TWENTY-NINE

W hat?" Jake gasped. This had to be a very bad joke or
some terrible mistake. But Kat was obviously deadly
serious. "Kat," she begged, a rush of panic threatening to overwhelm
her, "please look at me."

Kat did. But her expression was cold, unreadable.

"You can't believe that!" Jake pleaded, her eyes welling with
tears. She found it impossible to accept that she was a bounty
hunter—let alone even consider the possibility that she might have
ever intended to do Kat harm. She shook her head back and forth,
back and forth. "You can't be serious!" Her voice had a tremor in
it. "I could never hurt you, surely you know that."

Kat's expression softened, and she nodded. "You proved that
when you came out in the snow trying to help me." She looked
away for a moment as if lost in thought. "That was a brave and
selfless act, Jake." A hint of a smile appeared at the edge of her lips.
"Even if it was also an incredibly stupid thing to do." The warmth
returned to her eyes.

"But I believed in my heart even before that, Jake," Kat
volunteered. "I knew that something extraordinary was happening
between us. Something rare and very precious. And something
more powerful than anything in our pasts." She looked into Jake's
eyes for confirmation as she said this.

Jake nodded, tears spilling down her cheeks.

"I'm sorry I've kept things from you," Kat said, taking Jake's
hand. "I don't know who you are—your real identity, I mean. But
I got a heads-up about a woman bounty hunter who was coming
after me. Her name was Scout. Does that ring a bell?"

"Scout? No." Jake shrugged.

"Well, you fit the description and you showed up out here about the time I got the warning." Kat leaned toward Jake. "The car you were driving was stolen, and there was no ID on you or in the car. Both are pretty typical of people in our line of work. But what really convinced me was what I found in your trunk. A photo of me and a high-powered takedown sniper rifle, just like one I have."

Jake shook her head. An inner voice denied she was capable of any of this. She envisioned herself as a musician or artist. Something creative. She wasn't—couldn't be—a mercenary. A killer for hire. But then she still couldn't believe it of Kat either, despite what she had witnessed tonight.

A new thought occurred to her. "When did you find all this out?" she asked Kat.

Kat tried to think back. "Well, I suspected from about the first day," she said. "I knew the car was stolen almost immediately, and I found the photo and rifle when I went back to it the second or third day, whenever it was." Time had all jumbled together for her since the accident. The long periods without sleep and the lack of natural sunlight in the bunker made it difficult to tell how much time had elapsed between events. She rarely glanced at her watch.

"Then why did you save me?" Jake pressed. "Why go through everything you did if you thought I was here to kill you? I don't understand that at all."

"I don't think I had much choice," Kat replied. "That's the easiest way to explain, I guess. It wasn't something I normally would have done," she admitted. "But I felt compelled to get involved when I saw your car go off the road and flip over. Something just pushed me forward to help. And when I saw you...well, you were hurt, and vulnerable, and I just kind of felt protective toward you." She grew silent for a moment or two, fighting the hint of a blush that threatened to blossom on her cheeks. "After we...kissed..." she continued, looking down at their joined hands, "Well, that kind of sealed it for me."

Saying such things was incredibly difficult for Kat, who had never had an intimate relationship. For the first time in her life, she was fighting shyness, feeling incredibly inexperienced and naïve about how to go about getting close to the woman who had so captivated her. These feelings were extremely unsettling to Kat, even as they were exciting. She was used to being alone, being in control, using cold reasoning alone to make all her important decisions. She felt unprepared for this. But her logical mind had long ago given way to what her instincts and her heart were telling her to do.

"Jake," Kat said, determined to finish what she needed to say, "I've never really been close to anyone. Not really. I never thought I could be, doing what I do." Her hand began to caress Jake's as she spoke, and Jake responded in kind. "But I very much want to be close to you."

"I want that too. Very much," Jake said, her voice breaking on the last two words. Her hand gripped Kat's tightly for a moment for emphasis. "All of this is...difficult for me to believe, to say the least. I admit I'm kind of having a hard time with a lot of what you've told me. Particularly about my past. But I do know, I do very much believe, that we are supposed to be together."

Kat looked into Jake's eyes and let out a long breath. The creases in her forehead and around her eyes relaxed. The edges of her mouth curved upward into a hint of a smile. She moistened her lips with the tip of her tongue, and Jake's heart skipped a beat.

"Kat," Jake whispered. "Do you know anything more about my wedding ring?"

"No," Kat said. "I can tell you that bounty hunters often adopt other identities when they're pursuing someone. Well, some do, anyway. I've used a wedding ring on a few occasions myself. But I don't know whether yours is real or not."

"Well, I have to admit I hope it's a fake," Jake said. "I hope there is no one waiting somewhere for me."

Kat nodded in agreement. While they talked, both women continued the soft caresses of their joined hands.

"What are you going to do about those two men?" Jake asked. "And how did they find you?"

Kat's fingertips paused in their soft tracing of Jake's inner wrist and palm, a sensation that both women found eminently pleasing and increasingly distracting. "They followed the track I made getting you here from where the car crashed. But it's snowed a lot since then, so I don't think we have to worry about anyone else showing up." Her touch resumed its gentle path along Jake's smaller hands. Such delicate hands.

"As to what I'm going to do with them...Well, I'm going to keep them confined until you're well enough to leave. I'll have to give up this place anyway, now that it's been found."

She said this matter-of-factly, but Jake could tell from her wistful expression that Kat would really miss the bunker. She would too, she realized. She felt safe here, despite the last few hours.

"Speaking of getting you out of here," Kat said, nodding toward the forgotten food on the tray, "you have to get your strength back, and you need to eat to do that. So I'm going to go warm this up, and while you finish it, I'll work on your wrist and knee. Okay?"

"Sounds like a plan," Jake agreed. Her stomach was beginning to reassert itself at the mention of the food.

Kat rose and picked up the tray. "I'll have to go into town. We don't have enough food for four people for very long, and there are a few other things I'd like to pick up. Some antibiotics for your knee and some plaster so I can do a better cast for your wrist."

"When will you leave?" Jake asked.

"Soon. It's snowing now and will be for a while, so it will cover my tracks there and back. If I leave in a couple of hours, I'll get to town just as everything is opening up—when there are few people about." She smiled. "I'll be very quick. I bet you sleep through the whole thing."

I doubt that, Jake thought but didn't say. *When I'm not worrying about you, I'll be trying to picture myself as an assassin.* Not the kind of thing likely to induce nice dreams. "I'll try," she managed. "If you promise to be careful."

"Always," Kat confirmed, giving Jake a wink as she picked up the tray and headed for the door. She liked having someone concerned about her welfare.

So damn cute, Jake thought, watching her leave. Then she thought again about Kat's assertion that she had been headed here to kill her, and her stomach sank. *I hope I never remember.*

❖

Otter had a hell of a headache. That was the first thing that penetrated his consciousness. The second was the awareness that he couldn't move much. The third was the nauseating stench of dead fish that permeated his nostrils. His stomach lurched as he blinked his eyes, trying to remember what had happened.

He was lying on his side, his hands bound behind him, on a cold concrete floor. He could see a couple of snowmobiles, and if he craned his head, he could see what looked like a generator. As his mind hit upon what had happened to him he heard a cough from behind. He struggled to roll over, expecting to find Hunter gloating over him.

He had trouble adjusting his position. He had to scoot backward a couple of feet before there was enough slack in the chain for him to crane his neck around to see a big bear of a man studying him with a curious expression. The man was propped up, sitting with his back against the corner. Otter could see that they were both prisoners, bound together by a short chain, which was padlocked to a larger chain that was attached to the wall. He also noticed that the other man was somewhat more comfortably settled than he was, sitting on a down sleeping bag with a small heater nearby blasting what little warm air there was directly at him. "Frank, I presume?" Otter said.

"Yeah. You're Otter, right?" Frank asked.

Otter grunted in affirmation, trying to turn all the way over to better communicate with Frank. Because of the short length of chain connecting them, he had to back up until he was nearly in Frank's lap to accomplish this.

"Hey, man, don't get so close," Frank admonished as Otter awkwardly rolled to face him. The big man was trying to lean away from him. "You reek. I mean you stink really, really bad."

Otter didn't need the reminder. He felt just inches away from puking. He could tolerate most smells. He'd even hidden in a garbage Dumpster once. But he couldn't abide the smell of fish. Dead or alive. Raw or cooked. It had always made him profoundly nauseous.

Otter remembered that Hunter had taunted him about it rather maliciously the day they met, when he griped about her ordering salmon from room service. He wondered briefly whether she'd deliberately poured something on him or if he'd acquired this ungodly stench during the fight in the pantry. Didn't matter. Pissed him off anyway. *Bitch,* he seethed.

But Otter was amazed Hunter hadn't killed him. *She'll regret that.* He studied Frank, who was wrinkling his nose in distaste at Otter's close proximity. *Well, at least I have an ally.* An impressively big ally, at that. It would do well to be nice.

"Sorry," Otter said, trying to inch away as much as possible while still keeping an eye on Frank. "How long have you been here?" he asked, studying the room again but seeing no way to escape.

"Don't know. Hard to tell," Frank replied. "Several hours, anyway. You deal with her before?"

Otter's mind flashed back to their job together. Hunter abandoning him. Leaving him to prison or death. "Yeah. I have a score to settle with Hunter."

"Thought so. She said you wouldn't be too cooperative."

Otter snorted. "Cooperative? That's funny," he sneered. He couldn't figure out why she was keeping them both alive. He didn't really like thinking about what she might be planning to do to them before she killed them. He was certain they would die.

"She says if I cooperate, she'll give me some money and let me go," Frank said. He wanted Otter to confirm this was true. Otter knew Hunter, after all.

But Otter laughed. It was an empty laugh, devoid of humor. "Yeah, right. Stop dreaming, chum. Lying is what she does best. She'd say anything to keep you from trying to get out of here. You can't believe a word that bitch says."

Frank took in Otter's words, weighing them against Hunter's promise to be merciful if he didn't try to escape and kept Otter from getting out. Frank believed one thing for certain. If she caught them trying to leave, she would not hesitate to cut them both down.

Frank wanted to believe Hunter. He had to admit he respected her. She was one hell of a tough and beautiful broad, and she'd so far been pretty good to him, considering. This Otter guy, on the other hand, was obviously no match for her. And Frank found it hard to warm up to someone whose stench was making his eyes water. He'd just play it cool for now, see what developed. "Hey, man, what the hell happened, anyway? Why was Hunter in her underwear, and how did you both end up covered in food?"

Before Otter could answer, they both were drawn to the sound of the big steel door opening. Hunter was coming.

CHAPTER THIRTY

Kat got Jake to eat the warmed-over dinner while she iced her swollen knee and rewrapped the splint on her wrist. They didn't say much during the process. Jake's mind was still churning over Kat's revelations, and Kat was preoccupied with what she was doing. But they looked at each other frequently, warmly. Exchanging shy smiles.

When both were finished, Kat removed the tray and returned to the bedside. "Need a trip to the bathroom before I go?"

Jake nodded. She put her good arm behind Kat's neck as she was picked up. Without thinking, she threaded her hand through the hair at Kat's neck. She ran her fingers through the silky strands, lightly caressing the back of Kat's head and neck. Jake heard Kat's sharp intake of breath at the intimate touch and felt her stiffen slightly in surprise, but only for a moment.

Kat's mind was entirely on how fast her heart seemed to beat whenever she got close to Jake—it hammered now in her chest—when she felt the delicious touch of Jake's hand on her neck. She froze in place, halfway to the bedroom door. A soft groan escaped her lips as she relaxed into the caress. After a moment, Kat turned her head slowly toward Jake's, not wishing to break the caress but needing to look into Jake's eyes.

They were shining at her, pulling her in. She closed the inches between them and kissed Jake, softly at first, then deepening the contact, her tongue seeking Jake's.

Jake's lips parted and her tongue met Kat's. She moaned, a soft, brief hum more felt than heard. Her hand behind Kat's neck tightened its hold, pulling them even closer together.

A rush of heat enveloped Kat as the kiss grew more and more

passionate, making her suddenly wobbly on her feet. She pulled away enough to take a deep, unsteady breath.

Jake sighed in disappointment at the separation. Her eyes were half closed. She licked her lips.

Neither could speak.

Kat faced forward on rubbery legs and continued toward their destination. Jake's hand stayed entwined in Kat's hair, only reluctantly extricating itself when she was set down on the commode.

Soon after, Jake was back in Kat's arms, and then all too quickly back in bed. Still neither had said a word, but they hadn't needed to. The kiss was an affirmation of the profound attraction they could no longer deny and a promise of things to come.

Once Kat had Jake settled back in bed, she left to don a snowmobile suit and gather the things she'd need for her trip to town: her GPS device, binoculars, flashlight, cash, her small kit of lock-pick tools, and her Glock. She also retrieved her .38, which she carried with her back into the bedroom.

"I want you to have this with you while I'm gone," Kat said, holding out the revolver where Jake could see it. "I don't expect our two uninvited 'guests' to go anywhere. They're restrained, and there is a security door between them and you. But it doesn't hurt to take every precaution."

She extended the gun grip first for Jake to take it.

"It's loaded. Six bullets," Kat continued matter-of-factly. "Here's the safety."

Jake accepted it, but reluctantly. It felt cold and alien, and she once again pondered how she could possibly be the bounty hunter whom Kat had described. She hefted the gun in her hand. It was much heavier than she expected. It gave her a small measure of security, but she hoped she would never have to use it. She nodded toward Kat, who took it from her again and placed it under a pillow. It was out of sight but within easy reach of Jake's good hand.

Kat impulsively leaned down to kiss Jake on the forehead. "Get some rest. I'll be back before you know I'm gone."

Jake reached out with her good hand to touch Kat's forearm as she withdrew. "I'll know you're gone."

Kat went to her computer for one last check of the weather radar and forecast. It was still snowing fairly heavily. She headed for the tunnel, stopping to put on her boots and hat. She stuffed her mittens in a pocket. Then she went to the security panel and punched in the code to open the steel door.

❖

Kat stepped into the generator room to find both Frank and Otter staring at her. Frank looked like he'd been caught doing something he shouldn't. Otter glared at her with undisguised loathing. "Long time no see, little man," Kat said cheerily to the latter. She couldn't help it. He was such a worm, she had to taunt him just a little.

A part of Otter remembered how dangerous Hunter was and warned him not to egg her on. But he had waited too long and thought about her too much during those long years in prison not to seize the opportunity to say the things that had been festering inside him. "Fucking bitch," he spat at her. "You fucking *owe* me." His rage pushed aside any voice of reason that might have tried to intercede.

Kat smiled at Otter. It was a smile that warned him to shut up. But he was too worked up to see it. Frank did, and it made him wish he were anywhere else but chained to the guy who could provoke such a look in this dangerous woman.

"You're going to pay for leaving me there, Hunter," Otter wailed in fury.

Kat approached the two men, the ferocity of her smile matched by a predatory look in her eyes. Frank thought she resembled a panther stalking its prey.

She kneeled on the floor next to Otter. Leaned down and cocked her head so she could be face-to-face with him. Her eyes bored into his. But she said not a word. Daring him to say anything else. Finally he saw and understood the threat, and he knew his next words could decide whether he lived or died. He remained silent and looked away, his concession evident.

Kat leaned into him so she could speak directly into his ear. "I understand your anger, little man," she said in a voice full of menace. "But I've no more patience for you. We're even now. Don't tip the scales again and make me kill you."

She stood and looked down at Otter for several long moments—an open challenge for him to say or do something he'd regret. But he had learned his lesson, for the moment anyway. He stayed quiet and unmoving, keeping his eyes downward.

Kat glanced at Frank, who'd been watching her interaction with Otter with a look of growing trepidation. In the mood she was in, he really wanted her to forget he was even there. So he was stunned when the cruelty in her face suddenly melted away and she asked in an almost friendly tone, "Anything I can get you, Frank?"

He couldn't believe the change in her. The rapid transformation was startling. As much as he wanted to get away from Otter's stench, he wanted even more to be Mr. Agreeable to this unpredictable woman. He wanted her to have no reason whatsoever to look at him like she had at Otter. "No, I'm okay."

"Good boy. I knew we'd get along just fine. Be patient. And remember what I said," she added, tipping her head toward Otter.

Frank nodded.

Kat punched in the security code to open the main entrance. She started up her snowmobile, let it warm up a little, and took it outside, where she left it idling. She pulled Otter's snowmobile into the generator room and parked it where hers had been, pocketing the keys. She searched the vehicle and removed the tool kit and Otter's cell phone, which she examined a minute or two before she slipped it into her pocket. Then she checked the spare gas cans on the two rental machines and took the one that had been on Frank's. Still ignoring the two men, she left, shutting the panel behind her.

Otter rolled over to face Frank as soon as the door closed. They could hear the muffled roar of Hunter's snowmobile as she sped away from the bunker. "Okay. Whaddaya say we figure out a way to get out of here, huh?"

CHAPTER THIRTY-ONE

Evan Garner stared at himself in the mirror of the little bathroom attached to his office. He frowned at the dark circles under his eyes and splashed some cold water on his face. He looked haggard. His once impeccably pressed suit was wrinkled, and his usually clean-shaven face was marred by a shadow of stubble.

Garner couldn't live like this much longer, cooped up in these few rooms. He'd been barking at everyone within range until he was hoarse from hollering. He took a long swallow of water, considering his next move. Something had to break soon. This infernal waiting was driving him nuts.

He returned to his office and summoned Thomas. The bodyguard responded within a minute, appearing in the doorway looking none too fresh himself.

"Anything?" was all Garner said, moving to look out the wall of windows, his back to his aide.

"No, sir. None of them has called in. We do have two signals coming from the area. Scout's, which still hasn't moved from the wreck site, and another one we believe is Otter's. It's in the same general area, but it's still on the move."

"If Otter's all right, then why the hell hasn't he called in?"

"Well, sir, you remember Frank had trouble with his cell phone up there. He couldn't get a signal most of the time," the bodyguard replied.

Garner doubted that was all there was to it. "Send someone up there to track down the second signal and find out what the hell is going on with Otter." He went to his desk, dropping into the plush chair with a yawn. "And I suppose we still have no more takers on the contract?"

"No, sir," Thomas confirmed. He didn't add that he didn't think there would be any more, either. Word had gotten around pretty fast for such a secretive organization. The news that the three people who'd gone after Hunter were now all missing was being whispered in ever-expanding circles.

Garner sighed. "Up the contract to a million and a half, Thomas," he instructed. Much of the reward would come from his own personal funds, but he didn't hesitate committing the money. He just wanted to get rid of Hunter so he could begin living out in the open again.

"Whatever you say, boss," Thomas said, knowing that it would probably make little difference.

Jake lay awake in the dark long after Kat had gone. Her mind was working too hard for her to sleep, despite her injuries and exhaustion. *How can I be a bounty hunter?* her brain repeated over and over. It seemed so contrary to the inherent image she had of herself.

How many people have I killed? How could I forget that? Jake concentrated, trying to remember firing a gun, stealing a car. She couldn't. She reached beneath the pillow to put her hand around the cold metal of the gun. It sparked no memory. It still seemed a foreign object to her.

Jake seemed to have many more reasons not to remember her past than she did to recall it. If she had taken lives, she didn't want to have those memories haunt her the rest of her days. *How could I have lived without a conscience? I seem to have one now. I don't think I could kill anyone except maybe in self-defense. Or to save Kat. I think I would kill to do that.*

Even if you did do all that, things can be different now. You can be whoever you want to be, can't you? Isn't that what this amnesia does? Gives you a second chance? More and more, Jake wanted never to regain her memory. The only thing pulling her emotions in the other direction was the memory she had of her brother. She did want to remember him.

Jake didn't want to remember her spouse, if indeed she had one. She wanted to believe that she had used the wedding ring as a decoy, as Kat had suggested. *Then why the engraving?* her conscience nagged. *You wouldn't go to all that trouble for a prop. Unless maybe you bought it in a pawn shop?*

She suddenly wanted to take off the ring, but her left hand was too swollen.

Jake thought of Kat and the incredible kiss they'd shared. She began to relax and her mind drifted to what the future might be like. She could do anything she wanted, couldn't she? She knew that what she wanted most of all was just to be with Kat.

Kat seemed to want that, too. But she hadn't said what all that meant in terms of her own future job plans. *Will Kat continue to hunt down and kill people?* Jake wondered. *And how will I feel about that if she does?*

Kat's trip to Tawa in the hour before dawn was uneventful. Despite the rough terrain, she knew an indirect route that bypassed the worst of the hazards. She had taken it often enough that navigating it was no real problem even in the reduced visibility of the blowing snow around her. She was grateful for the conditions. Her track would be obscured within several minutes.

An added advantage of this particular route was that it took her well away from the site of Jake's car wreck some three miles from the bunker. She believed Frank was telling the truth when he said that was the last place he'd been able to report in by cell phone to Garner. So that was probably as close as her old boss could get in pinpointing the position of her hideout.

She intended to make it even tougher for him to find her. She took a wide detour around the perimeter of Tawa into a wetlands reserve well south of town. She parked the snowmobile and set out a short distance on foot over a frozen bog.

In no time she found what she was looking for amid the dead and dying trees that pervaded the swamp. Woodpeckers had drilled dozens of good-sized holes in a large dead oak. She put Otter's cell phone into one of the hollowed-out cavities, so that the homing device she'd found inside it would be protected from the worst of the elements.

She knew that Garner probably would not give up. Once he committed to something, he stuck with it. He would keep sending people after her, hoping one of them got lucky. He wouldn't care how many died trying.

Thanks to the heavy snowfall and having this cell phone as an extra bit of diversion, she and Jake were probably safe for now. But the bunker had gotten too hot, and keeping Frank and Otter captive there was inviting disaster. They'd have to move soon. As soon as Jake was able. And somewhere down the line, she'd have to deal with Garner personally.

As she walked back to the snowmobile, Kat began to consider the logistics of where she and Jake should go when they left the bunker. She frowned, thinking of the rough terrain Jake would have to be transported over in order to reach the nearest cleared road. Kat added one more stop to her mental list of places she needed to visit while in Tawa.

She'd hit the small clinic before it opened. Then the grocery, and on the way back out of town, the little airstrip where Sam kept his helicopter. She'd get him to pick her and Jake up in a few days near the bunker. She would give him a GPS position as a rendezvous point. She'd drop Sam off back at the airstrip and helicopter Jake to their next destination.

So the next big decision, then, is just exactly where is that destination to be?

Kat was in and out of the clinic in four minutes, two hours before it was to open. It was a typical small-town med station set up to treat routine injuries and complaints. It had simple locks and no alarm system. And she had scoped out the layout of the place and the location of the drug cabinet several months earlier when she was there on a legitimate visit.

It was something she always did—studied the details of the

world around her. The architecture of buildings, the layout of the rooms inside, the routines of guards and workmen, the hours of operation. It was mostly habit and exercise for her keen instincts and curious, analytical mind. And you just never knew when such information might come in handy.

She'd had to break into more than a couple of clinics and hospitals to get supplies to self-treat her wounds. So she'd memorized the Tawa clinic when she'd gone in for a shot after having an unexpectedly severe allergic reaction to multiple wasp stings.

Next stop was the grocery store, which had just opened. There were a few cars in the newly plowed parking lot out front, but they belonged mostly to employees.

Kat grabbed a cart and began wending her way through the aisles. She replaced the lost staples and stopped in frozen foods for a stack of TV dinners for Frank and Otter, thankful it was well below freezing outside. She also selected several items so she could whip up more elaborate fare for herself and Jake. She rather liked exercising her culinary talents for such an appreciative audience.

Kat's mind flashed back unbidden to the seductive look in Jake's eyes just before they'd kissed. It made her hurry her steps through the store to the checkout. She spent a few minutes securing her unwieldy load of groceries onto the snowmobile, then started up the machine and drove north out of town toward the isolated airstrip.

A pair of eyes followed Kat's every movement from the time she left the store until her snowmobile was out of sight. Several minutes later, a second snowmobile emerged from behind the grocery's Dumpster and began following the track of the first.

CHAPTER THIRTY-TWO

K at slowed the snowmobile to a stop twenty feet in front of the helicopter office. The sight of the familiar yellow crime scene tape sent all of her senses on high alert, but she doubted anyone was in the immediate vicinity at the moment. There were no cars, no tracks in the snow, and the place was dark inside.

She could see the helicopter still parked in its usual spot, and that was enough to propel her forward toward the office. She pulled her flashlight from her insulated suit as she approached the door, noticing immediately that the police seal that had been placed across it had already been broken. She picked the lock and went in, shining the light around the waiting area. Then she went to Sam's office.

The bright halogen beam picked out the fading chalk outline of a body on the floor, and Kat frowned with disappointment. She'd liked the pilot, despite his incessant need to hit on her whenever they did business together. Sam had a certain charm, and he'd been an invaluable help in ferrying supplies to the bunker.

Otter did this, Kat concluded as she studied the large bloodstain on the floor where Sam had died. *Otter was looking for me and figured I might be using a helicopter up here.* Her anger resurfaced at the pilot's needless death because of his association to her. She might have to reconsider her decision to let Otter live.

She rifled through the contents of the desk and scanned the office and waiting area, looking for the key to the helicopter, but came up empty. Next she searched the chopper. Still no key. She was frustrated she'd have to come up with a new plan to evacuate Jake. Airlifting her out of the bunker had seemed the perfect solution.

Kat returned to her snowmobile. It was still snowing. Her

tracks from town had been nearly covered during her time inside the office. The wind had died down, however, so visibility was good. She'd take a more roundabout way back to the bunker. It would take longer, but there were vast open places along that route, and high vantage points that would enable her to tell if she was being followed.

She started up the machine and pulled out her GPS device for a quick reading. She roared off to the northwest at a fast clip.

She was watched through a pair of high-powered binoculars. But instead of following her this time, the second snowmobile started off in the opposite direction, back toward town.

It took Kat four hours to make the trip to town and back, much longer than she'd expected because of the extra stop at the airstrip and the long, circuitous return route she'd taken to avoid a tail. She had spent a full half hour at one point parked on a high ridge, snacking on cheese and crackers while she scanned with binoculars the open area she'd just traveled through. She waited there until she could no longer make out her snowmobile track. Only then did she resume her journey back to the bunker.

She left her snowmobile idling outside the main entrance while she opened the hidden door. She glanced at Frank and Otter. They were as far apart as they could be given the short chain between them, but they remained bound and subdued in the corner.

"Hi, boys," she called out, projecting her voice over the sound of the snowmobile's rumbling. "Being good, are we? That's nice."

She pulled the snowmobile into the generator room, inching it as close to the two rental machines as she could. It was still well out of reach of her captives. She shut off the engine and closed the outside door, then opened the one to the tunnel.

She carried the groceries into the kitchen, having to make a couple of trips. Once the snowmobile was unloaded, she paused before the two men.

"I'll be back in a little while to take care of you," she said in a rather ominous tone that made both men wonder exactly what she meant.

❖

Otter tried to sit up. He looked at Frank. "Still think she's going to let you go?" he asked with a sneer. In the hours that Hunter had been gone, Otter had struggled against the handcuffs until his wrists were raw and had memorized every inch of the room they were in, still seeing no way to escape. His frustration was boiling over. He absolutely hated being confined again after all those years in prison. And he still felt ready to puke from the stink that seemed to pervade the entire room. Frank had been no help whatsoever. He'd hardly said a word the whole time, and he didn't seem to be working at all to free himself. *Just great. I get captured with a guy who looks like the Incredible Hulk, and he turns out to be a chickenshit.*

But Frank surprised him. He leaned into Otter until their faces were nearly nose to nose. "I'd watch your tone, friend," Frank said unpleasantly, as if he'd read Otter's mind. "Seeing as how I don't think she would mind if I kicked your ass."

Otter looked away and scooted to the full length of the chain that connected them. *Real smart,* he berated himself. He considered how he could make amends with the guy who might be his only help out of here.

Kat looked in on Jake after she had put the groceries away and was pleased to find her sleeping soundly. She changed out of her coveralls but kept her gun with her, tucking it into the back of her jeans.

She e-mailed Kenny, asking whether he had any more news about the contract on her life. She also wanted him to find out what he could about the murder at the Tawa airstrip.

She outlined what she knew about Sam, the pilot, but omitted her suspicions of Otter's involvement. She waited by the computer for a few minutes, but when no immediate answer arrived, she concluded Kenny must be away from his computer and logged off.

She spent a good hour cleaning up the mess in the pantry, salvaging what she could. By the time she was finished, she had decided to be merciful to Frank, if not to Otter, and let Otter change his clothes. It really was pretty inhuman, she decided, to force anyone to be subjected to that awful aroma in a confined space. She'd scrubbed the floor of the pantry repeatedly, but she could still smell it in the living room even with the door closed.

She took the insulated coveralls that Jake had been wearing, along with thick socks and a set of sweats, out to the generator room. She tossed them on the floor beside Otter.

As she reached down to unlock his handcuffs, Kat put her mouth near his ear. "I don't have to remind you not to try anything stupid, now do I?" she crooned, as she turned the key and freed his wrists. She stepped away from him and casually reached for her Glock, holding it loosely in her right hand as she watched him rub his sore wrists.

Otter said nothing. He expected her to kill him, so he couldn't understand what the change of clothes was for.

She gestured to the sweats with her gun. "Frank's been a good boy. He shouldn't have to pay for your clumsiness," Kat said. "Change clothes."

While Otter was happy to get out of his stinking suit, he didn't like taking orders from Hunter, and he didn't particularly relish having to strip in front of her at gunpoint. But he complied, peeling off his insulated outerwear and the layer beneath it until he was left standing in his ratty briefs. He reached for the clothes on the floor, but her voice stopped him.

"Everything goes. Everything stinks."

Reluctantly, Otter removed his damp underwear, trying unsuccessfully to cover himself with one hand. It was bitter cold in the room. He glanced down, then at her.

She had a smirk on her face.

Otter fought against his rising anger, focusing on getting out of his Jockeys and into the clean clothes. Once that was accomplished, he looked at her again. She motioned with the gun for him to turn around, and he did, putting his back to her and offering his wrists behind him to be handcuffed again.

As she locked the cuffs, she noticed the raw abrasions that

were evidence of Otter's struggles to free himself. She chained him to Frank and checked Frank's handcuffs closely. He hadn't tried to escape. She leaned over and whispered into Frank's ear. "Nice to see you're being smart. You'll be pleased with your reward," she promised.

Kat opened the exterior door and carried Otter's stinky clothes outside, disposing of them a short distance away under a large downed tree where they couldn't be seen. By the time she returned to the generator room and closed the panel again, the small room had been sufficiently aired out, but the temperature inside had fallen dramatically.

She returned to the tunnel and gathered up the coats that she had wrapped around Jake. She set them on the floor beside Otter so he would have some insulation against the cold concrete.

He eyed her suspiciously but took advantage of her apparent kindness, rolling onto the coats.

After he did, Kat leaned over him and looked directly into his eyes. "I've been meaning to ask you, Otter," she said, studying his face. "You didn't make a little stop at the helicopter office in town, did you?" She knew immediately from his expression that he'd done precisely that.

CHAPTER THIRTY-THREE

Why did you kill him, Otter?" Kat inquired evenly, not missing a beat. She watched the expression on Otter's face turn from surprise to confusion in rapid succession.

"I didn't kill him," Otter said, meeting her eyes. "He was dead long before I got there. I thought you did it. Cops are looking for a woman."

He said it so quickly, and with such assurance, she was pretty sure he was telling the truth.

"Maybe it was the blonde," Frank offered helpfully. "You know, that Scout chick."

Kat turned to look at Frank. She tried to keep her face expressionless, but he thought he'd detected a hint of surprise at his suggestion, as if she hadn't considered that possibility before.

"Perhaps," she acknowledged. She gave him a small nod and a half smile that acknowledged his attempt at cooperation.

She rose and turned to leave. She looked back at Frank before she closed the door. "Dinner will be in a just a little while," she said, ignoring Otter.

After she had gone, Otter turned to look at Frank. "What the hell happened to Scout, anyway?" he asked.

Frank debated not answering. But he'd been curious about the same thing himself. "Dead is what I think. Hunter wanted to know everything I knew about her, like she couldn't ask her herself." He paused, remembering. "At first I thought I was following Scout's track from the crash site—that somehow she'd made it here and then Hunter caught her. But now I think maybe Hunter caused the car to crash and she brought Scout back here."

"That doesn't fit," Otter said. "Hunter wouldn't have left such a clear track between the road and this place."

Frank shrugged. "Maybe. Maybe it was snowing and she thought the tracks would be covered up by the time anyone found the car. Or maybe she was in a hurry to get Scout here while she was still alive, to find out what she knew," he speculated, "but she died before Hunter got a chance to question her."

Otter pictured the hatch that had been left open—the hatch he had used to gain access to the bunker—and another scenario occurred to him. "I don't think Scout was that badly hurt in the crash," he told Frank. "I got inside through another entrance that had been left standing open. I think Scout used it to escape, and Hunter went after her."

Otter thought back to the short glimpse he'd gotten of Hunter in the TV monitor, just after he'd gotten into the bunker. "I saw Hunter on one of her surveillance cameras bringing Scout's body back here. She brought it through a door just like this." He nodded toward the main entrance beside them.

"It was this door, I bet," Frank said. "She brought something in she didn't want me to see. Made me turn my face to the wall."

"But if she killed Scout when she tried to escape," Otter wondered, "why bring the body back here? Why not just leave it out in the snow?"

That didn't make sense to Frank either. "Are you sure Scout was dead when you saw them? Maybe she's still alive and Hunter's got her in there somewhere."

The thought gave Otter a chill. What the hell was Hunter planning to do with all of them?

Kat returned to her computer to see whether she'd gotten any response from Kenny. His e-mail was waiting for her.

Good to hear from you. I was getting a little worried. The contract on you is up to a million and a half. I'm pretty sure Garner is behind it. There are rumors three people who went after you all are missing. (You wouldn't

know anything about that, would you?) I don't know if that includes Otter and the woman. The woman is going by the name of Scout. Can't pin down anything else on her. Let me know if you want me to keep looking. The helicopter pilot you asked me about had his throat cut a few days ago. No suspects, but police are looking for a woman client he was supposed to have met.

She e-mailed her thanks, saying she'd be in touch, and logged off. So Otter was telling the truth.

Kat could not picture Jake cutting Sam's throat. She didn't want to. But she knew that was probably what had happened. She felt none of the fury over Sam's death that she had initially, when she thought Otter had done it. It was no less brutal a murder, and Kat still regretted that Sam probably had died because of his association to her. But Jake meant too much to her now, and the woman had no memory of killing anyone.

It had been hard enough for Kat to bring herself to tell Jake the truth about Jake's past as a bounty hunter. She would spare her the vivid, violent details of what had apparently been one of her last acts before her amnesia. Kat wondered whether Jake had been fleeing the murder scene when her car had crashed. It kind of made sense. The airstrip was on the same lonely road where the wreck occurred.

It really didn't matter now. She knew what she had to do. The police were looking for Jake. That had to be considered in any plan to get them both to another destination. Kat didn't want to move Jake far if she didn't have to, but she had to at least get into another law-enforcement jurisdiction.

Kat was lost in thought, staring at the blank computer screen, when she heard a muffled cry through the closed bedroom door.

❖

Jake thrashed around violently in the bed, crying out "No! No!" in a voice filled with anguish.

Kat flung open the door so hard it slammed against the wall. She was at the bedside in an instant, fumbling for the light. She put her hands on Jake's arms and shoulders to pin her to the bed, to keep her from hurting herself further.

Gripped in her nightmare, Jake was feeling no pain from her injuries. "Let me go!" she screamed, struggling against the restraining hold Kat had on her.

"Jake, it's me," Kat said, trying to awaken her, but maintaining her firm grip. "Everything is okay, you're safe. It's Kat." She rambled reassurances until Jake finally did calm and opened her eyes.

"Kat?" Jake asked. The nightmare was already fading.

"I'm here." She took her weight off her hands, releasing her hold of Jake. But one hand remained on Jake's shoulder, lightly caressing it.

"Blood," Jake said in a strained voice. "There was a lot of blood." Mercifully, the details of the dream had already evaporated. All that remained was a large splotch of red in Jake's mind. She was still breathing fast, but the sense of panic was past.

Kat leaned over Jake and gently embraced her, pressing her lips against Jake's forehead, which was damp with sweat. "You're all right now, it was just a dream," she whispered.

"Was it?" Jake wondered aloud. "Or are my nightmares memories of things I've done?"

CHAPTER THIRTY-FOUR

K at held Jake in her arms, absently stroking her fair hair, until she finally relaxed and her rapid heart rate slowed to normal. But Kat could offer few words of reassurance. She knew of no way to avoid the subconscious hauntings of one's misdeeds.

"I'm okay now," Jake sighed, pressing her face into the warm flesh of Kat's neck. Kat's comforting embrace had chased away the terrible vision.

Kat released her and pulled back enough to look into Jake's eyes. "What can I do?"

"You've already done it," Jake answered. "Kind of hard to remember nightmares when such an irresistible distraction is so close."

Kat colored a little at the unexpected compliment. "Been kind of hard for me to keep my mind on anything but you lately, too," she admitted.

"So you made it to town?" Jake asked. "What happens now?"

"Well, first I'm going to get you patched up with some stuff I picked up at the clinic." Kat took two vials out of her pocket and shook a pill out of each. "I want you to take these. This is Cipro. It's an antibiotic. Your knee might have an infection. And this is Darvon, a painkiller. I'm going to have to reset that arm in a while, and it's going to hurt when I do. That'll help." She poured a glass of water from the pitcher on the bedside table and handed it to Jake with the pills.

As Jake swallowed them, Kat examined her injured arm. "The swelling's gone down quite a bit. I'll be able to reset it in just a little while. You'll get a proper cast this time."

"So you've had medical training too?"

Kat nodded, but didn't elaborate.

"Well, I'm lucky you're so multitalented," Jake said. "Speaking of which, will you play your cello again for me soon?"

"If you like," Kat responded. There wasn't much, she realized, she wouldn't do if Jake asked her to. *That's a switch.* "But how about I practice my cooking skills first. Hungry?"

"I could eat," Jake admitted.

Kat couldn't hide her smile. "Okay, I'll whip us up something and be right back." She started to turn to leave, but Jake reached out her hand and stopped her.

"Uh, Kat? I need another pit stop pretty soon," she said.

Kat nodded and immediately picked Jake up and cradled her in her arms in what was now getting to be a rather familiar position. They looked at each other, remembering what had happened the last time they were like this, and both smiled shyly.

Jake couldn't resist. She threaded her fingers into Kat's hair again and caressed the back of her neck as before as she grinned at Kat and raised her eyebrows expectantly.

Kat laughed and charged off deliberately toward the bathroom. "You'll never get fed if you keep that up."

"Aw, shucks." Jake snapped her fingers in disappointment.

Kat was still chuckling as she left the bathroom and shut the door. She leaned her back against it and closed her eyes. She couldn't stop grinning. She had never felt so comfortable with anyone while at the same time so unbelievably nervous and excited. It was an odd mix.

And she was just a little terrified at the prospect of letting her barriers down to be close to someone. She didn't know how. *I'm no good with words. Not these kind of words.*

"Okay, Kat. I'm ready."

Kat's hand was already on the doorknob. She had the door open almost before Jake stopped speaking.

Jake jumped a little at Kat's instantaneous response. "My, you're eager to please," she teased.

Kat's cheeks reddened, but she was still smiling as she took Jake in her arms and lifted her.

Kat did it so effortlessly that Jake could not help but run her hand over the taut muscles in Kat's upper back and shoulders as she was carried to the bedroom.

Kat bit back a whimper at the soft caress.

"Thank you," Jake breathed playfully in Kat's ear, just before they reached the bed.

Kat turned to look at her.

Jake had her eyes closed and lips pursed, ready to be kissed.

Kat chuckled. "You're dangerous," she said, setting Jake down gently on the bed.

Jake shrugged, and they shared another laugh.

"Well, I'm off to the kitchen," Kat said. "After you eat something, would you like to clean up? It will be a lot harder to take a shower once I've put your cast on."

"I would. My hair can really use it," Jake said, running her hand through her disheveled locks. She looked chagrined. "And I've probably started to ripen a little, haven't I?"

Kat smiled. "No," she reassured Jake. "Not that I've noticed. But I thought it might make you feel better, and it would just be easiest if we do it soon."

"Well, thanks. That'd be great," Jake said. "Now what's for breakfast? Or is it time for lunch?"

"It's whatever time your stomach tells you. Which will it be?"

"Doesn't really matter, I guess. Anything at all is fine."

Kat turned to go.

"Anything fast," Jake amended in a loud voice just as Kat disappeared through the doorway. "And I am pretty hungry!"

Jake settled back into the pillows and closed her eyes. She relished the easy camaraderie that was developing between them. If she'd ever felt like this before about someone, she certainly didn't remember it. She didn't believe it was possible. It was as though destiny had brought her here, wiping her violent past from her memory and delivering her to the woman who would complete her.

Despite her playful teasing, Jake was uncertain how to proceed. She knew one thing, though, for sure. She trusted Kat. The woman had saved her life heroically, not once, but twice—despite the fact she believed Jake had set out to kill her. Her actions spoke volumes about her true nature, and her heart.

But although Jake was anxious to get closer to Kat, she was incredibly nervous about it too. In a way, she was a tiny bit glad that her injuries would necessitate a delay in any real intimacy. She didn't want things to happen too quickly. It was too much fun savoring it as it happened.

Kat whipped up some potato pancakes for her and Jake. She relished having fresh ingredients again. She sautéed some apples to go with them and fried up thick slabs of bacon. She plopped a large dollop of sour cream on each of two plates, then filled both with the brunch ingredients. She set the plates on the serving tray, along with two mugs of coffee.

Kat needed the caffeine. She'd started to yawn midway through the cooking process and was finding it hard to stop. She didn't want to calculate how sleep deprived she was. She knew she needed at least a short nap pretty soon.

Kat carried the tray into the bedroom to find Jake waiting expectantly for her. As she approached the bed, Jake strained to see what was on the plates, sniffing the air like a bloodhound. Her eyes widened in pleasure when she spotted the full plates, and she wasted no time snatching up a fork when the tray was placed in front of her.

Kat grabbed her own plate dramatically off the tray, as if afraid Jake would devour that too. Jake played along, stabbing out toward Kat's plate with her fork as it was being pulled out of her reach.

"Can't help it if I like your cooking," Jake grumbled good-naturedly.

The two were mostly quiet as they ate, stealing occasional looks at each other as they both attacked the food with hearty appetites. Jake's plate was nearly empty when she suddenly stopped her single-minded assault of its contents and set her fork down. She looked up at Kat. "Uh, Kat?"

Kat met her gaze. "What is it?"

"Well, I-I was wondering how you thought we might manage

a shower for me. I mean, I don't think I can stand on my own very long," Jake stammered. The prospect of having Kat help her in the shower sent a flush of heat to her face. She didn't think she was quite ready for that much exposure. Not with their sexual chemistry crackling like a bonfire.

Kat had already considered that. "I have a big plastic tub you can sit on in the shower," she said. "I'll be close by if you need help, but you'll be able to reach everything you need." A grin found her lips. "I think if you can make it out of the bunker and halfway to Canada," she said, rolling her eyes, "you can manage this mighty challenge."

Jake laughed. "Great. It'll be nice to be clean again."

An hour later, Jake was clad in a pair of green flannel pajamas that were much too large for her, but toasty warm. The painkiller had kicked in, helping her endure her efforts in the shower and making her drowsy again. She was propped up in bed watching Kat put a cast on her arm.

It covered half of her palm and ended at her elbow. She couldn't remember ever having a cast before and wondered if this was the first time she'd ever broken anything. Kat had checked her ribs before she'd undressed for the shower, and they seemed to be much better. She hardly felt them now. Her knee was still swollen and she couldn't really put her weight on it, but it wasn't hurting as much since she'd taken the pills.

Kat finished and began toweling off her hands.

Jake flexed her arm, testing the cast. It was more comfortable and solid than the splint had been. She wiggled her fingers. The swelling was nearly gone. She tried again to take the wedding ring off. It moved but wouldn't quite go over her knuckle.

Kat noticed her efforts. "I really should have taken that off you when I first brought you in," she said. "It's something hospitals do routinely when there's swelling. But I didn't notice it at first, and then it just somehow seemed—well, like you should be the one to do it, I guess. But it's bad for your circulation to keep it on. Let me help."

She walked to the bathroom and returned with a small tube of hand cream. She slathered Jake's finger with it, and the ring slid off. Kat set it on the bedside table.

"Thanks," Jake said, staring at her finger. At the deep impression where the ring had been. Like she'd worn it for a very long time.

The ring evoked the painfully unresolved question of Jake's marriage. Jake's conscience reasserted itself—a nagging guilt that tugged at her despite her desire to be with Kat.

Kat wondered what Jake was thinking but didn't feel she could ask. She too saw the deep mark the ring had left. *You've worn that too long for it not to be real.* She herself had never worn a prop ring long enough for it to leave behind more than a faint, fleeting mark.

Kat wondered not for the first time what might happen if and when Jake remembered a spouse. *I couldn't bear it now if she left.* The thought sent an ache as real as any pain she'd ever felt through her chest. She suddenly needed air. The renewed thought that something might one day surface to come between them was unbearable. It was an enemy she didn't know how to fight.

"Try to get some rest," she said, adjusting the pillows behind Jake so she could lie flat.

The painkiller was making Jake awfully sleepy, and her mind welcomed the opportunity to stop its guilty tirade over the wedding ring. She lay back and closed her eyes. "Thanks, Kat," she mumbled.

Kat watched her for a few minutes until she was sure Jake was asleep. She leaned over and kissed her on the forehead. Then on the lips, barely touching. "Pleasant dreams," she whispered.

Kat stuck two TV dinners in the oven to cook for Frank and Otter and set the timer on the stove. She napped on the couch while they cooked. She'd always had a talent for being able to go long periods without substantial sleep, subsisting on catnaps she grabbed whenever she could. But the short rest didn't help much this time. She awoke groggy and knew she needed a long chunk of uninterrupted sleep very soon.

She carried the dinners, two paper cups, and a gallon jug of water out to the generator room. Frank was asleep on the sleeping bag, his snores so loud they overpowered the drone of the generator. Otter was lying on the coats, watching her.

She set the food and water down near the two of them. "Still determined to get back at me?" she inquired idly, digging in her pocket for the handcuff keys.

"You shouldn't have left me there, bitch," he sneered.

"It's the past, Otter. It's over and done with. I'd advise you to forget about it and think more about whether you'd like to have a future."

"Like you're going to let that happen." What the hell was she up to, playing these mind games with him?

"You really should get in a more cooperative frame of mind," Kat said, pulling her gun. "Lie face down now, like a good boy."

He complied, grunting as he rolled onto his stomach.

She stepped around him to unlock Frank's handcuffs. She nudged the snoring man awake. "Dinnertime, Frank," she said, backing away, keeping her gun trained on both men.

Frank blinked awake to find his wrists were free. He sat up and stretched, looking at Hunter, then his eyes fell on the food.

"Eat up," Kat encouraged.

"What about me?" Otter whined.

"You'll get your turn."

Frank picked up one of the Salisbury steak dinners and began eating. Kat had bought a package of plastic utensils at the grocery to feed the men with. Frank's flimsy fork broke midway through his meal. He stared at it just a moment before tossing it aside and reaching for the one in Otter's.

Otter glared at him but didn't object.

When Frank was done, Kat opened the door to the outside and motioned him through it. "Five minutes to stretch your legs and do anything else you need to do," she said, keeping the gun trained on him.

They stepped through the door into the chill air, and she closed it again to try to retain as much heat as possible in the generator room.

The snow was still falling. Kat was relieved to see that no trace of her snowmobile track remained. It was only midafternoon, but the thick cloud layer obscured the sun and made it seem later than it was. She breathed deeply of the crisp cold air, idly watching Frank turn his back to her so he could piss without her seeing.

Frank took his full five minutes, working the kinks out of his stiff muscles. He said nothing to her until his time was almost up. "Are you really going to let me go?"

She met his eyes. "Yes. You have my word. If you continue to do as you're told. Don't let Otter talk you into something you'll regret." She opened the door and waved him through it ahead of her, then shut it again.

"Lie face down, Frank. Hands behind you." She locked his handcuffs behind him again and secured him to the wall. Then she stepped over to Otter and unlocked one of his cuffs, keeping her gun pressed against the back of his neck as she did so. She stepped away, giving him a wide berth.

Otter rubbed his sore wrists as he sat up, watching her. He reached for his dinner, retrieved his fork from Frank's empty plate, and began eating. The food was stone cold, but he ate in silence, hardly glancing at it. He kept his eyes on Hunter.

When he was done, she let him outside as she had done with Frank, but she kept more distance between them.

Otter looked right at Hunter as he unzipped his coveralls and relieved his too-full bladder in her direction. But his arrogant display failed to provoke a reaction.

Kat watched him with a bored expression.

Otter walked around as much as he dared until his time was up, studying the surrounding area in the light of day. The dense trees around would provide good cover for an escape, but the fresh snow would make it too easy for her to track him.

"Let's go," Kat said. She punched in the security code and opened the door. Otter trooped ahead of her, watching for an opportunity.

From a short distance away, a pair of eyes followed them through binoculars as the two disappeared inside. The door slid closed.

CHAPTER THIRTY-FIVE

Kat crashed on the couch after she finished with Otter and Frank and got six full hours of uninterrupted sleep. She awoke with a plan. She looked in on Jake, who was still sleeping, then booted up her computer to message Kenny. It was time to call in a favor. He wouldn't like it, but she knew he would do it if she asked.

She spelled out what she needed him to do. She gave him the access number to one of her Swiss bank accounts and the GPS coordinates of a small clearing near the bunker. It was a measure of trust she had never afforded anyone, even Kenny, but it was necessary if her plan was to work. It would probably take her friend a couple of days to implement everything she needed him to do, but Jake could use the healing time before they tried to move her.

She sent off the e-mail and waited for his response. She didn't have to wait long.

Whatever you need. I'll be in touch.

Satisfied, she noted the time—10:00 p.m.—and logged off. If all went according to plan, Jake would be safely ensconced in a new location within seventy-two hours or so, and Kat would be free to deal with Garner.

Jake came awake to the feel of Kat's large hands gently stroking her hair, fingertips caressing her scalp. They traced a slow pattern from her hairline, just above her forehead, back along the top of her head to her neck. The pattern repeated, then again. Kat's thumb traced the outside of her ear as the caress passed by.

Jake, lying on her side, opened her eyes drowsily and smiled at Kat. She closed them again so the caress would continue. "I can't imagine a nicer way to wake up," she murmured. She enjoyed the touch immensely. It was sensual yet healing. Relaxing, but undeniably stimulating, too.

Kat chuckled, and Jake's eyes popped open. The caress halted when their eyes met.

Kat was in the chair, which had been pulled up against the bed near Jake's head. Her left elbow rested on the edge of Jake's pillow as her hand paused in its journey through soft blond hair.

"I can think of a nicer way," Kat said. A soft flush of pink colored her cheeks. Her fingertips resumed their slow, gentle tracings.

Jake smiled and reddened a little herself at the image Kat's admission evoked. *Being kissed awake in your arms. That would be nicer than this.* She wondered what Kat was imagining. "Care to share? Tell me what would be better than this," she drawled impishly.

Kat's blush deepened, but she didn't stop her slow caresses. "Maybe when you're better, I'll demonstrate," was all she would volunteer.

"I'll look forward to that."

"How are you feeling?" Kat put the palm of her hand on Jake's forehead, testing for a temperature.

Jake stretched. "Not too bad, really. Stiff and sore. The arm feels pretty good, but my knee still hurts when I try to move it much."

"Well, it's time to take your meds. That'll help." Kat got Jake into a sitting position and handed her two more pills and a glass of water to take them with.

"Thanks," Jake said, handing back the glass.

Kat moved to set it back on the table without really looking. She studied Jake's face. The bruising around her friend's eyes was better, and in her sleep-tousled state in the soft glow of the bedside light, Jake looked incredible to Kat.

As Kat tried to return the glass to the table, she bumped the wedding ring. It bounced with a thin, high *ping!* on the concrete floor and rolled to the door. Kat retrieved it, and when she went to set it back on the table, she noticed there was an inscription inside. *I knew it. It's real.* Her heart sank. She felt it inappropriate for her to read it. But she had to tell Jake it was there.

"There's an inscription in the ring, Jake," Kat said, holding the gold band out toward the woman.

"I know." Jake took it but set it back on the table, out of the way. "It doesn't mean anything to me. There's no clue in it as to who I am."

"You realize," Kat said, "that an inscription—and the fact that it's left such a deep impression on your finger—mean the ring is most likely real. You probably are married."

"Legally? Maybe. But I don't feel married." Jake pushed aside her nagging guilt. "I want you, Kat. I want us. That's the only thing I trust. It's where I belong."

"Good," Kat answered, the depth of her relief evident in the slight catch in her voice. "Kind of glad to hear that."

Jake hadn't realized until just that moment how much Kat had needed reassurance. This vulnerable side of Kat made her even more endearing. "Kat, you must already know that. Don't you?"

"Well, it's still kind of hard to believe. I mean, what's happening...between us." Kat smiled at Jake. "Kind of nice to hear it's mutual."

"Oh, very, very mutual." Jake confirmed, which made Kat blush again.

"You know, you should eat a little something with that medicine," Kat said, to change the subject. She cursed the unfamiliar shy streak that seemed to keep her on the edge of embarrassment whenever she was in close proximity to Jake.

"Whatever you say, Doc. I think I can force myself. What's on the menu?"

"Something fast, and lots of it!" Kat replied, chuckling, already heading for the door.

Kat whipped up a batch of clam linguine and set two more TV dinners—fried chicken this time—in the oven for her prisoners.

Although she protested that she really wasn't all that hungry, Jake ate all of her portion and nearly half of Kat's.

Kat was happy to give it up, though she was bewildered as to how Jake could put away the quantity of food she did and still look so incredibly tantalizing. Kat found herself staring at Jake's neck, wanting to kiss the soft, sensitive spot where she knew she could faintly detect the heartbeat just beneath the skin. She wanted to make Jake's pulse quicken and feel it when it happened.

She was lost in her daydream when she realized Jake had said something to her. "I'm sorry, what did you say?"

Jake grinned at her. "I said 'thank you, that was delicious.'"

"You're welcome. Glad you enjoyed it."

"And I said that you had a rather dreamy look in your eyes and I was wondering what you were thinking about."

Kat opened her mouth to answer. Shut it again. Took a deep breath. "One-track mind, I guess."

"Meaning?"

"That I was thinking about this," Kat said, following her impulse and leaning over the bed to kiss Jake softly on the spot she'd been staring at.

Jake inhaled sharply, jolted by the incredible, unexpected sensation. Kat's lips lightly caressed her neck, the tip of her tongue darting out to taste the delicate flesh. Jake reached up and cupped her hand behind Kat's head, arching her neck and pressing Kat's mouth harder against her, encouraging the touch.

As Kat's oral explorations deepened, Jake's hand moved of its own accord. It stroked Kat's neck, shoulders, and back. Jake felt suddenly too warm. Unbelievably aroused. Her injuries were forgotten.

CHAPTER THIRTY-SIX

A loud beeping sound brought them both abruptly out of the moment. Jake froze, thinking it was another security alarm.

But Kat just exhaled loudly in exasperation. "Only the stove," she explained. "Dinner for our guests." She pulled away from Jake reluctantly and they looked at each other, their mutual desire evident. She stood. "I'll take care of that and be back in a little while. Would you like something to read to pass the time?"

"Sure," Jake answered, leaning over to try to better see the books on the shelf under the bedside table. "Whatcha got?"

Kat smiled. "I don't think those would interest you. What do you like? Mystery? Biography?"

"A mystery sounds good."

Kat nodded and left. When she did, Jake leaned farther over until she nearly toppled out of bed, determined to read the titles of the books Kat thought she would probably not be interested in. "Ah," she said aloud when she finally was able to get a good look at them. The titles were all in Greek.

The beeping stopped, and a minute later Kat reappeared with a paperback in her hand. "Try this. It's set in Isle Royale National Park, just a bit north of here in Lake Superior."

Jake took the book from her and scanned the cover. *A Superior Death*, by Nevada Barr. "Thanks," she said, glancing up at Kat. She looked toward the shelf by the bed. "Greek?"

Kat nodded. She took a deep breath and suddenly seemed to withdraw into herself. There was a sad, faraway look in her eyes. "I was born on Cyprus," she said. "I've lived here—in the States— most of my life. But I guess Greek is still my first language."

Jake had no idea that she had just learned something that Kat had volunteered only once before. To Evan Garner.

"Do you go back there often?" Jake asked.

Kat wouldn't look at her, and it was a long moment before she answered.

"No," she finally replied in a soft voice, as if there was more to say but she would not bring herself to say it. Then Kat sighed and seemed to shake off the memories. "Better go feed our two guests. I won't be long. Anything else I can get you?"

"No, thanks," Jake said, her mind still curious about Kat's mysterious past. *Will I ever know you? Will you tell me what it is you're remembering that brings you so much pain?*

Kat took the chicken dinners out to the generator room and went through the cautious routine of feeding her prisoners and letting them outside. Frank first again, then Otter. The sky was still overcast, but the snowfall had diminished to a few scattered flakes.

While she watched them—her gun in one hand and a flashlight in the other—her thoughts strayed back to Cyprus and Kyrenia, the fishing village on the northern shore where she'd grown up. She couldn't go back there now if she wanted to. Even under an assumed name, it wasn't safe.

"*Koproskilo*," she spat, an expletive that literally translated to *dog shit* but was more the Greek equivalent of *bastard*. She meant it as a general curse toward all the people who kept her from her home, both past and present. Kyrenia was no longer Greek. Since 1974 it had been part of the so-called Turkish Republic of Northern Cyprus, a country recognized by no one but Turkey. To the rest of the world it was occupied Cyprus—the northern portion of the country still under military occupation by tens of thousands of Turkish troops. Turkish settlers now lived in her family home, a large estate outside the village.

It had been a glorious place to grow up. Her father's fame and celebrity paid for servants and parties and vacations in exotic places. She missed the little walled garden where she'd go to read in the late-afternoon Mediterranean sun. And she'd never seen water the same deep blue as that in Kyrenia harbor. Her father used to take her there to watch the fishing boats.

Father, would you forgive me the things I've done? You spent your life preaching conciliation, didn't you? She pictured him the last time she'd seen him—on the television, speaking before the United Nations. The news stations had run that tape a lot when her father and mother were killed just a week after the speech.

Thousands of her neighbors had fled Kyrenia and other villages in the north, abandoning their homes and belongings to become refugees in the south. They were the lucky ones. Her parents stayed to meet the invading Turkish troops.

Her father was convinced that his diplomatic status would protect them. But he and his wife were murdered in their sleep.

Kat was thousands of miles away at the time, spending the summer after her ninth birthday at an exclusive riding camp in Maine. *The woods there were a lot like this,* she remembered, her eyes taking in the dense stands of pine and mixed hardwoods about her. It was nothing at all like the terrain of her homeland, with its scattering of mountains and vast groves of lemon trees.

A sound jolted her back to the present. Otter peeing a short distance away.

Kat turned and shined the flashlight on the security panel to punch in the numbers that would open the secret door: 2-3-7-3. "Let's go," she said to Otter.

The address of the old estate, thought the assassin watching them through high-powered binoculars. *Sentimental one, aren't you, Katarzyna?*

Once Kat had tended to the men, she returned to the living room and went to her desk, glancing automatically at the monitors. One was black. She went into the tunnel to remove the jacket she'd thrown over the camera there when Otter was inside the pantry.

Better, she thought, returning to the desk to see all three monitors now operating normally. She couldn't believe she hadn't noticed that earlier. She felt relatively safe now that the snowfall had erased all the tracks. But she told herself she still needed to keep an eye on the monitors, especially with Otter and Frank here and part of the security system deliberately disabled. The keypad locks on the doors were still enabled, but she was going in and out of them so often now that she hadn't turned the alarm system back on. It had been off since Frank had arrived.

She turned on her computer to see whether there were any updates from Kenny. There were two e-mails from him, both short and sweet. The first read: **Transportation anytime after tomorrow 6 pm. Need four hours advance notice of rendezvous.** The second said: **Money transferred. Pickup 9 a.m.**

It was midnight. Kat shut down the computer and stretched, yawning. Despite the sleep she'd gotten, she could stand a few hours more. She headed to the bedroom to check on Jake.

Jake was propped up, her back against the headboard. She was so engrossed in the novel she was reading that she didn't immediately notice Kat standing in the doorway.

But within just a minute or so, she seemed to feel Kat's eyes on her. She glanced up and smiled. "Hi. How long have you been standing there?"

"Not long," Kat replied, crossing the room to drop into the chair beside the bed. "Enjoying the book?"

Jake bent the corner of a page to mark her spot and set the book on the table. "Very much. How is...everything?"

"If you mean our guests, they're fine. No trouble." Kat reached out a hand and laid it atop Jake's, which rested beside her on the fleece blanket. "And I'm working on a plan to get us out of here to a safer place where you can get back to 100 percent."

"As long as I'm with you," Jake said. "Have I thanked you recently for taking such good care of me?" Her thumb gently caressed Kat's palm.

Both pairs of eyes fell to their joined hands as Kat began to return the light caresses. The touch was electrifying.

Their eyes met, three feet apart.

Then two feet, as they leaned toward each other. Their intentions obvious, both women smiled slightly just before the final distance was closed and their lips met in a kiss that reflected the growing urgency of the attraction between them.

As their tongues met and their heartbeats accelerated, Kat's hand came up to Jake's cheek, stroking it softly, then more firmly. She reached around behind Jake's neck to pull them closer together.

The kiss deepened and Jake's hand found its way behind Kat's back, stroking between Kat's shoulder blades, pulling, urging her even closer.

Kat complied, her lips briefly breaking contact with Jake's only so that she could move to sit on the bed. They quickly came together again, mouths meeting hungrily, hands caressing in ever widening exploratory paths.

Jake raked her fingernails lightly across Kat's broad, softly muscled back. Down to her hip, then along the top of her thigh.

Kat's fingertips trailed along Jake's side and found their way beneath her sweatshirt, seeking naked flesh. Each touch edged tantalizingly closer to their areas of greatest pleasure.

Otter was dreaming he was back in prison when he was awakened by a loud noise, a cold blast of air, and a bright light in his eyes. The light moved away to shine on Frank's face.

Frank grumbled until he cracked open his eyes, squinting against the harsh glare, and remembered where he was. Then he grew silent.

A velvet-smooth female voice, an octave higher than Kat's, addressed the men. "Hi, boys," it drawled. "Are we having fun yet?"

CHAPTER THIRTY-SEVEN

Frank's mind worked a beat slower than Otter's. He was still trying to register that this wasn't Hunter, when Otter asked, "Who are you?"

The flashlight moved back to Otter. "I'll ask the questions. Where's Hunter?"

"Through that door," Otter said, nodding in that direction. *What a break!* "Probably won't be back for a while," he offered.

The flashlight beam found the steel door and security panel. The woman walked over to it.

Now that the flashlight was out of their eyes, Frank and Otter were able to see the woman clearer in the light provided by the twin bulbs on the generator.

She was short, probably 5'3" or so, but they couldn't tell much else about her. She was dressed all in black, her head encased in a balaclava. Her body was clad in a one-piece insulated snowsuit that made it hard to judge what her figure might look like under all that padding, but she seemed diminutive.

The two men looked at each other. Otter had a hopeful expression on his face; Frank still seemed in disbelief. Then they looked back at her.

She shined the flashlight all around the room, taking everything in, looking carefully up and down all the walls and in all the corners. "Does she have security cameras?" she asked without looking at them.

"Yeah, there's one outside that door you just came through," Otter said. The main entrance was still open and it was getting very cold in the generator room, but the woman seemed not to notice or care. "And there's one on the other side of that door as well," he added, indicating the steel door to the tunnel with another nod of his head.

Otter wasn't absolutely certain of that, of course; he'd been unconscious when he was brought through that door into this room. But he thought it looked just like the steel door he'd seen when he was inside the tunnel, so he was pretty sure that was all there was to the bunker.

He had the woman's full attention. She stepped toward him. "What else is on the other side of that door, hmm?"

"A tunnel. It connects this room to the house part. A big room with a bedroom and a bathroom off it. And a pantry," Otter added, flinching slightly as he recalled the whacks his head had taken.

"Alarm system?"

"Don't think it's on if there is one," Otter said. "I haven't heard any alarms." He looked toward Frank for confirmation.

The woman's eyes followed his, and she too stared at Frank.

Frank shook his head. "Me neither."

"Anything else?" the woman asked.

"There's another entrance to the place," Otter answered. "It goes up out of the tunnel, up to a hatch."

The woman returned to the security panel.

"Hunter carries a gun. She was wearing it in the back of her jeans," Otter supplied next. "And there may be someone else in there with her."

The woman turned to look at him again.

"You working for Garner?" Otter asked her.

"I ask the questions," she reminded him. "Who's in there with her?"

"A woman named Scout," Otter said. "Another bounty hunter. We followed her out here. She may be dead, we don't know. Or she may be in there."

"You say you followed this Scout? Explain that," the woman said.

"Well, her car crashed on a road a few miles from here. We followed some tracks from there to here."

"What kind of car? How did you find it?" she asked.

"It was a dark sedan," Otter replied. "I forget the model. We were following a homing device that was in her cell phone. It led us to the crash site."

The woman turned her attention back to the security panel. "I don't suppose you've managed to see what code she uses to get through this door, have you?"

"No," Otter said. "She's pretty careful."

The woman continued to examine the keypad. "So what happened to you two?"

Otter didn't answer for a moment. "I got in the other entrance and was going to ambush her. She cut the lights and I couldn't see a damn thing in there. She snuck up on me and knocked me out."

The flashlight swung from the security panel toward Frank, seeking his answer.

"She jumped me outside."

The beam returned to study the panel.

"Hey, how about helping us get out of these," Otter asked, rattling his handcuffs and the chain connecting him to Frank. "We can all jump her when she comes back to feed us. Make it fast and easy, split the money." He had no doubt this woman was another bounty hunter out to collect on Garner's contract. A million split three ways would still be a hell of a payoff.

The woman laughed. No, she *cackled*. "Make it fast? Easy? Now why in the world would I want to do that?"

The tone in her voice stopped Otter cold. There was something about this woman that wasn't...quite...right. "You want to do this alone, that's cool. But how about helping us first? You know—I did you a favor, you do me a favor?"

The woman came over to stand in front of him. She crouched down, her face inches from his. "But I've already done you a favor." She smiled. It was a smile absent any warmth at all. A crocodile smile. "I'm letting you live."

She rose from her crouch and went back to the steel door, dismissing any further consideration of the two men in the corner.

❖

Jake was long past conscious thought. Her body had taken over, and she had surrendered completely to the incredible sensations that were flooding her senses. Her skin was hypersensitive along the path that Kat's fingers were tracing. They had slipped beneath the oversized sweatshirt Jake had on and were slowly exploring her stomach and side. Every now and then they would stray to tease the curve of her breast. Jake's desire swelled until the anticipation was excruciating. Her tongue and lips pressed harder against Kat's while her hand tugged at Kat's shirt, pulling it from her jeans.

Kat was lost in her own sensual haze. Every nerve ending was on fire. She had never felt so incredibly aroused. Her previous sexual encounters had not prepared her for this. Her heart was pounding so hard she could feel it in her ears. A rush of blood coursed through her like liquid fire. When Jake's hand slid beneath her shirt and skimmed lightly across her already erect nipple, she could not suppress a moan of pleasure.

"Well, isn't this cozy," a high, feminine voice interrupted from the bedroom doorway.

Jake and Kat broke apart to look toward the door. Kat had her back to it. She turned, slowly, until she was facing the intruder. She shifted her weight so that her body would act as a shield between Jake and the new threat.

"Katarzyna Demetrious. At last." A woman dressed all in black held a gun on them. She leaned against the door frame as if she'd been watching them for a while. "I've been dreaming about this moment for a long time." She had shoulder-length, curly blond hair, matted down after its long confinement under the balaclava. She was an attractive woman, but with a detached cruelty in her eyes that Kat recognized.

Kat had not heard her full name in so many years it stunned her momentarily into inaction.

"Before we get acquainted," the woman said, taking slow steps toward the bed, "let's have your gun. Left hand. Very slowly." She kept her 9mm handgun pointed at Kat's head as she advanced to the end of the bed, keeping well out of Kat's reach.

Kat's hand moved slowly behind her and pulled her Glock out of her jeans. She tossed it on the bed near the intruder. The woman picked it up and shoved it into a pocket of her snowsuit.

During the millisecond the woman looked away, Kat's eyes darted toward the pillow that had concealed her loaded .38. Jake had moved it! She had rearranged the pillows to prop herself up to read. Kat had no idea where the gun was now.

"Good girl," the stranger said. She backed up a few steps to put a little more distance between them. She motioned Kat off the bed with the gun in her hand.

Kat hesitated.

The woman calmly cocked the 9mm.

Kat reluctantly complied, easing off the edge of the bed with a glance back toward Jake.

Jake's mouth was open, her eyes wide, staring in absolute horror at the woman who held them at gunpoint. She was breathing so fast, she was nearly hyperventilating.

Panic attack, Kat thought, unconsciously moving toward Jake to help her.

"Don't," the intruder warned, taking a step toward Kat with her arm outstretched at shoulder level. Her eyes focused through the sights on the gun on the center of Kat's forehead. She moved amazingly fast.

Kat froze.

The woman kept the gun trained on Kat, but she turned her head slightly to really look at Jake for the first time. "My, my. It is a small world, now, isn't it? You created quite a few problems for me, you know. It's been a while since I had to hot-wire a car, and I didn't appreciate losing my rifle. But now you're here, and I can take care of both of you at once." She laughed, shaking her head in disbelief at her good fortune. "Goody goody. Must be my lucky day."

Kat's mind worked furiously to try to comprehend what was going on. This woman had gotten in and snuck up on them. Kat had thought that impossible. *She is obviously a bit crazy and she knows who I am. And who Jake is, too, evidently.* Kat looked at Jake.

Jake still hadn't moved. She was gripped in a private terror, her eyes glued to the intruder. She had an almost glazed expression on her face.

"She doesn't seem to be doing real well," the intruder observed, glancing from Jake to Kat and back again. "Missing hubby all of a sudden?"

That finally brought a reaction from Jake, though not one

that anyone expected. Frozen one moment, a blur of motion the next, she suddenly had Kat's .38 in her hand. She pointed it at the intruder.

"You killed him!" she screamed, tears running down her face. The hand holding the gun trembled slightly.

CHAPTER THIRTY-EIGHT

Yes, I did," the intruder confirmed. "While you ran away." She seemed not unduly concerned by the turn of events. She continued to hold her own gun on Kat.

Jake's hand shook uncontrollably.

"And now you have a new lover," the woman observed, nodding toward Kat. "He must not have been much to mourn over."

Jake looked at Kat. Her look was full of anguish and pain.

Kat wanted to reach out to her, but she remained rooted in place. She held Jake's gaze, and with a slow, deliberate movement, blinked toward the gun and nodded very slightly. A signal she hoped Jake would understand. She wanted her friend to pull the trigger.

"How about her?" the intruder barked, drawing Jake's attention. "Will you mourn her? Pretty touching scene I walked in on."

Jake looked back at Kat uncertainly. Her whole upper body shook. She couldn't keep the gun still.

"Put it down, or she's dead," the woman warned.

Jake's head whipped back around to look at the intruder.

The woman had taken another step toward Kat. "Now!" She was only a couple of feet away and couldn't possibly miss.

Jake lowered the .38 and tossed it toward the end of the bed.

The intruder picked it up, pocketed it, and moved a few feet away again.

"Who are you?" Kat asked, her eyes darting between the woman and Jake, who had collapsed against the pillows.

"Who am I?" the woman repeated, as if she were considering

the answer. "Well, I guess that depends on who you ask. I'm using the name Scout at the moment."

The final pieces suddenly fell into place in Kat's mind. *Jake is—was—Sam's wife. Scout killed him, and Jake saw it happen.* But somehow Jake had escaped...in Scout's stolen car. It explained why Jake had been speeding like a bat out of hell on that lonely road. She was leaving the airstrip.

Kat looked at Jake. Her friend was not the assassin she'd believed her to be all this time. She was an ordinary woman who was ill prepared to deal with this kind of situation. Jake appeared to be in shock. *She can't protect herself.*

Kat looked back at the intruder. She still didn't know how this woman knew her real name, but she was certain of one thing—she was very, very dangerous. Scout had good reasons to kill them both, and she would apparently enjoy doing just that.

"Well, Scout. How about I save you some trouble. I'll double Garner's offer if you just leave now," Kat said.

Scout laughed. "Oh, it's no trouble, Katarzyna. Far from it. I can't tell you how much I've been looking forward to reminiscing about some of your past...accomplishments." She had a cruel, cold smile on her face. "And now I can also get to know your friend," she added, leering at Jake and licking her lips.

Kat's blood boiled at the prospect, and she had to fight hard against a sudden urge to throw herself at Scout. The woman was too far away and she'd already demonstrated well-honed reflexes.

Kat had to focus. Wait for the right moment. Push down the rage she felt at the image of Scout harming Jake. Her emotions could make her careless. If she failed, Jake would be defenseless.

Kat looked at Jake again. She was worried about the dazed expression in her eyes. "Jake?" she said, ignoring Scout for the moment in an effort to jar her friend back to reality.

"Jake?" Scout repeated. "Why do you call her Jake? Pet name?"

"It's Riley," Jake whispered, more to herself than to either of them. "Riley McCann."

"Oh, this is rich," Scout said. "You didn't tell her your name?" She looked at Kat. "And you didn't ask?"

"I didn't know it," Riley said without emotion. Her eyes were clenched shut.

Don't, Kat wanted to say. *Don't tell her anything.* She wanted so much to reach out to her. *Riley. That will take a little getting used to.*

"You didn't know it?" Scout snorted, disbelieving. "You didn't know your name?"

"No. I didn't remember my name, or anything else until..." Riley's voice trailed off as her eyes opened and focused on Scout. Her dazed expression seemed to clear.

Kat noticed the change with relief. The shock seemed to be wearing off. She wondered how much Jake—Riley—was remembering.

"Until you saw me? How sweet," Scout purred. She turned to look at Kat. "And how much have you told her, Katarzyna? Does she know about the estate where you grew up? Your famous father? The special academy you got to attend in Virginia?"

Kat tried to mask her shock. *How the hell does she know all this? How does she know about the Academy?* Her silence seemed to infuriate Scout.

"I bet she doesn't know about all the people you've slaughtered in their sleep!" Scout screamed, her face and voice suddenly conveying all the rage that was pent up inside her.

Kat still didn't respond.

"On the floor, Katarzyna! Face down, hands behind your back!" She waved the gun at Kat. When Kat didn't immediately move, Scout aimed the gun toward Riley, and her cruel smile reappeared. She pulled the trigger and the gun went off.

The bullet missed Riley's head by less than a foot. It slammed into the headboard, splintering it.

Riley flinched when the bullet hit and stared wide-eyed at Scout, who calmly cocked the gun again and took aim at Riley's head.

Kat dropped to the floor. Her instincts were screaming against it, but she knew Scout's threat was deadly serious.

Once she was on the floor, Scout approached her and put her gun to Kat's head while she fished in her coverall pockets for handcuffs. "Don't test me again," she warned. She put one knee on

Kat's back to pin her to the floor as she fastened the cuffs tightly to Kat's wrists.

"Who are you?" Kat asked again, her face pressed against the cold concrete floor.

"Justice," Scout replied, just before she brought her gun down hard against the back of Kat's head, knocking her unconscious.

CHAPTER THIRTY-NINE

K at came awake to the sound of Jake's voice. *Not Jake. Riley,* she remembered. Her head throbbed.

"Can you hear me? Kat? Please wake up and talk to me. Kat?" Riley pleaded in a loud whisper.

Kat opened her eyes. To darkness. Not quite total darkness. Her eyes were beginning to adjust. She could just make out a small bit of light around the closed door she lay opposite. It was enough to allow her to discern her friend's outline. Riley was on the floor several feet away.

They were in the pantry. The smell of the fish sauce had thankfully faded and was now annoying but tolerable.

"Please, Kat. Please wake up and tell me you're all right. It's Jake." Riley said.

"Thought your name was Riley," Kat replied in a low whisper.

"Thank God," Riley said. "I wasn't sure you'd remember. I was kind of hoping you might want to wake up to Jake. Are you all right?"

"My head is killing me." Kat tried to move. Her hands were handcuffed behind her and her feet were tied together. A short length of rope connected her hands and feet. She could tell from the dim light that Riley was similarly hog-tied, though her knees weren't bent back at such a sharp angle. "Think I'm all right other than that. What about you?"

"She didn't knock me out," Riley whispered. "Just brought me in here and tied me up. Then dragged you in here. My knee doesn't like this, but I'll live. I was worried about you. Your head was bleeding a lot."

"I'll be all right. How long was I out?"

"About ten minutes."

"Did she say anything?"

"She...well, she tried to screw with my mind," Riley said vaguely. "Unsuccessfully. I was too worried about you to think about much else."

"What did she say to you?" Kat asked, her temper rising.

"She...gloated," Riley said. "Over my husband's murder." Her voice was full of pain. "Said she might not have had to kill him if I hadn't interrupted her. Tried to make me feel guilty for running away. Told me she'd...get me back...for all the inconvenience I caused her."

"How much do you remember?" Kat asked.

"Everything. It all came back when I saw her. She killed Sam. My husband. I went to the airstrip. He's—he was," she amended sadly, "a helicopter pilot." She took a deep breath. "She had a knife to his throat. He was tied up on the floor, like we are now."

Her voice took on a slight tremor, as if it suddenly occurred to her that the same fate might be in store for both of them. "He had cuts all over his body," Riley went on. "His shirt and pants were bloody and he had cuts on his face."

Kat knew how painful this recollection was, but she had to let her continue. She had to learn everything she could about Scout to best prepare for whatever lay ahead.

"He started screaming as soon as he saw me. 'No, Riley! Run!'" Tears spilled down her cheeks. "She killed him as soon as the words were out of his mouth. She...she slit his throat." Her voice was full of anguish. "I didn't really have time to think. I did what he said. I ran. I took her car. She nearly caught me. She was chasing me, shooting at the car. I took off in the only direction I could. I don't remember going off the road, but I was really upset."

"How did you end up in her car?" Kat asked. Throughout Riley's recollections, Kat had been working at her bindings, trying to loosen them, so far without success.

"I parked my truck in back, next to Sam's. His wasn't running, and I had told him he could use mine while I was out of town if he'd give me a lift to the airport in Marquette. I was supposed to go to Vancouver that night for a job. When I walked around the building, I noticed the car parked in front. I glanced inside because I didn't recognize it, and I saw the keys were in it."

There was a long pause. "Sam and I had been separated a long time," Riley explained. "I was gone a lot, and he was always having affairs while I was on the road. It wasn't a bad breakup—we were still friends. But I guess I was just in the habit of noticing things—like who he was spending time with. Anyway, when I ran out of there, I just headed for that car because it was a lot closer than my truck."

Riley was silent another long moment. "I wonder if Sam might be alive if I'd done something differently. It just all happened so fast."

"Listen," Kat said. "There's nothing you could have done. This woman is a cold-blooded killer." She tried not to think about the fact that the description she'd just used fit her as well. "Riley, I'm very sorry about your husband." The next confession was hard. "I think he died because of me."

"Because of you?"

"Scout is after me," Kat said. "I knew Sam. Not well. I mean... I never knew he was married. I used his helicopter a lot when I was building the bunker and when I needed to resupply. I think Scout somehow figured out I knew him, and she was trying to get Sam to tell her where I was when you interrupted them."

Riley absorbed that news. "You're not to blame, Kat," she said finally.

"And neither are you," Kat said. "Scout's a nutcase. Any idea what she's doing now?"

"She said she wanted to find out all she could about you," Riley said. "Do you know what that means?"

"Maybe," Kat said. *Can Scout find the weapons room?* She thought it unlikely. *No, but she might be able to hack into the computer if she got into the bunker.* She thought about her e-mail correspondence with Kenny. *That could be trouble.*

"Jake? I mean, Riley, sorry—" Kat began.

"I don't mind if you call me Jake, you know," Riley said.

"Good, because I might slip now and then," Kat said. "Can you scoot over here closer to me?"

Riley had attempted several times when Kat was unconscious

to move toward her. But each time she did, the pain in her knee was so excruciating she nearly blacked out. "I can't, Kat. I tried to, but my knee is just too—"

"It's okay. I know you would if you could."

"I'm sorry," Riley said. "I'm sorry I didn't kill her when I had the chance. I know you wanted me to. I just couldn't take the chance she'd shoot you."

"It's all right, Riley," Kat said. "You're not a killer." There was a catch in her voice and Riley knew why.

"Kat," Riley reassured her, "Nothing's changed. Yes, I'm Riley, not Jake. A writer, as it turns out, and not a bounty hunter. But I still want to be with you. Just as soon as you get us out of this."

Otter was worried. He was so cold he could no longer feel his hands. He'd been flexing them to try to keep the circulation going. He'd even lain on them, hoping to warm them up that way. But it wasn't working. The little heater was ineffective against the open door. The wind outside had picked up, and frigid air was blowing in. His face was freezing. His cheeks and his nose stung, and his eyes watered.

"We've got to get out of here before we freeze to death," he told Frank.

Frank hadn't spoken in several minutes, but Otter had heard his chattering teeth and knew he was suffering too.

"Hunter is not going to help you, Frank. That woman got her, or Hunter would have come out to check on us."

"If she got Hunter," Frank said, shivering, "then why didn't she come back out here?"

"Who the hell knows? Maybe she went out through the other exit. Maybe she's in there torturing Hunter. Maybe they killed each other. Whatever the hell happened, nobody's gonna come help us. We got to help ourselves."

Frank had never thought he'd find himself hoping that Hunter prevailed, but he did. He hoped she'd get out of whatever was happening in there, because he didn't think he would survive otherwise. He thought there was no way they could get out of their bonds. *But perhaps,* he admitted, *it's time to really try. Just to make sure.* "Got any ideas?"

Scout hunched over Kat's computer. Trying to find the right password, she typed in several different numerical combinations, every number she knew that had been significant to her long-sought quarry. Phone numbers, addresses, birthdays. Then she tried words. Place names and family names and every false identity she knew that Kat had used.

Scout had been gathering information on Hunter for eight years in preparation for this day. It had been her obsession since she was released from a Belfast jail after serving two months for passing bad checks.

She'd awakened in a cold sweat in her cell that night, gripped in a nightmare she couldn't remember. The same night that Hunter broke into a remote cottage in Northern Ireland and killed four members of a particularly violent offshoot of the Irish Republican Army. Scout was the absent fifth member of the group. Her brother Ian, among the dead, was its leader.

She'll remember that day. With a little encouragement, she'll remember.

The presence of the pilot's wife makes all this a lot more interesting, Scout thought. *Especially since she and Katarzyna undoubtedly have the hots for each other.* Scout hadn't thought it possible that Hunter had a heart. Yet she seemed very selflessly protective of the injured Riley.

Katarzyna had been Scout's obsession. She knew more about her than anyone alive, and she'd never found evidence that Hunter was intimate with anyone, male or female. So what she'd witnessed changed her game plan a little. She was still working it out in her mind, how she might use the relationship between the two women to her advantage. She'd heard that her adversary had a very high tolerance for pain and could not easily be persuaded to give up information. *Perhaps she might be more easily convinced if her friend is the one being tortured.*

❖

It took Scout another hour to hack into Kat's computer files. She was patient. While she tried various possibilities, she spared a moment's thought to the two men. *Must be getting pretty cold out there about now.* Maybe she'd go shut the door for them after she'd gotten into the computer files. Maybe. First she had to think of a reason they might be useful and worth the effort.

When she finally got into the computer, Scout went to Kat's e-mail program and read the exchanges between Kenny and Hunter. *So Katarzyna does have a friend. Someone she trusts enough to give the access number of her Swiss bank account and the location of this place.* She read their entire correspondence. This Kenny was a good source of information as well as a good friend. He had warned Katarzyna about her, as well as someone named Otter.

I bet Otter is one of the guys in the garage, she reasoned. She was very interested to learn that Otter had dealt with Katarzyna before somewhere and knew Kenny. *Otter might be worth keeping alive after all. At least until I find out everything he knows.*

Scout composed her own e-mail to Kenny, asking him to personally deliver the cash and transportation he was arranging. She told him it was imperative that he speed up the process and get to the bunker as soon as possible. He was to e-mail back when he knew precisely when he'd arrive. She signed it "Hunter" and sent it off. *I have to make sure I take care of everyone important to you, Katarzyna. Just like you did for me.*

She turned her attention to Kat's Swiss bank account. She accessed the bank's online customer service page and set to work arranging an electronic transfer of all remaining funds from the account into her own account in the Cayman Islands.

CHAPTER FORTY

It took Kat fifteen minutes to get across the pantry floor to Riley. Her head pounded from the exertion, and she was soaked in sweat despite her body's contact with the cold concrete. Trussed up tightly as she was, she could move only by inches. Both women remained quiet while Kat worked so they could listen for Scout's return. Kat maneuvered herself behind Riley and positioned herself so she could reach her bindings.

"Okay, reach out if you can with your good hand," Kat whispered. It was awkward. Kat had to operate blindly with her hands cuffed behind her, but she flailed around until her fingers finally found Riley's outstretched hand. "Got you." She grasped it firmly and gave it a brief squeeze before her fingers moved to Riley's wrists.

Kat was surprised to discover Riley was not handcuffed. Scout had tied Riley up with the same type of nylon rope that she'd used to hog-tie Kat's feet to her hands. She realized Scout couldn't handcuff Riley because of the cast. Perhaps that was the break they needed. Kat had excelled in all the courses at the Academy, but she'd actually had fun in the class entitled Breaking Out And Breaking In. She was especially good at picking locks and at tying and untying every possible kind of knot.

She had Riley free in less than ten minutes. As soon as she could straighten her leg again, Riley felt worlds better, and she could move without unbearable pain.

"See if you can untie my feet from my hands," Kat whispered. While Riley worked at her ropes, Kat closed her eyes and tried to visualize the contents of the pantry. What had been there before, what remained after the fight with Otter, and where she'd rearranged things on the shelves. She was mentally searching for a small—*That's it!* A possibility came to her.

"How's it coming? Any progress?" Kat lay on her side.

Riley was sitting up now, her bad leg stretched out in front of her.

"Yes, getting there," Riley whispered back. "Slow but sure. The cast makes this harder than it should be, and I've never seen knots like this before." She kept at it, glad to be doing something to help them get out of there. Her small fingers actually worked to her advantage, enabling her to manipulate the knots better than if she'd had larger hands. After a few minutes, she untied the final tight knot that bound Kat's feet to her hands. Kat extended her legs gratefully, stretching the cramps out.

Riley shifted position to begin working on the knots that bound Kat's feet, but Kat stopped her.

"No, that can wait. Think you can stand up?"

"Yes. What do you want me to do?"

Kat rolled over to face her. "Over in the corner behind you, I think on the top shelf, are a couple of small cloth sacks of grits."

"Grits?" Riley repeated, as she hauled herself to her feet.

"Grits. Cloth sacks within plastic bags. See if you can find one and bring it over here."

"Right," Riley whispered, pulling herself along the wall. She squinted in the dim light, feeling about for the bags with her good hand. She found one and carried it back to where Kat lay.

"Okay. Rip off the plastic bag," Kat said.

Riley did.

"Now if I remember right, there should be a small piece of metal wrapped around the top of the cloth bag to close it," Kat whispered.

"Found it."

"Unwrap it and put it in my hand," Kat instructed.

Riley did. The metal was stiff and difficult to work with, but she was able to straighten it with some effort. When she did, she had a small metal rod about two inches long. She placed it carefully into Kat's outstretched fingers.

"Now you can start working on the knots on my feet," Kat said.

As Riley set to her task, Kat bent the length of metal into an L shape and picked the locks on her handcuffs. She had them off long before Riley got her feet free.

"I'll finish that," Kat said, sitting up and rubbing her wrists.

Riley impulsively leaned into Kat and kissed her on the cheek. "I know we'll get out of this," she whispered, feeling more confident by the minute.

Kat put her hand on Riley's shoulder and squeezed it briefly before she began working at the knots at her feet. "We will. I won't let her hurt you."

"I don't want her hurting you either," Riley whispered back. "So take care of yourself too, all right?"

Kat smiled. "You bet. We have some unfinished business, as I recall."

Riley warmed at the remembrance. "Yes, we do."

It took Kat only another minute to free her legs. She got to her feet and helped Riley up.

"What now?" Riley whispered.

It took no time at all for Scout's Grand Cayman account to reflect the addition of the $640,000 she transferred from Kat's Swiss bank account just before she closed it.

It was a lot of money, but Scout was disappointed. Together with the $400,000 that Kenny had already withdrawn, which he would be bringing to the bunker, Scout would get a total of more than a million dollars of her adversary's money. But Katarzyna had been born into wealth, and she was a legend in the business, so Scout expected a lot more. Hunter hadn't blinked when she offered to double Garner's offer. *That's two million right there. She has to have more accounts somewhere.*

She could find little else of value in the computer. Apparently Hunter wasn't the type to keep a lot of confidential information on her hard drive.

Scout tried the desk drawers. Locked. She reached into a pocket of her coveralls, which were lying on the floor beside her, for the key ring and loose key she'd taken off Kat after she knocked her out. Scout had shed her heavy outerwear in the warmth of the bunker and now wore a black fleece top and black flannel-lined jeans.

She found that the loose key fit the desk. She opened it and began going through the contents of the drawers. From the bottom one she withdrew Kat's file folders and skimmed through them.

They were cases. Past assignments she had taken, or perhaps just considered taking, it was hard to tell. Scout did not find a file about her group's assassination, but she didn't expect to. It had happened too many years ago.

She picked up the photograph that lay face down in the drawer and studied the faces. Father, mother, and daughter. A formal portrait of an affluent family. The daughter, six or seven, had brown hair, high cheekbones, and dark eyes. Katarzyna was startlingly beautiful even then. Mother had the same cheekbones and was dressed expensively, with jewels at her throat and around her wrists. But Katarzyna got most of her handsome looks from her father. His hair was longer than most middle-aged men would wear, but it suited his dark Mediterranean ruggedness. Like his wife, he was impeccably dressed. His expensive navy suit was perfectly tailored to fit his tall, athletic frame, and a starched white shirt provided crisp contrast to his dark olive complexion. He had his hand on Katarzyna's shoulder, and the expressions on their faces suggested a shared secret. Father and daughter had identical broad smiles, as if captured in a moment of perfect happiness that Mother didn't quite share. Her subdued smile seemed forced for the picture.

Scout knew all about them, of course. She had researched Katarzyna's family thoroughly and was frankly disappointed to find they were already dead. But now perhaps she had a suitable means of justice. She would kill the two people closest to Katarzyna: her lover and her friend. Scout placed the photograph on the desk.

She decided to check on the two men in the other room to see if one was Otter. If so, she wanted to know what he could tell her about Katarzyna and Kenny, who would soon join the party.

❖

Otter and Frank had tried everything they could think of to break free. The chains held them fast. Otter had begun to panic a little at the loss of feeling in his hands. Frank too, finally, had used every ounce of strength left in his six foot three inches of brawn, but he was unable to budge the handcuffs or heavy links of chain.

When it became clear they could not free themselves, the men huddled together for warmth. They tried to wrap the coats and sleeping bag around them, and it did help to ward off the biting winds blowing in through the open door. They lay uncomfortably pressed together, discussing in low voices what might happen if the woman who had broken in returned.

The men agreed she was dangerously unpredictable, so they tried to think of ways they might convince her to help them and then let them go.

Kat poured a bit of vegetable oil over the pantry door's hinges before she tried to open it. She turned to Riley and whispered, "Don't move."

With excruciatingly slow movements, she turned the knob and cracked the door open a fraction of an inch. With her ear to the opening, she detected faint sounds from the outer room. Fingers hitting the computer keyboard. Silence. More typing. A desk drawer being slammed shut. Kat opened the door a few more centimeters and peered out. She couldn't see Scout. The desk was off to the right of her limited field of vision.

Kat was still considering her next move when the loud creak of the desk chair being pushed back broke the silence. Scout was moving.

Kat froze, her senses on high alert. She glimpsed Scout as she crossed toward the bedroom or bathroom. A minute or so later, Scout crossed through in the opposite direction, and then Kat heard the unmistakable sound of the door to the tunnel opening and closing.

Now was their chance.

Kat opened the pantry door and scanned the outer room. She scooped Riley up in her arms and hurried to the wall of bookshelves.

She set Riley down just long enough to get to the secret button to open the weapons room. She pressed it and heard the sharp click of the lock releasing; then she replaced the book that had concealed the button. She swung the door panel open and helped Riley through it, then pushed it shut again once they were both safely inside. The room went black.

"You're full of surprises," Riley whispered. She reached out, seeking Kat's reassuring presence.

Kat was already moving toward her. They met in the darkness and held each other, Riley's arms encircling Kat's waist, Kat's arms around Riley's shoulders.

Riley blew out a long shaky breath, trying to calm her racing heart.

Kat embraced her tighter. "How are you doing?" she whispered as she stroked Riley's back and hair.

"Better now," Riley whispered back. "Can she find us in here?"

"Don't think so. If she does, we'll be ready for her. We're in my weapons room."

Riley had gotten only a brief glimpse of the room when she'd been hurried inside. All she'd noticed were three very large safes. "Weapons? That sounds reassuring."

Kat moved to loosen their embrace, but Riley was loath to let her go. She kept her arms tight around Kat's waist.

"I'll be right back. Just going to get us a little light in here," Kat said. She kissed Riley on the forehead, and Riley reluctantly released her.

Kat found the small chain that led to a bare 40-watt bulb above them. She tugged it, and the room was lit by a soft glow. The women caught each other's eyes, and both smiled. Kat closed the distance between them, and they resumed their embrace.

"She won't be able to see the light?" Riley whispered.

"No, the doorway is a tight seal," Kat replied. "And I don't think she can hear us if we keep our voices low—that partition between us is pretty thick. But I've never really tested it, so we'd better be careful."

Riley nodded, her head pressed up against Kat's chest.

"We can't stay in here forever, obviously. There's no food and no water," Kat said. "And it won't take Scout long to figure out we haven't left the bunker. But this gives us some time to plan on how we'll confront her, and it evens things out a bit."

Now that she had access to her arsenal, Kat would have liked to go out immediately to confront Scout. But Riley complicated things. Keeping her safe was Kat's main priority now. She didn't want to act in haste and underestimate Scout, who had already proven to be a particularly tough and unpredictable adversary.

The main danger would lie in the moment she opened the panel to leave, Kat reasoned. Scout was patient and determined, as evidenced by her unbelievable knowledge of Kat's history. So she would surely think nothing of waiting a few more hours until Kat made a move.

Scout's most likely plan would be an ambush, Kat was certain. The only question was where she would lie in wait. If she hadn't yet discovered the weapons room, she could be anywhere. But if she knew where Kat and Riley were hiding...

Even in the best scenario, Riley would be vulnerable until Kat got through the doorway and closed it again.

Better to wait a while, let Scout stew over our disappearance. No one could go without sleep forever. Scout's search for them would exhaust her, Kat hoped. Eventually she'd have to rest and let her guard down. In the meantime, Kat would get a little shut-eye and be refreshed and alert for their confrontation. Riley could use some rest too, she knew. She just wished she had Riley's medicine and some provisions to make their wait more comfortable.

"How's the knee?"

"Not great," Riley admitted. "Probably better to get my weight off it."

Kat glanced around at the cold concrete floor. She gently extricated herself from Riley's embrace and moved to one of the safes. She opened it and reached inside for her Sig Sauer handgun—the 9mm P226 model popular with law enforcement and the military. She checked to make sure it was loaded before sticking it into the back of her jeans. She put a second magazine containing ten rounds into one of her front pockets.

Next she withdrew a belt pack from the safe. Kat kept it loaded with emergency gear. She pulled out a survival blanket made of a thin aluminum and polyester polymer developed for NASA. She unfolded it on the floor. Then she took her bulletproof vest from the safe and placed it atop the blanket to add a bit more insulation from the cold floor.

"Come on," Kat said, helping Riley to the makeshift pallet. "See if you can get some rest."

Riley lay down and Kat kneeled beside her. She wrapped the blanket around her friend, cocooning her in the shiny material.

"What about you?" Riley asked as Kat tucked her in. "You took a pretty good hit to the head."

"I'll join you in a little while," Kat replied. First she intended to survey the contents of her safes. Select what she would use against Scout and see what else they might use while they were trapped in here.

But Riley reached up and grasped Kat's arm. "Please?" She opened the thin blanket, scooting over to make room for Kat.

Kat relented and slipped into Riley's open arms. The blanket was not big enough to cover them both. It was now only a thin insulation against the concrete. Kat enveloped Riley in an embrace, careful to avoid her injured knee.

They stayed wrapped in each other's arms for a long moment before Riley broke the silence. "Katarzyna Demetrious? Is that your name?" She'd wanted to ask her about the things that Scout had made oblique reference to—things about Kat's past. There hadn't really been an opportunity until now.

Kat stiffened, but only for a moment. She stroked Riley's back with one hand. "Yes," she affirmed quietly. "I've not told anyone my real name in..." She paused, remembering. "In many years. I don't know how Scout knows it." There was a long silence. "My father was Konstantin Demetrious. He was the Cypriot ambassador to the UN when I was a child."

The name sounded vaguely familiar to Riley, but she couldn't recall why.

"He was well known as a peace negotiator," Kat continued, a catch in her voice. "When I was six, he became a special ambassador-at-large for the UN itself. He traveled around the world to all the hot spots, trying to resolve conflicts, bring warring sides together."

She paused. "He was up for the Nobel Peace Prize. There was talk of making him the next UN secretary-general."

There was another long silence.

"What happened?" Riley asked.

"He was killed," Kat said. "When Turkish troops took over northern Cyprus, he and my mother were murdered in their sleep."

"I'm sorry," Riley said, caressing Kat's stomach. "I can't imagine how painful that must have been for you. How old were you?"

"Nine. I was here in the States at summer camp when it happened." Kat relaxed a little under Riley's soft caresses. "I stayed here. The home where I grew up was taken over by the Turks."

"You never went back?"

"I went back to Cyprus once—when I was older," Kat replied. She wanted to tell Riley everything, but the next confessions were the hardest.

"My father was rich, so I didn't lack for money," she explained. "An uncle in Greece—my only surviving relative—arranged for me to attend boarding school in Connecticut under an assumed name, so that I wouldn't be a target for the media and for those who might exploit me for my father's wealth. My uncle couldn't take me in. He was an old man. He died less than a year later."

Kat's voice grew husky, her emotions close to the surface. "I was...very angry for many years about what happened to my father and mother. Both of them, of course, but I was particularly close to my father. My mother was...formal, proper. I think she was disappointed in me because I was a tomboy, always getting into mischief. 'Katarzyna!' she'd scold. 'Look at you! Company is coming and you're a muddy mess!' You know, I can't remember her ever hugging me or telling me that she loved me."

Kat unconsciously drew Riley even closer to her as she continued. "But my father..." Her voice trembled. Her eyes welled with tears. "He called me Kat. When he'd come home from a trip, he'd yell 'Here, Kitty Kat!' and I'd come running, both of us laughing. He'd scoop me up in his arms and swing me around and tell me how much he'd missed me. Then I'd sit on his lap and he'd talk about all the unusual things he'd seen. All the fascinating people he'd met, the strange food he'd eaten." She exhaled a long, slow breath. "He told me once he'd named me Katarzyna because it meant 'pure.' He wanted me to do good. Follow his example. Live a life of service to others."

Riley, understanding now the reasons for the pain that Kat hid so well, felt her own eyes fill with tears.

"But I chose another path a long time ago. When all I felt was rage over their deaths, and the need for revenge." Kat's shame threatened to overwhelm her, but she needed to finish.

"I was an athlete in boarding school. Track, basketball, fencing. Sports were a distraction against loneliness. I didn't have many friends. In college, I took up martial arts and won a national title. It was then that I met Evan Garner—and became a killer for hire."

CHAPTER FORTY-ONE

Scout found Frank and Otter huddled together beneath Kat's coats. Their heads popped out of the covering when they heard the steel door open. Both men looked at her expectantly, but neither spoke. They had discussed a variety of things they might say to the stranger if she returned, but each wanted the other to be the one to risk raising her ire. Seeing her now, knowing she evidently had overpowered Hunter, did nothing to ease their trepidation of her.

Scout had not bothered to put her coveralls back on. She didn't intend to be out in the cold very long. But the temperature in the room had dropped to fifteen degrees and the wind blew in fiercely, so she closed the outside door. "What are your names?" she asked the men.

"Otter."

"Frank."

"Move apart," she instructed as she fished in her pocket for Kat's keys.

They obeyed her, separating as far as they were able. Both men fixed their eyes on the keys in her hand. A trace of a smile appeared on Otter's face when she stepped behind him and unlocked the chain that connected him to Frank.

Scout saw the smile and jerked Otter up hard by his handcuffs. She was stronger than she appeared, and the movement sent pain shooting up his arms. He grunted and tried to turn to look at her. But she yanked him hard again when he did. With her free hand, she dug her knife out of her pocket, clicked it open, and held it to his throat. It took only a few seconds.

"You're not a part of my plan," she hissed. "So I'll be happy to get rid of you right here and now if you don't do exactly as I say."

Otter nodded, afraid to speak. Perhaps this wasn't the positive development he'd hoped it to be.

Scout shoved him toward the steel door without another look at Frank. Otter stumbled the first few steps. His legs were cramped and stiff from the cold confinement. Once they were through the door, Scout slammed it shut.

Frank tried to cover himself with the coats and sleeping bag, wondering if he or Otter was now in the more enviable position.

"I want to know everything there is to know about your previous dealings with Hunter," Scout said without preamble as she shoved Otter forward in the tunnel toward the living room.

So that's why I'm getting the special treatment, Otter thought. *This might not be such a good thing,* he realized. *Especially if she thinks I was once any friend of Hunter's. Or if I'm only useful to her as long as I can tell her something she wants to know.* His mind worked feverishly on how to respond.

"Evan Garner sent us on a job together once. Her, me, and a kid. This was years ago. I got to know her pretty good. How she thinks, how she plans." Otter exaggerated his knowledge of Hunter in an effort to prolong his value to the stranger. But he also had to make sure she knew he was no friend. "The job went off without a hitch, but the damn bitch left without me. I ended up in prison for seven years because of her."

"This kid," Scout said, as they entered the living room, "What was his name?"

"Kenny. I think he was only like seventeen or eighteen, but really smart—" Otter's words were cut off when he was shoved violently forward.

The woman behind him shrieked.

Otter lost his footing and fell hard on his shoulder. He saw Scout rush to the pantry. The door to it stood open.

"Damn it!" Scout cursed. Her eyes scanned the pantry floor,

taking in the open handcuffs and the rope. "How the hell did they get away?"

"They?" Otter wondered aloud from his place on the floor. This couldn't be good. Hunter had apparently escaped, and this woman was not at all happy about it.

Scout turned toward his voice. "Shut up. Shut up and let me think. They can't have gotten far." She pocketed her knife and pulled out her gun before checking the bedroom and bathroom. She slipped her coveralls back on, donned her balaclava and gloves, and was out the door.

As soon as she was gone, Otter stumbled to his feet. His eyes darted around the room, looking for some means to get out of the handcuffs. The kitchen.

He got several cabinet doors open with his teeth. Plates, glasses, mugs, pots and pans, spices. He tried to open a couple of drawers the same way, but most were too heavy to budge. The one he was able to open was a shallow junk drawer, containing a mishmash of utensils and assorted odds and ends. He stared at the contents, seeking something small enough to fit into the handcuff locks.

Scout entered the tunnel and headed straight up the emergency exit, believing it to be the only way the two women could have escaped the bunker while she was in the generator room. She struggled for a few minutes with the hatch, not realizing it was locked. Then she had to figure out the odd locking mechanism. Finally she had it open. She scanned the area around her with her flashlight, looking for tracks.

There were none. The pristine surface of white from the new snowfall was unmarred.

What the hell?

❖

Otter froze when the door crashed open again and Scout came

through it, cursing. She turned in his direction with an angry scowl. All around him, cabinet doors stood open like accusing sentinels.

"What do you think you're doing? Didn't you understand me when I said I will kill you if you try anything?" She pulled out her knife as she came around the kitchen counter toward him.

Otter retreated until his back was against the sink. He didn't at all like the crazy look in her eyes. "Take it easy, I'm sorry. I was just trying to find something to get myself a drink," he lied.

She stopped in front of him and cocked her head as if she was considering what to do with him. She twirled the knife in her hand.

Otter didn't like her obvious familiarity with the weapon. He had to do something. "Look, if Hunter's escaped, I can help you look for her," he offered.

She seemed to consider this for several moments. Finally she nodded as she pocketed her knife and pulled out her 9mm. "Turn around."

Otter obeyed.

She placed the gun against the back of his neck. "I presume I don't need to remind you how I want you to behave?"

"No, I'm clear. No trouble." The gun remained pressed against Otter's neck as the cuffs were unlocked. He brought his hands slowly in front of him to rub his sore wrists, but even when the cold metal was removed from his neck, he did not move until she acknowledged he could.

"Okay, turn around," Scout said.

Otter slowly pivoted to face her.

She was still pointing the gun at him, but she'd backed up several feet. She tossed him Kat's key ring. "Unlock the other guy and both of you start searching every inch of this place. They're either hiding somewhere or there's another entrance than the two we know about. If you find them, come get me. I want to be the one to take care of Katarzyna...Hunter."

Katarzyna? This woman knows Hunter's real name? Otter was impressed. Though he didn't want to make her angry, he wanted to know what he was up against if he was going to be searching unarmed. "Uh...the other one we're looking for, that's Scout, right?"

"No, moron. I'm Scout. You're searching for Hunter and her little blond girlfriend. Just get going." She waved him toward the door with the gun. "The code to the steel door is 8-9-7-7."

Otter took off at a trot.

After he had gone, Scout went to the monitors and looked for tracks leading from the bunker. Nothing. She turned on the computer to see if there was an update from Kenny. *If she's hiding, this friend will be useful to flush her out.*

Kenny had indeed responded to what he thought was Hunter's missive. **Understand urgency. Will be at your location 11 am with cash.**

Scout looked at her watch. It was 2:00 a.m. Nine more hours. She'd have liked it to be sooner, but it would have to do.

She stripped off her coveralls and emptied the pockets of weapons. She stuck her own gun in the front of her jeans and pocketed her knife. She locked in the desk the rest of the guns and ammunition she'd taken off Kat.

Scout examined the room she was in. The concrete walls and floors seemed unmarred by lines. That decreased the areas she would need to search for a secret portal. Her eyes fell on the bookcases. *That's a possibility.* The kitchen, the pantry, the shower, around the bed, the monitor wall—they were also areas that would need to be gone over carefully. And she'd need to get another look at the tunnel.

Scout decided to start her search in the pantry, where she had last seen the women. She began pulling shelves out, spilling what was left on them onto the floor.

As Otter ran through the tunnel, his eyes fell on Hunter's toolbox. He considered taking a wrench or hammer from it. He didn't like the idea of flushing out Hunter without a weapon. But then he remembered the monitors and worried Scout might see him do it. *Better wait.* At least he was out of the handcuffs and free to move around.

Otter punched in the code Scout had given him and went

through the steel door. He walked over to Frank, jingling the keys in his hand.

"Here's the deal," Otter said, freeing Frank. "Hunter got away somehow, along with some girlfriend of hers that was in there. That blond chick who broke in and captured them—that's Scout, but don't ask me to explain it. I haven't a clue. She's pissed as hell they're gone, so I talked her into setting us free to search for how they got out or where they're hiding. We're not supposed to try to take 'em. Scout wants to be the one to kill Hunter."

Frank got to his feet and massaged his wrists and forearms. "I ain't in no hurry to kill Hunter."

"We better do what this broad says," Otter said, heading toward the tunnel. "She's got a hell of a temper and says she'll kill us if we try anything. I believe she means it. Still," he said, waiting for Frank to join him, "doesn't mean we can't look for an opportunity."

They were nearly to the living room when they heard a shout from within. They hurried toward it.

Scout found nothing useful in the pantry. The place was in ruins by the time she was finished. She stepped back into the living room, perspiring heavily from her efforts. She listened for a minute but could hear no noise from within the bunker save for the soft hum of the refrigerator. Her frustration was growing with every moment. "I'll find you," she shouted, hoping the two women were within earshot. "The longer it takes, the worse it will be for you!"

She heard running footsteps in response to her plea, but it was only Frank and Otter. They froze when they came through the door and saw her, gun in hand, her face red and her anger palpable.

"Get to work!" she ordered. "Find them!"

Otter sprang into action, hustling toward the bedroom because it was away from her.

Frank followed his lead and darted into the bathroom.

Scout eyed the wall of bookshelves and moved toward it, looking for something unusual or out of place. The shelves extended from floor to ceiling and were filled with hundreds of books.

Nearing them, she saw that Katarzyna had carefully arranged them by topic and author, as meticulous as any library. She grunted in satisfaction as she began ripping them from the shelves.

CHAPTER FORTY-TWO

Evan Garner approached me after I'd won the national karate title," Kat said, tightening her arms around Riley. The recollection of her most painful memories was eased by the comforting proximity of her friend.

"He invited me for coffee. Said he had a proposition for me." She took a deep breath. "He told me he worked for the government and was always on the lookout for young people with an aptitude for what he called 'extraordinary achievements.' He looked the part: clean cut, blue suit, a flashy ID that said Justice Department. He'd found out a lot about me—what I'd studied, and even that I had no next of kin listed on any of my enrollment forms. He didn't know who I really was, though. Only the headmistress at the boarding school I'd attended knew that, and she had vowed to seal the records.

"Anyway," Kat continued, "Garner told me he wanted to send me to a special school to learn to be an operative for the government. I'd be trained in weapons, infiltration techniques, close-quarter combat. It was attractive to me, because I thought I could use those skills to do the one thing that I'd been dreaming about for years. Kill the men who murdered my father.

"So I went to the Academy and learned several different ways to kill people, among other things. By this time I trusted Garner, so I told him who I really was and what I wanted to do. Somehow he found the men who killed my father. And he made all the arrangements so I could get in and out of Cyprus safely. I got my revenge. And then I owed Garner. I started to work for him."

As she opened her mouth to continue, they heard Scout's

muffled shout through the wall. It was just loud enough to be able to make out the words. "I'll find you," the voice shrieked. "The longer it takes, the worse it will be for you!"

A shiver ran up Riley's spine at the words. She once again envisioned Sam's brutal murder.

Kat felt the tension in the other woman's body. She stroked Riley's hair. "Don't worry, you're safe here."

They listened for another minute or two but could hear no more voices from outside the hidden chamber.

But Kat's sensitive hearing did pick up something, although it took her several seconds to identify what it was. Faint noises a few feet down the wall from where they lay. "Stay still and keep quiet," she whispered. She took a moment to wrap the thin survival blanket around Riley before she crept toward the area where the sounds originated.

Kat put her ear to the wall. Indistinct but steady sounds. Moving slowly down the wall at knee height. *She's pulling books off the shelves.*

It wasn't that Kat didn't expect this might happen, but she didn't think Scout would be quite so quick about it. Kat went to one of her safes and pulled out her MP5 submachine gun, which was capable of firing single shots, three-shot bursts, or full automatic fire—800 rounds per minute.

She loaded the MP5 and slung the strap across her shoulder before returning to the wall. The sounds had moved higher—about to the height of Kat's head. They were still moving steadily down the length of the wall. Kat thought she heard a muffled curse from the other side but couldn't be certain. Abruptly, the sounds stopped.

When the noises hadn't resumed after a minute, Kat returned to Riley.

"What's happening? Can you tell?"

"Scout was pulling books off the shelves looking for us, but she's stopped now. My guess is she's done all she can reach. The latch is a couple of shelves higher." Kat laid the submachine gun on the concrete floor and scooped Riley up, blanket and all.

"I want you over in the corner," she whispered. "Away from the door." Kat set Riley down so she was sitting up with her back against the wall. She opened the blanket and removed the bulletproof vest. "I want you to put this on," she said, then realized the cast was too big to get through the armhole. "That's no good," she amended. "Well, put your right arm through, anyway," she prompted, and Riley complied. The vest was very big on her and could be closed over the cast if Riley just kept her injured arm at her side, pinned against her body. It was snug and uncomfortable, but Kat hoped it wouldn't be for very long.

"Kat, you should wear it. You'll be in more danger than I will," Riley pleaded.

"No arguments. I'll be distracted less if I know you're as safe as I can make you." Kat's head jerked abruptly back toward the wall when the faint sounds resumed, several inches higher. "Keep very quiet," she whispered. She picked up the MP5 and moved to the door. She put the gun on full automatic. *Shouldn't be long now.*

It took Frank only a few minutes to thoroughly search the bathroom. But he lingered there, pacing back and forth, trying to think of a way out of this mess. He could hear Scout's grunts of rage and frustration from the living room, along with the muted cadence of books hitting the floor or crashing against the wall. Every now and then, he'd stick his head out of the door to watch her.

Scout attacked the bookshelves with single-minded fury until the living room was in chaos. Books were scattered everywhere. Torn pages littered the floor. The coffee table and easy chair were overturned. And almost everything breakable—Kat's cameras, the photographs on the walls—had been smashed into bits.

The bunker grew silent.

Frank peeked out of the bathroom doorway.

Scout stood before the bookshelves, breathing heavily.

"Get in here!" she commanded.

Otter appeared in the bedroom doorway as Frank emerged

from the bathroom. They glanced at each other, and Otter started to speak, but Scout cut him off.

"Anything?"

The men shook their heads.

"You!" she gestured to the taller man with her gun. "What's your name again?"

"Frank."

"Come over here and pull out the rest of these. Look for a way through the wall," she ordered, waving the gun toward the bookshelves. Only the top two still contained books. The rest were empty.

Frank negotiated his way through the disarray and began clearing the lower of the two shelves, dropping the books on the floor. He glanced over his shoulder as Scout plopped down onto the couch behind him. Small beads of sweat glistened on her forehead.

She turned toward Otter, who leaned against the bedroom door frame watching her. "You. Go search the kitchen."

Otter nodded and headed toward it. He had to briefly pass behind her, and she watched him as he did.

It was while Scout's attention was on Otter that Frank began clearing the top shelf. He had to reach above his head. He removed *The Secret Garden*, and his fingertips lightly grazed the button that unlocked the hidden door.

Chapter Forty-Three

Frank's eyes widened and he froze, just for a moment, when he realized what he'd likely found.

Scout didn't see it. By the time she looked back at Frank, he was progressing on down the wall as if nothing had happened.

Frank got to the end, removed the last book, and turned toward Scout. He could tell she'd not noticed that he'd found what they were searching for. He shrugged. "Nothing," he said, just a little too loudly. "I don't think they're back there."

Scout waved the gun toward the desk. "Try over there. See if those monitors come out of the wall."

Frank nodded and did as he was told. *Now what do I do with this interesting little bit of information?*

Kat's hearing was hypersensitive by the time the faint sounds neared the location of the button that would expose them. She pressed her ear against the panel. The sounds seemed to pause there briefly, but then continued on. She faintly heard Frank's voice and realized it had been he who had been removing the books. He told Scout he'd not found anything, yet she was fairly certain he had. *What are you up to?*

Kat remained where she was for several more minutes until it seemed the immediate threat had passed. She heard nothing more from the outer room. She kept the submachine gun with her but returned to Riley's side.

"We need to be quiet now. Try to rest," she whispered as she sat down and put her arm around Riley.

Riley leaned into the crook of Kat's shoulder and closed her eyes, letting her exhaustion overtake her.

Kat remained vigilant, the MP5 on the floor beside her.

As she drifted off, Riley thought about the life she'd had and what she wanted now. She wondered what else there was to Kat's story. *And what do you want, Kat, when we get out of this? We have so much to talk about,* she wanted to say, but she was too far into sleep to speak.

Kat should have been plotting their escape, but her mind was preoccupied with Riley. There was still so much she hadn't told her. Kat hadn't admitted that much of what Garner initially had told her had been a lie. She hadn't worked for the government. Not officially. She was one of a group of expendable, anonymous trained killers assigned to jobs that neither law enforcement nor the military could do.

Some of the money for Garner's group surely came from government coffers, but she also got assignments that were paybacks. Hits financed by rich individuals who had scores to settle but couldn't get their own hands dirty.

She'd taken the assignments until she'd felt she'd long paid her debt to Garner. Then she went freelance so she could make her own decisions on what jobs she would take. Only targets who were dangerous and unredeemable. People who had done things that earned them no mercy.

Garner had exploded when she told him her decision. His tirade and threats of retribution finally made her see that he was not the father figure she'd believed, but a manipulator who cared only about how her talents could be exploited. After she left his office that day, she dropped out of sight.

Apparently her former mentor had now decided to make good on his threats and make her an example to others who wanted to leave. The contract on her life was only a surprise because of its timing. More than five years had elapsed since she'd left Garner's employ. *Why now, Evan?*

Kat's attention was diverted by a muffled clatter from the other room. It had a discordant musicality to it, and she realized with a heartsick certainty that her prized cello had become the latest target of Scout's rage.

❖

By 5:00 a.m., Scout was ready to give in to exhaustion. She hadn't slept in nearly two days. Her anger over having been outsmarted had initially kept her focused on the search for the two women. But she was struggling to keep her eyes open, and she couldn't stop yawning. She needed sleep. She couldn't afford to be careless.

Frank and Otter sat on the couch, having just completed a third search of the tunnel. Otter leaned back and closed his eyes. Frank eyed Scout warily, awaiting her next orders.

She stood with her back to the bookshelves, her head less than five feet from the button that would admit her to the hidden room.

Frank resisted the temptation to look toward the spot.

"I want you two to go outside and search for tracks. Get warm stuff on, you'll be out there a while." She nodded toward the tunnel.

The men suited up, and Scout handed Otter a flashlight.

"Up there." She pointed toward the emergency exit with her gun.

He started climbing.

"I'll keep an eye on the monitors," she called up to Otter as he exited the hatch. "Come back in two hours unless you find something earlier."

"All right."

Scout turned to Frank. "Go up and lock the hatch. You're going out the other way."

He did as instructed.

When he returned, Scout motioned Frank toward the generator room. She punched in the code to open the outer door, shielding the panel from him so he would not know how to get back in. "Two hours." She handed him a flashlight and shut the door behind him.

She returned to the living room and went to the monitors. Both men were still in camera range near the exits, as though reluctant to wander far from the bunker. Scout didn't think they'd find anything. She was convinced the two women were hiding somewhere inside. But the men's absence would at least allow her to rest. Her hopes now hinged on the arrival of Katarzyna's friend in less than six hours. Perhaps Kenny would be incentive enough for her quarry to come out of hiding.

Scout went into the bedroom and locked the door. She lay down on the bed for a short nap, gun in hand. *If that doesn't work, I know something else I bet will. Fire.* She didn't want to resort to it unless she had to. Scout wanted her enemy to know who she really was and how clever she had been. And she wanted the satisfaction of seeing Katarzyna's face as she died.

Fire would be much too quick.

Frank and Otter spent several minutes checking around the exits before ranging farther with their flashlights. Neither worried about being able to find his way back. It had stopped snowing, and the tracks they made were easy to follow. Both remembered how to get from one exit to the other, so they worked their way toward each other.

Frank had no intention, at least not yet, of divulging where he believed Hunter was hiding. Still, his attitude toward Otter had softened somewhat since they had been chained together, and he wanted to see if the other man had any ideas.

Otter knew his chances of getting out of this were greatly increased if he and Frank worked together.

The two men were drawn to each other's flashlight beams and met under the shelter of a large evergreen.

"Find anything?" Otter asked.

"Nothing. You?"

"Nah. I don't think they got out. But damned if I can figure out where they went, either. Hunter's got a hell of a hiding place." The cold air was helping Otter fight off the drowsiness that had threatened to overtake him in the bunker. "I'm worried about what Blondie's gonna do when she accepts she ain't going to find 'em. She's nuts."

Frank nodded.

"And she'll have no further use for us," Otter added.

"Yeah, I thought about that, too. Got any ideas?"

"I'd like to just take off right now," Otter said. "But I had a hard enough time getting here. Without a snowmobile and a path to follow, I don't like our chances in this cold. I have to say this—Hunter picked a good spot to hide."

"Yeah," Frank answered. "I haven't a clue how to get out of here either. And if we tried, Scout could track us down pretty easy if she wanted to."

"So that's out," Otter agreed. "At least for now. I looked for a map while we were searching but didn't find one. I did grab this." He pulled a large crescent wrench from the pocket of his coveralls. "I'll hit her if I get a chance. But she's been pretty careful."

"Yeah. I've been wondering if she sent us out here just to get rid of us. You don't think she'll keep us locked out, do you?" Frank asked.

"Who knows with that broad? I think we should look for a chance to jump her when we get back in. We could load up a couple of snowmobiles with food, water, and extra gas. It'll be light soon. Easier to see where we're going even if we don't know what direction to take. We gotta hit a house or somethin' eventually."

Frank nodded. "Okay. I'm with you." He thought it a reasonable plan if they could overpower Scout. But he would also look for a chance to use the information he had. He hoped Scout wasn't even now rechecking the bookshelves, but he thought it unlikely.

The men split up and resumed their search of the woods around the bunker. At 7:00 a.m., as the sun was coming up, each man returned to the exit he'd used and waited to be let back in.

A half hour passed.

Then an hour.

Still no Scout.

Both men fidgeted impatiently, wondering whether she did indeed intend to leave them there outside in the cold to fend for themselves.

Scout awoke groggy. She glanced at her watch, surprised she had slept so deeply and so long. It was nearly 10:00, and Kenny was due in an hour. She stretched. Her stomach rumbled loudly. She couldn't remember the last time she'd eaten anything.

She went into the living room and glanced at the monitors. Frank leaned against the rock wall, waiting to be let back in. Otter was nowhere to be seen, but the area around the hatch was well trampled with footprints. She wondered whether he'd been dumb enough to take off, but decided it really didn't matter.

She threaded her way through the books on the floor and made her way to the kitchen. A little breakfast, then she'd think about whether she had any further use for Frank.

Riley had napped, but fitfully. Her fears and anxiety kept her from truly restful sleep. She lay on her back on the floor, Kat's lap her pillow.

Kat had forced herself to remain alert despite her overwhelming fatigue. The lack of any further noise from the room outside worried her. She couldn't believe Scout would be content to just wait for her to show herself. Unless...Frank had told her where they were?

CHAPTER FORTY-FOUR

Kenny pulled up the collar of his overcoat. The helicopter had a small heater, but it was not enough to fight off the bitter chill that seeped in around the door to his right. He had Hunter's $400,000 in a large duffel bag behind his seat.

Kenny didn't particularly like helicopters, but he was happy to be able to do something for Hunter. She rarely asked for more than a little information now and then. When Hunter left Garner's employ, she took Kenny with her—secreting him away to a safe location several states away and setting him up in his own computer consulting business. She financed everything until the business took off, and refused all offers of repayment.

Kenny glanced at the pilot, an ex-Navy man who'd been recommended by one of his military contacts. He'd been told the man was trustworthy enough to do a job without asking questions and would keep his mouth shut. But Kenny still was cautious. He had been entrusted with very sensitive information. He'd given the man only a set of GPS coordinates and told him they were to make a delivery and pickup, nothing more.

They were in a four-seat Bell Jet Ranger helicopter, flying low over a sparsely populated wooded area. Kenny looked at his watch and spoke into his headset. "How much farther?"

"We should be there in another hour," the pilot answered. "Maybe a little less."

Kenny nodded. They were making better time than he'd predicted and would arrive at their destination at least a half hour early.

❖

Otter was convinced Scout meant to leave them in the cold. After waiting outside the hatch for more than two and a half hours, he made his way to the other entrance to meet up with Frank.

As he neared the rock wall, Otter saw the big man with his back to the sun-warmed surface, his eyes closed. *How can he doze off standing up? Must be even more exhausted than I am.* "Hey, Frank."

Frank opened his eyes and stretched.

"How can you sleep? You're not worried she's going to leave us out here?"

Frank studied Otter a moment and bit back a sharp retort. It wouldn't help for them to carp at each other right now. Sure, he was worried. But he was also more tired than he could ever remember being. "Yeah," he finally answered. "Sure beginning to look like she isn't gonna let us back in. Think we should start walking?"

"I don't think we have any other choice." Otter looked around. "I think I came in that way." He pointed. He remembered his approach on the snowmobile, his headlights shining directly onto the rock wall.

"Yeah, that seems right."

Both men grew silent, staring out at the endless landscape of trees and snow.

Otter was remembering the trail to the bunker. It had taken all sorts of crazy twists and turns. There were boggy areas and lots of hills.

Frank had the same pictures in his head. He wondered how they'd ever find their way to the road on foot.

"Let's do it, then," Otter said, setting off.

Frank pushed off from the rock wall and followed him.

They had gone only forty feet or so when a sound behind them made them both spin around. Scout stood in the entrance grinning at them, gun in hand. "Going somewhere, gentlemen?"

They glanced at each other and headed back toward the bunker. Otter jammed his right hand into the pocket of his jacket and wrapped his fingers around the crescent wrench. *Just let me close enough, bitch.* He hated the smug smile she had on her face as she watched them. She was as bad as Hunter.

She backed up as they neared her, as if she knew Otter's intentions. "So, I take it you didn't find anything?"

"No," Otter said, a little too sharply.

Frank shook his head.

Scout was about to close the door when her hand froze over the keypad.

"What's the matter?" Otter asked.

"Quiet!" she barked. She ran to the generator and shut it off. The lights went out as the drone from the machine died, but Scout could still see the men clearly by the sunlight streaming in through the open doorway.

Now all three could hear the unmistakable sound of a helicopter. It was still some distance away but drawing closer.

Kat found the MP5 by her side within just a few seconds of the lights going out. She hadn't expected this. The darkness didn't really bother her, but it would make it more difficult to protect Riley. And she didn't know if Scout now had Otter and Frank working with her, and that complicated things.

She moved Riley's head from her lap so she could stand, and Riley woke up.

"Kat? What's happening?"

"Not sure. Someone's shut off the generator." Her hand found Riley's and squeezed it. "Don't move."

Kat picked up the MP5 and made her way to the wall.

She put her ear to the panel and listened.

Scout stood in the doorway of the generator room, trying to spot the helicopter. The trees around the bunker entrance made it impossible to see anything that wasn't almost directly overhead. The sound grew louder and seemed to come from her right.

In her reconnaissance of the area, Scout had seen a clearing in that direction—undoubtedly the GPS coordinates that Hunter had given to Kenny. Scout glanced at her watch. *You're early.* A sound from behind her made her wheel around just in time to see a flash of metal aimed at her head.

Otter knew when he heard the helicopter that it would provide his best chance to overpower Scout. Her attention was on the approaching chopper, and the noise would help conceal his effort to creep up behind her.

He spared a quick glance toward Frank, but the other man was too far away and was staring out the door. It was now or never.

Otter closed the distance to the blonde. He withdrew the wrench just as she glanced at her watch.

He swung at her, but Scout ducked and the wrench glanced off her forehead. Otter brought the weapon up again as she twisted away from him, but she was faster than he was. Before he could connect a second time, Scout kicked him hard in the groin.

Otter crumpled to the floor with a groan. The tool slipped from his fingers. He grimaced and struggled to his knees. When he looked up at her again, she was pointing her gun at him.

Scout was breathing hard. Blood trickled down her face.

"Stupid shit," Otter heard her say, just before she pulled the trigger.

Chapter Forty-Five

Otter felt a flash of heat in his thigh and looked down in horror to see a hole in his pants, blood already forming a dark stain around it. He looked up at Scout. His mouth worked but no words came out.

Scout brushed a trickle of blood from her eye before aiming the gun at Otter again.

She fired into his other leg.

He screamed.

Scout turned to Frank. "Don't move." She took off in the direction of the clearing. The sound of the helicopter was very close.

Frank stepped over to Otter.

Otter lay as he'd fallen, one leg skewed awkwardly beneath him. He was still conscious. He groaned. "Help me."

Despite his initial disdain for the other man, Frank felt a certain kinship with Otter now because of all they had suffered together. He didn't think he could just leave him to bleed to death.

Frank glanced around the room. Scout had left the steel door to the tunnel open. Now might be his only chance to get to the hidden room and warn Hunter. But if Scout came back and caught him, he would surely get the same treatment as Otter. Or worse.

His mind made up, Frank fished his flashlight from his pocket and went into the tunnel. He came back with a couple of long scarves and wrapped them tightly around Otter's wounds. The two bullets had passed through, and the wounds were bleeding heavily. The scarves would not be enough for long. But Scout apparently had missed the major arteries. There was no copious spurting of blood that Frank knew from experience meant certain death. Perhaps Otter had a chance.

Frank snatched up his flashlight and ran to the living room. Stumbling over the piles of books on the floor, he went to the bookshelves. "Hunter, it's Frank," he shouted. "I know you're in there, but I won't give you away. Scout's outside, meeting a helicopter. She'll be back soon. I have to get back, but I'll help you if I can. Oh—and she shot Otter, he might not make it." He waited just a moment, hoping for a response.

When none came, he went into the bathroom and grabbed gauze, tape, and antibiotic ointment, stuffing them into his pockets. Then he detoured into the bedroom to pull the sheet from the bed. He returned to the generator room and crouched beside Otter.

Scout was nowhere in sight.

Blood had already soaked through the makeshift bandages, and Otter's face was pale. He seemed to be in shock.

Frank took off the scarves and made thick compresses of gauze to put over the wounds, coating them liberally with ointment and binding them tightly with long strips he ripped from the sheet. He lifted Otter and placed him on the sleeping bag. He covered him with the heavy coats they'd huddled under together and shoved his hat under Otter's head. It was all that he knew to do. He noticed after a few minutes that his first-aid efforts seemed to have slowed the blood loss.

"Don't move around. You'll bleed more if you do." Frank wasn't sure if the wounded man could hear him.

Otter's eyes were closed. He wasn't moving.

Kat had her ear pinned against the panel when Frank's voice broke the silence. She heard him nearly as clearly as if he were standing in the room with her. She could read the tone of his voice, and she believed he meant every word he said.

So a helicopter is coming, Kat thought. *Scout's way out of here? Reinforcements from Garner?* Another option was even more disturbing. Kenny? *Did she get into the computer and summon Kenny? Oh Jesus. No.*

❖

Scout was oblivious to any pain from the cut on her forehead but aware enough of the wound to take the right precautions before she met the helicopter. She didn't want to alarm its occupants prematurely. She washed her face with wet snow and pulled her black balaclava over her head. Only her eyes were visible.

She saw the chopper through the trees, coming down in the clearing. She put her right hand in her pocket and curled her fingers around the grip of her 9mm. *There are getting to be entirely too many witnesses.*

For a while in her pursuit of Katarzyna, it hadn't mattered to Scout what happened to her—she would even have died if she'd had to, as long as Katarzyna paid dearly for killing her brother and her friends. But now with the money she'd be getting, she decided she might want to stick around after all.

With a little swing in her step, Scout walked toward the helicopter as it touched down and the engine was cut. The massive blades began to slow. She waved as she approached the pilot's side.

The pilot opened his door and smiled at her.

But instead of speaking to him, she addressed the man in the other seat. She had to talk loudly to be heard over the sound of the dying rotors. "Are you Kenny?"

"Yes," he confirmed. "Where's Hunter?"

Scout turned toward the pilot. Her right hand came out of her pocket, too fast for him to react. "I won't be needing you."

She put the gun to his head and pulled the trigger.

CHAPTER FORTY-SIX

Kenny flinched as the gun went off. Blood and brain matter splattered the interior of the copter. Kenny was covered with it—his face, neck, the front of his coat. It had happened so fast it took him a moment to register what had happened. He recoiled in horror at the sight of the pilot's head. Half of it was missing. Then he turned to look at Scout, his mouth open and his eyes wide.

Scout leveled the gun at Kenny's forehead.

He raised his hands. They were shaking. "Please. I'll do whatever you say," he managed. His throat was dry. "And forget I ever saw you," he added. *Where the hell is Hunter?*

"You might be useful," Scout said, pulling off her balaclava. Her wound had nearly stopped bleeding, but dried blood clung to her hair. "Did you bring the money?"

"Yes. It's behind the seat, in the duffel."

"Do you have any weapons? Any in the chopper?" she asked.

"No. Not that I know of," Kenny said.

Scout reached in to the copter and grabbed the keys. "Okay. Come around to this side and pull his body out." She nodded toward the pilot and backed away from the chopper. "Put him over there." She motioned with the gun toward a large fir tree.

While Kenny took care of the odious task, Scout grabbed the duffel bag and opened it. Inside were neat stacks of currency. Packets of $100 bills, bound by bank bands that read $10,000. She smiled. *You can buy a lot of trouble with this kind of cash.* She searched the bag for a weapon before zipping it shut again.

When he finished with the pilot, Kenny tried to wipe the blood and brain bits from his face, head, and neck with snow. The smell of it made him nauseous.

"Let's go," Scout barked. "That way." She gestured toward the tracks she'd made from the bunker.

Kenny started in that direction. She lagged several feet behind.

"How well do you know Hunter?" she asked after they had taken a couple of steps.

Kenny started to turn around to answer, but her voice stopped him before he got halfway.

"Keep walking."

"She's a-a friend," Kenny replied. Volunteer nothing, Hunter had always told him. Suddenly he realized who the woman behind him was. *Scout.* She fit the description perfectly. Then he remembered something else. *Has a thing for knives.* Kenny swallowed hard.

"I want to hear everything," her voice said from behind him. An audible click followed her statement.

Kenny glanced over his shoulder. His stomach dropped out from under him.

Scout's left hand held her gun. Her right now casually twirled a very wicked-looking switchblade knife.

Frank spotted them approaching through the woods. He tried to make out the man in the lead. *Friend of Scout's?* he wondered. Frank positioned himself in front of Otter, trying to shield him from view. He hoped Scout wouldn't notice the bandages.

When they got closer, Frank could see stains on the man's coat. Bloodstains, he realized. Just then, Scout stepped out from behind the newcomer, and Frank saw the gun and knife she held on him. *Nope, he's no friend.* The man didn't seem injured, so Frank wondered whose blood it was that covered his overcoat. This wasn't good at all.

❖

During their short walk from the chopper to the bunker, Kenny kept talking but tried to offer only vague, innocuous information. He told Scout he'd known Hunter for a few years, but not very well. He admitted they'd worked together but volunteered no details. He said their contact was mostly via computer and not face-to-face. He told her he hadn't actually seen Hunter in "quite some time."

Scout didn't prod for more. In fact, she hadn't said another word as he'd rambled on about Hunter. Kenny's apprehension grew with each step as he thought of the knife and wondered what had happened to his friend.

As Kenny stepped into the bunker, he blinked several times, adjusting from the bright sunlight to the relative darkness of the generator room. His eyes met Frank's.

Scout was behind Kenny, so Frank risked a quick nod to the newcomer—a signal of camaraderie he hoped the man could understand.

Kenny's eyes widened slightly, then he blinked his eyes in a slow, deliberate motion in return. *And who the hell are you?* he wondered.

Scout stepped from behind Kenny and glanced at Frank, then to the floor behind him. "What have you been up to?" She motioned with the gun for him to step aside. Scout stared down at Otter. She kicked away the coat that covered him to expose the bandages around his legs. "Well you're a regular Florence Nightingale, aren't you, Frank? How touching."

Frank didn't reply.

Scout turned the generator back on, restoring lights and power, and shut the outside door. She kept her distance from Kenny and Frank. She couldn't be careless now. She was too close. The helicopter parked outside marked the location of the bunker, so she needed to wrap this up before anyone else showed up looking to collect on Garner's contract.

"Okay, let's go," she said, motioning the two of them toward the steel door. "Time to end this game of hide-and-seek. Now is when the real fun begins."

❖

Kat was startled by the sudden restoration of light. But she didn't move from her spot, keeping her ear pressed against the panel that separated the weapons chamber and the living room. She wished she'd installed a peephole when she'd put in the secret room, but she'd never expected to be hiding in it.

She turned her head to look at Riley, still propped in the corner farthest from the door.

Riley watched Kat, awake and alert now, both women sensing an impending showdown.

They exchanged resolute smiles, their prolonged eye contact reaffirming the depth of their desire for each other.

Scout's voice, muted but audible, broke the silence. "Come out, come out, wherever you are," she shouted in the singsong manner of children in a schoolyard.

Her next words were spoken in a much different tone. Shrill, angry, and out of patience. "If you don't reveal yourself, Katarzyna, I'll have to start taking out my frustration on your buddy Kenny here."

Scout put her gun to Kenny's head. They stood in the middle of the living room, his back to her, his arms in the air. She didn't expect an immediate response. But she was alert. Her eyes scanned the perimeter of the room.

Frank was seated several feet away on the couch watching them, fighting a persistent urge to glance at the bookshelves.

After a minute or two of tense waiting, Scout addressed Frank. "Get the desk chair over here."

He obeyed, pushing the wheeled chair the last few feet to avoid getting too close to her.

Scout shoved Kenny into the seat.

"Get me the handcuffs and rope from in there," she told Frank, nodding toward the pantry.

He found them and tossed them to her, then backed away again.

"Hands behind you," she snapped at Kenny.

He complied, wrapping them around the back of the chair.

Scout fastened the handcuffs and tied Kenny's legs together with the rope. There wasn't enough of it to also bind him to the chair.

She turned her attention to Frank.

He was hard to read. He'd worn the same neutral expression all along. And he hadn't leapt in to help Otter try to overpower her. He hadn't tried anything at all. In fact, he had been careful not to.

Scout reached the same assessment Kat had of the man. He was an enforcer. A guy who didn't take chances and who followed orders. Probably any orders, at the right price.

Scout stepped to the kitchen counter, where she had set the duffel full of money, and motioned to Frank to join her.

"You've seen what I can do," she said.

He nodded.

"I might be able to use you. If I can trust you."

"I'm your man," he said.

Scout reached into the bag and pulled out two stacks of bills.

She handed them to Frank, whose eyes widened in surprise. He shoved them into his pockets.

"You're gonna take care of Hunter's friend." She moved to stand in front of Kenny.

Kenny tried to remain calm. He didn't want her to see how afraid he was. But his heart was pounding in his chest.

"Babysit him. If he moves, stop him. Like this." Scout raised her gun and brought it down against the side of Kenny's face.

Kenny tried to duck, but she connected with enough force to make his vision swim. He groaned. Blood trickled from a cut on his cheekbone. Grimacing against the pain, he averted his eyes.

"Convince him it would be extremely foolish to try to get away," she continued, smiling down at Kenny. "You can hit him as hard as you like. Just make sure he's still able to talk."

"And Frank," she added, finally turning away from Kenny to look at the big man, "if you try to help him or get away yourself, I'll make your death most unpleasant." She said it so matter-of-factly that Frank's palms began to sweat.

"I understand."

"If you do as you're told," she promised, "you'll get more cash, one of the snowmobiles...and you get to leave here alive."

Frank nodded.

"Okay, let's see what you can do." She nodded toward Kenny as she stepped back.

Frank looked at her, momentarily confused. Then her intent became clear. A cruel test. One he had to pass convincingly. Frank stepped in front of Kenny and put his back to Scout. As he did, Kenny's eyes rose to meet his.

Frank tried to convey apology in his expression as he brought his hand back and balled it into a fist. He slammed it into Kenny's midsection with enough force to knock the wind out of him and cause one hell of an impressive bruise later. But Frank had pulled the punch enough not to break any ribs or damage any internal organs. One thing he knew was how to hit someone.

Kenny slumped over and gasped for air.

Frank glanced at Scout as he brought back his fist again. "Want me to hit him some more?" he asked with a half smile.

Scout laughed. "Maybe later," she said. "I get my turn first."

Kat strained to hear what was happening on the other side of the door. She was faced with an impossible choice. She would gladly have sacrificed herself for Kenny if that were the only decision she had to make. But to reveal their hiding place would probably do nothing to save her friend. She was pretty sure Scout would kill him anyway to leave no witnesses.

No, she couldn't come out. To do so would put Riley in Scout's hands as well. She couldn't watch both of them die.

Her hands clenched into fists as she imagined what Scout might do to Kenny. When Kat pictured him, she still saw the face of the boy he'd once been. Though they e-mailed each other frequently, they had not seen each other in several years. He'd come all the way out here, put himself at risk because of their friendship. Could she listen to him being tortured and do nothing?

CHAPTER FORTY-SEVEN

Kenny fought to catch his breath. He knew Frank could have hit him much harder. He had seen the look of regret in Frank's eyes, and he felt a glimmer of hope at the realization. His cheek still throbbed from Scout's brutal assault, but he was determined to endure whatever the woman had planned for him. He didn't want Hunter to risk her life to save him.

❖

Kat's frustration boiled. She could hear nothing of what was happening in the other room. She glanced at the MP5 slung over her shoulder. If she had to leave their hiding place, it would not be the right weapon. Scout would be using Kenny as a shield.

She returned the submachine gun to its safe.

She took out a small buck knife and slid it into her left boot. Next she removed a case containing three throwing stars, each with four razor-sharp points. She slipped one into each back pocket and the third into the top of her right boot.

She also withdrew a .38 from the safe and loaded it. She handed it to Riley. "It's loaded. Safety's off. Don't use it unless you have to."

Riley nodded and took the weapon.

Kat returned to the panel to listen.

❖

Scout stood facing Kenny, cruel intent written in the smile on her face. Her gun was in her left hand, switchblade in her right. She kept glancing around the room as if expecting Hunter to appear at any moment.

Scout put the knife to Kenny's throat and caressed him with the razor-sharp edge, forcing his head up to look at her. Her voice was soft. "Call out for your friend, Kenny. I know she'll want to come out and play when she hears you're here."

Kenny remained silent. He tried to free his hands.

"Need a little encouragement, eh?" she purred. "I kind of hoped you would."

She drew back with the knife and slashed his forehead—a cut three inches long, and deep.

Kenny cried out. Blood poured into his eyes. He struggled harder to free his hands.

"Stop that!" she snapped.

Kenny froze.

Scout got behind him. Kenny's wrists were red and raw from trying to get out of the cuffs.

"Go get those chains and padlocks she used on you and Otter," Scout ordered Frank, waving him toward the generator room.

Frank nodded and headed for the door. As he reached it, he glanced back.

Scout circled Kenny, trailing the point of her knife in a path along his body. It went around his neck, paused at his ear, and followed his arm to his fingers. "I'm through playing around," she snarled. "You're going to start losing body parts unless you call out to her. Now!"

Her words echoed in Frank's head as he ran to the generator room.

Kat heard Kenny's muffled cry of pain. She fought the overwhelming urge to burst out of the hidden door to confront Scout and rescue her friend. She held her Sig Sauer so tightly in her right hand her knuckles were white. Her left hand gripped the latch that would unlock the door.

She thought she heard Scout say something, but she couldn't make it out.

Then Kenny's voice. "Hunter," he shouted hoarsely. "It's Kenny."

The lights blinked out again.

❖

None of them expected it.

So when the lights went out, there was at first a moment of shocked silence.

Then everything happened all at once.

Kenny's chair skittered across the floor.

Scout shrieked in frustration and lunged out after him just as Kat slipped into the room, fifteen feet away.

Kenny careened into the desk. He howled in pain as his hands were pinched between the chair and desk. He kicked off hard with his feet again to keep moving. His chair hit some books on the floor and stopped abruptly. He kicked again and rolled into the wall near the bedroom door. He froze there and listened.

Scout followed the noise of the chair. When it stopped, she headed in that direction.

Kat slipped her gun into her pants at the small of her back. She couldn't use it now. She risked hitting Kenny. And if she shot at Scout and missed, the flash from her gun would give away her location.

She reached for her buck knife and held it loosely in her right hand while her other hand rested against the wall of bookshelves to her left.

It took her only a few moments to pick up Kenny. His heavy breathing was in front of her and to her right. She crept forward.

Kat opened her mouth and inhaled, tasting the air. She faintly smelled Kenny's sweat. Then the coppery tang of fresh blood. She gritted her teeth. She could hear nothing, smell nothing, of Scout.

There were obstacles in her path. Books. She inched forward, nudging them aside with her feet as quietly as she could.

Kat imagined she was only six feet or so from Kenny when she heard a scuffle. Kenny grunted. Then the chair skittered across the floor again. It hit the wall, and through her fingertips Kat felt a slight vibration from the impact.

Kat tuned out Kenny's sounds as she crept closer to him. Finally she could detect a new sound—Scout's slightly accelerated breathing, near where she had heard the scuffle.

Kat focused on that sound with her eyes closed as she sheathed her knife and reached for one of her throwing stars.

The stainless steel was cool in her hand, the weight and the feel of it familiar, though it had been at least a year since she'd thrown one. Her fingertip caressed the throwing edge as her mind went through its checklist: the grip, the pressure on the blades, the flick of her wrist that would give it just the right spin at the moment of release. She let it fly.

The star struck Scout in her left shoulder and penetrated deep into the muscle. She screamed and her gun clattered to the floor.

Kat shot forward, her hands outstretched, seeking Kenny. Her left one found his head.

Kenny cried out.

Kat clamped one hand over his mouth. The other grabbed the back of the chair and yanked hard, pulling Kenny toward the bookshelves and farther from Scout, who was gasping loudly in pain.

The chair rolled several feet before a pile of books halted its progress. Kat leaned down until her lips were against Kenny's ear. "It's me," she whispered, taking her hand from his mouth. She felt for his bindings. She discovered he wasn't tied to the chair. He was just unable to raise his hands over the high back to free himself.

She sliced through the rope around his feet. Then she put her arms under his armpits and lifted him.

Kenny struggled to his feet, his hands still cuffed behind him.

Kat put her hand to his mouth again. She could no longer make out Scout's labored breathing.

She put Kenny behind her, reached down, and picked up several books. She threw them rapid-fire in a scatter pattern toward Scout's last location until she heard a startled grunt of impact. She reached for another star and hurled it hard at the sound, gratified by the cry of pain that followed.

Kat reached up and skimmed along the bookshelves with one hand while her other remained on Kenny's shoulder. She found the latch and pressed it. The click of the door lock seemed unusually loud.

She pushed the panel open and shoved Kenny through it, then closed it again. She listened. She picked up a few more books and threw them in Scout's direction. Nothing.

Scout was on the move.

Frank cursed himself for not picking up a flashlight before he'd cut off the generator. He got to his hands and knees and groped around on the floor beside Otter, searching for the one he'd had earlier. Finally he found it and clicked it on.

Frank remained still for several seconds, considering his next move. He was tempted to just get the hell out of there while he could. The emergency exit beckoned him. *But then what? Wander around out there until you freeze to death?*

He went into the tunnel and took a hammer from Hunter's toolbox. Then he continued on to the door to the living room, but didn't open it. He pressed his back against the wall and clicked off the flashlight. A good place to wait, he decided, comforted by the heavy heft of the hammer in his hand.

The second throwing star cut deeply into Scout's left arm. It could have been much worse. It struck where her head had been a second earlier. But Scout was alert to Kat's presence now, and she had instinctively dodged to the side after the book had hit her, marking her location.

The adrenaline pouring through her body helped her ignore the pain. Scout gripped her switchblade in her right hand as she crept toward the center of the room. She heard a click in the direction of the bookshelves.

Riley heard the click of the panel door, then the shuffling of feet. *Thank God, Kat's back.* Her relief was short-lived, however, when she next picked up soft grunting sounds. *Someone struggling, or in pain.* They had a distinctively male sound to them, Riley decided. Her heartbeat accelerated at the realization. She pointed the .38 in the direction of the sounds.

CHAPTER FORTY-EIGHT

K at and Scout were ten feet apart.
Scout stood in the center of the living room, listening. Nothing. But she knew Katarzyna was there. Near the bookshelves. She began to inch her way behind the couch to flank Kat's position.

Kat had no idea where Scout was. She crouched down, feeling around her. More books. To disturb them would risk exposing her position. The only way out of the makeshift obstacle course was the way she'd gone to rescue Kenny. Toward the bedroom. She crept in that direction.

The two women moved farther and farther apart. Fifteen feet separated them. Then twenty.

Kat encountered fewer and fewer obstacles the farther she got from the bookshelves. Every few steps she paused to listen, but she could still not tell where Scout was.

Scout closed in on the bookshelves, knowing she had to be close to where she'd heard the noise. She worried Kenny and Katarzyna had escaped into the secret hiding place. She picked up several books and threw them toward the shelves. They clattered off the walls. Nothing. Scout gritted her teeth. *You won't get away from me,* her mind chanted. She reached for more books.

Kat listened to the books hitting the wall and narrowed her keen hearing until she could make out two different types of sounds. Just prior to each thud against the wall, there was a faint whoosh, a fluttering of pages as the book sailed through the air. It gave her a general idea of where Scout was. Still in a crouch, she crept toward that location.

Another flurry of books was launched, this time right at Kat.

The first sailed to her left. Then her right. She dodged the third by mere centimeters, catching the faint rustling of pages at the last moment as it flew directly at her face.

But Scout was tossing the books one after the other at close range, and Kat couldn't react quickly enough to successfully evade the next one. It hit her square in her chest and dropped noisily to the floor.

Kat dove to her left, but she was not fast enough to evade Scout's switchblade. It sank into the flesh of her right arm, halfway between her shoulder and elbow. She could not suppress a wail of pain as her own knife clattered to the floor.

Blood dripped into Kenny's eyes from the slash on his forehead. He was having no luck trying to free himself from the handcuffs. His wrists were raw.

He explored the area around him with his feet, hoping to come upon something he could use to get the blasted things off. His left boot found something solid. He put his back to it and explored with his fingers. Metal. Big. He felt the dial on the door of the safe and recognized it for what it was. He continued on, taking shuffling steps. Another safe, the door open.

Kenny felt awkwardly behind him until his hands found a canvas strap. He followed it to a submachine gun, hung on a rack. Below it hung a rifle. He couldn't reach high enough to tell if there was anything above them.

He crouched to examine the floor of the safe. With his fingers, he identified a pair of binoculars. A rifle scope. A canister of some sort. A box. He shook it. It rattled. He pried it open. Bullets. Continued on. Three more boxes of bullets. His hand closed around a pistol. Not what Kenny was looking for, but he stuck it into his back pocket. Convinced he had explored the contents of the safe as best as he could, Kenny stood and resumed his shuffling search.

He had gone a few feet when he heard a gun cock. It came from very close by and near to the floor. It took him several seconds to reach for his own pistol.

Unable to aim the weapon, he cocked it, hoping the sound

would be enough to dissuade the other person from shooting him. The sound echoed in the small space.

❖

Riley tried not to make a sound. Her heart was pounding. She held her breath.

She listened to the intruder noisily search the gun safe. She imagined that one of the two men who had been chained up had discovered the secret room.

She gripped the .38 in her hand and pressed herself into the corner, hoping the man would get what he was after and leave.

But his shuffling steps came nearer until she was sure he would be upon her any second.

She cocked the gun, alarmed by how loud the sound was. *Stupid.*

Her fear was confirmed when she heard the answering call of the intruder's gun being cocked.

❖

Kenny couldn't believe Hunter would have gotten him away from the blond psychopath only to place him in more danger. So despite his shock at discovering someone else in here with a gun, he knew he had to find out for sure what the hell was going on.

He kept his voice to the slightest whisper, afraid that the room he was in wasn't soundproof.

"Don't shoot. I don't want to hurt anybody, and I hope you don't either." He paused, hoping for a response. Silence. "Are you a friend of Hunter's too?"

After a long pause, a feminine voice whispered back. "Hunter? Who's Hunter?"

Kenny frowned. "Tall, beautiful, mysterious? Owner of this fine establishment?" He hoped a little humor might prompt the woman to put away the gun that was trained on him.

"Kat," Riley whispered. "Her name is Kat. Why do you call her Hunter if you're her friend?"

"Well, I am her friend," Kenny insisted. "And she's been

Hunter as long as I've known her."

"How long is that?"

"Seven years or so, I guess," he whispered, "Since she saved my life."

"She has a habit of saving people, it seems. She saved my life too. More than once," Riley said.

"Can I suggest we agree not to kill each other, then?" Kenny asked. "Probably would really piss her off."

Riley had to smile despite the situation. "Okay," she answered, carefully releasing the hammer of the gun. "What's your name?"

"Kenny. You?"

"Riley. What's happening out there? How did you get in here?"

Kenny crouched beside her and filled her in on everything that had happened since his arrival.

Riley in turn briefed Kenny on what she knew, and soon both had a clearer picture of how ruthless Scout was and how determined she was to kill Kat.

Together, they grew anxious as the minutes ticked by with no further word from their friend.

When Scout's switchblade sliced into her arm, Kat cried out and her hand jerked open in reflex. Her buck knife clattered to the floor. But then her years of martial arts training and close-quarter drills at the Academy kicked in. She shut out the pain.

She anticipated Scout would charge her. Her left hand came up to search for what had impaled itself in her right arm. Her fingers closed around the handle of the switchblade. She withdrew it with a grimace and swept a wide arc before her with the weapon, just as Scout launched herself forward.

The knife met fleshy resistance. Scout screamed.

The scent of blood hit Kat's nostrils. A thin spray of warm wetness hit her face and neck.

Scout was wounded, but it didn't slow her down. She charged, and both women went down hard.

Kat landed on her back, Scout on top of her.

The impact knocked the wind out of Kat and sent the switchblade cartwheeling from her hands.

Scout scrambled to sit on Kat's chest, pinning down Kat's arms with her knees.

Kat's handgun cut into the small of her back, unreachable. Scout's left knee pressed down hard on the knife wound in her right arm. Kat thought she might pass out from the pain. She had trouble focusing.

Scout punched Kat hard in the mouth—once, twice, three times. She put her hands around Kat's neck and started to squeeze.

Kat arched her back, putting all the strength of her long legs into it, and sent Scout flying forward, off balance.

Scout flew face first toward the hard floor over Kat's head, but put out her hands to break her fall.

Kat rolled to one side, gasping for breath.

That led Scout back to her. She lunged at Kat, throwing haphazard punches, connecting with Kat's face, neck, abdomen, shoulder.

Kat tried to fight back with her left hand. Her right arm was useless. Her fingers sought Scout's neck, but Scout moved too fast, successfully evading her.

Kat shifted her weight with a loud grunt and managed to get Scout off her again. She kicked hard with both feet and sent Scout crashing into the kitchen counter.

Kat rolled painfully onto her right side and reached behind her for her gun. She fired blindly with her left hand.

On the fourth shot, Scout cried out and Kat heard her hit the floor.

Kat got to her feet. She found Scout with her outstretched boot and nudged her a couple of times. Scout reacted only with pained groans, so Kat crouched and found her head. She placed the cold tip of her gun against Scout's temple. "Who the hell are you?" she demanded.

No reply. The blonde wouldn't, or couldn't, answer.

"Frank!" Kat shouted into the darkness. "Frank! It's Hunter. I've got her. Turn the lights back on!"

❖

Frank opened the door to the living room just a foot or so. Just enough to peek inside. It was unmistakably Hunter's voice, but was it a trap?

He clicked on his flashlight and swept it in a quick arc across the room until it landed on a grisly tableau. Hunter, poised over Scout. There was blood all over both of them, and Scout wasn't moving.

"Right away, Hunter," Frank said. He headed for the generator room.

Frank's flashlight blinded Kat momentarily, but she'd still gotten a pretty good look at Scout's injuries. There was a widening pool of blood around her. Kat didn't think she could survive long. She relaxed a little.

"Who are you?" she repeated. The anger was gone from her voice, replaced by curiosity.

The blonde coughed, a gurgling sound. "Maggie O'Rourke," she answered in a strained voice.

Kat couldn't place the name. "Why?"

No reply.

Kat leaned down over the woman. "Why?" she asked again, her lips inches from the blonde's face.

"Clogher," the blonde rasped out.

And then Kat knew. She remembered her only visit to the village in vivid detail. The IRA members she'd killed.

The splinter group had begun its reign of terror with ambush attacks against British soldiers. Then they had set bombs on buses in Dublin, killing dozens of men, women and children. Kat remembered she'd been told to expect five targets—one a woman—but she'd found only the four men when she broke into their cottage stronghold.

The lights flashed back on. Distracted by her grim memories, Kat was startled and had to squint her eyes to adjust.

Scout sprang to life. She clasped her hands together and slammed them into Kat's hand. The gun went flying.

CHAPTER FORTY-NINE

S cout rolled over and struggled to her feet. Kat launched a side kick that swept Scout's legs out from under her and sent her crashing to the floor.

Scout tried to rise, but Kat kicked her again, this time a roundhouse blow that connected with Scout's jaw.

She remained where she had fallen. The fight was gone from her. She moaned and then fell silent.

Frank reappeared in the doorway. He paused, eyeing Kat warily.

"You did real good, Frank," Kat said in a tired voice. "Get rid of the hammer and come help me, will you? Frisk her, get any weapons. Then carry her out to the generator room."

Frank nodded and bent over Scout. He searched her, then lifted her and turned toward the tunnel. He paused at the doorway. "You should take care of yourself. You're bleeding an awful lot too."

Kat nodded, a hint of a smile appearing at the corner of her mouth. "Wait out there for me. I won't be long."

As soon as he was gone, Kat unlocked the door to the weapons room. "The crisis is over, you two," she hollered. "Hold your fire."

She pushed the panel open and stepped into the inner chamber.

Riley and Kenny spoke at once as soon as they saw her.

"Thank God," Kenny said.

"You're hurt!" Riley cried.

"I'll be fine." Kat smiled down at Riley, then stepped over to Kenny.

"You've grown up," she remarked as she examined the cuts on his face. "We need to get you to a doctor to get these sewn up. Hate to have anything mess up that pretty face of yours." She put her hand on his cheek. "I'm sorry, Kenny," she whispered.

"Oh, don't worry about me. I'll be okay." He gave her a cocky grin. "Can I call you Kat now too?"

She nodded and tried to smile. "Yes, of course."

"And how about getting me out of these?" he said, turning to show her the handcuffs.

Kat patted her pockets for her keys before remembering Scout had taken them. "Soon. I'll find something to get them off. Come on, you two, let's get out of here." She reached out with her good hand to help Riley up.

When she got to her feet, Riley threw her arms around Kat and hugged her. The two women stood there a long moment, clinging to each other.

Kenny's eyes widened in surprise. He felt a pang of envy, but he was grateful someone had managed to break through and touch Hunter's heart in a way he'd been unable to.

The three emerged into the living room. The bunker looked like a bomb had gone off. In the middle of the chaos was a large pool of blood, the edges of it already turning dark.

"Is she dead?" Riley asked.

"Not yet," Kat said. "But soon." She turned to Kenny. "The helicopter pilot?"

Kenny cringed. "Dead. She shot him when we touched down. His body's out by the chopper."

Kat nodded and tried to flex her right hand. The pain was excruciating. "Then we have a problem. I can't fly us out of here with my right arm the way it is."

"Maybe you can't, but I can," Riley offered. "Sam taught me to fly. Between the two of us, we should be able to manage."

Kat's eyebrows went up, and she leaned over to kiss Riley on the cheek. "A woman of many talents. I have a lot to learn about you." She winked at Riley.

A blush colored Riley's cheeks.

"Let me grab a few things, and we'll go," Kat said. She checked the bathroom for bandages, but the supplies she'd gotten from the clinic were gone. She went into the bedroom and searched among the disarray for clean clothes. She stuffed them into a bag.

She locked up the weapons room and got her gun from the debris in the living room. She spotted the duffel bag on the counter, unzipped it, and looked inside. She glanced at Kenny. "This is the money you brought, right?"

"Yeah," Kenny said. "It's not all there. She gave some to Frank."

"She what?"

"To ensure his cooperation. But he was the one who turned out the lights, right when she was getting pretty ugly with me."

Kat nodded. She thought Frank had helped them, but she was surprised to find he'd done it despite getting money from Scout. She slung the duffel over her good shoulder, along with her bag of clothes. She looked at Riley. "Can you make it? Can't carry you this time, I'm afraid."

"I'll be fine if I just go kind of slow," Riley answered, smiling. "Lead on."

❖

Frank was crouched beside Otter when Kat, Riley, and Kenny entered the generator room. He glanced up at the trio. "She never woke up," he said, nodding toward Scout's body, which lay near the door.

Kat went to stand over Otter, who was either asleep or unconscious. "Nice patch-up job, Frank."

"Bleeding seems to have stopped. The bullets went right through, but he hasn't come to," Frank said.

"I wondered where all the first-aid stuff went," Kat said. "Since you did such a good job on him, how about fixing up my arm and Kenny's head?"

Frank looked at Kenny. "Hey, sorry about the punch."

"Forget about it," Kenny replied. "If you hadn't cut the lights, I'd probably be dead by now."

Frank looked over at Kat. "I had to hit him to get her to trust me."

She put her hand on his shoulder. "I owe you, Frank. And

you'll get your reward, just like I promised. But how about patching us up first? Start with Kenny while I try to find something to get him out of those handcuffs."

"Otter had the keys," Frank said. He searched Otter's pockets and came up with the key ring. He freed Kenny and went to work dressing their wounds.

When he was done, Kat opened the main entrance. She had lost track of time and was surprised to find it was light out. It was cold, but clear.

"How many seats in the helicopter, Kenny?" she asked.

"Four."

She looked at Frank. "Well, Frank, you get to choose who gets the fourth seat. I can take you, or I can take Otter. If you want him to live, you'll have to take a snowmobile."

Frank looked at Otter. "I don't think I can find my way back to the road," he confessed.

"I can help you with that," she replied.

"Then he can go with you."

Kat nodded. "Take him out to the chopper, will you? You can use my sled. Follow those tracks, they'll take you right to it. Then come back and get her." She gestured toward Scout. "The pilot's body is out there by the chopper. Put hers next to his, out of sight from the air."

Frank put Otter on the toboggan and headed toward the clearing.

Kat turned to her friends. "Kenny, grab us some coats from the tunnel, would you? Give us a minute?"

"Sure," he answered, leaving the women alone.

"I brought some clean clothes for the both of us. Think you can manage?" Kat held up the bag.

Riley nodded.

They dressed quickly. As they finished, Frank reappeared and took Scout's body away. Kenny came back with coats and hats.

Kat went back into the living room to get supplies for Frank. By the time he returned to the generator room, they were ready to leave.

Kat handed Frank his wallet, a compass, the keys to his snowmobile, and a map. "Follow the compass west by southwest," she instructed. "I've marked the way on the map. It shows where the hills and swamps are so you can follow the terrain back to the road. You have plenty of gas. You should make it back to town within a couple of hours."

Frank studied the map as Kat retrieved the duffel bag. She withdrew $100,000 and stuffed the money into her coat. She closed the bag and handed it to Frank. "There's $300,000 there—including whatever Scout already gave you."

His eyes got big. He unzipped the bag and glanced inside. "Thanks, Hunter."

"One more thing I'd like you to do for me," Kat said. "When you reach the road, destroy the map and forget you were ever here."

"I think I'm coming down with amnesia. What's your name again?"

She chuckled. "It's your choice if you want to work for Garner again, but I'd like you to wait a couple of weeks to report back to him if that's what you decide to do."

"I think I may just take a very long vacation somewhere and think about what I'll do next. Somewhere warm," he added, smiling at her.

"Better get going while there's still daylight."

As his snowmobile roared away, Kat turned to the others. "Time to go."

CHAPTER FIFTY

Two hours later, Riley set the chopper down in Canada beside a clinic at the edge of a remote village. As the rotors slowed, a tall, middle-aged man with a graying beard and white coat emerged to investigate the noise.

When he spotted Kat getting out of the helicopter, he walked toward her, shaking his head. "I should've known," he shouted over the roar of the decelerating blades.

She smiled and hollered back, "Got some work for you, Eddie. Start with the guy in back. We'll need a stretcher."

Kat and Kenny talked in low voices in the corner of the exam room while the doctor looked at Riley's knee and wrist. Kat sported a sling, and Kenny's facial wounds had been stitched and dressed.

Riley watched them. Kat did most of the talking. Every now and then Kenny would nod. Just as the doctor finished, Kenny left and Kat came to stand by the bedside.

"You patch her up?" the doctor asked Kat.

She nodded.

"Nice job." He turned to address Riley. "You just need some bed rest and you'll be fine." He nodded toward a new brace he'd fastened around her knee. "That'll help you get around better. And I can write you a prescription for some pain pills if you want them."

"A few, maybe," Riley answered. Her knee ached badly from flying the helicopter.

The doctor pulled out a prescription pad and started writing.

"You can get this filled at the pharmacy in town. Pick up some crutches while you're there, too." He handed the paper to Riley and turned to Kat. "Need a place to stay?"

"Kenny is taking care of that, thanks," Kat answered. "Riley will be staying at the Trapper's Inn, Eddie. Would you look in on her from time to time over the next couple of days?"

"Sure."

Kenny reappeared. "Cab is here. Ready to go?"

"Yup," Kat answered. She turned to the doctor. "Thanks, Eddie. You sure you don't mind keeping Otter here while he recovers?"

"No. I'll be careful when he's strong enough to cause trouble," Eddie replied. "He woke up briefly while I was treating him, by the way. He was surprised to be alive, and doubly so when I told him who brought him in."

"I bet." Kat turned to her friends. "Ready?"

The three of them made their way to the taxi. Kenny sat beside the driver, and Kat and Riley got in back.

As soon as they were underway, Riley turned to Kat. "You said I'll be staying at an inn."

Kat nodded. "Kenny will keep you company. I have to take care of something."

"What are you planning?" Riley asked.

"Tell you later."

They rode the rest of the way in silence. Kat weighed how much she was going to tell Riley. She would rather her friend not know precisely what she was going to do—but there was a chance she might not come back.

❖

Riley kept quiet only until she and Kat were in their hotel room. "Well? What are you up to?"

"Come sit down, get off that knee," Kat said. She helped Riley to the bed and got her comfortable, propped up against the headboard. Kat sat down on the edge of the mattress.

"I need to see Garner. He'll keep sending people after me until I stop him. Before we can think about the future..." She paused and looked into Riley's eyes. "I need to take care of this. I have to make sure you're safe."

"But you're hurt," Riley argued. "You're not in any shape to confront a man who wants you killed. Can't you wait until your arm is better?"

"No. It has to be now." Kat wanted nothing more than to remain with Riley while they both healed, but she knew she'd never be able to resist the temptation to consummate their relationship here in the privacy of the romantic inn. And she couldn't allow herself to take that step while they were still in danger, knowing she might not return. It wasn't fair to Riley.

"Once it's done..." Kat stroked Riley's cheek. "We can get to know each other without my having to keep looking over my shoulder. Take some time just for us and shut the world out," she promised. "I have plenty of money. We can go wherever you like, do whatever you want to do. I just have to take care of this first."

Riley leaned forward and hugged Kat. "Please be careful. I want to be with you more than anything. When do you leave?"

"As soon as Kenny gets here with the rental car."

"That soon? Shouldn't you rest?"

"I can sleep on the plane," Kat said. "Don't worry. I won't rush into anything I'm not up for. It may take some time to figure out the best way to get close to him. But I'll be back as soon as I'm able, I promise."

There was a knock on the adjoining door. Kenny called out, "I'm back, whenever you're ready."

"Be right there," Kat answered. She gazed into Riley's eyes for a long moment before she leaned in to kiss her. Slowly, gently, conveying the depth of her emotions in a way she never could with words. Their bodies pressed tighter together, and the growing passion between them surged through their bodies in a warm, enveloping wave.

Kat broke the contact. "Rest. I'll be back before you know it, and then we can finally..." She paused, searching for the right words, and a faint blush appeared on her cheeks. "Well, we can finally...be together. Without worrying about someone interrupting us."

Riley put her hand behind Kat's neck and pulled her close to kiss her again. This time the kiss grew more heated. Sparks flew. A promise of things to come.

Riley released her hold on Kat's neck, and their lips separated. "Please come back to me."

"I will." Kat kissed Riley on the forehead and left without looking back.

A week later, Kenny and Riley sat in the inn's restaurant drinking coffee and eating pie. Riley poked at her nearly untouched piece of rhubarb.

"Stop worrying," Kenny repeated for the tenth time. "She'll be fine. You've seen her in action. She probably just decided to rest her arm before going to see him."

"Then why hasn't she called?"

They had been over this so many times Riley knew Kenny had no answers. She knew he was concerned too, just better at concealing it. She put her fork down, her appetite gone.

CHAPTER FIFTY-ONE

Evan Garner's office was on the twenty-fourth floor of a nondescript steel-and-glass office complex that looked from the outside much like any other. Except for the high fence topped with razor wire that surrounded it.

Once inside, it was apparent that this was not a typical nine-to-five workplace. Security cameras were everywhere. Armed guards patrolled at irregular intervals. Nearly every door required a key card to gain access. And the top floor—Garner's floor—was accessible only by a private elevator that required a four-digit code. Normally the code was changed every six months, but in recent weeks, it had been changed every two days.

After watching the complex and Garner's home for three days, Kat concluded that her former mentor was in hiding, probably in his office. His car had not moved from its spot in the parking lot.

She accessed the building's personnel files on her new laptop and searched for the employee she would impersonate to gain entry. She focused on the food service people who worked in the cafeteria on the twentieth floor. She knew its layout well, and it faced the private elevator to Garner's floor.

Kat selected Bob Tarleton, a night-shift cook. He was single, roughly her height, and had a full beard and mustache.

She followed Tarleton for three days. She memorized his routine, walk, and mannerisms. She tapped his phone so she could learn and imitate his speech patterns. Then she went shopping for the supplies she'd need to complete her disguise. A week after she had left Riley and Kenny in Canada, she was ready to confront Garner.

Bob Tarleton glanced bleary-eyed at the alarm clock on his nightstand as the insistent pounding on his front door continued without pause. Six o'clock a.m. He'd only been asleep for two hours. He stumbled to the door and yanked it open, prepared to launch a stream of obscenities at the idiot who dared disturb him at such an ungodly hour.

His jaw dropped. He shook his head. *Must be dreaming.* He'd swear he was looking in a mirror. But his mirrored self smiled as he himself frowned in confusion. Before he could react, his grinning twin pushed by him into the room and pointed a gun at him.

"Hi, Bob," his twin said, in a voice eerily similar to his own. "Shut the door."

Tarleton didn't hesitate to tell Kat everything she wanted to know. Kat was pleasantly surprised to learn that the shaggy-haired cook was an observant man who noticed things. Yes, Evan Garner was indeed staying in the building. The cafeteria workers had compared notes on seeing the man at all hours of the day and night, looking more and more haggard and disheveled. Tarleton volunteered that the same was true of Thomas, the big guy who seemed to be Garner's shadow whenever he came into the break room.

Thomas's hands were occupied with two oversized cups of coffee. It was 1:00 a.m. and Garner had insomnia again. The bodyguard reached awkwardly with an outstretched finger toward the elevator button. He felt a presence behind him. He glanced over his shoulder just as one of the cafeteria cooks reached around him and hit the button.

"Your boss just called down for this," the cook said, opening a small Styrofoam container. Inside was a large piece of lemon meringue pie.

Thomas nodded. Garner's favorite. He had been eating at least a slice a day. If the boss wasn't careful, he'd soon have trouble fitting into his custom-made suits.

As the elevator door slid open, the cook tried to give the pie to Thomas, but the bodyguard already had his hands full.

Thomas frowned. "Ride up with me." He stepped into the elevator.

"Sure." The cook got in too and went to stand slightly behind Thomas.

"Hold this." Thomas turned to hand one of the coffees to the cook. He reached for the keypad to punch in the elevator code. He was careful to block the cook's view as he did.

The elevator began to rise.

Thomas's world went black.

Evan Garner lay on the couch in his office with his eyes closed and the lights off. It was fruitless to try to sleep. He was hoping a good jolt of caffeine might make him alert enough to actually get some work done. He heard his office door open and close.

"How many times do I have to tell you to knock?" Garner rubbed his eyes as he sat up.

"How many times did you tell me the importance of the element of surprise?" a familiar feminine voice asked. The lights flicked on.

"Hunter." Garner gaped at the figure in the white cook's outfit.

She was five feet away and had a gun pointed at his head. "Evan. Been a long time."

"Yes, it has."

"I'd have come to see you sooner but I've been pretty busy, as I'm sure you're aware."

"T-Take it easy, Hunter," Garner stammered. "Don't do anything rash."

"That's a lot of money you put on my head. You must want me dead real bad."

"You gave me a good reason." He began to sweat. Garner

had a stale odor about him. His suit was badly wrinkled and his face showed several days of beard growth, a contrast to his usual impeccable grooming. "Look, Hunter. We have a history. I gave you opportunities that made you a rich woman. You can't just kill me in cold blood."

"I can find the strength to kill anyone I need to," she said. "Wasn't that what you always told me when I objected to an assignment?"

Garner stood up and started to pace, keeping his distance from her. *Where the hell is Thomas?* All the lessons he'd taught her on how to detach herself emotionally from the people she had to kill came back to haunt him.

"I want you to tell me something, Evan. I want to know why. Or rather, why now? You said you'd come after me, but that was five or six years ago and I've kept out of your way."

Garner's forehead furrowed. "What the hell are you talking about? You're the one who started this. You and your death threats. Sure, I was mad when you left. But I calmed down. You did your time for us. I wouldn't have hurt you."

"Death threats? What death threats?"

"The messages I got from you. Said you were coming after me to get back at me for ruining your life?"

She shook her head and shrugged.

"You didn't send them?" he asked.

"Nope."

"But they came through secure channels, with the code we gave you for identification purposes."

"Wasn't me," she repeated.

"Well, I wouldn't have issued the contract otherwise. It was purely self-preservation, Hunter. I've been living in my office, for God's sake! Afraid you were lurking out there somewhere waiting to ambush me."

Kat suspected Garner was on the level. Something funny was going on. The answer came to her. "How did you come to hire Scout? Where did you find her?"

"Scout?" He stopped pacing and leaned against his desk. "I didn't find her. She just showed up. Somehow figured out I was the one behind the contract and worked out how to find me. Didn't say how. She was an odd one." He shook his head, remembering. "I thought she had her own agenda. She didn't seem as interested in the money as she should have been."

"You were right," Kat answered. "She was after revenge. Remember that IRA group I took out, eight or so years ago?"

"Yeah, I remember." It had been a lucrative contract. "So what does that have to do with this?"

"She was the missing member," Kat replied. "The woman I was told would be there."

"No shit?"

"She must have been following me for years. She knew all about me. My real name, my past. Stands to reason she could have gotten the identifying codes too somehow and sent you the threats in my name. Probably bought out someone working for you and got a look at my old files."

Garner chewed his lip. He'd never had a traitor in his midst before, but it would explain how Scout could know so much about him too.

"She suspected you'd react to the death threats by ordering people to hunt me down," Kat speculated. "She wanted to be one of them, and this was her way of turning the heat up—to flush me out of hiding."

She glared at Garner. "And you played right into her hands."

Garner's left eye began to twitch. "I didn't know, Hunter. You can't hold me responsible."

"You're not in a position to tell me what to do, Evan."

The twitch got worse. "I was just trying to protect myself," he insisted.

Kat studied him in silence for a few moments.

"Come on Hunter, for old times' sake. Just let it go."

"Just like that?"

He shrugged. "I-I'm sorry, Hunter. Katarzyna. I truly am."

Kat had never known him to apologize to anyone. She put her gun away. "So you'll call off the contract?"

Garner relaxed. "Right away. Not that there have been any takers recently. Is Scout dead?"

Kat nodded.

"Frank? Otter?"

"Both all right."

"Then you've dealt with them all," he told her.

She nodded. "I'd like you to do me one last favor," she said. "To make up for putting me through a hell of a week."

"Name it."

She walked to his desk and wrote something on a slip of paper. "These are the GPS coordinates for a clearing in the woods near Tawa. Send a helicopter. Scout's body is there, along with the body of a chopper pilot she killed. He was ex-Navy. His ID is on him."

Garner nodded.

"Retrieve the bodies and get some money to the pilot's widow, if he has one. Oh, and she killed another guy—a helicopter pilot in Tawa named Sam McCann." Kat wrote the name on the slip of paper and handed it to him. Her handwriting was barely legible. "Get the case closed. I want all this done with the discreet kind of cover-up you're so good at."

"I'll take care of it. If you've left me with any staff to give orders to."

"No one's dead, Evan." She smirked. "Thomas will be asleep for a while, though. He's just outside the elevator door." She turned to leave. "What's the code today?"

"5-0-4-5," Garner answered. "Nice job getting in here, by the way."

Kat nodded.

"Hunter?"

She paused at the doorway.

"Is there anything I could say to get you to come back and work for me?"

She shook her head. "Those days are long gone, Evan."

"You'd get to choose," he pressed. "Do the kinds of jobs that really make a difference—get the real bad guys."

"No, Evan," she said as she turned away and stepped over the threshold.

But even as she spoke the words, she wondered whether she would miss the thrill of the chase and the rush of adrenaline she got when she found herself in dangerous situations. She had unique talents, and she liked to test them.

And she had to admit that some of her kills had indeed made the world a safer place for innocents like Riley.

"The offer is always open!" Garner called out after her as she closed the door behind her.

KIM BALDWIN

CHAPTER FIFTY-TWO

Riley sat in a screened-in porch in the north woods, surrounded by the reds and yellows of autumn, a symphony of bird calls and the wind in the trees. It was a bucolic setting, but she could not enjoy it.

She wanted to doze—she hadn't been sleeping well lately—but the constant tap, tap, tapping of a woodpecker nearby kept her awake. It droned on and on, incessant.

Riley opened her eyes, startled to find she was not in the woods at all but lying in bed, and the tapping sound was someone knocking on the hotel room door.

Her disorientation turned to mild alarm when she glanced at the clock on the nightstand. She'd fallen asleep with the light on. It was 2:00 a.m. *No one knocks on your door at 2:00 a.m. unless it's bad news.*

She got out of bed and wrapped a hotel robe around her. She padded to the door and looked through the peephole, then fumbled with the lock in her haste to get the door open.

"You're here!" she squealed, throwing herself into Kat's arms. She hugged her fiercely. Tangible evidence this wasn't a dream and Kat really was back, safe and sound.

"Sorry to wake you. There was no one at the front desk, and I forgot to take a key with me."

"Don't be ridiculous! Get in here! I was so worried about you!" Riley relinquished her hold just long enough to get inside, where the embrace resumed. "I missed you so," she whispered into Kat's neck. "Is everything all right?"

"Yes. Sorry I took so long," Kat hugged her back, her heart so full she was unable to speak. They remained like that for several moments, the joy of their reunion overwhelming them.

Riley realized Kat was embracing her with both arms. "Your arm." She pulled back and gently ran her hand over the spot where Kat had been stabbed. "It's all right?"

Kat stretched it out and flexed the fingers on that hand. "Almost back to normal. I saw a doctor in D.C." She put the arm around Riley again and pulled her close. "How about you? How are you feeling?"

Riley released a long, contented sigh. "Perfect at the moment."

Kat chuckled. "I meant your knee and wrist, silly."

"I'm fine. The cast comes off in two weeks. The knee really doesn't bother me unless I'm on it too much. Which I probably have been lately—pacing back and forth worrying about *you*." Riley poked Kat in the chest with one finger. "Why didn't you call me?"

Kat opened her mouth. Closed it. Nodded toward the bed. "Come on, let's get you back under the covers."

Riley watched Kat as she shed her robe and crawled under the covers. Kat had avoided her question, and now she was avoiding her eyes. "What's wrong?"

Kat sat on the edge of the mattress. She licked her lips. Her mouth was dry. She stared at her hands. "Riley, I-I wasn't sure that I should come back."

Riley's eyebrows shot up and her mouth gaped open. "You're not serious?"

Kat shook her head. She couldn't look at Riley. "I've lived a violent, dangerous life, Riley. Done a lot of things I'm not proud of."

Riley took Kat's hand in hers and squeezed it. "Stop beating yourself up over your past."

"You don't know everything I've done," Kat whispered.

"I don't need to know, honey. I know the person you are now."

"Riley, it's more than that. I'm not sure I know how to...love you." She stumbled over the words. "I mean, I've never been...like this...with anyone. You deserve a lot better."

Riley's hand went to Kat's chin and gently forced it upward so Kat would look at her. "I don't think we choose who we love, Kat," she said. "It just happens. Don't you feel it?"

"Yes," Kat replied, so softly that Riley barely heard her. "I do. That's why I came back. Maybe it's selfish. But I can't bear to be apart from you."

Riley blew out a long breath. "Well I'm glad that's settled! You had me worried there for a minute. Don't *do* that again."

Kat smiled. "So how have you and Kenny been getting along?"

"Great," Riley replied. "But he's worried about you too. Have you told him you're back?"

"No, I'll talk to him in the morning. I have a job for him."

"Problems?" Riley asked.

"Nothing to worry about. Scout cleaned out one of my bank accounts. Maybe Kenny can get the money back. If not, it's okay. I have others. Plenty to do whatever we want. Speaking of which, where do we go from here? Given any thought to that?"

"Doesn't matter to me, as long as we're together," Riley answered. "That's the good thing about being a writer. You can work from anywhere."

"What kind of writer are you? Have I read anything you've written?"

"Maybe. I've done mostly magazine articles—travel pieces, profiles. I was always on the road. I think that's what prompted Sam to start looking elsewhere." Tears sprang to her eyes. "Poor Sam. I shouldn't have married him. We were high-school sweethearts in a small town, and it was just kind of expected." Riley looked at Kat. "We never had what you and I have. This just feels so different."

Kat nodded. "You make me feel things I never thought possible."

"What about you?" Riley asked. "Is there something you'd like to do? Anywhere you'd like to go?"

"Well, I've thought about that. I'd like to go back to Cyprus. Maybe I can't go home, but I think I can find some comfort there now, and closure, if you're with me."

"Cyprus it is, then." Riley stifled a yawn.

"It's late. You should get back to sleep."

"No way," Riley replied. "I'm not that tired." She wiggled her eyebrows.

"Not, huh?" Kat smiled.

Their eyes met. They came together in a searing kiss fueled by days of anticipation. Their tongues found each other.

Riley's hand curled behind Kat's neck. Her fingers entwined in Kat's hair. She pulled their mouths more firmly together, deepening the kiss. *Such soft lips,* Riley thought. *No, it was never like this with anyone else. And now I know it to be true.*

Kat's hand found its way under Riley's oversized T-shirt. Her fingertips trailed up Riley's abdomen and teased the curve of her breast. *Those breasts. How could I resist those breasts?*

Riley leaned into the caress and moaned into their joined mouths.

Kat's fingertips found Riley's nipple and brushed across it. It was instantly erect. Kat's heartbeat accelerated.

Riley broke their kiss and pulled away. Her pupils were huge. She was breathing hard. "Come to bed. I need to touch you."

The invitation sent a wave of heat through Kat that settled between her legs. She stood beside the bed and began to strip. The nervousness she expected to feel was nowhere to be found. Her body felt electrified. Her eyes never left Riley's.

She pulled off her socks and shoes, jeans, pullover. Then, more slowly, her black silk bra and panties.

Riley watched as each enticing body part was exposed to her. Long legs, firm thighs, taut abdomen, and full, round breasts, with dark nipples hard as pebbles. She licked her lips.

The subdued glow of the bedside lamp softened the scars that marked Kat's life as Hunter.

"Beautiful," Riley breathed. She slipped off her T-shirt and tossed it on the floor. She wore nothing else. She pulled back the covers, exposing her nakedness. Ivory skin, lightly freckled on her shoulders and chest, trailing away into the valley between her breasts. They were high and firm with vivid pink nipples. The triangle of hair below was the same honey blond of her head.

Kat's breath caught in her throat. She slipped beneath the sheets and moved into Riley's outstretched arms. "You have an incredible body," she whispered. She shifted her weight so their bodies pressed against each other along their full length. She shuddered at the satisfying flesh-on-flesh contact.

"God, you feel so good." Riley breathed a long sigh. Her breath was warm against Kat's neck. "I've ached for you."

The confession turned up the heat pouring through Kat. She claimed Riley's lips, her tongue demanding entrance. There was more urgency to this kiss. One of Kat's hands trailed down Riley's back to her ass and caressed one firm cheek.

When they parted to breathe, Kat's lips and tongue moved to explore the soft skin below Riley's jaw.

A needy moan escaped Riley. She arched her neck to allow Kat greater access.

Kat sucked gently on Riley's earlobe, then nipped at the tender flesh at the base of her neck. Her lips and tongue caressed the place beneath Riley's jaw where she could feel her heartbeat—it drummed away just beneath the surface of the skin.

"Mmm," Riley purred. Her right arm encircled Kat's waist. She tugged at Kat, urging her on top.

Kat shifted and Riley opened her legs, inviting Kat between them.

Kat left fluttering kisses on Riley's heated skin as she climbed atop her. She tried to distribute her weight on her elbows and knees, afraid she would crush Riley.

But Riley wrapped her arms and legs around Kat, urging their bodies even closer.

They began to move together, breast to breast, the friction of their contact doubling their excitement.

Riley moaned again.

It brought Kat's mouth to hers as their hips increased the rocking motion that fueled their arousal.

Kat kissed her hard, then broke away. Her lips moved from Riley's mouth to her cheek, then to her neck. She slid down Riley's body, keeping as much contact between their naked skin as possible.

Her lips and tongue tasted Riley's cleavage and drew closer and closer to Riley's breast.

Riley laced her fingers through Kat's hair and brought her to her nipple. When Kat's lips closed around it, Riley moaned again.

The sound of that long, throaty sigh drove Kat wild.

Riley arched her back and stroked the back of Kat's neck firmly, seeking harder contact. Kat complied, her tongue and teeth nipping and caressing the sensitive nipple, then giving equal attention to the other, until Riley could stand the sweet torture no longer. Her whole body throbbed. "Please, Kat, please!"

Kat continued her oral adoration of Riley's left breast while her hand began to trail a teasing path. Down the soft skin of Riley's stomach. Along her outer hip. Down the outside of her leg and across the knee. Then slowly up the sensitive inner thigh.

Riley whimpered. She pressed herself against Kat's hand.

Kat inhaled the musky scent of Riley's arousal. It was heady, intoxicating. Her fingers closed in on Riley's soft, wet folds.

Just before they reached their destination, Riley reached down and put one hand under Kat's chin to bring her head up. Their eyes met.

"Together," Riley whispered in a low, breathy voice. "I want to touch you too."

Kat trembled as she moved up Riley's body to kiss her again. Her blood was roaring in her ears.

Riley's hand slipped between them and found the swell of Kat's breast. Her fingers closed around the rigid nipple as their lips joined.

Kat shifted until she straddled one of Riley's legs, remaining on top of her. Their kiss deepened as their eager hands found and caressed the sweet evidence of their readiness for release.

They stroked each other, exploring, teasing. Finding all the places that evoked the greatest response. Groans and sighs, one echoing the other. Moving in tandem. Deeper, faster. Mouths parting to gasp for breath. Finally, both peaked. Exquisite explosions. Riley first, Kat seconds behind, pushed over the edge by Riley's cry of release.

They held each other for a long while, both unable to speak. Their overheated bodies cooled and heart rates returned to normal.

Finally Kat's voice broke the quiet. "I have no words to tell you how I feel."

Riley shifted to look into Kat's eyes. "I love you, Kat."

Kat's eyes filled with tears. "I love you too." Words she'd never said, except to her father. Words she never expected to say again.

Riley saw the tears forming. "You okay?"

Kat caressed Riley's cheek with her fingertips. She smiled and nodded. "More than okay." She winked at her lover. "I'm just Jake."

About the Author

Kim Baldwin is currently at work on her third novel for Bold Strokes Books. *Hunter's Pursuit*, Author's Edition will be followed by the release of her romance *Force of Nature* in September, 2005. A short story, "Overdue," will appear in the Bold Strokes Books anthology *Stolen Moments: Erotic Interludes 2*, also in September. Nature, romance, and adventure are key themes in her stories. She lives with her partner in a cabin in the north woods.

Look for information about these works at www. boldstrokesbooks.com.

Other Books Available From
Bold Strokes Books

Distant Shores, Silent Thunder by Radclyffe. Ex-lovers, would-be lovers, and old rivals find their paths unwillingly entwined when Doctors KT O'Bannon and Tory King—and the women who love them—are forced to examine the boundaries of love and friendship and the ties that transcend time. (1-933110-08-2)

Hunter's Pursuit by Kim Baldwin. A raging blizzard, a remote mountain hideaway, and more than one killer-for hire set a scene for disaster—or desire—when reluctant assassin Katarzyna Demetrious rescues a stranger and unwittingly exposes her heart. (1-933110-09-0)

The Walls of Westernfort by Jane Fletcher. All Temple Guard Natasha Ionadis wants is to serve the Goddess, and she volunteers eagerly for a dangerous mission to infiltrate a band of rebels. But once she is away from the temple, the issues are no longer so simple, especially in light of her attraction to one of the rebels. Is it too late to work out what she really wants from life? (1-933110-24-4)

Change Of Pace: *Erotic Interludes* by Radclyffe. Twenty-five hot-wired encounters guaranteed to spark more than just your imagination. Erotica as you've always dreamed of it. (1-933110-07-4)

Fated Love by Radclyffe. Amidst the chaos and drama of a busy emergency room, two women must contend not only with the fragile nature of life, but also with the mysteries of the heart and the irresistible forces of fate. (1-933110-05-8)

Justice in the Shadows by Radclyffe. In a shadow world of secrets, lies, and hidden agendas, Detective Sergeant Rebecca Frye and her lover, Dr. Catherine Rawlings, join forces once again in the elusive search for justice. (1-933110-03-1)

shadowland by Radclyffe. In a world on the far edge of desire, two women are drawn together by power, passion, and dark pleasures. An erotic romance. (1-933110-11-2)

Love's Masquerade by Radclyffe. Plunged into the often indistinguishable realms of fiction, fantasy, and hidden desires, Auden Frost discovers a shifting landscape that will force her to question everything she has believed to be true about herself and the nature of love. (1-933110-14-7)

Beyond the Breakwater by Radclyffe. One Provincetown summer, three women learn the true meaning of love, friendship, and family. Second in the Provincetown Tales. (1-933110-06-6)

Tomorrow's Promise by Radclyffe. One timeless summer, two very different women discover the power of passion to heal and the promise of hope that only love can bestow. (1-933110-12-0)

Love's Tender Warriors by Radclyffe. Two women who have accepted loneliness as a way of life learn that love is worth fighting for and a battle they cannot afford to lose. (1-933110-02-3)

Love's Melody Lost by Radclyffe. A secretive artist with a haunted past and a young woman escaping a life that proved to be a lie find their destinies entwined. (1-933110-00-7)

Safe Harbor by Radclyffe. A mysterious newcomer, a reclusive doctor, and a troubled gay teenager learn about love, friendship, and trust during one tumultuous summer in Provincetown. First in the Provincetown Tales. (1-933110-13-9)

Above All, Honor by Radclyffe. The first in the Honor series introduces single-minded Secret Service Agent Cameron Roberts and the woman she is sworn to protect—Blair Powell, the daughter of the president of the United States. First in the Honor series. (1-933110-04-X)

Love & Honor by Radclyffe. The president's daughter and her security chief are faced with difficult choices as they battle a tangled web of Washington intrigue for...love and honor. Third in the Honor series. (1-933110-10-4)

Honor Guards by Radclyffe. In a journey that begins on the streets of Paris's Left Bank and culminates in a wild flight for their lives, the president's daughter and those who are sworn to protect her wage a desperate struggle for survival. Fourth in the Honor series. (1-933110-01-5)